His Bonnie Bride is "charged with highly sensual love scenes . . . thrilling battles and delightful characters."
—*Romantic Times*

"I KNOW WE ARE ENEMIES, BUT MUST YE MAKE ME PLAY THE WHORE TO GAIN MY FREEDOM?"

Cupping her face in his hands, Tavis teased at her lips with his while saying, "Ah, lass, I didnae mean those words. They were spoken in anger. What I am about to do has naught to do with ye being my prisoner. Nay, nor your ransom we have yet to gain. This is solely the burning need of a man for a woman. I couldnae bear the thought of ye being sent back to Hagaleah without tasting the sweetness of ye."

As his lips moved down her slender throat, he groaned, "Touch me, lass. I want to feel those bonnie wee hands move o'er my flesh. Touch me, Storm. Discover the man that aches for ye."

"Nay, I must not. I . . . ah!" she cried softly when he cupped a breast in his hand and his lips closed over the hardened tip. "I am lost," she whispered. . . .

Other *Leisure* books by Hannah Howell:

ELFKING'S LADY
BEAUTY AND THE BEAST
STOLEN ECSTASY
COMPROMISED HEARTS
PROMISED PASSION

HANNAH HOWELL

His Bonnie Bride

LEISURE BOOKS   NEW YORK CITY

A LEISURE BOOK®

January 2004

Published by

Dorchester Publishing Co., Inc.
200 Madison Avenue
New York, NY 10016

ISBN 0-8439-5301-2

Visit us on the web at www.dorchesterpub.com.

His Bonnie Bride

1

A cool wind blew across the battlements, nipping at the skirts of the women gathered there to watch the men of Hagaleah ride off to battle. As they had so often in the past, they were riding to meet the Scots, most particularly the clans MacBroth and MacLagan, ancestral enemies of the Eldons of Hagaleah and the Fosters of Fulaton. The rising sun reflected off their armor as they rode away across the moors to do as their fathers had done and their fathers before them, on into the mists of time.

Lord Eldon's wife sighed, mostly in envy and anticipation of a long, boring wait for the men to return. She was his second wife, a young girl from a prominent Sussex family. Lady Mary Eldon was beautiful, spoiled and heedless. Having grown up in the verdant, peaceful south, she had little under-standing of the constant state of warfare along the border or the danger of raids. In her mind the battle would be as a tournament, something glorious and exciting.

"I intend to watch that battle, Hilda. I see no reason for us to be marooned here."

Hilda stared at her mistress in amazement. "My lady, you cannot. Think of the danger."

"Nonsense. There is a well-covered knoll within sight of where the battle shall take place."

She turned and proceeded back into the keep, her

7

small retinue at her heels frantically trying to talk her out of her rash plan yet not make her angry. Lady Eldon's anger was swiftly becoming legendary. She did not like opposition of any sort, as many of the keep's servants had discovered to their cost. None of those following the headstrong Lady Eldon wished to lose their privileged positions.

To their horror, the lady's cousin, soon to wed Lord Foster's heir, also thought the idea a good one. The unthinking young ladies were turning the venture into a picnic. Mary ordered food to be packed and even instructed the nursemaids to bring the children, six in all, including Lord Eldon's two by his first wife. The hope that the few men left behind would stop Lady Eldon vanished quickly as servants scurried to hitch up carts and open the gates. A sizable entourage was soon heading for the knoll overlooking the battlefield. Only the older servant women and Lord Eldon's eldest child, a daughter, remained somber. The other women, lady and servant alike, and children began to act as if on an outing to the fair.

Little Robin Foster, a plump boy of eight with blond curls, tugged at Storm's braid, thinking yet again that the color was an odd one, rather like marigolds in that it was a red that was near to orange. "Why must we stay here? Cannot we sit with the ladies, Storm?"

Storm looked at the boy from her height of two years' seniority, her amber eyes scornful. "No. 'Tis safer here. We can hide amongst the bushes if need be. This is a foolish move for my new mother to make. We should be tucked up in the castle, not frolicking within the grasp of the Scots."

"But the Scots will be fighting down below, sister," piped up Andrew, her six-year-old brother, his fiery red curls thrashing in the breeze. "I should like to see our father in battle."

8

"Aye, and we would be seen too. We with our hair as bright as any beacon. You can see well enough from here." She quieted all protests from her five underlings with one sweeping glare. "Now, listen all of you before the harsh sounds of battle drown out my words. If I say to move, ye move and go where I tell ye with no wailing. Think ye not that the Scots would like to catch their enemies' spawn?"

"You are frightening us," protested four-year-old Matilda Foster, her hand nervously twisting her blond braid.

" 'Tis as well. Ye will move faster if need be. Here now, the armies prepare to face one another."

At first it was much like a pageant as the armies aligned themselves to face each other. The gleam of steel, the waving of pennants and the ringing of armor stirred the audience upon the hill. It all looked glorious, even awe-inspiring. A person could not help but be moved by the sight, but then the cries of "Foster! Foster!" "Eldon! Eldon!" "MacBroth! MacBroth!" and "A MacLagan! A MacLagan!" roared through the air, the battle was engaged and things changed with ominous speed.

The armor still rang as sword hit sword, but now there were screams as it was pierced. Steel soon lost its gleam as it was covered with blood and the mud churned up by so many men and horses. Formation was all but forgotten as man grappled with man, knights upon horses wedged their way into the battling mass of infantry and the wounded were, when possible, dragged, carried or assisted to the rear in the hope that they would live for another battle.

As the fighting spread, flowing outward to the sides, the knoll was no longer safe. It was placed more to the Scottish side of the field, the enemy edging ever nearer to the now silent on-lookers. Even the more bloodthirsty of the women began to falter

9

as the increasing heat of the day strengthened the scent of warfare, the light summer's breeze bringing along with it the smell of the fighting men's sweat and blood. The children made no complaint as Storm began to edge them toward the bushes.

Suddenly matters took a dangerous turn. A group of battling men reached the base of the knoll. Within moments, a band of Scottish knights were racing toward the knoll to assist their harried kinsmen. The Fosters and the Eldons were falling back under the bludgeoning force of the Scotsmen. The women of the castle, already in a high state of tension, panicked when a cry from one of the Scottish knights indicated that they had been spotted. Screaming, they fled to their carts. A few Scots gave chase, trampling the bright blankets and scattering all the festive eating arrangements. In the confusion, Storm hustled the children off, remembering a shearer's hut and deeming it a good place to hide, unwittingly shepherding her charges closer to the enemy.

The shearling was in a poor state of repair, but it remained a niche in which to hide. Storm guessed at her error when the tents of the Scots became visible, but there was no turning back for she could hear the swift approach of armed horsemen. Pushing the children within the doorless hut, she sat before them and, putting a hand on her knife, was ready to protect the smaller ones should they be discovered.

Scotsmen were soon returning from the field, passing the hut all unknowing of the treasure it held. Storm began to think they would escape detection when suddenly a small knot of men paused before the hut so that one could sit and rest. She easily recognized the laird of the MacLagans, for he had a number of distinctive qualities, not the least of which was his silver hair and the scar that ran the length of his face in a jagged line from forehead to chin. When his blue eyes, darkened by pain, met and held hers she felt her heart had stopped. Her mind conjured up a multitude of fates.

"Weel, look what we have here, lads," Colin MacLagan drawled in a husky voice. "Look, Tavis."

The young man turned to follow Colin's gaze. His eyes, the blue of a summer morning's sky and so clear in his swarthy face, fixed upon the children. When the tiny girl with her brilliant hair pulled a knife from a pocket in her skirts a smile brightened his harsh features.

"Now, lass, what do ye intend doing with that?" Tavis asked, his eyes dancing.

"Stick ye like a pig if ye come any closer," Storm replied tersely, frowning fiercely when the other men seemed amused. "I mean it," she warned when Tavis stepped closer.

"There's no need o' doing that, lassie. We're nae going to harm ye," said the laird.

Storm's eyes narrowed, for that rather contradicted the stories she had been told. However, even covered in mire and blood as they were, none of the men struck her as the sort to cook and dine upon children. The five youngsters clutching and trying to hide behind her skirts were plainly not so sure. It struck none of them as strange to look to Storm for protection; she was not only the eldest, but had always been the strongest one. Storm carefully considered her next move.

Tavis edged nearer to his father, saying softly, "What fool do ye think let them near the battle?"

"God knows. With that hair, methinks we may have some Eldon spawn. Strange little lass."

"Aye. Cat's eyes and that hair. 'Tis a wonder. I have never seen the like before." He grinned at his father. " 'Tis taking her awhile to decide whether or not to stick one of us." They laughed softly.

"I want your oath," Storm spoke up. "Your oath that ye and none of your men will harm us. Your word of honor." She watched them carefully.

"Ye have it, lass," the laird said gravely. "We'll just be holdin' ye for ransom."

"Fair enough." She tucked her knife back into her skirts and then scowled at the other children. "Will ye leave go my skirts? All your trembling is near to shaking my teeth loose."

Two men helped the laird to stand, and Tavis looked at Storm, motioning her to join them.

Ushering the children ahead of her, Storm fell into step beside Tavis. When they reached the camp the surprise of the men there was plain to see. The Foster and Eldon men captured and being held for ransom became vocally upset, needing a few minutes of rough persuasion to quiet them. The children were kept near the laird and his sons, two more of whom had come to his side. They were barely settled before a tent when some men came up dragging an upset and untidy Hilda, who fell upon the children, hugging and kissing them as she wept copiously.

"Enough, Hilda." Storm escaped her clutches. "Ye will surely drown us. How are the other ladies?"

"They got away, lass. I could get none o' the lot to help me look for ye."

"What were ye doing so close to the battle?" Colin asked Storm as his armor was removed.

"My new mother thought to watch the spectacle." Contempt was heavy in her voice. "She and the Foster heir's bride-to-be and a number of servant women drove out to the knoll. 'Twas a picnic. Then, when your men drew near, the silly cows fled screeching. Seems only Hilda remembered we children."

"And whose children do we have? I wish to be exact in me ransom demands."

"Well, m'lord, ye have Storm Pipere Eldon," she said with a curtsey, "eldest child of Lord Eldon, and his heir, Andrew. These two are Fosters, the heir's

12

two by his first marriage, Robin and Matilda. The brown-haired twins are my cousins, Hadden and Haig Verner. The lot are at Hagaleah for the Foster heir's wedding in a fortnight."

"B'God," breathed the laird, "the future of both families in one catch. That woman should be thrashed within an inch o' her life. 'Tis a fair ransom we will gain from this." He turned his attention to his messenger, who would ride to Hagaleah with the ransom demands.

"Hilda, we children are well, but our men held there may need your nurse's touch," Storm suggested and watched with a half smile as Hilda forced her way to the captive knights, full of the importance of her errand, before turning to scowl at the way Iain MacLagan was tending his sire's wound. " 'Tis a right poor job ye are making of that," she told the young knight. " 'Tis like to kill him, not cure him."

"Oh? Ye can do better?" Tavis drawled with a touch of sarcasm, but his eyes revealed his delight in the small girl. "By all means, make us privy to your knowledge."

"I will if I can, despite your cynicism, sir." She ignored the chuckles of the men and looked around for what she required, spotted it and ordered Andrew to go fetch it.

"I won't," her brother said stubbornly. "I do not see why I should get dirty."

Storm looked at this sign of rebellion in the ranks with contempt and half raised her fist. "Ye will or your stub of a nose will be peeping out of the curls on the back of your head."

Andrew went but tried to salve his pride with a lot of grumbling concerning his sister's many faults. Storm busied herself getting a bowl and clean water and tearing her petticoats into clean strips. She washed her hands, washed the wound and cleansed

13

the needle she would use. When Andrew returned she made her poultice, neatly stitched the laird's wound after dousing it with whiskey, treated it and expertly bound it, even to tying a sling for the laird's arm.

The MacLagans watched with amused admiration. Not only was the child not made squeamish by the ugly wound, but she had a definite skill. As she worked she talked to the dark, scarred Scottish laird just as a nurse to a child, much to the amusement of him and the other men.

Tavis, having recently reached the manly age of nineteen, was fascinated. Storm Eldon was an elfin child, small and slender. Her small, long-fingered hands held a grace far beyond her years. The thick hair speedily escaped the restraint of her braids and looked startling against a skin of alabaster hue. Her face was heart shaped, and the wide, slanted, amber eyes, set beneath tilted brown brows and heavily lashed, seemed to fill it, leaving little room for the delicately shaped nose and full mouth. He could not even begin to catalogue the many facets of her character.

"How old are you, child?" he asked as she washed her hands.

"I turned ten a month past." She handed Iain the remainder of her homemade salve, instructing, "You keep the wound clean, change the dressing thrice each day, and dab a bit more of this on it until it begins to close. In about a week or ten days ye can cut the stitches. I hope Papa did not get hurt, for he likes me to tend to him. The others fuss over him too much."

"There was no sign that he had been," Sholto MacLagan, the youngest of Colin's three sons, said.

They were brought some food, for it was thought that it would take some time for the Eldons and the Fosters to gather the ransom. The six children sat quietly eating, unaware that the MacLagans dis-

14

cussed them. Hilda glanced toward them every now and then, but the captive men needed her attention more.

"Do ye think the lass has poisoned ye?" Sholto jested when he saw the laird touch his bandage.

"Nay. I was just thinking it a job well done. Never seen such neat stitches. The lass has the touch. I have seen me a muckle lot of wee lasses in my years, but none the like of her."

"Aye," Tavis agreed. "I was thinking much the same. Hard to believe she is an English lass."

Colin grinned. "Aye. Too much spirit in her. Stick ye like a pig indeed." He laughed but stopped suddenly, his eyes on the children. "Oh ho. Trouble in the ranks."

Robin Foster was suffering from bruised pride. It was a sore point to recall how he had cowered behind Storm's skirts when faced with the enemy. Now it rubbed to have her holding sway over all of them, a position he felt should be his. When she told him to take his sister's plate it was one thing too many. He leapt to his feet, tossed his plate to the ground and glared at Storm.

"No, I will not. I do not have to take orders from you. 'Tis an insult."

Storm slowly rose to her feet, hearing the insult to her behind his words. "How so, young Robin?"

"I am destined to be an English peer and I'll not take orders from a half-Irish bastard."

"I'm no bastard and well ye know it. My father married my mother ere I was born."

"Minutes before," Robin sneered. "We have all heard the tale. Well, Robin Foster takes no orders from the spawn of some Irish whore," he yelled, his words echoing in a suddenly quiet camp.

His words were barely spoken when Storm's fist sent him sprawling to the ground. She flung herself upon him and began the fight in earnest then, her skirts not hampering her in brawling as well as any lad. They were equally matched. The men moved in closer to watch, thus stopping Hilda from putting an end to it. Matilda watched silently, but Storm's brother and cousins were highly vocal in urging her on to victory. Even the captives took sides.

"Irish blood, eh?" Colin mused as he watched the children fighting. "That explains it. I wonder where and how his lordship found himself an Irish lass?"

"She has him now. This will sore wound his pride," Tavis said, laughing.

Storm had Robin pinned to the ground. "Do ye yield?" she asked with one fist raised near his face.

For an instant Robin hesitated, but his body had already suffered too much from those punishing little fists. "Aye, aye. I yield. I yield."

"Now take back those words ye said about my mother."

"Taken. Will ye get off?" he wailed, sure that his nose was broken as well as a few other things.

Tavis lifted the little girl off her defeated foe and Hilda rushed over to help Robin, moaning, "Lass, lass, it ain't right for ye to be tussling about like a stablehand."

"He called my mother a . . . one of those," she cried, defending her lapse from gentility.

"And bad it was for him to do so, there's no denying, but it wasn't right for ye to answer the insult with yer fists. That ain't the way of a lady."

"No," Storm snarled, "the way of a lady is a bit of poison in the meal. So much more refined." She tried to yank free of Tavis's grip, but he ignored her struggles, seating her next to Colin.

"My mother was no whore," she grumbled as Tavis began to clean her up, checking her for anything worse than a scrape or a bruise, "and I am no bastard. I could not let him get away with those lies."

One look at her troubled, beseeching face told

Tavis that Robin's words were an often flung insult. "If your parents were wed before ye were born then ye are no bastard and she no whore." He knew that was far too general a statement, but he would not try to explain that marriage did not always stop a woman from being a whore. "It looks like ye just missed having this eye swell."

She shrugged. "I have had one or two before. They were late wedding for Papa was off to battle, but ere I saw the light of day they had taken their vows. My mama was beautiful and a lady."

"I'm sure she was," Tavis murmured as he continued to bathe her face.

With that fine sense a child often has, Storm realized the man was murmuring soothing nothings. "Well," she drawled, "I cannot see what her being Irish has to do with it."

Tavis paused in his ministrations, saw her dancing gaze and grew wary. "Quite right."

"After all," she looked at him, appearing quite innocent save for the twinkle in her unusual eyes, "she could have been Scottish." She met his disgusted look with a peal of laughter so light, carefree and lovely to the ear that many a mouth smiled in response to it.

Unraveling what remained of her braids so that he could free her hair of twigs and leaves, Tavis grinned at her. "You are a wretched wee lass that ought to have been beaten thrice a day."

" 'Tis what Papa says, yet he never does it." She eyed him as he combed his fingers through her hair, ridding it of foreign clutter, and began to adeptly rebraid her hair. " 'Tis a skill ye have for that. Do ye have a wife then?" Tavis shook his head, and she looked at Colin with a grin. "Frisky, is he?"

"Sit still." Tavis gently yanked on her hair as his family laughed. "Why the name Storm?"

" 'Twas the weather the night I was born. They

had expected a son, so had no girl's name chosen. So, too, did my Mama believe that as I was born midday on the summer's solstice in the midst of thunder, lightning, wind and rain that my character, perhaps even my life, would be stormy so 'twas a fitting name. I fear I have too oft proven her right." She looked down at her dirty, tattered dress and sighed. " 'Tis plain for all to see that I have been in a tussle. Papa will be angry."

"I think your papa will note little save that his bairns are well and whole," Tavis predicted.

2

The great hall at Hagaleah was the scene of hectic activity as the highest-ranking men of the Eldon and Foster households gathered in various states of health. The squires saw to the care of the armor and the weary men relaxed in their shirts and breeches. Conversation centered around what had gone wrong in the battle.

"Leave it be," Lord Eldon snapped at the young maidservant who had started to see to his small wounds. "Find my daughter. Storm has the touch I need, and where the hell is my wife? Find her." When the young girl fled to do as he commanded Lord Eldon turned his brown eyes upon Lord Foster. "Did they catch many of our men? A heavy ransom would be unwelcome at this time."

"Not many, and few of any standing." Lord Foster ran a grimy hand through his blond hair. "We may have lost the battle, Eldon, but our loss of men was not as high as I had feared," he said halfheartedly, and the talk turned to trying to recall exactly who had fallen that day.

"What mean you her ladyship cannot come?" bellowed Lord Eldon when the maid returned with no one. "Where is my daughter then? Or Robin? He e'er rushes to his father when the man returns."

"I cannot find them, m'lord. The ladies are abed and looking pale. Aye, as are their maids. I cannot find Hilda, nay, nor none o' the wee ones. They weren't any o' the places they oft go."

"Get her ladyship and Lord Foster's fiancée down here, wench, if you have to drag them. Now," Lord Eldon snarled and watched the girl race off before turning to Lord Foster. "I cannot like it. Not at all."

He liked it even less when the ladies arrived. They looked ill and terrified. Their personal servants huddled near them, acting as if they were headed to the gallows. He exchanged a look with Lord Foster, and they both began to tense, especially when the women began to weep piteously.

"Where are the children?" demanded Lord Eldon in a voice that silenced everyone. "Cease that damnable caterwauling and answer me."

"We do not know," whimpered Mary, and she cringed when her husband leapt to his feet.

"When did you last see them?" Lord Foster barked as he moved to tower over the women.

"On the knoll near to the battle." The dark looks growing on the men's begrimed faces caused Mary to cringe and begin to babble. "We just wished to watch the battle. All was well until suddenly the Scots were coming from all sides. We fled for our lives but, once safe, Hilda and the children were gone." Her words ended on a scream as her husband's open hand connected with her cheek, snapped her head back and sent her sprawling into the other women. "There was nothing we could do," she wept as she shielded herself behind the others.

"Sweet Mother of God! Nothing you could do?" he bellowed. "Your recklessness has handed the enemy our heirs. My brother-in-law's as well. If they let the children live, the ransom they will ask could ruin us. You managed to save your own precious neck though, didn't you?"

"It all happened so quickly." In an attempt to pacify him, Mary moved closer, saying softly, "I am so sorry, but you can have other children. I can give you children."

He grabbed her by the hair and hissed, "Have no fear, wife, you will an I can stomach seeding you." With an oath he flung her away. "Heed me, if my children are returned, they, and any future ones I may have, will not come into your care. I will choose who cares for them and they will answer only to me."

Lord Foster strove to shake free of his shock. "Are you sure Hilda is with them?"

"We think so, m'lord," replied one of the maids. "Mistress Storm kept the wee ones to the back near the shrubs, and they were gone when the heathens stormed the knoll. Hilda was with us, but when she saw that the children were not she was like a mad-woman. She leapt from the cart whilst it was moving and disappeared." The girl began to weep quietly. "Lord, it looked as if she ran straight into the enemy."

"Be gone," roared Lord Eldon, sending the errant ladies scurrying for their quarters. "My God," he groaned as he sat down, "how could I have wed such a woman? If she were not so incapable of thought, I would wonder if this action was planned to rid her of the obstacles 'twixt my estate and any children she and I may have. I hope old Hilda comes to no harm."

Nodding, Lord Foster sat down next to him. "If she and Storm are with the babes, they'll not be so afraid." A smile suddenly broke out on his face. "Now, I wonder what the Scots make of Storm?"

A laugh, weak but true, broke from Lord Eldon. "Sweet Jesus, she no doubt told them in great detail of the many ways she would alter their anatomy." A sadness came and went in his eyes. "She is so very much like her mother. 'Tis glad I am she is but a child and not a woman grown."

Thinking of Storm as a woman grown, Lord

Foster shuddered, knowing full well how the girl would be used. "God, yes. Even now a man can see that the lass will be a true beauty."

"I pray they do not harm them. I feel a wretch for I seem more worried for Storm than the others, but there is no denying she is dearer to my heart. Mayhaps 'tis the matter of her birth, that I was there to help her into the world. Ah, then, too, there's that temper of hers, her healing touch, the way she can cut to the heart of a matter, be so adult one minute then so delightfully childlike the next."

"I know. Feel no guilt, my friend, she touches us all. Even I, though she will insist on shaming me by thrashing Robin." He exchanged a weak grin with Lord Eldon. "Come let us decide what we have to meet the ransom demands that must come soon."

They were working hard on that when the Mac-Lagan messenger arrived. Both men ground their teeth as the Scot was ushered in. It was hard not to race up to him, demanding to know the children's fate.

"The children are unharmed?" Lord Eldon demanded before the man had begun to speak.

"Aye, m'lord, as is the nurse, though there was no need o' the woman rushin' at us and demandin' tae be taken tae the bairns. The wee lass with the odd-colored hair was managing. The demands?"

"Aye, aye. Tell us what is asked for." Lord Foster frowned as the messenger related all that was asked for the safe return of all whom they held; although it was not as bad as they had feared, it was steep. "Tell MacLagan he shall have it. We will deliver what he asks on the morrow, an hour after first light."

"We will be left sorely strapped after the morrow," Lord Eldon sighed after the messenger had left.

"For now, but we can call in debts owed us, Eldon, and recoup nicely. Mayhaps, if that fails, we can appeal for a contribution from all our kin as we have oft aided them in the past."

Little rest was found at Hagaleah that night. By the light of torches and a full moon, the ransom was gathered. The tale of how the ladies from the south had placed the children of both castles into the hands of their ancestral enemies spread to the lowliest peasant. Even the townspeople, so often protected by the men of both houses, contributed. What worries were held about how such a loss of goods and money would affect them over the winter if not replaced were not aired. One look at the lords' faces told them that the men had enough on their minds for the moment.

A few knights suggested a rescue attempt, but the idea never took hold. The paying of ransom was custom and, once agreed to, it would not be honorable to do other than peaceably deliver it. There was also the fear of harming the children. It was galling to hand over so much to their enemy, but there was no other way.

The gray light of dawn found Lord Eldon, Lord Foster and a select group of knights on their way to the enemy camp under a flag of truce. Many a person watched grimly as a large slice of their livelihood was led away; although starvation was not really a specter on the horizon, winter could turn out to be very hard indeed. It was especially hard to think on the fact that their enemies would doubtless be very comfortable.

"They're coming, and it looks as if they have fully met our every demand." Sholto grinned.

Colin grinned back. "Ye and Iain take a few men and start a tally. Their lairdships can come and sit with their bairns if they've a mind to."

Storm's eyes widened as she saw what her father had brought, and she looked at Tavis, who had the role of guard. "This could mean a lean winter for our

23

people. Ye have asked for a lot."

He gave one of her braids a tug. "Consider what we hold, lass. We could have taken it all."

She nodded. "Twould be fitting and just if they went and claimed from the lands of their ladies' kin."

There was a touching moment of confusion as Lord Eldon and Lord Foster were reunited with the children. Lord Eldon was slightly unbalanced as his own two offspring plus his two nephews hurled themselves at him. When things quieted down a little both men noticed the state of their eldest children.

"Have you taken to brutalizing children then, MacLagan?" snarled Lord Eldon, causing an immediate rise in tension at the camp.

"Oh no, Papa!" Storm gasped, gripping her father's hand which had gone to his sword. "Robin and I did this to ourselves. Truly we did. These men have been all that is kind. My word on it."

"What did you and Robin fight about this time?" Eldon asked with weary patience.

Knowing ths could not tell the truth, Storm put her hands behind her back and crossed her fingers. "Robin called me a sharp-tongued, nasty-tempered hag who would no doubt end up as a wizened, bitter old maid, for no sane man would take me to wife. So I fought him to a draw."

Lord Eldon had a strong feeling she was lying, for she looked far too angelic. His eyes narrowed, but before he could say anything Lord Foster drawled, "To a draw you say, Storm?"

"Aye, m'lord." Storm hoped the overly bland faces of all who had heard her lie would not give her away.

"Strange, is it not, that Robin looks in a poorer state than you?"

"Not at all, m'lord. Being the gentleman he is, he

was hindered in the fight for, of course, he felt he would not strike me as hard or as oft as I would him. I took unfair advantage of that."

"Ah, aye, of course, I should have recalled that from the last draw between you." Lord Foster did not need the sudden epidemic of averted eyes and coughing to tell him he was being fooled.

"I wish to talk to you, Storm. Excuse us, Foster." Lord Eldon led his eldest child out of earshot, accepted the stool offered him by Sholto MacLagan and then looked at Storm, who stood calmly before him. "While it is clear in my mind and we are idle as they tally up the ransom, I feel I must speak to you. You must cease this brawling, Storm. 'Tis unbecoming. Ladies do not resort to fists. Think of how many enemies you could make. No lad likes to be thrashed by a bit of a girl. That could well be a sore point in the years to come, a shame they long remember. I want you to give me your word that this will cease. Your word, Storm."

"I fear I cannot give it, Papa," Storm said quietly. "My temper is such that I would break my word, and that would grieve me as much as displeasing you. I will promise to try not to get in any more fights, to try to control my temper." She kissed his cheek. "Will that suit, Papa?"

Trying to ignore the amusement of the MacLagans who stood close by, Lord Eldon said, "I gather it must. You are a wretched wee lass whom I should have beaten with far more regularity."

Storm smiled. "I know, Papa. That man said the same thing. Do ye know he fixed my braids as well as Hilda ever did, but he is not married. Now where do you suppose he learned?"

Grinning, Lord Eldon tugged one of her braids. "Impertinent little wench." He stood up and took her by the hand. "Come, we will sit with the others and pray that Hilda ceases her wailing."

Glancing back at Iain, Storm said accusingly, "You have not changed his dressing yet."

Watching Lord Eldon and Storm rejoin the others, Sholto mused, "I cannae say I like seeing how the mon is when we arenae fighting. I'll feel it sorely an I run my sword through him, for now I ken the ones that will be left greeting for him if he dies afield."

" 'Twill nay stop ye, though, will it, lad." Colin understood his son's sentiments well.

"Nay, just grieve me to deprive the bonnie wee lass of her father." Sholto started to move away. "I'll see that the tally is being done right. We left Robbie doing it."

The tally was soon done and the English party prepared to depart. Lord Foster took his daughter up before him and his son behind. Hilda was set in a cart, along with the wounded. Lord Eldon tossed his nephews up with two of his escort before putting his son on his horse. He then mounted and helped Storm swing up behind him, something she did nimbly.

"It cost me," Lord Eldon said to the MacLagans, "but I thank you for not harming the children."

"We do not make war on bairns, m'lord." Colin suddenly grinned. "Then, too, the lass was all set to skewer me eldest if I didnae give me word not to harm them."

Lord Eldon groaned and held out his hand, into which Storm dutifully placed her knife. "Storm, you should have been a boy." He tucked the knife away.

"I have oft told ye that, Papa," she said with an unrepentant grin as they started off. "Good morrow to ye," she gaily saluted her former captors.

"Lass, you must not be so amiable toward the enemy," Lord Eldon admonished genially.

"Oh, then I gather I should not have tended to the laird's wounds."

"You what?!" her father bellowed, but she laughed and winked at the MacLagans, grinning when Tavis winked back.

Despite the hefty ransom felt by all at the manor and surrounding it, there was much rejoicing when the children were returned. The houses of Foster and Eldon had always done well by their people, protecting them and caring for them as few other lords did. It was a relief to all to see that the direct lines were once again assured. They would continue to have as good a life as one could expect in such troubled times. Hagaleah resounded with cheers as the troupe arrived.

Only two people felt no joy. Mary Eldon watched her husband's return with a set face, and Lord Foster's fiancée slept, having wept herself into exhaustion for fear that her nuptials would be canceled. Once the shock of what she had done had faded, Mary began to feel herself ill-used. She felt her husband lacked understanding, was too harsh in his judgment, for, after all, she was born and bred in Sussex and did not understand the way of life along the border. Now, instead of being allowed to learn from her error, she was to be forever punished for it, her standing at Hagaleah greatly reduced.

Briefly she thought of seducing her husband into a gentler attitude, but soon forgot that. Even before they had wed she had guessed that his children by his first wife, an Irish nobody, were as important to him as the blood in his veins. By putting them at risk she had lost what little place she had managed to grasp in his affections. Now he would treat her as little more than a brood mare, a vessel to bear him more sons to act as insurance, to guarantee that the line would pass to one of his own blood, and she would not even be able to regain her stature through her children, for she did not doubt that he would keep them from her as he had sworn to.

Her gaze settled upon the bright head of the one she considered the root of her troubles, the one who had caused her problems from the start. Jealousy raged through Mary as she thought of how strong a hold Storm had upon the lord of Hagaleah. The bitterness Mary felt over the destruction of her plans to be the grand lady of such a powerful holding was directed at the little girl. Logic and rationality had little to do with her thoughts as Mary swore that someday Storm would pay for her disgrace.

Storm settled down in her bed, unaware of the malevolence directed toward her. She felt content, for she was home again, her father had survived the battle, Hilda was again her nurse and she had had an adventure. Caring little for the woman, Storm had not noticed her new mother's absence from the festivities. She felt no real animosity toward her, but had known from the start that they would never be friends. Therefore, Storm made an effort to have as little to do with her stepmother as possible.

"Hilda?" she called softly before the woman could leave the room.

"What is it, lass?" Hilda moved to the side of the bed, her eyes soft with honest affection.

"Why do we fight the Scots?"

"Ah, well, I think 'tis for the land mostly. They think 'tis theirs and we say 'tis ours. Of course we have fought and raided each other for so long I don't think anyone really knows or even thinks about the why of it. What's made ye ask that, child?"

"They did not seem much different from us so I was not sure why we were enemies."

"Men always have enemies. They would be lost if they had no one to fight. 'Tis the way of it."

"Why have we been told such lies about them, and they are lies, aren't they, Hilda?"

"Aye, most of them. They kill, loot and rape, but

28

then our men do too. I do think they be a bit wilder lot, but be they Scot, Englishman, Frenchman or any other breed, a fighting man is a fighting man. Put a sword in their hand and 'tis time for the women and children to hide." She sat on the bed. "I think 'tis the blood and battle which changes them from the men we recognize to beasts with naught else but killing, firing homes and raping women on their minds. Ye could meet a man who's all courtesy and smiles, a true gentleman, but ere the next day, in a battle with a sword in his hand, his softness fades and, because they are now enemies, he could kill the man he drank with not long ago or toss a lady whose hand he had kissed so genteely but nights past and treat her no better than a tavern wench. 'Tis all a mystery, I fear."

"So, if I had been a woman grown the nice man who did my braid would not have been so nice. He may well have dishonored me instead."

"Aye, lass, I've little doubt of that if for naught else than it would have been a blow at your sire."

"Ah, well." Storm yawned, and her eyes closed. "I shall not see them again, I am certain."

Hilda stood up and stared at the sleeping child. "I hope not, lass. I surely hope not."

Once the English had left the Scots headed home. Colin MacLagan rode in a well padded cart to protect his wound, his sons riding to his side and behind. It had been a successful venture, far more so than he could have hoped, and he was pleased. His gaze fell on a pensive Tavis.

" 'Twas a good battle. Few men lost and much gain to show. I cannae remember one so successful."

"Nor I, Father. The bounty we have gained should ease the greeting a wee bit."

"So why are ye looking so pensive, laddie?

Thinking on a wench, are ye?" Colin grinned.

A slow smile touched Tavis's handsome face. "Aye, ye might say that. A wench, and a visit I have sworn myself to making six or eight years hence."

3

It was warm for a night so early in the spring. A full moon turned the budding greenery to silver. The soft light also strove to outline a group of men moving stealthily with an assortment of animals. Only the keenest of eyes could have spotted them within the shadow of the trees and only the sharpest hearing could have picked up a sound, so quietly did they go about their thievery. Suddenly their leader held up a gloved hand. All movement stopped, and he was joined by two others.

"What is it, Tavis? Why have we stopped?" queried Robbie, the burly master at arms, but then the sound of hoofbeats reached his ears and his hand went to his sword. "We are discovered?"

"Nay. Rest easy. We have merely stumbled upon a tryst." Tavis's smile gleamed briefly. "Take the men on, Angus," he directed a stocky man. "Robbie, you, Jaime, Donald and Iain stay with me. Wait for us by the horses, Angus. I do not plan to be long, but this interests me."

As the others moved on, Iain hissed, "Why do we risk this? Let us go and leave the lovers be. The raid was a masterwork. This pair can mean naught to us." Iain could not understand Tavis's actions.

"They can when the lass has hair of a color I've seen but once, seven years past," Tavis replied softly and, when he edged closer to the clearing where the couple were meeting, Iain was close at his side.

Although fully aware of the folly of her actions, Storm made her way to the stream that wove its way through her father's land. She needed the quiet, the isolation. Not another instant could she have born it within the walls of Hagaleah. Life had become a trial. She needed time to think.

"Oh Lord, Papa, where can ye and Andrew be? Ye are sorely needed at home," she mourned softly as she tossed pebbles into the stream. "The bitch from Sussex is set to ruin us."

She sat down, uncaring that the grass might ruin her gown. Since her father and Andrew had gone to take a turn at fighting the French, leaving Hagaleah in the hands of his steward, things had gone wrong. The steward did whatever his lover, her stepmother, requested. Storm could not even appeal to the Fosters, for the men there who would have helped were also in France. She could only sit by helplessly watching the woman drain the wealth, antagonize old, dear friends and mistreat the peasants.

One of the few things in which she had managed to thwart Lady Mary was the matter of her cousin, Phelan O'Conner, who had arrived from Ireland but a fortnight before her father had left. By some miracle the scrawny boy of nine had made his way, alone, all the way from Ireland. A note written by her mother before her marriage, which gave an O'Conner the right to seek aid of any sort from his English relations, had given him the chance for something besides poverty and starvation. He was now being tutored in skills that would serve him well when he became a man and, by force of will and guile, Storm had ensured that the boy had stayed when her father had left and things had begun to change. Phelan's Irishness was enough to make him unwelcome to Lady Mary.

The sound of a horse fast approaching sent her

heart into her throat. When she recognized the rider her fear changed to anger. Her stepmother was determined to wed her to Sir Hugh Sedgeway. He was not ill-favored, being of medium height, with blond hair and brown eyes, but his character was abhorrent to her. Crude, violent and lecherous, he was everything she disliked. Storm had no intention of becoming his wife and spending her days surrounded by by-blows or watching him lust after everything in skirts. Even more important, she would have nothing to do with one of her stepmother's lovers, one of her partners in the orgies that grew more frequent. Tensed and ready to react, she watched him secure his mount and stride to where she cautiously rose to her feet.

"This is unwise of you, Storm. 'Tis a good thing I saw you leave and followed you."

"Is it?" She stepped back when he moved closer. "I sought some quiet and privacy."

"Ah, aye, 'tis a lovely spot." He reached for her, but she deftly eluded his grasp. "Now, lass, you should not be wary of your husband-to-be."

"Your plans advance beyond reality, Sir Hugh. Never will I be your wife."

"Not a tryst then," murmured Iain, his gaze running over Storm's small but shapely form. "She's still a bonnie wee lass. Just what are ye planning, Tavis?"

"I am not sure." His gaze went slowly from the brilliant hair done in a coronet of braids on down her slim length, noting the full breasts, tiny waist and gently rounded hips. "She has grown up fine indeed."

Sir Hugh shook his head, his brown eyes glittering with anger over the way the girl continued to oppose him. "Why do you fight me so, lass? We will be wed." He suddenly lunged, clasping her tightly in his arms. "Cease your struggles, wench. I intend to show you the joys of matrimony." He laughed loudly, a laugh that was cut short by Storm's knee connecting forcefully with his groin. "You bitch!"

"Robbie, you and Donald circle round behind our wounded knight. Jaime, you stay here. Iain and I will circle round behind Mistress Eldon. With the stream as our ally we will entrap the pair."

Free of Sir Hugh's grip, Storm glared at the hunched-over man unsympathetically. "Joys, is it? Spare me that. Ye'll get no pleasures from me, Sir Hugh, now or ever, so I suggest ye hobble home. We both know my father would ne'er agree to our wedding. Ye'll nay dishonor me to ensure the match."

"You are a cold-blooded bitch, Storm Eldon," he snarled. "You are enough to freeze a man."

"Not like my dear stepmama, eh, Sir Hugh?" she sneered.

"I don't know what you are talking about," he said with an overdone confusion.

Storm's laughter was derisive. "Think ye that I've not seen the pair of ye slipping off to dark corners to grope about like frenzied animals? I daresay our esteemed steward would be interested to hear how ye visit Lady Mary's chambers of a morning. My God, I doubt the heat of him has ere left the bed."

"We do nothing wrong," bellowed Sir Hugh, silently cursing his luck at having been found out.

"No? Playing backgammon, are ye? My, I have not realized what a physical game it was ere now. All that grunting and moaning and crying out. 'Tis the tossing of the dice, I imagine."

Iain watched, bemused, as Tavis buried his face in his arms to stifle his laughter. It was a rare thing for Tavis to laugh. As his eldest brother had grown he had become more solemn, even hard and cynical. Many had ventured a guess as to why the man had become that way, but no one really knew, for Tavis was a private man, keeping too much inside of himself. Suddenly Iain decided he would say nothing, whatever Tavis had planned for the lass. She could prove the tonic needed to lighten Tavis's soul.

With a bellow of rage, Sir Hugh lunged at Storm, sending them both to the ground. She realized her taunts had driven him into one of his furies. Fighting him with all her strength was useless, and she knew it, but did not cease. Suddenly she was firmly pinned as he straddled her, one of his strong hands pinning hers above her head. He smiled coldly and she fought her fear.

'Not so haughty now, are you," he sneered, his free hand nimbly unlacing her gown.

"Ye do this, Sir Hugh, and I shall see ye dead if 'tis the last thing I do."

Her voice was so low and cold that he hesitated briefly before laughing. "I'm sure you'll try." He stared at her heaving breasts and then roughly parted her unlaced bodice, exposing their alabaster firmness to his greedy eyes. "God, but you are well made, wench." His hand reaching to cup one, he suddenly found a sword at his throat and felt another at his back. "Sweet Jesus, what . . ."

"Get up very slowly, Sir Hugh. Lay one hand on the lass and I cut your throat," came a deep, soft yet icy voice with a definite if subtle Scottish accent, a voice that teased a memory free in Storm's mind as she waited for Sir Hugh to get off of her.

Sir Hugh blanched as he faced skewering from both sides. The moment her hands were released, Storm drew her clothing together and struggled to redo her laces. By the time Sir Hugh had slowly risen to his feet, she had accomplished enough to give her the barest semblance of modesty. A hand grasped her arm and pulled her to her feet. She was not overly surprised to find herself facing Tavis Mac-

Lagan as, for reasons beyond her, she remembered him well. The head-to-toe black he was adorned in hindered her recognition not at all. It was his voice and eyes that she had most recalled.

"We meet again, Mistress Eldon," Tavis drawled as he sheathed his sword and began to redo her laces.

She eyed him calmly but with humor. "I see ye have as much skill with laces as ye did with braids."

"Do you know these men?" Sir Hugh asked with some incredulity, for he knew they were Scots.

"Why, aye. This is Tavis MacLagan, and the man next to him is his brother Iain. Seven years past they held me, Andrew, Robin, Matilda, Hadden and Haig for ransom. How healed the laird's wound?"

"Quickly and neatly, mistress," Iain replied with a grin. "Ye have a good memory."

"Ah, well, it was an adventure of the best sort for a child. Exciting yet leaving no scars."

"What do we do with this?" asked Robbie, nudging Sir Hugh with his sword.

Tavis's eyes narrowed as they rested on the Englishman. "Strip him and bind him o'er his saddle."

Dislike of the man and temper aside, Storm felt for the shame that would bring Sir Hugh. "Oh, sir, can ye not leave him his attire? It will be shame enough for him to be sent back across his saddle."

"I need no wench to plead for me," snarled Sir Hugh.

Goaded, Storm glared at him. "Fine. Return to Hagaleah with your backside out for all to see. I daresay most of the women will recognize it well as it's occupied most every hedge, bed and hayloft there."

Flushed with impotent rage, Sir Hugh sneered, "A man needs some relief when he makes the folly of pursuing the cold-blooded spawn of some Irish whore."

With an incoherent sound of rage, Storm lunged

at him, the long fingers of her delicate hands curved into talons. As he stepped back to avoid her, Tavis grasped her from behind. His strong arms wrapped around her slim form like the bands of a cage and he held her until her struggles ceased. He was surprised at the strength she displayed, for she barely reached his shoulder and was as slim as a reed.

Calming down as the red mist of rage cleared from her brain, Storm felt the tight bonds encircling her ease slightly. She kept her eyes fixed upon Sir Hugh as he was roughly stripped of his clothing. There was no denying that he was a fine figure of a man, but she was unmoved, knowing well the rot that the attractive edifice tried to disguise. She watched with the detachment of a physician, her features set and cold.

Releasing her, Tavis glanced from her unreadable face to the naked man. "Like what ye see?" he purred.

Meeting Sir Hugh's eyes as he was tugged to his horse, Storm replied clearly, " 'Tis a fine enough form, though I have seen too few to judge well. Nay, I was merely wondering what draws so many women to his bed or causes them to invite him into theirs. The attraction eludes me, though I daresay he serves Lady Mary well enough, for her tastes have e'er been less than exacting." She ignored Tavis's soft laughter and continued to meet Sir Hugh's gaze, refusing to flinch beneath his rage and hate.

She watched as Sir Hugh was slung over his saddle with little consideration for his lack of clothing. He was tied down, and the rump of his horse given a sound slap. The animal trotted toward Hagaleah for a few yards before slowing to a walk. It would be a long while before Sir Hugh reached the castle. His threats and curses served to entertain the Scotsmen but failed to prod the horse onward.

Turning to look at Tavis, Storm said, "What do ye

plan to do with me, sir? I fear if 'tis ransom on your mind ye are lost. Lady Mary will give naught for me e'en if ye threatened to send me home piece by piece. She runs Hagaleah now and she would rejoice to see me dead or gone."

"Where is your father then?" He took her arm and urged her in the direction of the rest of his men.

"France. Our king felt his services would be of more use there than along our fractious border."

"And ye feel the man left in charge woundnae see to your safe return?" Tavis asked.

"He is completely under Lady Mary's control." Storm struggled to keep pace with the man so that his hand upon her arm stayed as a guide and not a drag. "They just need not tell anyone. I fear 'tis as bad at the Fosters, for Lady Mary exerts a great deal of control over the lady there. What I truly fear is that the lords and their heirs may not return, and I speak not of an honorable death in battle."

"What would it gain them?"

"They have each borne a son, and Sir Hugh is sure of being appointed guardian." She looked at the animals the men had stolen when they reached the place where the remainder of the raiders waited. "A successful raid, I see. It would ne'er have been so easy if things were as they should be. Was anyone hurt?"

"We left a few bound up who'll suffer a sore head on the morrow," Tavis replied. "It did occur to me that the raid was far too easy," he mused. " 'Twas little guarding going on."

Storm sighed. " 'Tis sure to ruin us. So, sir, what do ye plan to do with me?" She was not at all sure she liked the way he smiled, for she was no child now but a woman.

Tossing her upon his horse, Tavis mounted behind her, grinning at the way she tried to tug her skirts down over her slim legs. "I am sure there'll be some benefit from your abduction." Slipping an arm around her tiny waist, he started his mount on the way to Caraidland, the keep of the MacLagans.

Tavis was not at all clear on what he would do with Storm Eldon. All he knew was that he wanted to keep her with him for a while. There was also a very healthy desire for her involved but, although he could take her at any time, he strongly wished for her to succumb willingly. He certainly did not want to send her back to Hagaleah so that Sir Hugh could maul her.

He was puzzled by his attitude toward her as, for a long time, he had felt women were good for only one thing and aside from that he had no use for them and less interest. Yet, when Sir Hugh had attacked the girl a white-hot rage had seized Tavis far in excess of any offended sense of chivalry or honor. He wondered if it was because he still saw Storm as that engaging child of the past.

Storm was no less confused. It was a wonder to her that she was unafraid. It was well known what a man did with a woman captive, yet she could not seem to conjure up any real fear. Some instinct told her she would not be tossed out as amusement for the men. That same instinct told her that Tavis was not taking her along simply to reminisce about their meeting in the past.

Despite that, she felt relatively calm. A part of her acknowledged that she would prefer Tavis MacLagan to steal her virtue than Sir Hugh, who was plainly not going to give up and so would therefore eventually succeed. That thought managed to stir up a little resentment over the way that men simply took as they pleased with little or no thought to the lady involved. The fact that it had always been so did little to ease that resentment.

Several hours later they halted, although they had not gone far. Driving the stolen animals made it impossible to gain any speed. Storm was also sure that they were not all that far from Caraidland, but the men were plainly in need of a little respite. She sat calmly on a rock as the animals were secured and a guard chosen. As they seemed to, she doubted there would be any immediate attack put forth. Her father would have hesitated for fear of endangering her, but those at Hagaleah now would be slow due to unreadiness.

Tavis handed her a blanket, watching quietly as she rolled herself up in it, pillowing her head upon the moss as the men did. He then wrapped himself up in his plaid and lay down beside her, his sword away from her but near at hand. She was an uncomplaining captive, but he did not doubt that she would try to escape if given half a chance. He fixed his gaze upon the gentle curves of her blanketed form and his eyes were slow in closing.

Thoughts of escape were indeed in Storm's mind, but she could see that her chance would not come yet. A part of her was glad, for the idea of trying to get back to Hagaleah alone in the dark was terrifying. She sighed silently, wishing she were a man, for then she would only face ransoming. Then, too, she would have been better equipped to plot escape, manage it and elude her captors. As she began to close her eyes a movement in the forest just beyond caught her notice. She stiffened for she feared she knew what it was.

Like some specter and with as little noise, the small figure crept over to her. It was at her side when Tavis suddenly sprang to his feet, his sword raised. With a small cry and no thought to her own safety, Storm placed herself between Tavis and her cousin Phelan.

"Do not harm him. 'Tis but a boy." She saw that the other men had roused quickly, ready for battle.

Tavis did not put away his sword, but he held it less threateningly. "I can see that. Who is he?"

"Phelan O'Conner," the boy replied in a clear child's voice that held no fear.

"How come ye here?" Tavis was noting the bright hair and odd eyes so like Storm's.

"I followed Storm to the glade. Ye should ne'er go out alone," he scolded her. "When ye took her I followed ye. I thought I could aid her to escape," he said flatly, his shoulders sagging with the weight of failure.

"Ye followed us on foot? Alone?" Tavis was duly impressed by such a feat.

"Aye. Ye were not traveling at a very fast pace," the boy replied with the air of one unaware that he had done anything worthy of note. "I left when ye did so I know not what they do at Hagaleah."

"What is this boy to you?" Tavis asked Storm.

"My cousin from my mother's kin in Ireland."

Tavis told his men to return to their rest, fetched another blanket and tossed it to Phelan. "I would send ye home, but I ken ye'd nay go. Better to keep ye with us than to have ye yapping at our heels. Ere ye bed down for the night, laddie, I'll be having that knife ye have tucked in your boot."

"I would ne'er kill a sleeping man. T'would be cowardly," Phelan said as he handed over the knife.

" 'Tis a comfort to know that, but I prefer ye unarmed. Get some rest, laddie."

When they were again settled Tavis listened to the cousins' whispered conversation. At times he was hard put not to laugh out loud. He did not want the boy along, but he knew there would be no keeping the child away from Storm. It was his fervent hope that there would be no others showing up.

"I had hoped to rescue ye, cousin."

"Not to worry, Phelan. Mayhaps next time."

Silence reigned for a moment before Phelan said, "Are ye feeling a bit cold, cousin?"

Storm bit her lip to stop her laughter, unknowingly mimicking Tavis, for she knew it was not the cold that made the boy wish to be nearer. "Aye. 'Tis a bit sharp. What do ye suggest?"

With the air of one making a sacrifice, Phelan replied, "We could huddle a bit closer for warmth."

"An excellent idea. Come along then." She let the boy snuggle up to her, the back of him fitting closely to the front of her. "That is much better. Good sleep, cousin."

"Good sleep to ye as well."

"I am glad ye are here," she said softly and meant it, for even though he was but a child he was family, and somehow that made things seem less bleak.

4

Caraidland burst into life when the raiding party
rode up, their bounty on the hoof very welcome after
a long winter. Storm sat before Tavis upon his
stallion and watched her father's stock praised and
sorted out. Knowing how easily that vital stock had
been gained by the MacLagans was yet another
grievance to lay at Lady Mary's door. Despite her
years at Hagaleah, the woman still failed to really
understand the way of things. For that misjudgment
the people who worked her father's lands would
have less food in their bellies. Storm knew that
would not bother Lady Mary at all.

Tavis dismounted, helped Storm down and left
her standing next to her cousin with Angus to keep a
close eye on them. He always saw to the stabling of
his mount himself. After a last quick glance at
Storm, who looked tiny next to the stocky, muscular
Angus, he turned his attention to caring for his
horse.

"They surely did well for themselves," Phelan
remarked softly.

"They surely did. Some of our best stock. T'will
mean a few less lambs, a few less calves, a few less of
everything, for one loss leads to another. Lord, but I
wish my father had not gone away from Hagaleah."

" 'Tis not his fault, cousin. How could he know
what would happen? He believed your steward

worthy of his trust. 'Tis not his fault that the man's a lecherous bastard who's easily led by his . . ."

"Phelan!" Storm cried, cutting off the boy's too candid commentary, and then she flicked a quelling glance at Angus, who quickly turned his laughter into a fit of coughing.

"Sorry, cousin, but sometimes I forget ye are a lady."

"I suppose that is a compliment," she murmured, her eyes dancing with laughter as they met Phelan's.

For a moment they simply stood and watched the people of Caraidland watch them. Although somewhat used to stares because of their unusual hair color and catlike eyes, it was, nonetheless, unnerving. These people were, after all, the ancient enemies of the Eldons. It was difficult to guess what thoughts lay behind those steady looks.

"Ye may hold my hand if ye are feeling a wee bit afraid," Phelan said quietly.

Biting back a smile when she recognized yet another of Phelan's attempts to behave as the child he was, yet not lose face, Storm said, "Why, thank you, Phelan. I believe I am feeling a bit faint of heart."

She held out her hand and he clasped it with his, which was not all that much smaller. Storm saw a brief flash of approval in Angus's solemn face. It puzzled her that she should feel pleased.

"They are not like the Northmen, are they?" Phelan asked with a hard-won casualness.

"No, of course not. Where did ye hear tales of those men?"

"From my grandfather. The Northmen oft raided the coast of Erin. They were a savage lot."

"Aye, they were that. These people are not like that. They are not all that different from the men at Hagaleah. We have raided each other and fought each other since the first Eldon set up housekeeping

44

along the border. Ye must not believe all the tales ye are told."

Nodding, Phelan was content for a moment, but then his eyes widened and his agitation grew very apparent. "They may be men like those at Hagaleah, but e'en your father's men—when they catch a woman—with a woman they . . ." A glance at Angus's suddenly unreadable face did not aid Phelan at all.

A chill snaked up Storm's spine, but she calmly said, "I would rather not discuss that, Phelan."

Phelan's concern was not so easily quelled. "But ye cannot be blind to the dangers, cousin. Ye must . . ."

"I am not blind, but that does not mean I must constantly stare at them either. Acushla, a woman unguarded is ever at risk. I was not safe in my own home. Sir Hugh was not reading me poetry, was he? Let us leave the subject. Allow me my temporary ignorance, for it eases my soul. There is naught we can do about it."

Again they fell silent. Storm struggled to heed her own words while Phelan wished himself a man full grown who might give Storm more of the protection she would need. Though only nine, he was far from ignorant of the way of a man with a woman. He could read the look in the men's eyes, especially in the one named Tavis. That man wanted what Sir Hugh had sought, and he could take it as he pleased.

"Oh, look there, Phelan," Storm cried, honestly surprised but also seeking something to lighten the sad look upon the boy's face. "Is that not the mare called Cornelia? The one so carefully shipped to us from Sussex?"

"Aye, it is," Phelan exclaimed, a grin splitting his face. "I recognize those white markings."

Starting to laugh, even as she wondered how she could, Storm said, "Oh Lord, Lady Mary's personal mount. I wish I was there to see her face when she discovers that the mare was taken. She will be livid. T'will be glorious. Such a pity to miss it."

"Can ye see it?" Phelan began to laugh as helplessly as Storm. "The lady standing about with her gilded saddle and nary a mount to display it upon. I could almost pity that pretty groom of hers come discovery."

" 'Tis sweet justice, is it not?" Storm gasped and was struck by another seizure of hilarity.

Tavis arrived and looked to Angus for an explanation of the prisoners' good humor. Prisoners were not known to do much laughing. As he waited, his own mouth twitched with laughter, for the open, unaffected laugh Storm possessed was infectious. Angus, a rather stolid man not given to laughter, looked very near to joining the cousins in their uninhibited amusement.

"Seems we hae taen Lady Mary's personal mount," Angus explained with a smile.

A grin split Tavis's face. "Have we now." He looked at the two cousins whose remarkable eyes were still bright from laughter only just halted. "Ye are still a wretched wee lass," he told Storm.

"I know. Still, 'tis funny to think of m'lady with her elegant saddle and her personal groom, who was chosen for his beauty and dressed so fine, but no horse. She had the mare brought up from Sussex. She will only ride Sussex mares."

Shaking his head over such wasteful eccentricity, Tavis took her by the arm. With Phelan hovering close by, he led her into the tower house that their laird called home. As they walked, Tavis marveled that she could look so fresh after the long night and the rough trip. It was a strength he would not have attributed to an Englishwoman.

It was a good strong building that they entered, one which Storm felt could withstand most anything if by some miracle an enemy breeched the outside walls. From what she could see as they made their way to the hall, the MacLagans were not without funds. Here was no simple border landholder but a family of power and prestige. Her nose and eyes also told her that ventilation was very good, something not often the case even in the best of fortified residences. She became reluctantly impressed as she was led along the corridor.

The hall filled up quickly when they arrived. After a brief glance around, noting such things as tapestries of excellent quality, rugs from the East and other signs of well-being, she looked at the people seated at the massive head table. She quickly recognized Sholto MacLagan and the laird, although he did not look well, but wondered who the relatively young woman was who looked so imperial and lovely. Phelan's hand slid into hers as Tavis and Iain went to greet their father, leaving Angus as a guard yet again.

"Sweet Mary, I'd nay have thought Eldon would be so easy to steal from," remarked Colin when he had a full accounting of what had been seized as well as the ease of the raid.

"He wasnae home," said Iain. "Off to France to fight for the Sassanach king. His steward's in charge."

"Weel, we could make a very fine profit if this is how the man cares for his laird's property." Colin squinted toward the captives. "And what have ye got . . . God's teeth, ye have taken the wee lass again."

"Aye." Tavis let his gaze rest upon Storm for a moment. "Aye. The lad's her cousin. He followed us. Had a thought to free the lass." He grinned at his father. "Truth to tell, I had to rescue the lass ere I could steal her. A Sassanach gentleman was behaving verra ungallantly. Had her down upon the grass and

47

all."

"Things are in a tangle from what the lass says," Iain reported. "The steward is cuckolding the laird and nay a one o' the ones with responsibility are using it. 'Tis easy to see, for there were few guards and watches posted. So, too, I cannae believe Eldon would let a man stay at Hagaleah who is sore bent on bedding the lass and nay too subtle about it. That man had no fear of retribution, though he was set on raping the only daughter of the laird." Iain then went on to tell his father of what they had done to Sir Hugh, and his father laughed heartily.

"She said we'd get no ransom," Tavis added. "She claims the Lady Mary would as soon see her sent back piece by piece. The lass e'en feels her kin will ne'er return alive from France and 'tis no death in battle that she fears. Lady Mary has her own bairns readied to be laird and her lover to be the children's guardian."

For a moment Colin said nothing, simply frowning in thought. He pondered on the girl's claims and felt that there was a chance they were the truth. Once the opportunity for a ransom was negated, Colin quickly came to the only other possible reason for Tavis to abduct the girl. Colin looked at his eldest son, noting that Tavis's gaze never faltered.

"Ye'll no take the lass if she's unwilling. I owe the lass me sword arm. I could have lost it that day, for 'twas a deep wound. It healed weel and the physician said 'twas due to the good and quick care I got."

"Aye, 'tis true. I dinnae want her unwilling." Tavis smiled slightly. "Nay, I will have the lass say aye first."

"A firm aye, ye rogue. Nay a one seduced out o' her. I'll have ye ask ransom for her first as weel."

Tavis nodded. "I will send the demand out right away. Care to pass a wee word with her?"

Colin nodded, ignoring his young wife's frown of

disapproval. It had been seven years since he had seen Storm Eldon. He was curious to see what changes had been wrought in the taking child they had known so briefly. One thing was clear to see and that was that, although small of stature, Storm Eldon was now a very beautiful young woman. Colin could easily understand his eldest son's desire, but he would ensure that that desire was not satisfied by force.

Hesitating briefly when Tavis signaled her to come to his side, Storm wondered what plans had been made. As she moved to stand between Tavis and Colin as instructed, she noticed that the young woman seated at the table was looking none too pleased. With lovely chestnut hair and gray-green eyes, the woman was beautiful but, at the moment, those eyes flashed with dislike and the voluptuous figure was stiff with outrage. Storm wondered if the woman meant something to Tavis and surprised herself by finding that she did not like the idea of that at all. Shaking her mind free of such puzzles, Storm turned her attention to Colin MacLagan.

The puzzles returned when Colin introduced the young woman as his wife, Janet, for Storm found herself feeling distinctly relieved. She also found that she still did not like the woman, a feeling that had nothing to do with the fact that Janet was a healthy 25 or so years younger than Colin. Many a man took a woman much younger than himself as a second wife. Storm only knew that there was something about Janet that chilled her. Telling herself that she was giving her imagination too free a rein helped not at all. It was clear enough that the brothers cared little for the woman and from Tavis Storm sensed an even stronger emotion than mere dislike or disinterested intolerance. Things at Caraidland were plainly not very calm and cozy.

"So, Mistress Eldon, our ways cross yet again."

Colin met her wary look with a smile. "And the lad?"

"Phelan O'Conner, sir," the boy replied in a clear, firm voice that revealed none of his nervousness.

"Ah, from the Irish half of your family, eh, lass?"

"Aye, m'lord." She smiled at Phelan. "He appeared at our door a short while before my father left. When my parents were wed my mother left a note for her kin telling them to come to Hagaleah if they were ever in need of aid. My young cousin here found it when he was left without kin there and took it upon himself to make his way to our gates to see if we would honor that promise."

"Ye traveled from Erin on your own, laddie?" asked Colin in an amazement shared by all there.

"Aye. The note bade come if help was needed. I needed it so I came." It all seemed very logical to Phelan, who had wondered from the first what people found so astonishing about his journey. "Folk take small note of a thin, ragged boy with no horse and no pack save to boot him out of the way. I paid to sail to English soil and then begged my way to Hagaleah." He shrugged to say it was all that simple.

Colin shook his head in wonder. "Ye could have gone astray at the verra least."

"Nay. I knew twas on the border, so I kept to that as near as I could. Had to near it ere long."

"Of course," Tavis drawled, his eyes alight with laughter, " 'tis verra logical. I can see that."

"Can ye now." Colin turned his attention to Storm again. "Ye have grown into a verra bonnie woman." He smiled widely when she blushed.

Phelan frowned. "How can ye say that? She looks just like me." He frowned even more when the men suddenly took to coughing. "Well, she does look just like me."

"Nay," Storm said. "Ye look just like me. I looked

this way first and have for eight more years than ye."

Grinning, Phelan nodded. "Aye, 'tis true enough. Still and all, I shall be taller."

"Oh, I do hope so." She laughed with Phelan, but then looked at Colin. " 'Tis no guarantee of a ransom this time, m'lord. I would not be surprised to find my father's second wife holding a celebration," she added with a small smile. "She would be fair pleased to see the last of the Eldons she began with eight years ago."

"Och, weel, we shall give it a try, lass. We will put her in the west tower room, Tavis. The boy can bed down in the room just beneath her."

"Nay," Phelan cried, and his gaze was fixed upon Tavis even though he spoke to Colin. "I will stay with Storm even an I must needs sleep upon the floor. 'Tis true I will be little protection an a man wants to visit her, but, if naught else, my presence will make seduction awkward. I swore to her father that I would watch out for her and I shall."

"Then ye shall," said Colin, oblivious to Tavis's obvious displeasure. "Lay him out a pallet in the west tower room. Tavis, lead them to their quarters. I ken they may like to rest a wee bit, mayhaps wash up."

Tavis gave Phelan a harder shove than needed to make the boy move along. He had not really thought to creep to Storm's room like a thief in the night, but the boy's clear intention to stay constantly at her side would make a wooing very difficult, if not impossible. There would also be the problem of what to do with the boy when the time was right to collect his treasure. It was just another obstacle that he did not need.

"Why do ye give the best room to that Sassanach slut? Is she not a prisoner?"

Looking at the woman he regretted marrying

51

more with each passing day, Colin replied, "Aye, a prisoner, but also the daughter of an enemy I respect and a lass who once did me a good turn. Lord Eldon is a man of honor. I will treat his kin as I would expect him to treat mine if they fell into his hands."

"If ye want her treated weel, then ye best keep Tavis from sniffing round her."

" 'Tis expected to use a woman taken a captive," said Sholto. "Lord Eldon will think naught else."

"Aye, 'tis expected," agreed Colin, "but I'll nay have the wee lass abused. I have Tavis's word that he will seek a ransom first, and his word that he'll nay take the lass to his bed if she is unwilling. 'Tis all I can do."

Janet thought it very little indeed. She had wanted Tavis since she had first seen him four years ago. It had seemed such a simple thing to seduce him into her arms, but it had not been. Unlike other men she had known, Tavis MacLagan had proven immune to her, his sense of honor and his deep loyalty to his father proving an unbreakable wall. She had accepted the occasional presence of Katerine MacBroth in his bed, for she knew Tavis only used the young woman, that he would never wed her nor care for her as the girl hoped he would. However, it had taken Janet but a moment to see that Storm Eldon was a very real threat. She hoped fervently that Hagaleah would quickly come forth with the ransom. It seemed impossible that the girl's kin would refuse to pay any ransom. Lord Eldon could easily survive to return to power at Hagaleah and need to be answered to.

"Recovered from your ordeal, Sir Hugh?" Lady Mary purred, her full mouth slipping into a smile.

"I am so pleased I was able to provide your lady-ship with some amusement." Sir Hugh was unmoved by the sight of Lady Mary in her bath, her voluptuous charms barely concealed by soap and water. "Do you plan no retaliation for this raid?"

"I have seen to the watches being strengthened." Her lovely face hardened. "The arrogance of them."

"But what of that which they have stolen from us?"

"The stock will be replaced. I am, nonetheless, enraged by the theft of my mare. However, I will not persue those heathens into their own den. It would cost me more than it would gain."

"I speak not of your stinking horse," Sir Hugh snarled. "What of Storm? Your husband's daughter?"

Lady Mary shrugged as she stepped out of the bath, and her maids rushed to dry her off. "The swine will no doubt cry for ransom. They usually do when they catch one of our people. That fool Roden would even ransom the peasants."

"Ah, then you will pay. Mayhaps it will not be too steep."

Wrapping the towel around herself, Lady Mary sent her maids off before turning to Sir Hugh. She resented his apparent immunity to her as well as his deep interest in Storm. Despite that, she did not fear that he would become too uncontrollable. Not only did she know how to stir his passion despite the apathy he now displayed, but she could also use his greed to maneuver him.

"I care not how much or how little they ask, for I will not pay. Not right away. Mayhaps not ever."

Sir Hugh turned an unhealthy shade of red as rage threatened to overcome him. "You promised me the girl and, through the girl a fortune. God's teeth, woman, you know very well how she will be used."

"I knew not that virginity held such an attraction for you, Hugh."

" 'Tis not that, but I would rather she had not been bedded by all and sundry."

"Well, I cannot see them doing that to her. She is too high-bred. The sons, mayhaps the father, but that is all. There is honor among these heathens. There is also a respect betwixt these two old enemies, even an odd liking of each other. I doubt Storm will return to Hagaleah as innocent as she left it, but she'll not have been abused. Think of it as training." She laughed and lay down upon the bed on her stomach as a pretty young maid entered the room. "They will teach her all she needs to know."

"I hardly need their help," Sir Hugh grumbled. "I could have done that upon my own."

Lady Mary sighed as the silent maid removed the towel and began to massage into her body a scented oil that kept her pampered skin soft. "No doubt, but I think 'tis her spirit that causes you the most trouble. Some time with the rough Scots will cure Storm of that. She'll be easier to handle. Do not forget the feet, wench," she told the maid. "The winter's cold floors have roughened them."

Watching the maid rubbing the softening oils into every inch of Lady Mary's back was swiftly curing Sir Hugh of his disinterest. "I could have done so given time," he murmured hoarsely when he recognized the maid as one he knew well, a certain well-endowed girl named Agnes.

Turning over, Lady Mary saw that his disinterest had fled, and made a soft, purring noise as the maid began to gently rub the oils in upon the front of her body. "You wish to wed the girl. She does not wish to wed you." Her smile widened as Sir Hugh began to shed his clothes. "A touch of shame and humility could serve you well. If she is dishonored, she will think again before she turns down your offer, for she will know full well that there will be few others, perhaps none."

"It will make me look the fool," he said as he moved to the side of the bed.

"A rich fool," she murmured as he settled down beside her.

"Mayhaps." His brief frown fled as the maid, at Mary's signal, began to shed her clothes. "Still, it will wound my pride, and I had wanted to be the first."

"Worry not, Hugh. Mayhaps the Scots will teach her a few tricks."

"Ah, my'lady," he said softly, "if they can teach her to be as you, they can keep her for as long as they wish." He laughed and both women joined him as they fell into his open arms.

5

Phelan sat on the large bed, watching Storm struggle to fix her hair. "It has been near to a week."

Storm sighed and smoothed the skirt of the dress she wore, glad that she had been provided clothes, for she shuddered to think that she might have had to continue to wear only what she had arrived in. So agreeable was it to have a change of clothing that she could not only ignore the fact that they were Janet's, but the ill grace with which they were lent to her. The laird had told her to adjust them to fit, but Storm had merely basted the tucks needed to make them fit her smaller frame. She did not think Janet would do so, but, if the woman wished, the dresses could easily be returned to their original size and owner.

" 'Tis not when the MacLagan man returns, but what the reply to the ransom demand is that is important to us. We are well treated, if watched constantly. 'Tis as comfortable as Hagaleah."

"Aye. They are not bad folk. 'Tis easy to forget we are enemies. Yet I had thought that Sir Hugh would push for your rescue or ransom." Phelan grinned when his cousin made a face. "He does want you."

"Sir Hugh wants anything female that is neither too old nor too ugly. My attractiveness is vastly increased by the fortune he would gain were we to wed. My father has given me a sizable dowry."

"Then surely he would rush to gain your release ere ye be abused and made useless as a wife." He frowned. "He'd not want to wed you ere ye are dishonored by a man or men. Nay, especially when 'tis by a MacLagan."

"I think Sir Hugh is in sore need of funds and would wed me ere I had been made whore to the whole clan. Lady Mary will no doubt soothe any qualms or wounded pride the man suffers."

Phelan bit his lip as he thought and then said, "Tavis is after sharing your bed."

A murmur of doubtful acknowledgement escaped Storm as she thought on Tavis MacLagan. He was a man a maid often dreamed of. His black hair was thick and as glossy as a raven's wing. Taller than most men, he was leanly built, with the well-developed muscles of a fighting man. His face was hawkish with high, well-defined cheekbones, a long, straight nose and sturdy jaw, but his glorious eyes, so heavily lashed and set beneath gently curved brows, could soften the harsh lines. So, too, did the smiles that so rarely seemed to touch his finely drawn, thin-lipped mouth, a mouth that had yet to kiss hers.

That was a puzzle to her, for she, too, sometimes got the feeling that he wanted her. She truly doubted that Phelan's presence restricted Tavis. There was nothing to stop him from simply tossing the boy out of the room, yet Tavis did not even try to do that. In fact, there had not even been the hint of a kiss. Storm smiled a little when she recognized that she felt piqued. She certainly did not want to be ravished, but she could not help but wonder why, when it was his perogative as her captor, Travis MacLagan had not touched her.

"What is that smile for, cousin?"

"I am smiling o'er the vagaries of a female's vanity." She grinned. "I do not wish to be ravished yet 'tis annoyed I am that it has not been tried. 'Tis

58

starting me to wonder where or how I am lacking." She laughed along with Phelan. "Ah," she moved to open the door when someone knocked, "our escort to dinner."

Angus led them down the hall, he and Phelan chatting amiably about the hunt that day. Everyone, save Janet, had been quite friendly. If it were not for the guard always at their side, it would be easy to forget that they were prisoners. It would also be easy to forget that the MacLagans were the hereditary enemies of the Eldons, that the reiving and the fighting had been going on for generations.

Storm knew she was in danger of forgetting that fact with Tavis. The time spent talking, laughing and arguing with the man had served to obscure that. It took a greater and greater effort for her to remember it. It was the same with most of the others she had come to know at Caraidland but, with that insight into herself that so often helped her, Storm knew it was far worse, far more dangerous with Tavis. She not only forgot that he was the enemy, her captor, but she was rapidly falling in love with him. That was not only foolish, but could lead her down a path to a great deal of pain.

Tavis greeted her at the door of the hall as he had all week. It was hard for him to keep up a casual demeanor, for he wanted her more with each passing day. Yet, he found himself enjoying getting to know her. Here was a woman who was not swayed by empty, artful phrases, one who had the opinions of a well-informed mind and was not afraid to voice them and defend them, and one who had a sense of humor as well as the ability to laugh at herself, her frailties and errors. He had discovered that, while she possessed a temper and an open, beautiful laugh, she also had a ready wit, pride, honesty, modesty and many another quality that he had lately found rare in a woman.

The one thing that truly amazed him was her lack of awareness concerning her own beauty and attraction for a man. Features that had promised beauty on the small girl had fulfilled their boast. Her wide, slanted amber eyes still seemed to fill her small heart-shaped face, thick, long brown lashes giving them a sensual look, and the tilted brown brows accentuating their shape. No changes had occurred in the satiny alabaster skin, but the full mouth had lost its childishness and now begged to be kissed. Tavis did not think she had grown all that much taller, but she had gained all that was needed to heat a man's blood and carried it with a graceful, unconscious sensuality that was seduction itself.

It was as the meal drew to a close that the MacLagan messenger finally returned from Hagaleah. The sinking feeling that Storm experienced as the laird read the missive with an easily discernible frown told her that she had been foolish enough to harbor the small hope that the ransom would be paid, that she and Phelan would be released. She was curious as to whether her father's wife had openly tossed her to the wolves or was employing a subtle delaying tactic. The laird's face as he handed her the reply told Storm that she was not going to like it.

The blatant falsehood that excused Lady Mary from immediately paying the ransom made Storm laugh softly. There was little chance that she would have chased her father and brother to France. Even if she had not enough sense to fear the war, she would have feared her father's wrath. However, it gave the woman the needed excuse for delay, requesting proof that the MacLagans did, indeed, hold her and her cousin Phelan as prisoners, for the ransom was too high to hand over without such proof.

"I daresay my head on a salver would be the proof she craves," Storm drawled, smiling faintly. "So what do ye do now, m'lord? 'Tis my thought that

60

this delay will soon become an outright refusal."

"Aye," Colin agreed with a frown, but then he smiled. "Your head is indeed the answer. A lock of that hair. 'Tis a rare color. There'll be few that have it. 'Tis proof enough. We'll send it and see what she replies. I cannae believe she is so confident she can see to your father's end, therefore can refuse to aid ye. We have tried for years."

Storm nodded. "As my father has always expected ye to. 'Tis true," she continued when she saw that she had everyone's full attention, "that the marriage is no marriage despite my two half-brothers. My father knows of Lady Mary's many faults, but he does not see her evil nor her cunning. He feels that she should be content in that she wants for naught and thus pays little heed to her. As with most men, he would not look to a woman for his final fall, he being a strong knight, a skilled fighter."

"Why should he?" asked Sholto with the scorn of a man possessing an agile, strong sword arm.

"She has allies. I doubt not she could raise an army to fight him if she but called upon all her lovers," Storm drawled.

"Aye, but he has fought us often and come away alive, most oft unscathed," Iain pointed out.

"Would ye draw a sword upon the man ye trusted to run your lands ere he had drawn one upon you? Nay, I thought not. My father would expect no threat from that quarter. Being an honorable man, my father would ne'er expect a knife in the back, and I fear that is my stepmother's way." Storm shook her head, a sadness settling upon her face. "I did not see her plan until 'twas too late to warn my father. She will do her best to see that he and Drew do not return."

"And ye?" Tavis asked, his mind on the fact that the ransom had been refused, so he need not go softly with her any longer, could at last indulge in more than a gentle wooing.

"She would rejoice to be free of me as well. The woman detests me. Has always done so. I made matters worse by aiding Mistress Bailey, a widow who would no doubt be the next Lady Eldon if Lady Mary died. Mistress Bailey has been my father's mistress and the wife of his heart for five years now. She has given him two children. Lady Mary had a plan to be rid of the woman as soon as my father was gone. She hired men to attack Mistress Bailey and the babes as they traveled to relatives. I was able to get warning to her so that the plan failed, but I fear Lady Mary found out what I had done."

"Hagaleah sounds a right bed of intrigue," Iain said with a shake of his head. "I cannae believe a woman could kill a man like your father. A woman isnae made for plotting a murder so coldly."

"Is she not? I mean no faulting of my sex for we, as men, have our good and our bad, but I think a woman is very much capable of it. A woman is a creature of strong emotion and has not been filled from birth with ideals of honor. I know men feel we have none, do not understand it. Have none of you gentlemen found yourself the victim of some female machination, some ploy you failed to see until she had gained her end?" She nodded when she saw uncomfortable recollection flicker over many a man's face. "A woman can have cunning, and her very softness makes it more effective. Aye, a woman can plot a murder, mayhaps better than a man, for I believe she can hate better, hate with a cold clarity that oft eludes a man."

"Ye really believe she'll not send the ransom for ye," Colin commented. "I will try again, ye ken."

"Aye, ye can try all ye like, but I think the lady will delay until she feels sure that my father will ne'er return or, mayhaps, until Sir Hugh urges her to fetch me. She will not honor the usual way of ransoming, I am thinking. The woman will be loathe to hand over a bag of rotten meal for me and Phelan." She looked at Colin, one shapely brow quirked in question. "So, m'lord, what plan ye for us if I prove right?"

"Ye'll stay here," Tavis replied, cutting off any reply his father could have made.

Storm noticed the sudden silence at the table and frowned. From the various expressions and the pointed lack of such on the faces around her she knew they were aware of something she was not. For a brief instant she feared death, but the fear was quick to fade, for she felt sure the MacLagans would not kill a helpless woman and child. Without a chance of ransom, however, she saw no point in them keeping her and Phelan at Caraidland. She could not see them keeping her and Phelan until her father returned either, for his return was uncertain at best. It was a very large puzzle to her, and growing larger.

Tavis watched the confusion flash across her lovely face. He thought wryly that he must have behaved himself very well indeed if he had left her with no idea of what he wanted or, at least, so little a one that it was not the first to come to mind. It would soon be the first thought upon her mind, however, for now that the ransom had been more or less refused and would probably not be forthcoming at all, he no longer felt bound to go gently as he had promised his father. She could look upon it as a ransom of sorts. He would have her and it would be soon.

"What is the point if I can bring ye no ransom?" she queried in bewilderment.

"Ye'll stay here, ransom or nay, 'til I say ye may leave," he said softly, turning to look fully at her where she sat at his side. "So I'll hear no more questions about it."

His autocratic tone put fire in her eyes, her precarious position as a prisoner forgotten for the moment. " 'Tis my right to know what ye want with me, why ye insist that I stay here when there can be no profit in it for ye."

"So ye wish to ken what I want with ye," Tavis drawled as he grasped her by the shoulders. "Allow me to demonstrate," he purred, yanking her into his arms as he had wanted to for days.

At first Storm was so surprised that she was still in his arms. It was when his warm, soft lips began to stir a heat within her that she came to life. She quickly found that it was not easy to fight a man's hold while sitting down. Despite the fact that fury, a fury increased by the audible amusement of the others at the table, gave her added strength, Storm also discovered that trying to fight Tavis was akin to beating her head against a wall. Although being kissed before an audience was not at all to her liking, most of her fight came from a fright of the response her body was showing. She knew a surge of white-hot rage when he released her and grinned at her. It blinded her to the fact that he was clearly moved by the kiss.

The blaze in her amber eyes fascinated Tavis almost as much as the kiss had pleasured him. He did not think he had ever seen a woman look so gloriously angry. It disappointed him somewhat when, in a typical outraged-maiden tactic, she moved to slap his face. He easily caught her wrist, but then suddenly felt a surprisingly strong little fist connect with his jaw, catching him unawares and sending him off the bench to sprawl on the floor. Tavis was caught up in a mixture of anger and amusement. The snickers he could hear his family and the men indulging in mattered little to him. He was too interested in Storm.

"I forgot what a wee scrapper ye are, but now ye

ken why ye'll stay here," he said, watching as she left her seat to stand and glare at him, her lovely hands planted firmly on her slim hips.

"Oh, I understand. Slow to grasp your intentions I may have been, but 'tis clear as a bell now. Ye are no better than that slimy toad Sir Hugh."

"An I was, lass, ye'd be well used by now," he snarled as he stood up to tower over her, his temper having gained the upper hand when she compared him to the Englishman.

"Used mayhaps," she sneered, "but 'tis a question as to whether it be well or nay."

Colin briefly thought of putting a halt to the swiftly worsening argument, but only briefly. The couple had squared off before and he found it far too entertaining to end. If the subject was not exactly genteel, it was of little consequence, for all there knew what Tavis had planned for the girl. It was simply a question of when he would take it and how hard he would have to work for it. Tavis never having suffered a problem with the women, it was of inerest to them all to see him meet resistance.

Grasping her by the wrists, Tavis growled, "Weel, mayhaps we should go and see how weel I use ye."

Storm could not hit him as she wanted to, but she was not totally disarmed. She gave him a kick in the shins and he yelped gratifyingly. It was hardly the way to ingratiate herself to the man who held her fate in his hands, but she was too furious to think on that. Since the day she had become a woman she had suffered from men's unwanted advances, her status as only daughter to a powerful border lord not serving as all that much protection. Long ago she had given up trying to politely repel such advances.

"Spare me, please. I have just dined." She fruitlessly tried to free her wrists from his grip.

Although Tavis had never been repulsed by any

woman he had set his eyes upon, it was not solely her reluctance that stirred his anger. He felt he could understand her reluctance. After all, she was gently born, a woman whose virginity was guarded as well as any castle and was considered as great a prize. Any man who wed her would expect her innocence to be intact, and to lose that could mean that her future was irrevocably altered for the worse. His anger stemmed from the fact that he ached for her as he had for no other woman, yet she seemed not to suffer at all from the same malady.

"Then I'll remember to catch ye atween meals," he purred.

She recognized the soft tone that was indicative of his rage but ignored it. "Ye'll catch me not at all, MacLagan, or ye best watch out for your life," she hissed. "I will kill the man who dishonors me."

"And how will ye do that?" he scoffed. "Ye havenae any weapons, lass."

Her voice was a soft, chilling purr as she said, "An I must, I will tear out your throat with my teeth."

So startled was Tavis that he lost his grip, and she broke free to head toward the door, her slim back stiff with anger, Phelan at her heels. Angus quickly moved to take up his post as guard and escort. Tavis strode over to her, catching her by the arm before she went out of the hall. Neither cared nor really noticed that everyone was very quiet in the hope of hearing every word spoken.

"Aye, retreat to your chambers, lass, but ye'll nay escape me. Those at Hagaleah seem loathe to pay a tithe for ye, so we'll settle the cost o' your release another way, a way to please me."

Indicating that she must act the whore to gain her freedom was not the way to dampen the anger that seethed through her, and Storm wondered how he failed to see that. "Pleasure is the last thing ye will gain ere ye touch me, MacLagan. And I cannot stop ye, I'll be as cold as the coin Hagaleah denies ye. So come if ye will and have your lust taste ice. I'll nay give ye e'en the pleasure of a poxy tuppence whore."

" 'Tis a challenge ye offer me, lass, and 'twill ne'er be long before I pick up the gauntlet."

" 'Tis nay a challenge for a man of your strength to subdue a lass. 'Tis merely rape, sir, a common enough amusement practiced by many a man. None of ye can heed a nay as I have learned well."

What Travis was prepared to reply to that was lost, for their argument was abruptly interrupted. A buxom young woman several inches taller than Storm with midnight-black hair, creamy skin and hazel eyes burst into the hall and flung herself at Tavis. The ensuing embrace did little to calm Storm, but she refused to examine why the sight of the two kissing should cause her insides to knot up, telling herself that the proof that her dishonoring would merely be another careless tussle for the man was the cause.

Dislodging the woman who had served his basic needs for two years was not easy for Tavis. She had a fierce grip on him. He cared not at all for her past a surface desire and was furious that she had come without invitation. The undisguised scorn he read in Storm's lovely eyes only added to his anger, for he did not want to rape Storm but make love to her. The presence of his mistress would certainly aid Storm in fortifying herself against any persuasion he could bring to bear. It suddenly came to his attention that, despite Kate's impassioned embrace, he still held on to Storm. Kate's notice of that as well as her narrowed eyes made Tavis think Kate would solve his dilemma herself. She had ever been hot-tempered and jealous, expecting of him what he had never offered.

"Who is your guest, Tavis?" Katerine asked between clenched teeth.

"Storm Eldon, the daughter of Lord Eldon of Hagaleah, and my hostage. Storm, meet Kate Mac-Broth."

Neither woman did more than nod curtly to the other, and Kate turned a seductive smile upon Tavis. "She'll bring ye a handsome ransom. Let Angus take her wherever she was headed. I heard naught from ye upon your return from the raid and feared ye had come to harm."

"As ye can see I am in good health. There was no need for ye to come. I have enough to occupy me," he added softly with a meaningful look at Storm.

While Katerine seethed, Storm freed her arm from Tavis's light grip and gave him a smile that was anything but sweet. "Do not let me disrupt your routine, sir."

"My routine shall ne'er be disrupted by my plans for ye, m'lady," he drawled.

"Methinks ye have far too great an opinion of your stamina, sir." Storm marched off, ignoring the laughter her remark stirred, including that of Angus, who followed her.

6

The smile that had slowly come to Tavis's mouth in reponse to Storm's parting remark was quickly erased by Katerine. She knew well what Tavis intended for the Sassanach woman, just as instinct told her that it was more for Tavis than the taking of a female captive, something that was so common it was often considered a right. For two years she had plied her charms and skill upon the heir of Caraidland, seeing her longevity as proof that she was more than just a vessel for his lust, yet the look in his eyes when he gazed at Storm Eldon was enough to destroy that idea. Katerine had no intention of losing out to a scrawny Sassanach girl with cat's eyes and orange hair.

"So ye think to have a wee tussle with the Sassanach lass, do ye? There isnae a muckle lot to tussle with," she purred as she moved to take Storm's seat at the table.

Deciding it was neither the time nor the place to discuss the matter, Tavis refilled his goblet and retook his seat, drawling quietly, " 'Tis none of your concern, Kate. Planning a long stay?"

Her hands gripped her goblet tightly until her knuckles whitened as she fought to subdue the rage she felt, a rage inspired by Tavis's indifference and the amusement of the others. " 'Tis nay the weather for me to return home. A spring storm is upon us. I barely escaped a drenching." She looked to Colin, ignoring the laughter in his eyes. "What have ye askit for a ransom, or have ye nay askit it yet?"

"Aye, a week back. 'Tis less than wililing they be to give it to us. We are negotiating."

That was far from welcome news to Katerine, for it meant that the woman would be around for a while, and she scowled only to pout with false sympathy when she spotted a bruise upon Tavis's jaw. "There was a wee bit o'. trouble on the raid?" she asked, lightly touching the spot.

Even Tavis laughed. "Nay." He rubbed his jaw and winced a little. "The lass and I have a wee argument. She was making a point and I was not really on my guard. The vixen," he murmured.

There was a tone to his voice that grated on Katerine. "Ye must needs show the wench who is the prisoner and who is the captor. Her arrogance is unpardonable."

"I insulted her," Tavis said curtly.

"Aye, ye did that, laddie. I ken ye made a promise. She didnae look too willing to me." Colin chuckled as he recalled the sight of his eldest son sprawled on the floor. "The lass still has her spirit." He signaled to his man Malcolm. "I am to bed. 'Tis past time I can make a night o' it." He sighed.

Tavis watched his father leave. The man continued to grow weaker, his color was bad and he ate nothing, for it was near to impossible for him to keep the food down. It was hard to watch a strong man fade away, let alone his own father. He refilled his goblet, scowling at the way Katerine cuddled up to him, her touch far too possessive.

Throughout the evening Tavis continued to drink heavily, his mind on his father's ill health as well as Storm Eldon. He was mostly oblivious to Katerine's many subtle and then not so subtle attempts to stir his ardor. His desire for her had never been very fierce, merely convenient, despite

70

her unquestionable talent in bed. It had even occurred to him often, once past the first six months of their affair, to be rid of her, but convenience proved a hard thing to forgo. Since there was little chance of his partaking of her charms during this visit, he felt she would soon understand that their affair had come to an end.

As the liquor ran through his veins, he grew angrier at Storm as well as himself for his promise to his father. Tavis convinced himself that he would not seduce Storm, merely reveal to her how much she did want him. It was inconceivable to him that he could burn so strongly for her and she not feel the same. He felt sure that, once he got her into his arms, her repulses would prove to be a sham.

Katerine ceased trying to stir Tavis. A more direct approach was needed, but that could not be put to use before an audience. She allowed Janet to take her to her room, although she had no intention of staying there. As soon as Janet was gone, Katerine made her way to Tavis's chambers, shed her clothes and made herself comfortable in his bed. He'd not remain cold and, perhaps, the combination of drink and passion would make him less careful. Although she had no desire for a child, she felt she could suffer the trial once in order to secure her place in Tavis MacLagan's bed.

Storm lay abed with little chance of finding any sleep, her mind too full to allow her any rest. She now had a clear understanding of the cause of most of her anger, and it was not to her liking. That kiss had shown her that she was a lot nearer to loving Tavis than she had thought, if not already at that point. As a result, her desire now carried on a raging battle with her morals. Her innocence should be a gift for her husband, which Tavis MacLagan could never be, yet she knew he would not have to fight very hard to gain that prize. Even the knowledge that she would return to Hagaleah dishonored while he stayed at Caraidland to play with another did not still her wanting him. Telling herself that Katerine could see to his needs only brought her pain. All she could see ahead was a great deal of trouble, even the pleasure bringing grief in the end.

"The laird does not look well," commented Phelan from her side, the pallet not used once since it had been made up for him. " 'Tis as if he is wasting away."

Glad to leave her thoughts of Tavis, Storm replied, "Aye, 'tis an odd affliction."

"How so, cousin? I have heard of a wasting sickness before. 'Tis not so rare."

"True, yet I have seen it, and 'twas not really like this from which the laird suffers."

"Let us think on what symptoms we have seen. I know he is prone to fainting and nosebleeds."

"Ah, I did not know that. I have seen that he is increasingly listless, his skin grows drier each day, he eats little for he cannot keep it in his belly and oftimes I do not think that he has much feeling in his hands."

" 'Tis indeed an odd affliction," Phelan mused aloud. "Ye know the art of healing. What could it be an 'tis not a wasting sickness? Enemy he may be, but I cannot like to watch a man die in such a way. A man such as Colin MacLagan should die fighting, not fading away slowly."

"Nay, 'tis sad. I believe even Papa would feel so. I must think on it a bit. Something is not right, not right at all," she murmured.

Phelan lay quietly, letting her turn the matter over in her mind. The more Storm thought on Colin MacLagan's ailment, the less she liked it. Put all together, his symptoms indicated that there was treachery afoot in Caraidland, a plot aimed at the removal of the laird. She shivered as her thoughts crystalized.

"He is being poisoned, Phelan. I am sure of it," she said very softly.

"But by whom?" he asked, not questioning her conclusion, for he trusted her judgment completely in such matters.

"I do not know. We must needs watch everyone, Phelan, and I mean everyone. Even his sons. I find it hard to believe one of them is guilty, but I know them little. Sons have been known to murder their fathers."

"What do we watch for?"

"Mother of God, I do not know. Someone is slipping it to the man." She rubbed her temples as she struggled to think of things. "I think we must watch for someone who always performs the same task. Mayhaps always serves him his ale or wine, gives him a potion, such as that. Even rubbing it onto his skin."

"That makes for a lot of watching. Still and all, we have little else to do whilst being kept here."

"True. 'Tis one he trusts, as well. We must not speak of this yet."

"I thought the same, Storm. We could well give a warning to the scoundrel." Phelan thought for a moment. "If we do uncover treachery and the laird regains his health, we could gain our freedom."

"So we could. An only 'tis in time. For him as well as I," she added softly, but Phelan heard her.

"Aye." He took her hand and gave it a comforting squeeze. "Tavis grows tired of waiting for ye. I will do me best to keep ye safe, cousin," he added, although he knew there was little he could do.

"Phelan," she began hesitantly, needing to speak her thoughts to someone, " 'tis not really rape I fear."

"I know. Nor dishonor. 'Tis your own feelings for Tavis MacLagan. Am I right?"

"Ye are too perceptive for a lad. Aye, 'tis exactly what I fear. I have ne'er felt drawn to a man before. Ah, Lord, 'tis my wicked luck to be drawn to a Mac-Lagan. 'Twas just a fear 'til the man kissed me. 'Tis still a fear, but now I cannot ignore it for 'tis a fact as well. All of which means that if he comes to me, is gentle and loving, I am lost. In all honesty, I'll not be able to cry rape, and my dishonor will all be upon my shoulders, for what man pulls away from a willing maid?"

"Nary a one that I have heard of. Mayhaps he would take ye to wife."

" 'Tis not to be thought upon, Phelan. I am an Eldon and he is a MacLagan. The families have fought each other for too many years. Then, too, I get the feeling that Tavis can be a lover, but that he does not love. He would be all a woman could want until his desire was spent, and then he will coldly discard her for another. I may be able to suffer dishonor and the loss of my virtues outside of marriage, which is a sin, but I could not bear to watch my lover's passion wane, his heart harden and his arms reach for another. 'Twould kill me."

"Then I must see that he does not come near ye, cousin."

"Ah, Phelan, 'tis good of ye, but nay. There is little telling how a man will act when his blood is hot. I will not have ye harmed trying to save something that most all at home will have thought lost to me ere now. An he does come to my chambers, ye are not to argue overmuch with the man. Leave that to me." She swallowed her pain as she added, "We may speak on a problem that will ne'er arise. He has his mistress now."

"She did not stir him enough to make him leave go of ye," Phelan said quietly.

"He was not expecting her," Storm argued, ignoring her own increasing nervousness. "Now to sleep,"

74

she commanded, knowing it was easier said than done, especially whe her mind kept drifting to Tavis.

Thoughts of Storm kept whirling through Tavis's increasingly muddled mind. Drinking and jesting with his brothers and the other men did little to keep his desire for Storm at bay. It had been his hope to drink enough to enable himself to pass into a deep, dreamless sleep, but that plan seemed to be failing. All that was happening was that his mind was turning more and more to Storm, conjuring up images that made him close his eyes against his need. She was a fever in his blood and he was already at the crisis point.

"Ah, Tavis, ye are a lucky bastard," teased a none too sober Sholto, "with twa lovelies to choose from."

"Care an I comfort the one ye dinnae visit?" queried Iain with a grin.

"Nay. Ye ken where Kate usually sleeps."

"Och, weel, I was hoping t'would be the other," sighed Iain, his turquoise eyes alight with laughter.

"Mayhaps I'll take them both," mused Tavis, his laughter blending with that of the others.

"Ye would ne'er see the dawn. One o' the lasses would kill ye for being with the other."

"Sholto's right," Donald laughed, a burly man who was their first cousin. "I would put my coin on the wee lass from Hagaleah. She be a feisty bit o' woman. 'Tis the hair, I ken."

Refilling his tankard, Sholto sighed heartily. "I would fair love to see it down and free, out o' those neat braids. I wager 'twould be a glorious sight for a man to see."

"I'll remember to tell ye how it looks," remarked Tavis as he finished his drink and stood up.

In a low voice, so that the others could not hear, Iain said, "Recall, ye swore nay to touch the lass unless she be willing. 'Tis a small thing Father asks, a small pleasure to give him when he's ailing so."

"Aye, she'll be willing." Tavis frowned. "What do ye think ails our father? He grows even weaker."

Iain nodded. "Aye, aye, he does, but there seems naught to do but watch him fade. God's wounds, but it makes a man feel helpless. He has nay lived a bad life. He deserves a better death, nay this slow one."

There was little Tavis could say, for the same thing troubled him. He gripped Iain's shoulder in a brief gesture of sympathy and understanding. However, as Tavis made to leave, Iain grasped him by the arm. With one brow raised in silent query, Tavis met Iain's somber look, noticing that the man was far more sober than he.

"Dinnae hurt the lass, Tavis. Eldon she may be, but she's a bonnie wee thing, sprung from the loins of a man I respect, though he be my foe, and 'twould grieve me if she suffered at your hands."

Leaning down so that only Iain heard him, Tavis replied, "I dinnae intend to hurt the lass."

"I ken I cannae ask ye to leave her be, to nay dishonor her."

"Ye ken right. Few will believe she's nay been touched ere she leaves here. 'Tis a fever with me."

Nodding, Iain released him. Grinning in response to many a ribald remark, Tavis left the hall. He headed to his own chambers, for he wished to bathe. A part of him hoped that a hot bath would ease his ache, cause him to seek his own bed and leave Storm Eldon alone, but he doubted it would.

In a small chamber between his and Iain's quarters, Tavis had his bath set up. The lack of a window, the small size of the room and the fireplace kept the room draft-free, a perfect place to bathe. As he washed, he fought a hard inner battle, but neither his conscience nor his body won. Stepping out of the tub to towel himself dry, he merely swore not to force Storm, to cease if she resisted him too vehemently.

She was his prisoner, he rationalized. He had a right to do as he pleased with her. Then, too, he had no intention of hurting her, only giving her pleasure. There had been the flicker of a response when he had kissed her, so he felt he could do that. She had also shown no true dislike of him in the week she had been at Caraidland. He simply could no longer silently suffer the aching need to possess her.

He stepped into his room to find his robe. As he picked it up off a chair, Katerine sat up in his bed, bringing a harsh oath to his lips. Putting on his robe, he strode to the bed.

"What in the devil's name are ye doing here?" he snarled, feeling nothing but fury as his gaze flickered over her thick black hair and the full breasts bared to his view.

" 'Tis where I belong. 'Tis where I have slept each time I have come to Caraidland." She rose to her knees and slipped her arms around his neck. "Come to bed, Tavis, and let me pleasure ye as I have so oft in the past." She began to kiss his throat. "I have waited hours for ye to come to bed."

"I didnae ask it of ye." He pulled her arms away from his neck. "I ken I made it plain in the hall this night that 'tis not what I want. Go to your own chambers, Kate."

The chill in his voice combined with his flat rejection shattered Katerine's resolve to be conciliatory. "Ye would leave me for that scrawny Sassanach bitch?" she screeched, and swung at him.

Catching her wrist with ease, Tavis flung it from him. "Aye. I would."

"How can ye treat me so after I have given ye twa years o' me life?"

"I didnae ask it of ye and I ken those years

werenae solely mine. Nay, 'twas ye that sought out my bed, Kate, much as ye have tonight."

"My family will make ye pay for this insult," she snarled, catching her clothes as he flung them at her.

"A man has a right to choose his bedmate. They'll do naught and weel ye ken it."

"Ye made promises. They expect us to be wed."

"If they do 'tis because ye lied to them, Kate. I made ye nary a promise save to give and take pleasure, and that promise has been fulfilled. Ye were nay an innocent. Ye had kenned a man ere I had ye." He laughed softly. "Aye, and weel we ken who it was, for ye were far from discreet. Your family kens as weel. Nay, they may wish I will wed ye, but I dinnae think they expect it. An I take a wife it willnae be one of the women Alexander MacDubh has used and tossed aside."

The color fled from Katerine's face, for she had not realized that Tavis knew about her affair with Alexander. " 'Tis a lie," she bluffed.

"Is it?" He shrugged. "It matters not." He made no move to help her as she struggled into her clothes. "I cannae turn ye out, Kate, as ye are a MacBroth, and they are all welcome at Caraidland. Ye will, nonetheless, stay to your own room. 'Tis over, and we both ken it. Let it die. Find another man. Ye might e'en find one fool enough to wed ye, e'en though ye have the morals of a cat."

Choking with anger, Katerine strode to the door. Part of her fury stemmed from the discovery that Tavis knew far more about her than she had thought or had wanted, as well as the fact that her plans to get with his child would never reach fruition if he kept her from his bed. Furious though she was, she did not plan on giving up. Her stint as his mistress was too well known. There would be few men who would wed her now. She could not lose Tavis, for he could well be her last chance to get a husband.

"Go to the Sassanach whore then," she hissed as she stood in the doorway. "Ye will soon tire of her and want a real woman. Ye best hope when that time comes that I am in a forgiving mood."

He winced as she slammed the door upon her exit. It was not to his liking that the ending was so acrimonious, but he doubted that it could have been any other way. Storm was not the only reason for freeing himself from Kate. The woman had gotten to be too possessive as well as a liability. Tavis was fairly sure that she was planning to become pregnant, and he wished to be away from her before she could succeed.

It was not that he wished no wife, for he knew he must needs get one before too long, nor that he cared all that much that she be a virgin, although it would be nice. In the case of Katerine, it was simply her character. He doubted he would have even taken her for his mistress if she had not initiated the relationship. She was too much the cold, grasping sort, and she had no concept of fidelity, the one thing he would demand of a wife, for he had no wish to spend his years as a cuckold or guessing the paternity of his children. Kate was much like many another woman he had known.

A crooked smile touched his finely chiseled mouth as he made his way to the tower where Storm slept. It appeared he would have some difficulty in finding a wife if he was after a woman he could trust. In his six and twenty years he had found that breed very rare. Only once had he trusted a woman, just to end up looking the fool, a hard thing for a proud man to endure.

Recalling Mary always brought a surge of bitter anger. He had loved her to the point of near worship. Finding the woman he thought so pure and perfect in the arms of Alexander MacDubh, with her skirts tossed up like some whore, had been a shattering blow. From that moment on he had trusted no woman, treating them all with a callousness he thought they deserved, an attitude that none had yet been able to change. It had also been the start of a somewhat acrimonious rivalry with Alexander Mac-Dubh, a rivalry that never broke out into open warfare, for Tavis did not hate the man, but he could not fully disassociate him from a time of painful disillusionment.

Something in him craved to find Storm worthy of trust, to find her character little changed from the open honesty she had shown as a child. Her image had returned to him many a time since that first meeting. Yet, he told himself, she was a woman now. She was also an Eldon. Neither was a good foundation for putting his trust in her.

When he reached her door he stared at it thoughtfully while the guard roused himself to unlock it. Tavis was rather glad that Angus was not there, for the man had developed a fatherly fondness for the pair and would no doubt have made his disapproval felt. Shaking away all moral questions about what he planned to do, Tavis stepped into the room, signaling the guard to follow. Tavis wanted Storm with a desire that was nearly crippling, and he intended to have her.

7

A dying fire lit the room with a soft glow. Upon the large bed Storm and Phelan lay in each other's arms, the woman looking as much the child as the boy. Their slender bodies made little impression beneath the covers they were so snuggly wrapped in.

"Get the boy and secure him elsewhere," he told the guard with a voice made husky from the vision of thick, brilliant hair spread over the pillows. Phelan woke as the guard lifted him from the bed. The resultant confrontation woke Storm. In a calm voice and in the tongue of Erin she told Phelan to go quietly.

"Are you sure?" he asked in the same language, his gaze fixed belligerently on Tavis.

"Yes." She also looked at Tavis, thinking it cruel that fate should allow her to bestow her heart upon a man who was not only her enemy but merely wished to use her. "It is inevitable, my darling boy. If not now, it will be later, for he desires it and I love him. I think the best thing for me to do is to get what pleasure I can out of it, so go, Phelan, and worry not about me. There is nothing that can be done."

"If fate is kind, he will suffer from the withers," Phelan said and marched out of the room.

Moving to stand by the bed once they were alone, Tavis looked down at a giggling Storm. "What did ye and the lad say to each other?" he asked quietly.

"I told the boy he could do nothing so to go quietly. He wished upon ye an affliction that will make what ye plan an impossibility." She wished she was not so aware of how attractive he was when he smiled.

Sitting down on the bed, Tavis grasped her by the wrists and held her hands on either side of her head. "Do ye still intend to fight me, lass? I'll warn ye now," he bluffed, "a fight willnae deter me."

"That I had judged upon my own," she drawled. "Nay, I will not fight ye for 'twill bring me only pain."

He brushed featherlight kisses over her flushed cheeks. " 'Tis true. This way I can bring ye pleasure."

"I said I would not fight ye. I did not say I would cooperate." As his lips continued to move gently over her face, Storm had the distressing feeling that her body would go its merry way despite her wishes.

"Mayhaps I can change your mind, lass. Since ye must give in, why not gain what ye can from it, sweeting?" He pulled the covers down and began to unlace the silken chemise she wore.

Storm could feel the heat of desire seep into her veins despite her battle to quell it. The light from the dying fire and the candle he had brought with him made it fairly easy to see what he was doing, something that was proving a heady experience. She realized with a touch of bitter self-recrimination that if she had fought him it would have been a very short battle. The only way she could save any face would be to feel no pleasure or to hide that which she did feel, but she knew instinctively that she would not be allowed even that small victory. Her heart was her worst enemy. She could only pray that he would never realize how fully he held her in the palm of his hand.

Tavis eased the garment off of her, wishing she

did not hold herself so limply. When his gaze fell upon her full, ivory breasts, his breath caught in his throat. It was not only her beauty that moved him, but the indication that her disinterest was a total sham. Her breathing was already becoming erratic, the perfect rosettes upon her breasts were hardening before his eyes, calling out for his caress, and the pulse of her elegant, slim throat was pounding in such a way that it showed him her blood was racing through her veins as much as his was. The desire within her was clearly winning out over her other wants.

Slowly his gaze moved to her tiny waist and lingered on her flat, satiny stomach. His survey shifted quickly to her small lovely feet, eased its way up her slim, well-formed legs and riveted greedily upon the nest of coppery curls that hid his final prize. Turning his gaze back to her face, the blush in her cheeks apparent even in the dim light, he shed his robe.

"Ye are perfection," he said, his voice soft and hoarse with need. "I think ye are blushing all over."

"No man has e'er looked upon me as ye do now. 'Tis shame that brings the color to my face."

"Ah, lass, if there be any shame in this, 'tis mine and glad I am to bear it an it means I can possess the loveliness I now look upon. So cease your blushes, sweeting. They gain ye naught."

A fact that she would rather die than reveal was that some of the color in her cheeks was caused by blood heated nearly to boiling by the vision of his un-clothed body. As his eyes had drifted over her, so hers did over him. Tavis MacLagan made Sir Hugh look like a wizened cripple.

Her gaze skimmed over broad shoulders and a strong, lightly furred chest with a delight that was hard to conceal. As she ran her tongue along sud-denly dry lips, her gaze followed the thin path of dark hair past a trim waist and lean hips. Following the perfect symmetry of his long, muscular legs, she returned to the spot she had shyly evaded earlier. A flicker of virginal fear rippled through her as she saw the bold proof of both his desire and his masculinity. She suddenly felt very small. A shudder went through her when he joined her on the bed and she was held close to all that virility.

"Do not do this, MacLagan," she pleaded in a final attempt to stop what seemed inevitable. "I am a virgin. I have known no man. My innocence should be a gift to my lawful husband."

The image of another man possessing what he now held seared through Tavis's brain, and it took him a moment to quell a nauseating rage he did not understand. "Ye ask too much, sweet. I am but a man. To turn away from this is more than I can do."

"Can ye not satisfy your lust upon your mistress? She would know better than I how to please you." Even as she voiced the suggestion, nearly choking upon it, a part of her prayed he would not heed it.

"Nay, lass, I cannae." He ran a hand down her side, luxuriating in the hollows and rises. " 'Tis a puzzle to me, but ye have entered my blood. Kate was in my chambers, waiting and willing, but for all I told myself 'twould be best to turn to her, I found myself sending her away." He slid a hand up her rib cage to gently cup her breast and experienced a small sense of triumph upon feeling the nipple bore into his palm with impudent invitation. "I have lost all taste for her charms. The time was o'erdue for her to be away."

"I know we are enemies, but must ye make me play the whore to gain my freedom?" she cried, stoutly ignoring the urge to pull him into her arms in reaction to the joy his words had given her.

Cupping her face in his hands, Tavis teased at her lips with his while saying, "Ah, lass, I didnae mean those words. They were spoken in anger. What I am about to do has naught to do with ye being my prisoner. Nay, nor your ransom we have yet to gain. This is solely the burning need of a man for a woman. I couldnae bear the thought of ye being sent back to Hagaleah without tasting the sweetness of ye."

His kiss was a gentle seduction, nearly clearing her mind of all thought save of him and pleasure. However, a small, rational voice hung on, telling her that the man was a practiced deceiver, a skilled charmer. He knew just what to say to break down the wall she had tried to build. Even so, as his tongue explored her mouth, she had to clench her hands into tight little fists to still the urge to touch him. Her body cared nothing for her mind's warnings.

As his lips moved down her slender throat, he groaned. "Touch me, lass. I want to feel those bonnie wee hands move o'er my flesh. Touch me, Storm. Discover the man that aches for ye."

"Nay, nay, I cannot," she moaned in a voice she did not recognize as her own. " 'Tis not right."

"Storm, bonnie Storm, dinnae make me angry. I am nay too sane just now and I could hurt ye, which isnae what I want at all." He brushed kisses over the swell of her breasts. "Touch me, Storm."

"Nay, I must not. I . . . ah!" she cried softly when he cupped a breast in his hand and his lips closed over the hardened tip, sending shafts of fire through her as his tongue flicked over the nub, creating an ache that he eased with a gentle suckling. "I am lost," she whispered, her hands burying themselves in his thick hair while her body arched against him in graceful need.

" 'Tis the purest nectar," he murmured as he gave her other breast an equal service, his hand moving in a slow caress down her stomach. "Your skin is like the finest silk."

85

Storm bit her lip in an attempt to stop the soft sounds of passion trying to escape her. It was in vain, for they exploded in her throat, sounding very much like a contented purr. He was turning her into a mindless receptacle for his lust, yet she could not stop her body's response to his practiced caresses. Her hands touched him wherever they could reach, moving with a shy but greedy delight that she could not control. As his kisses moved over her soft mid-riff, his hand slid between her legs to caress and probe. She tensed slightly, briefly, then slid over the edge into a mindless state, aware only of her pleasure and an aching need that was rapidly growing within her.

Tavis sensed her final capitulation and gave a soft, triumphant laugh. He had felt the passion within her, felt her tremble as she fought to subdue it, and had used all his skill to make passion the victor. His reward was the way she was coming alive beneath him, her thrashings and the sounds of pleasure escaping her stirring him in a way he had never experienced before. As his mouth edged its way back to her breasts, his fingers sought out the heart of her, readying her for his final possession and luxuriating in the warm moistness of her, a warmth that would soon know him more fully.

He wanted to savor his passion, the like of which he had never known before, but soon reached the limit of his endurance. Her small hands with their shy, unpracticed touches were driving him near to madness, giving him more pleasure than he had ever found beneath the skilled touch of others. His strong hands upon her slim hips to hold her steady, he eased into her, met the obstruction of her innocence and shattered it, his mouth swallowing her startled cry of pain. His teeth gritted against his body's urges, he lay still, letting the pain subside and her body adjust to his intrusion.

"It hurts," she whispered a little tearfully. "Can ye not leave now?"

"Nay, 'tis the sweetest haven I have e'er known." His lips moved gently over her face as his hands stroked her body, easing away the tension. His hand on her thigh, he said, "Wrap these slender beauties around my waist, sweet Storm. Cradle me to ye. Hold me close atween these silken thighs."

With a passion-induced obedience she did so, and shuddered along with him as he deepened his possession of her. Her eyes locked with his where he hovered above her, raised up on his elbows. A soft gasp escaped her as he began to move slowly; what was left of her pain was forgotten as a nearly painful pleasure grew within her. Unaware that her eyes had turned to a deep molten color, she was held in the fierce light of his gaze. After a moment she began to move with him in nature's own rhythm.

"Aye," he groaned in a voice trembling with passion as his lips teased at hers. "That is the way of it. Parry my ilka thrust. Take me so deep inside ye that I cannae find my way out. So sweet. So verra sweet," he rasped, and took her lips in a greedy kiss as he began to move faster.

Storm met his growing fierceness with an equal one of her own. Her slender arms joined her legs in holding him close while her tongue played with his as their kiss matched the growing frenzy of their movements. She was only dimly aware of his husky mutterings, his voice thickened by passion nearly beyond her comprehension. Suddenly the feeling within her grew to a point that alarmed her. She felt balanced on the edge of some precipice, her body drawn back like a bowstring ready to be released. Despite her growing fear she could not bring a halt to things, and that only increased her agitation. Suddenly she was an unwilling passenger on a journey she did not know the destination of.

"Tavis, I . . . oh, God, please, something . . . Tavis, I fear to shatter. Help me, please. I am afraid."

Cupping her face in his hands, he strove to articulate clearly so that he might ease her fears before they dimmed her passion. "Dinnae fight it nor fear it, sweeting. Give yourself to it. Give it to me. 'Tis the glorious ending of of our journey. Savor it."

He held her gaze and read her release there even as his ears heard her impassioned cry. His body luxuriated in her tremors of inner delight. With one fierce thrust he sought his own escape, seeing in her face the way her body greedily accepted his passion's tribute before he collapsed in her arms. For a moment they lay intimately entwined, letting their minds and bodies slowly returned to normalcy.

With her return to sanity, Storm found herself caught in a growing sadness. She knew some of the reason for her tears was the sense of loss, the realization that she was no longer innocent, her childhood irrevocably put aside. The greatest cause of her depression was the knowledge that something so beautiful to her was simply the use of a woman to the man she held. Though not one given to weeping and fully aware that it was mostly self-pity, Storm found herself too caught up in her crying to stop.

Leaving her arms, Tavis fought to quell the guilt that had swiftly grown from a small twinge at the start of her weeping. With a damp cloth he washed them both clean of the signs of her lost childhood. Returning to the bed, he took her into his arms, ignoring her slight resistance.

"Dinnae greet, lass. I cannae give it back. E'en an I could, I would just take it again."

Storm hoped he would never gain a full accounting of what he had stolen from her. " 'Tis easy for ye to speak so. It matters not how many women a man has. They can even find a pride in their conquests. 'Tis different with a woman ere she wants to wed. A

88

man expects his wife to be pure, untouched by any man. Ye have ruined my hopes for marriage and a family."

" 'Tis not quite as bad as all that," he said quietly, although he thought it might be.

"Nay," she snarled, wrenching free of his gentle hold, " 'tis always easy to find those who will take me for my fortune. Men such as Sir Hugh or mayhaps another of Lady Mary's past or present lovers."

It was not a pretty picture. Tavis grew angry, for she was stirring up his guilt again, a feeling he was not overly fond of. The cynicism he had so often brought to the fore failed him. He could not say it mattered not to him and mean it. Then, too, the thought that no other man might want her now was fleetingly pleasant, but only fleetingly, for he knew it was not true.

"The bride gift may not be so sweet, but ye'll nay be left to wither on the vine."

"Would ye take a wife that was no virgin?" she snapped, already sure of his answer.

Tavis smiled slightly when she registered open-mouthed surprise at his answer. "Aye, an I kenned 'twas nay her fault. A lass is no match for a man. 'Tis wrong to blame her for what she couldnae prevent. There'll be enough men willing to overlook your lack of a maidenhead, for ye be highborn, pretty and wealthy. Just dinnae tell them how much ye enjoyed it." He laughed softly and easily parried her blows, pinning her beneath him on the bed. "What is this ye wear, lass?" he asked, picking up the amulet she wore around her neck, which he had disinterestedly pushed aside earlier.

Looking at the circle of amber he held, a lovely butterfly forever caught in full wingspread within, Storm relinquished some of her anger. "It was my mother's. She found it when she was a small child and had it hung upon this chain. When she fell in love with my father she gave it to him. As she lay dying, she told me to wear it and do the same. 'Tis not often ye find such beauty caught in amber, nor caught so perfectly. She felt it was a perfect love token, for 'tis unique and the shade of our eyes.''

"And ye have nay found a man to give it to as yet?''

"Obviously not,'' she drawled, trying to ignore a twinge of pain that came with recalling her circumstances.

Ignoring her reference, Tavis stared into her eyes, truly fascinated by their coloring. "Aye, 'tis the same color, and your eyes can snare a man as well as this resin did the doomed butterfly.''

"I have no intention of snaring anyone,'' she snapped indignantly.

"Nay?'' As he cupped her face in his hands, his thumbs caressed her cheeks with a slow, gentle motion.

"Nay.'' She could feel herself reacting to his touch, as well as the lean strength of him pressed so closely to her. "Well, now that ye have had what ye wanted, ye best scurry back to your own bed.''

"I never scurry.''

Biting her lip against a rising annoyance, as well as a growing passion, she gritted out, "Then walk, run, trot, lope or do as ye please, but ye best get to moving.''

"I am not going anywhere, lass.'' He smiled as her eyes widened.

"Ye cannot stay here. 'Twould be known by all what ye have done come the morning.''

" 'Tis common knowledge now. I made my plans plain enough ere I left the hall.''

For a moment Storm was speechless with embarrassment and outrage. "Did ye have to? How can I face all the others on the morrow? Could ye not have kept my disgrace a private matter?''

Shaking his head, Tavis found her naïvete hard to believe. "Ye are my prisoner and a bonnie wee lass. Not only your kinsmen will question your innocence when ye leave here, but my folk have wondered why I have nay touched ye. Those that didnae ken I had not all thought I had. Near half the folk ye have faced all week have thought ye in my bed or I in yours. Think on it no longer, my sweet little one."

"How unjust of them," she whispered. "Do ye not care that they think ye a ravisher of maids?"

"Nay." His hands began to stroke her slim length and he felt her tension being replaced by desire. "I've nay ravished ye. Seduced, mayhaps, but nay ravished." His tongue tracing the outline of her mouth, he murmured, " 'Tis here in your arms I intend to stay until ye are given back to Hagaleah and England."

Neither paid much mind to how uncomfortable the mere thought of separation was. Even so, it killed what little resistance Storm had. Tavis became all the more desperate in his need.

Iain paused outside his father's door, saw a shaft of light, heard voices and rapped. Following the command to enter, his gaze settled upon Janet, a woman he neither trusted nor liked. He said nothing until his father finished off his potion, handed the goblet to Janet and she had left the room.

"Putrid rot," Colin grumbled. " 'Tis little help it gives me, yet I feel I maun suffer it."

"Tavis is with the Eldon lass."

Colin sighed. "Aye. 'Twas due. I hope he isnae going to hurt the bairn."

"Nay. He might not keep to the letter of his promise, but he'll not harm her. She's an Eldon."

"I ken that weel enough, and many's the man who'd say 'Have at it, Tavis,' but she's a good wee lassie and I cannae wish her hurt. Muckle's the year

Eldon and MacLagan have faced each other at sword's point, but the man doesnae deal in treachery and butchery. Many's the time I wished I could have a friend at my side as worthy as that foe. I cannae like visiting dishonor upon his child. Then, too, there's the wee matter of me sword arm," he finished, touching the smooth scar at his shoulder.

"Aye. All this I can see weel, but 'tis more than that, is it not?"

"I have ne'er seen the lad in such a fever for a lass."

"Nor have I. 'Tis what drives him to go against your wishes, mayhaps against his own."

Hesitating, Colin held his son's gaze and then decided that Iain was very probably of a like mind, so would not find his growing qualms foolish ones. "I fear Tavis is sowing himself a harvest of grief," he said quietly, and Iain solemnly nodded.

8

Ignoring the tension that was building within her with each step she took, Storm followed Phelan into the great hall where dinner was to be served. Since Tavis had begun to share her bed there had been less of an air of imprisonment to her stay at Caraidland. Tavis did not like someone hanging around all the time, yet Storm knew she would not get many steps away if she tried to flee. There was always someone near, always a pair of eyes following her.

The fortnight had brought yet another reply from Hagaleah, couched in such terms that, although it was a refusal, it could not be acted upon as such. When Storm had presented Tavis with what she considered a reasonable tally for her nightly services and suggested that he deduct it from the ransom there had been a spectacular argument. She thought it a little hypocritical of him to use her like a whore, but then become enraged and outraged if she dared to call herself one in even the most subtle of terms. Nevertheless, she was careful not to, for they found quite enough to argue about as it was.

Then there were Janet and Katerine. They did all they could to make life miserable for her. They were proving to be experts in the field. It had reached the point where Storm feared an immediate outbreak of hostilities. More and more the subtle remarks flew, anger simmered and reaction was forced down to grow greater and fiercer.

Kate's reason for being vitriolic was plain to see. It had taken Storm a while to understand Janet's. When she did she wished fervently that she had not or that she would be proven wrong. Instead, as Colin grew weaker, Janet's reason for resenting her became all too clear. Janet plainly wanted Tavis, desired her own husband's son.

A silent groan rose up in Storm as the ever weakening Colin was led out of the hall, no longer able to linger with the others after the meal. The ritual of the women preparing to retreat to a far corner of the hall and leave the men alone to talk but the men inducing them to stay was gone through. Storm preferred staying at the table, for she really had little in common with the other two women, and the men afforded some protection from the vicious remarks and rising animosity. She was not afraid of the women, but did fear a humiliating scene if things were not kept curbed in some way.

Storm continued to feel that someone was slowly poisoning Colin but, although she had a very strong suspicion as to who it might be, she could not yet accuse someone. The watching she and Phelan indulged in had left them with only one firm conviction: Malcolm was the only one they could wholeheartedly exonerate. Their reasons for doing so were rather vague, but they did not care. If nothing else, they had to trust someone soon or Colin would die. Storm wondered how she could get to Colin's room to talk privately with the devoted Malcolm. There was little time left. It amazed Storm that Colin still lived, for he looked so very close to death.

"So your people still refuse to buy ye back," drawled Katerine, her eyes hard as they flickered over the way Tavis's hand rested upon Storm's knee with an unconscious possessiveness.

"Lady Mary would not part with a brass farthing to save her own mother," Storm remarked calmly.

"Aye, and mayhaps she kens ye be working off the ransom," Janet purred too loudly.

"Janet," Tavis growled warningly into the sudden hush that had fallen over the table.

Refusing to let the woman anger her, Storm coolly retorted, "Ah, well, I did present Tavis with what I considered a reasonable tally, but mayhaps I estimated too low, for he was loathe to accept it."

Tavis's hand tightened on Storm's knee in warning as snickering erupted around the table. He did not like to hear Storm referred to in such terms. Despite the situation, he did not think of her that way and did not want her or any other to do so.

Kate had reached the limit of her endurance. For a fortnight she had struggled to entice Tavis away from the girl but had failed miserably. The way her former lover treated Storm made Kate grind her teeth in jealous rage. Even when the couple fought there was a casual intimacy between them she had never achieved with Tavis.

"Methinks 'twas too high," sneered Kate, rising to stand next to Storm. "A skinny wench like ye wouldnae bring a ha'penth on the streets."

"Enough!" Tavis bellowed, leaping to his feet to glare at his former mistress.

Wine, frustration and desperation robbed Kate of pride, and she clung to Tavis. "How can ye toss me aside for her? Her folk arenae going to ransom her, 'tis plain. Send her back and return to one who kens how to pleasure ye. She cannae ken the ways o' loving. She's naught but a cold Sassanach bitch. How can ye nay see that I am the woman for ye?"

Storm watched the pair for a moment before standing up to leave. Her insides were knotted with a jealousy that grew with each caress Kate offered Tavis. It mattered little that he did not return them.

He neither pushed Kate away nor told her to cease. In fact, Storm thought he looked as if he was thinking about all the woman had said. Storm decided to leave before she lost control, revealing her jealousy and fear to everyone.

"Slinking away?" purred Kate, who also took Tavis's silence as acquiescence.

Turning in her advance toward the door, Storm looked Kate over with ill-concealed scorn. "Nay, I simply do not find groveling an entertainment to my liking."

The soft snickering that reached Kate's ears fueled her rage, and she moved to stand directly in front of Storm. "Ye just cannae stomach being set aside, can ye?"

"I believe I will survive," Storm drawled. "If ye wish to take back a man who has ignored ye for a fortnight, consorting with another right before your eyes, then, please, feel free to be such a fool. Just do not ask me to sit and watch a member of my own sex debase herself so."

With a cry of inarticulate rage, Kate backhanded Storm across the face. Tavis would have interfered, but Iain stopped him, saying quietly that the confrontation was past due. Storm was nearly sent sprawling from the force of the blow. She reacted automatically. With a strength increased by anger suppressed for too many days and a healthy jealousy, she struck back. Bringing a small fist up from her hip in a smooth swing, she dealt a blow to Kate's jaw that sent the larger woman sprawling to the floor and kept her there. A surprised silence fell over the hall.

"She's all yours, Tavis," she said quietly, "though I fear ye will have to rouse her first."

Tavis was too amazed to move after Storm and merely stood staring at the unconscious Kate while Storm strolled out of the hall, Phelan right behind her. It was a long moment before he could rouse himself enough to do anything. Picking up a tankard of ale, he tossed it into Kate's face, watching with no sympathy at all as she spluttered and wakened. He wondered how he had ever managed to bed her and ruefully admitted that lust gave little thought to the character of the vessel in which it spent itself.

"That bitch hit me," wailed Kate as she struggled to her feet unaided.

"Ye struck her first," Tavis pointed out in an icy tone. "I think it best if ye go home on the morrow." He strode out of the hall, oblivious to the curses Katerine screeched after him.

He went to his chambers to wash up. Although he spent every night in Storm's bed, he had not moved himself in with her for reasons he did not fully understand himself. Just as he slipped into his robe, Janet quietly entered his room, shutting the door after her and leaning against it.

With her hair loose and dressed in a diaphanous gown, Janet was beautiful, but Tavis was unimpressed. "What do ye want?" he growled.

"Ye shouldnae be so rude to your stepmother," she purred as she moved toward him. "I thought ye might be ready for a change from the squabbling bairns ye have bedded o' late."

" 'Tis only Kate causing the uproar, and she will be gone come the morn," he said coldly, not reacting in any way when she pressed her full curves against him.

"Ah, Tavis, how soon ye forget," she murmured, trailing kisses over his jaw. "Do ye not yet want to retaste the passion we shared that night?" Her hands slid inside his robe.

Grabbing her by the wrists, Tavis flung her away from him. "So ye claim, but I cannae recall any."

" 'Tis the guilt ye feel that tries to erase the memory. Ye must not feel so, Tavis. Your father hasnae been a husband to me in many a month." She tried hard to touch him again.

Stepping around her, Tavis opened the door. "Ye are still his wife. Good night, Janet."

Clenching her fists in anger, Janet watched him leave. Time was running out. Katerine had failed to keep Tavis from the Eldon girl, who seemed to have bewitched him. Despite the fact that Colin was but a heartbeat from death, Tavis still clung to his chivalrous ideals and would not succumb to her entice ments. Janet strode out of the room, deciding that it was time to urge events along.

Storm glanced at Tavis when he entered her room and sprawled on her bed. He lay on his stomach, watching the card game she and Phelan were playing on the floor. There was trouble written upon his handsome features, and she could read an inner torment in his eyes before he veiled his look. Telling herself she was a fool to feel so did not lessen her concern for him. The anguish she sensed in him became her own.

"Did Kate fail to wake up?" she asked idly as she played her card.

"A dose of ale served the trick. I left her raining curses upon my head. She leaves on the morrow. I cannae tolerate her shrewishness another day. She has become tedious beyond bearing."

"That is not what troubles ye, is it?" she asked softly, meeting his eyes.

"Nay, but it will pass."

"Will it? I have seen this trouble in your eyes before. It oft helps to talk about it." She continued to meet his gaze, noticed his hesitancy and said softly, "Is it Janet? She desires ye. 'Tis plain." A small frown crossed her face as she watched him pale slightly. " 'Tis not your fault if she does."

"Is it not?" he replied in an agonized

whisper. "Mayhaps I have given her encouragement. Why wouldnae a woman desire a man that has taken her to his bed? Disgusting, is it not? God's teeth, 'tis near to incest."

Silently Storm shook her head, her eyes wide. "Nay. Nay, I cannot believe that of ye."

With a groan, Tavis turned onto his back, wondering why he was revealing so much of himself, his secrets. "I dinnae want to either, but there is no ignoring the fact that I woke up with her in my arms about six months past, both of us naked. I cannae e'en use my drunkenness as an excuse. Drunk or nay, I shouldnae have lain with my own father's wife. 'Tis hard to ken that I am that much of a bastard."

The card game was forgotten as Storm climbed up on the bed to look into Tavis's face. She could not believe him the sort to cuckold his own father, drunk or not. She frowned as her suspicions grew. If he had been with Janet, Storm could not believe he had instigated it. It was probably small comfort, but she could not stand to see him so tormented. His next words increased her suspicions.

With a harsh laugh, Tavis said, "An I maun suffer for my pleasure, 'twould be nice an I could remember taking it. An I had a good time, I might understand it more."

"Ye do not remember taking your pleasure with Janet?" Storm asked.

"Nay, only waking with a sore head and my arms full of a very naked stepmother." He sighed. "I have tried to recall that night, but it willnae come. Mayhaps 'tis too painful. I would rather forget it."

"Ye have not forgotten enough, though. I think ye should try to recall the whole night."

"I cannae," Tavis growled. "I try and I come up against a wall. Leave it, Storm."

"Nay, I cannae," she mocked him. "Something is

not right." She reached to untie his robe.

"Eager are ye? Hadnae ye best send Phelan away?" He grinned when Phelan giggled.

She ignored both of them. "I am going to help ye recall all that happened that night. Get beneath the covers and lie upon your stomach. I have the strongest feeling that ye have been played for the fool, MacLagan."

Doing as she asked, Tavis inquired, "How can ye make me remember when I cannae?"

" 'Tis your sense of shame that hides your memories. You tense at the subject of that night, and thoughts cannot run freely when that happens. I will relax ye in a way I have oft used with my father when he wanted to think clearly. A Moor from Spain taught me this. He was in father's retinue for a time." She got a pot of oil from amongst the toiletries gathered for her use and then straddled him. "Now ye are to relax and let your thoughts drift unfettered by guilt and shame. Tell me of the smallest thing ye can remember of that night e'en if you think it of no importance. Would it not be better to know for certain at last? Be it good or ill?"

"Aye," Tavis said uncertainly, but her hands were already massaging away his tension.

Beneath her oiled hands Storm felt him begin to grow lax. "Start with the moring of that day."

"We went out on a raid," he replied in the tone of a man totally relaxed. "That feels good."

"Never mind that. Keep your mind on that day. Step by step ye must go through it." She was enjoying the gentle massage of his strong back, feeling each fit muscle relax beneath her ministrations, and smiling fleetingly over the way his voice began to thicken.

"It was a good raid, a success and only a few wounds to show for it. We put ourselves ahead for the winter. 'Twas reason enough for a celebration and the mead and ale flowed freely. Aye, and nay just a wee bit o' the *uisge beatha*. I ken I maun have drunk deep o' it all."

"Were Janet and the laird at this bacchanalia?"

"Aye, in the beginning. They retired fair early, for my father was suffering from a chill." He sighed as his eyes closed in pleasure. "He hasnae recovered yet. I fear he'll nay last much longer."

"Do not clutter up your mind with other worries now. Did ye stay much longer at this drinking orgy?"

"Mmmm. Much later. This would be muckle fine after a long ride or a battle."

"Father thinks so. When did ye go to your chambers?"

"I think 'twas far past midnight. I got undressed, nay, Alex helped me undress. Aye, Alex had to help me take me clothes off, I was that fou. Tucked me up in bed like a wee bairn."

"So," Storm drawled, ceasing her massage, "ye did not retire alone. Alex saw ye to bed."

"Aye, but I cannae remember a thing after that until the dawn. 'Tis the first time I have recalled Alex."

"Phelan, go get Alex."

"Why do that?" asked Tavis as the boy raced off. "Alex wouldnae have stayed with me long."

"Long enough to know just how able ye were of making love to a woman."

Tavis sat up quickly, sending Storm tumbling off him. "Of course! An I was in a drunken sleep, I couldnae have taken Janet." He pulled Storm into his arms for a hearty kiss. "Now that is tasty."

Pressing her down upon the bed, he indulged in another deep kiss, which led to several more. That was how Phelan and Alex found the couple. Phelan laughed while Alex loudly cleared his throat. Keeping an arm around Storm, Tavis turned to Alex, his smile indicative of his high hopes.

"Do ye recall that last raid ere winter set in?"

"Aye, Tavis." Alex grinned. "A muckle lot o' drink were consumed that night."

"Ye put me to bed, right?"

Alex nodded, his grin widening. "Ye couldnae e'en find the bed."

"So I was in no state to have me a woman," Tavis said in a thoughtful voice.

Laughing, Alex replied, "Nay. There isnae a woman on this earth could have found pleasure with ye that night. Ye were snoring loud ere I stepped out o' the room. Our enemies could've burnt Caraidland doon aboot your ears and ye would have slept on. Ne'er seen ye so fou."

"Thank ye, Alex," Tavis said, finding it hard to hide his elation. "Ye can go now. Sorry to drag ye up here." He pulled Storm deeper into his arms. "Aye, and ye can take Phelan with ye."

"I ne'er thought to see a man so pleased to hear that he was so disgustingly drunk," Storm said when they were alone. "Ye ought to be thoroughly ashamed of yourself."

Wrestling her beneath the covers, Tavis began to remove her nightdress. "An I wasnae so relieved I would find that bitch and make her pay dearly for putting me through such a torment. I cannae understand why, what game she plays."

"Ye can be very stupid at times. She wants ye. I think she hoped to weaken your resolve when she crawled into your bed and mayhaps felt that, if ye thought ye had already cuckolded your father, ye would no longer hold her at a distance. Are ye not flattered?"

"Nay. Disgusted. As I said, 'tis almost incest. Do ye think my father kens what she is about?"

"Mayhaps, though he has been ailing. He could be

blind to it all." She caressed his face. "He would not have believed her if she had told him ye had lain with her." She smiled impishly. "Ye may be a bastard, but e'en I could not believe ye would act so dishonorably."

"Ye shall pay for that insolence, wench," he threatened, but his form of retribution was very much to her liking and her cries were of pleasure, not pain.

Much later, as he held her languid body in his arms, he murmured, "Thank ye, Storm."

"For what?" she mumbled, feeling sated and content as she snuggled close to his strength.

"For freeing me from my torment. I could almost think ye cared."

"More fool you. Go to sleep."

He laughed softly and had soon obeyed her teasing command. Storm determinedly fought her own tiredness. As soon as she felt him relax into a deep sleep, she eased out of bed. Donning her night-dress and his robe, she crept from the room. She could wait no longer to voice her suspicions to Malcolm.

"What do ye want?" Malcolm asked when he answered her knock at Colin's door.

Pushing him aside, stepping into the room and shutting the door, Storm said, "I know what ails him." She spotted a beaker of something on a bedside table and picked it up. "What is this concoction?"

" 'Tis a potion his lady brings him each night. He wasnae awake sae he hasnae drunk it yet."

"Thank God." She dipped her finger into the milky liquid and tasted it, surprised at the strength of the poison. "This one was meant to be the last he would ever take. Colin MacLagan has been slowly poisoned. Taste this." She nodded at the shocked look on Malcolm's thin face. "She plainly felt 'tis time to hurry things along."

"Lady Janet?" croaked Malcolm, and Storm nodded. "But why?"

"So she can marry my son Tavis," came a weak voice from the bed, causing both Storm and Malcolm to jump in surprise. "How'd ye guess, lass? Are ye sure?"

"Near positive, m'lord. I am sorry."

"Och, 'tis past pain I am. I learned quickly that I had erred in wedding Janet. Have ye proof 'tis her?"

"Not enough, but I do have a plan."

"Weel, let us have it then. I'd send the bitch off, but I'd sore hate to inflict her upon another."

"To start with, ye are going into a coma so we can have time to get the poison out of ye and put some strength back in."

Colin smiled. "Aye? And then what, lass?"

Storm smiled and then elaborated, earning a great deal of approbation for her cleverness. It was fully two hours before she returned to her own chambers. She opened the door to bright light and a furious Tavis.

Tavis had woken up to an empty bed and a massive attack of suspicion. Lighting nearly every candle in the room, he waited for Storm to return. The longer she took, the more sure he was that she had gone to another man. When she walked into the room he leapt from the bed and slammed her up against the door.

"Where the devil have ye been?"

"Visiting your father. I could not sleep, recalling how poorly he was, but there is naught I can do." She met his gaze without flinching, feeling a little hurt by his suspicions. Glancing at his naked body, she murmured, "Ye best get in bed or ye'll catch a chill."

Muttering in Gaelic, Tavis slid into bed, pulling her into a rough embrace when, after putting out all the lights save for one candle by the bed, she joined him beneath the covers. Snuffing that last candle, he decided not to mention the matter any more. He had made a big enough fool of himself. Tugging off her nightdress for the second time that night, he lost himself in her silken loveliness and forgot all about her lengthy absence from their bed. Storm did her best to ensure that for, if her plan were to work, even Tavis had to remain ignorant.

9

There was an air of grim anticipation hovering over Caraidland. For three days the laird had lain in a coma, hovering on the brink of death. Now, even the most optimistic could not ignore the fact that Colin MacLagan was dying. Only Malcolm and Storm were allowed into the laird's chambers. No one questioned Storm's place, for her healing abilities were already well respected. Storm suspected there would have been a large number of very angry people if they could have seen behind the thick door of Colin's chambers.

"I think 'tis time for ye to come out of your coma," Storm mused from where she sat next to a rapidly improving Colin. "I think ye are strong enough to perform your death scene now."

Colin laughed and toasted her with a mug of ale. "I look forward to it. Where shall it be, lass?"

"Since ye are well known to be a stubborn man, none will think it strange that ye demand them all in your room to hear your last will and testament. They could easily believe ye would come back from the brink of death just to do that."

"Aye, but dinnae I look a wee bit too healthy now? They may not believe I am dying."

"A little powder and paint will serve." She produced a small sack. "Malcolm had best rid the room of all the signs of your returning appetite. As soon as I have ye looking ready to gasp your last, we will fetch up your family. I shall be glad to see the last of their long faces."

"Are ye sure the bitch'll give herself away?" asked Malcolm as he tidied the room.

"Oh, aye. Tavis plans to send her on her way if Colin dies. I doubt the laird's death rattle will have ceased echoing in the room ere he tells her to pack her things and go. Then there is our little *coup de grace*."

"Ye are a devious lass. I ne'er would have thought it o' ye." Colin chuckled softly.

"Needs must when the devil drives," she mumbled as she put the finishing touches on Colin's death mask. "There. Ye look like ye have been buried near a week. Mayhaps I overdid it. Not to worry. Ready for your performance, sir?" She grinned at Colin. "Shall I gather the audience?"

Tavis was the first to greet her when she entered the hall. Storm looked at his haggard face and felt guilty for causing him grief with her machinations. It was only a fleeting twinge, for she knew what she was doing was both necessary and right. The one who had tried to kill Colin had to be exposed. She delivered her prepared speech and led the solemn grou> to Colin's chambers.

Colin lay, slightly propped up by his pillows, the hollows of his face starkly accentuated by the light and Storm's skilled work with the paints and powders. He watched his sons' faces tighten as they fought to hide their grief and felt guilty, both over the deception and the pleasure he felt at this proof of their caring. It was hard to conceal his rage when his eyes settled on his wife, but he managed, knowing one error would ruin all they had accomplished so far.

"I ken ye are aware o' how I wish to disperse my holdings, but I wanted to say it one more time afore witnesses so there be no doubt," he said in an appropriately failing voice as Storm moved to stand by him. " 'Tis no surprise that I leave Tavis Caraidland and all that goes with it and the house in Edinburgh, plus half my wealth. Sholto and Iain, ye can sort out the rest as ye will. In my writing table ye will find a paper with instructions concerning a few others, such as Malcolm here."

"What of me, darling?" Janet asked when Colin closed his eyes and said no more.

"Och, weel, I leave ye what ye brought to Caraidland and no more." He grasped Storm's hand. "See that the lass here gets back to her folk," he gasped before passing away with a trembling sigh.

Thinking that he had done that very well, Storm crossed her arms over his chest. "He's dead."

She stood by the bed to block any chance of the unknowing seeing anything suspicious. With a sardonic look she watched Janet burst into tears and fling herself into Tavis's arms. Storm felt badly for the brothers, who plainly struggled to remain manly in their grief. Their unaffected sorrow erased the tiny, lingering suspicions she had so unwillingly harbored that one of them was in league with Janet.

With a harsh oath, Tavis flung Janet away from him. "Cease that false noise, woman. An I could do so, ye'd be on your way within the hour, but 'tis best an it waits until after the burial."

"Send me away?" Janet gasped. "How can ye be so heartless? I have nowhere to go, Tavis."

"Ye'll find a hole quick enough," he hissed, "so stop your weeping, or do ye weep for the gold me father didnae leave ye? 'Tis nay grief that sets ye to wailing. I ken that weel, as does many another. I'd nay be surprised to find ye had a hand in his death, ye had so little feeling for the man ye wed."

"Perfect," thought Storm, her eyes moving just quickly enough to catch the flash of panic in Janet's eyes.

Janet gasped, a hand dramatically fluttering to her throat. "I would ne'er do such a thing."

"Aye?" growled Malcolm, stepping in precisely on cue, "if ye be sae free o' guilt, go near the body, m'lady."

"What would that prove?" Janet asked haughtily, but her gaze darted nervously toward Colin.

" 'Tis said that an a murderer nears his victim's body, the body will give a sign such as a movement or blood flowing anew from an old or new wound. Care to try it, m'lady?" Storm asked.

"Peasant superstition," she scoffed, staying right where she was.

"Then it cannae hurt ye, can it?" Malcolm goaded. "Then again, ye may be guilty."

Glaring at her tormentor, Janet strode to Colin's bed. Storm and Malcolm feigned shock almost as well as the others did when blood began to seep from the old wound in Colin's shoulder, soaking the front of his night shirt. It was plain to see that the three brothers wanted to deny what their eyes saw. In the enlightened year of 1362 such magic was scorned, or so it was hoped. Janet blanched and backed away from the bed, shaking her head.

"It seems ye did have a hand in his death," drawled Storm her eyes settling accusingly on Janet, hoping that the woman would condemn herself with her own words.

Janet looked around at the accusing faces turned her way. Her guilt proved to be her own worst enemy. She turned to Tavis, her hands held out beseechingly. All along she had held to the delusion that only Colin kept Tavis from her side. Now she felt sure that his passion for her would be freed and therefore he would help her. Instead, she met nothing but contempt and suspicion, even open dislike.

"How can ye look at me so, Tavis? Can ye not see? Now we can be together."

Tavis's revulsion at that idea was plain to read upon his face. "I ne'er wanted to be with ye."

"That's not true!" She clutched at the front of his tunic. "How can ye forget the night we made love? All the words o' sweet love ye spoke to me? Now we need not keep it a secret."

"There's naught to be kept a secret," he snarled as he shoved her away. "Ye crawled into my bed and I was too fou to boot ye out. We did naught. I ken that now. Ye played me for a fool, bitch, but dinnae delude yourself as ye tried to delude me. I dinnae want ye. I ne'er have."

"But I did it all for ye. I kenned we couldnae be together whilst he lived," she screamed, then gasped in horror when she realized what she had said. "Nay."

"It was in the potion, was it not?" Storm asked quietly.

"Nay! I did naught! Ye have got me all confused. I ken not what I be saying."

"Ye ken right enough," came a voice from the bed, and Colin sat up to glare at his wife, shocking his sons into open-mouthed speechlessness and sending Janet one step closer to madness.

"Nay, nay, ye are dead. No man could have survived that last dose I gave ye," Janet moaned as she stepped further away from the bed, her eyes wide with horror. "Ye be haunting me, that be all."

"He is not dead, Janet. He did not drink your last potion, the one that was so strong."

"Ye have tricked me," she hissed, her wild eyes fixing upon Storm. "Ye bitch! Sassanach whore!"

Before anyone could react, Janet pulled a dagger

from a concealed pocket in her skirts. She lunged at an unsuspecting Storm, who had turned to help arrange the pillows behind Colin. Storm had no time to fully react to the cries of warning. With a snarl, Janet plunged her knife into Storm's slim shoulder. She had aimed for Storm's back, but Storm had already begun to turn, ruining her aim. Storm felt a flash of pain strong enough to make her swoon and collapsed upon Colin. Before Janet could try a second time, Malcolm swung at her with the fireplace poker. Janet fell to the floor with hardly a whimper, blood seeping from a wound at her temple.

"Is she dead?" Colin asked, holding on to Storm, trying to staunch her wound's bleeding with his own bed linen. "A neat swing, Malcolm. Could have been a bit quicker, though."

"She's dead," Iain said as he rose from examining Janet.

"How is Storm?" Tavis asked as he bent over the wounded girl. "Is it bad, Malcolm?"

"Nay as bad as it could be," muttered Malcolm as, after ripping open Storm's dress, he proceeded to wash the wound clean. "The knife was meant tae go deep into the wee lass's back, but she moved in time."

"So, 'twas all a ploy," breathed Sholto as he moved to the foot of his father's bed.

"Aye. 'Twas the lass's idea. She guessed that 'twas an unnatural illness I suffered from."

"How did ye get the wound to bleed?" asked Iain.

"Chicken's blood in a pig's bladder afixed 'neath me arm. The open end pointed to me shoulder. All I had to do was squeeze it a wee bit and it looked as if me old wound bled anew."

"Ye were ne'er in death's sleep, were ye," commented Tavis as he held Storm firmly to the bed so that, even in her unconscious state, she would not move as Malcolm stitched her wound.

"Nay, that was Storm's idea as weel. It gave me time to recover, get me strength back."

"How did she discover ye were being poisoned?"

"She kenned the symptoms, Sholto," Colin replied. "I'm right sorry ye were kept in the dark, but we felt it better that way. Ye'd act more natural and Janet'd be more apt to confess the truth."

"The poison was in the potion she mixed ye?"

"Aye, Tavis. An ancient one—arsenic. A slow death so it would look like a wasting sickness and raise nary an eyebrow. It was a clever plan that nearly worked."

"I wonder how the lass kenned what it was. 'Tis not common knowledge," Iain mused.

" 'Twas how her mother died," Malcolm said as he finished bandaging Storm. "They caught it too late and, being a wee lady, she hadnae the strength to fight it like the laird did. Some woman did it. Gather the lady felt 'twas time for the laird o' Hagaleah tae take a new wife."

Tavis suddenly recalled a small, girlish voice saying, "The way of a lady is a bit o' poison in the meal. So much more refined." Even then he had wondered at the bitterness in Storm's voice. Now he understood. As he brushed the hair from Storm's flushed face, he wondered how she had come through such trials with her innocence and optimism intact. Life had not treated her very kindly.

"I cannae like her color, Malcolm," Tavis observed, his eyes on Storm's deepening flush.

"Take her tae her own bed, lad," Malcolm ordered quietly. "Let's hope 'tis only the shock. I cannae do anymore for her wound, save change the bandage and keep it clean."

" 'Tis too bad we didnae get the receipt for that salve she gave me so long ago," said Colin as he watched his son pick up Storm with the air of one handling fine glass.

113

"Phelan might ken it," was all Tavis said as he left with his precious burden.

Colin fixed his gaze upon Malcolm. "Ye do your best for the lass." After Malcolm had left he smiled at his two younger sons. "Weel, what do ye think o' my miraculous resurrection?"

"Dinnae get too puffed up," drawled Iain with a grin that swiftly turned into a frown. "I may be wrong, and God kens I'd like to be, but I ken our Tavis is fair caught, though he may not see it."

"Aye, I fear 'tis so." Colin was beginning to feel a bit tired. " 'Twill be a grief for the lad, but there is naught I can do. I'm fair weary, lads. Take that woman to her room and see that she's readied for burying. I would have liked to keep this quiet, but with a stabbing and a death, I fear I cannae."

"We'll do what we can," Sholto promised as he lifted up Janet's body. "Ye get your rest."

"Keep me informed of the lass's progress," Colin called softly as they left. "I now owe her my life."

That was the thought on most minds of Caraidland as the tale of what had occurred in the laird's chambers spread like wildfire. Those few that had held Storm's birth against her now moved firmly into her camp. Colin was a very popular laird, and his clan now felt nothing but good toward the small English lady who had saved his life. None grieved for Janet. She had done little to make herself popular amongst her husband's people. They now did all they could to aid Storm's recovery, even if it was but to include her in their prayers, and not one of them felt that it was odd to do so.

Tavis took Storm to her room, stripped her and tucked her up in bed. He was honestly afraid for her, a fact he spent no time reviewing, but simply accepted. She had lost a fair amount of blood before her wound had stopped bleeding. He saw only how small she was, worrying that she could not recoup the loss. When Phelan and Malcolm arrived he left her in their capable hands and sought out a strong drink. The day had been a long one, too full of surprises for Tavis's liking.

"How's the lass?" Iain asked in greeting as he handed Tavis a full tankard of ale.

"I cannae tell. She's still unconscious. I left Malcolm and Phelan doing what they could." Tavis took a long drink. "She's such a wee thing, and 'tis a deep wound that has lost her a lot of blood."

"Aye, but she has strength," Sholto remarked as Tavis sat down at the table.

"I cannae believe Janet tried tae kill Colin," Donald mused aloud. "She maun hae been mad."

"I think she was a bit." Iain shook his head. "She had built a dream wherein she and Tavis would rule once Colin was gone. She thought 'twas only Colin's presence keeping Tavis at a distance." He fixed Tavis with a look that demanded a truthful explanation. "What night was she raving about?"

It was only family at the table, men he knew could be trusted to be quiet, so Tavis explained. "So," he continued, "I went about for near to six months thinking I had done as she had said. There were times I couldnae look our father in the eye, I was so eaten with guilt."

"How did ye find out ye hadnae?" Angus asked.

"Storm made me review all that had happened that night. She rubs your back and neck, aye, and your head until ye feel near to sleep and will say most anything." Tavis's voice held a remembered amazement. "She learned the trick from an infidel. Without the tension the memory always brought, I was able to recall that Alex had aided me to bed. He took away my last doubts by saying that I couldnae have made love to any woman." He shook his head. "I think Janet had convinced herself of her own lies. She was near to mad."

"Ye and the lasses, laddie," Angus sighed, causing the first laughter to be heard at Caraidland for three very long days.

The rest of the day proved hectic for Tavis. What work he had to do was periodically interrupted so that he could look in on Storm and then report to his father on her condition. When he retired for the night Storm still had only the mildest of fevers, and he began to relax. He crawled into their bed, careful not to disturb her, but her eyes were open when he turned to look at her.

"Janet tried to kill me, did she not?" she asked in a whisper that was hoarse with the pain that seemed to be radiating throughout her body from its origin in her shoulder.

"Aye, lass." He gently brushed the hair from her face, relieved to find it relatively cool.

"Sweet mother of God, it hurts," she croaked. "Is it a very bad wound?"

"It could have been much worse, sweeting. The bitch was aiming for a mortal spot upon your back."

" 'Tis my own fault. I should have planned for it. Aye, should have known it was unwise to turn my back on a murderess."

"I think ye did enough planning." He saw her brief look of worry. "I'm nay angry with ye for keeping it all silent, lass. 'Twas the best way. We are no actors and could have given the game away. I thank ye for my father's life." He grinned at the way she blushed and looked away in embarrassment. "Ye must cease saving your enemies."

She smiled weakly. "I could not let him die such a death, and I believe my father would think it wrong too. 'Tis a man of battle Colin is. He should die fighting bravely, not wasting away from a cup of poison handed him by such a treacherous wife."

"Aye, that he should. Janet is dead, lass. Malcolm felled her with a blow from a fireplace poker."

For a moment Storm was silent. "I do not understand how she could wed Colin if she had such a lack of feeling for the man. She was not forced; it was not arranged for her."

"Nay, she wooed and wed him at Stirling. She was from a poor family and dowerless. My father offered her the wealth and position she'd nay gain in another way. He realized too late how she really saw him. She cozened him. My father is nay a young man any longer. I imagine he was flattered to think that such a young, beautiful woman found him attractive. He fell victim to an old game."

"Ye are a cynic," Storm murmured as she caught the bitterness in his voice. " 'Tis a shame she did that, for I think there is many a fine woman nearer his age that would have thanked God daily for a man such as he. There are a good many widows. Colin is a man that likes to have a wife. He is not a libertine rogue like ye are," she added with a slight return of her old spirit.

"He may yet find a good woman to keep him company during his declining years."

" 'Twould be nice if ye said that with a bit of conviction."

"I cannae. I have yet to find a good woman."

"An I was not so weak, ye would pay dearly for that insult, Tavis."

"Thank God for small mercies," he teased. "Get to sleep, little one. Ye need your rest to get weel."

Storm obeyed without complaint. Despite her pain, she was weary enough to go to sleep, the short conversation using up what little strength she had. She was surprised at how gently Tavis held her, keeping her close enough to absorb the comfort of his strength but being very careful not to cause her any pain. It was nice to feel so cherished by him even if his reasons for doing so were not those she wanted.

She wished she were home safe with her father,

and Lady Mary sent far away along with Sir Hugh. It was not that she was unhappy at Caraidland. She had, in fact, settled in very nicely. Storm knew that the greatest danger was Tavis. With each passing day she fell more in love with him. As she fell asleep, she knew that the pain she would suffer for loving Tavis MacLagan would make her current pain seem like nothing at all.

It proved a long night. Although Storm escaped suffering from a fever and seemed safe from infection, her pain made her restless. Several times Tavis woke to her moaning and thrashing. He would steady her, check her bandage and once gave her a draft to ease the pain. His reward was that, in the morning, her forehead still felt cool and her wound looked untainted.

As he donned his robe preparatory to leaving the room, he paused to study her. Asleep, she looked like a child. Thick curves of lashes splayed over her delicate cheeks and her full lips were parted slightly. He was constantly astounded that such a tiny, innocent-looking woman was capable of the passion she revealed in his arms. She was proving a constant surprise.

He brushed a kiss on her forehead and then hastily departed, a little embarrassed over his unseen display of tenderness. Yet again he sensed that he was in deep, that she was a danger to the feelings he had so successfully buried. Although he recognized that, he could not stay away from her. Without even trying she drew him back into her arms as no woman had done before.

10

Storm winced as she tried to brush her hair. The wound was healing very nicely but was stiff. It was not a fear of reopening it that made her cautious, for it would take a lot to do that, but the twinge of pain it often gave her. Nevertheless, she was determined to go down to the hall for her meal. She could not face another night lying on her bed, staring at her ceiling and wondering what everyone else was doing.

There had been visitors. Colin had come to play chess with her. A lot of time had been spent teaching Angus about playing cards. Sholto and Iain had come to entertain her with nonsense now and again, although Tavis did not seem to like that. Tavis spent as much time as possible with her, as did Phelan. Despite all that and then some, for others had drifted in and out, she was bored. It was the confinement within her room that bothered her, and that was what she was determined to put to an end.

"Let me help you, cousin," Phelan offered, taking the brush from her hands. "I am becoming quite good at this."

"Aye, ye would make a fine lady's maid," she teased with a grin, and they both laughed.

" 'Tis not so bad here." He began to braid her hair. "The men are teaching me a lot."

"I am glad, Phelan. 'Tis a shame Father had to leave when he did, for that meant your training was cut short." She sighed as she watched Phelan start the second braid. "I pray that Lady Mary fails in her scheme."

Phelan nodded in solemn, heartfelt agreement. Although he had not known Lord Eldon long, he had instantly liked the gruff-voiced, quick-tongued but gentle-natured man. He also knew how much it would hurt Storm to lose her father, and the very last thing Phelan wanted was for his much-loved cousin to be hurt.

When they entered the hall a few minutes later Tavis went immediately to her side. He thought she looked far too attractive in the gold gown that accentuated her eyes so well. Since he could not convince her to stay in her room, he wished she could have looked haggard or dowdy at least. There were to be guests for dinner, and he did not want her looking as attractive as she did.

"I still think 'tis too early for ye to be up and about," he groused, touching her pinned-up braids.

"Tavis, I was wounded in the shoulder. My legs were not lopped off," she replied calmly but winked at a grinning Colin, who handed her a tankard of ale.

"Thank God for that," Tavis drawled with a leer directed toward those slim limbs.

"Your conceit is only exceeded by your vulgarity," she said haughtily, but her eyes danced with laughter. "Are ye having a celebration of sorts? Ye are all dressed so fine."

"Surprised are ye? Weel, m'lady, I ken ye think of us as naught but rogues and pirates, but we have a skill or twa aside from raping and pillaging." Tavis met her scowl with a grin.

Phelan stared up at Tavis innocently. "Aye and well ye love to hear the screams of the women ye pillage."

"Phelan!" Storm had to force the scolding tone into her voice, for she wanted to laugh as the others

120

did. " 'Tis not a subject for jests," she said with appropriate reproach although her lips fought a grin. "I merely asked if 'twas a special occasion, for I have no wish to intrude."

"Nay, ye'll not be intruding, lass. Ye will be company for Angus's wife Maggie and Lord Mac-Dubh's wife Helen. They and their son Alexander are our guests. 'Tis old friends they are. Ah, here is Angus now," Colin murmured.

Angus's wife Maggie was a plump woman with a cheerful, comely face that was a great contrast to her husband's usually dour one. Her dark hair held a few strands of gray but Storm knew the woman was still of child-bearing age, for she had just given Angus his fourth son and could only just be finished with her lying in. Her blue eyes were friendly and honest, brimming with the sparkle of good humor.

" 'Tis glad I am tae see ye oot of your room, lass," Maggie said with a smile.

"Aye, freedom is so sweet," Storm expounded dramatically. " 'Tis the chains weighting down my poor starved limbs that I am gladdest to be rid of." She met Maggie's laughter-filled glance with one of her own. "Of course I shall have my revenge. I have already planned it."

"I should hope so. May I ask what it is?" Maggie had known from Angus's tales that she would like this little amber-eyed Sassanach lady.

"Well, as he lies abed asnoring away . . ."

"I dinnae snore," protested Tavis, but his eyes revealed his amusement.

"I shall paint him blue," Storm continued as if he had not spoken. "Pale blue."

"Pale blue?" Maggie queried in a slightly choked voice.

"Aye. I have thought from the start that he was a bit too dark." She started laughing along with Maggie.

"Angus, I didnae ken that your wife had such a strange twist of humor just as my father," Tavis drawled with a glance at a chuckling Colin.

" 'Tis something I have tried tae keep a secret, much like a deformity."

"Angus!" Maggie protested laughingly. "Ye wretch tae speak o' your wife so. Oh! The guests."

Tavis's good humor fled immediately, although he was all that was polite as the MacDubhs joined them. The minute Alexander MacDubh's eyes settled appreciatively upon Storm, Tavis began to plan on a way to get her back to her room as soon as possible. Not once did he name the emotion he felt as the jealousy that it was, but called it a natural sense of possession. Storm Eldon was his until she was returned to Hagaleah and what was his, stayed his.

Storm greeted Lord and Lady MacDubh with all the respect due their position. She thought, irrepressibly that they looked like twins, both short, plump and silver-haired, although Lord MacDubh was a jovial, garrulous sort, while his wife was quiet and shy. Then she turned to meet their son, Alexander, and was stunned.

She did not think she had ever seen such a beautiful man and fleetingly wondered how the two plump, rather ordinary parents had produced such a tall god of a son. His fair hair was thick and wavy and crowned a face of such perfect proportions that it could have been cut by the finest artist from the marble his skin resembled. As tall as Tavis, Alexander's body was a woman's dream. His soft green eyes reflected appreciation as they met hers, and Storm felt herself blush slightly. He exuded sensuality and, to her surprise, for she loved Tavis, Storm felt a response stir within her. Here was a man who could stir a nun, she thought, and then silently apologized for her irreverency. Suddenly she thought that such abundance of perfection was almost repelling and felt herself no longer drawn to him.

No matter what he called it, the green-eyed monster was getting a firm grip upon Tavis. He saw the slightly glazed look on Storm's face and ground his teeth when she blushed. Alexander MacDubh's effect upon and success with women was nearly legendary. Tavis saw Storm swiftly joining those ranks. He ignored Alex's fleeting, sardonic glance as he put a possessive hand upon Storm's slim arm.

Although a little surprised by Tavis's action, Storm did not wonder about it long. She found it a little amusing that she and Phelan were being treated much like guests instead of the hostages they were. The MacDubhs were obviously too polite to point out the absurdity and joined in the game. Despite the way she was treated, who she was was not forgotten as the conversation over the meal soon proved.

Whenever any conversation about matters that could aid or interest her father was begun it was abruptly halted and another started. Storm thought she ought to feel uncomfortable but she did not. She had been invited, after all. However, she decided to retire to her room as soon as possible. It did not seem quite fair or polite to stay when she knew her presence restricted everyone in a way.

For once the women retired to a far corner of the hall at the end of the meal. Phelan joined the three ladies, sitting beside Storm on a settee before the fireplace. Storm quickly discovered that Lady Mac-Dubh was not as shy as she had first appeared. Away from the men, Lady MacDubh lost some of her reticence.

"Do you really believe that your stepmother means to refuse to pay a ransom?" Lady Helen asked. "Would she not fear Lord Eldon's wrath when he discovered what she had done?"

"If he discovered. If he returns from France,

would it not be easier for him to believe that some unknown fate befell me or that the MacLagans, for reasons unknown, have not stayed with the usual rules concerning hostages than to believe that his wife tossed his only daughter to the whims of fate?"

Maggie nodded solemly. "No matter how failed the marriage is, he'd nay want tae believe that."

"But to leave you here to be, weel, Tavis is . . ." Lady Helen stumbled to a blushing halt.

"Using me?" Storm completed. " 'Tis no secret in this keep, m'lady. I have little doubt that my father's wife finds that possibility something to savor. She was born a whore, if ye will excuse my blunt speech. My innocence was e'er an irritation to her."

Lady Helen found Storm's calm a curiosity. "But do you suffer no shame?" she asked with no reproach.

"For what, m'lady? What purpose would it serve? From the first night there was no return for me. I will ne'er be a maid again. I did not ask for the place I now hold, so why should I condemn myself? I did not throw myself at Tavis's feet, crying wantonly 'Please, take me.' " Maggie giggled and Storm smiled.

Storm sighed. "I was not safe within Hagaleah. My father's wife had chosen a husband for me, one of her lovers in need of a fortune." She nodded in response to the ladies' shocked gasps. "I naturally refused, but he planned to dishonor me, e'en get me with child, to gain his ends. Shameless it may sound, but as a ravisher I prefer Tavis MacLagan to Sir Hugh Sedgeway. Dear Sir Hugh has a liking to give more pain than pleasure."

"Oh. One of those." Lady Helen shook her head. " 'Tis hard for a woman with no protectors at hand." She frowned. "Has Tavis given no thought to the retribution Lord Eldon will try to extract when he returns?"

"The MacLagans and the Eldons have always

124

fought each other. This battle will just have a more tangible cause. Then and all, my father is a reasonable man. An I talk to him first, a real blood-letting could be avoided." Storm shrugged. "Then again, men do love a battle. 'Tis their life."

"All too true," sighed Maggie, and she glanced at Phelan. "A life they dutifully train the wee lads to. I fear for me Angus each time he rides away. 'Tis hard tae watch him go when I ken he may ne'er come back alive."

" 'Tis the Eldons he rides against more oft than not, yet ye seem to befriend Lord Eldon's very daughter."

"But, Lady Helen," Phelan spoke up, "could that not be because she knows that Storm suffers the like when her men ride against the MacLagans? Sure 'n' there's naught either of them can do to stop the battles."

"Aye," Maggie agreed. " 'Tis a thing that gies us a bond strong enough tae overcome who we are."

"That I can understand." Lady Helen studied the delicate English girl seated across from her. "I must ask it, though it be forward, mayhaps impertinent, but curiosity compels me. Ye have been here a number of weeks and most of those with Tavis. Living with him in such, er, intimacy," she blushed, "is there not a chance that ye could fall in love with the man?"

Smiling crookedly, Storm replied, "Every chance in this world, m'lady. 'Tis the one thing I fear," she added, feeling no need to point out that it had occurred a long time past.

Maggie adroitly turned the conversation to matters of household and fashion. Seeing that some of the men were now standing about in groups, Phelan slipped away to join them. It was not long after his escape that Maggie also departed, for she was nursing her new son and it was nearly feeding time again. Storm found herself alone with Lady Helen and soon saw that the ways of polite conversation differed little either side of the border. A woman of the Scottish court, Lady Helen had an abundancy of idle chatter.

When Alexander MacDubh strolled over and Lady Helen moved away to join her husband Storm was less than pleased. The man had so much in his favor that he overwhelmed her. She did not like the feeling. As she looked to Tavis for rescue, she frowned, for she had sensed that he had been watching her yet he was now apparently unaware of her presence. She edged away from Alexander as he sat down close to her.

Tavis was fully aware of Storm's presence, where she was and who she was with. Since Mary, he and Alexander had shared the favors of many women. The contest had been to see who could gain access first, a contest they were virtually tied in, or to see if one could draw a woman from the arms of the other. Since Mary, Tavis had found Alex's knowledge of his women, whether before, during or after his own use of them, only an annoyance until now. Now, for reasons he refused to clearly acknowledge, it meant more than it even had with Mary.

"How do you find the way of life upon this side of the border, m'lady?" Alex asked, leaning closer to her.

Storm felt his smooth, deep voice caress her and almost smiled, for the man was a perfect instrument of seduction. " 'Tis little different from what on the English side. People and their manners differ little if at all."

"Nevertheless, ye will be glad to return to your own home."

"Would not anyone in my position?" she asked smoothly.

"Exactly what is your position, Mistress Eldon?"

His gaze moved over her in a subtle caress.

"I think ye are well aware of what it is, sir." She wished he were not so close, but had no more room upon the settee to move away and could not be so rude as to suddenly stand up, at least not yet.

"You are a hostage who is treated much like a guest. It makes for some confusion, ye must admit."

"I see none. I can hardly pose a threat to a strong man. There is little chance that I will try to fight my way out of here or take a hostage myself. The chains may be invisible but they are there."

"Mayhaps the chains are not only those of a captor but of a lover," he said softly.

"Ye step out of bounds, sir. Hostage or nay, I am still a lady and should be tendered respect."

Alex smiled slightly, for here was one that was out of the ordinary. She was in a position that should rob her of dignity, yet she had it in force. There was also no coyness in her. She did not blush or try to deny what everyone knew, but simply pointed out his tactlessness in mentioning it.

"I merely wish to be sure that what I hear is correct, for I thought to offer you an alternative."

"I think ye needed no confirmation, but tell me of your alternative. Curiosity abounds."

"The MacDubhs are friends and connections of the MacLagans. Ones of long standing. I could speak to Colin, convince him that you would be better off in our keeping."

"Would I?" She mused idly that it was most unfair for one young man to have so much in his favor.

"You would be treated as the lady you are, one of high birth and breeding. I would ever be the gentleman."

"Think ye that Tavis does not treat me as a lady?" Somehow she felt there was more to his offer than a wish for her company or to shelter her from harsh treatment, but she could not guess what it was.

"I think not for, let us be open with each other, m'lady, he has brought dishonor to you."

Briefly she thought about putting the man in his place but decided it was absurd to act as if she and Tavis were not sharing a bed since all knew they were. "And ye would not?"

"It is not my way to force my attentions upon a lady."

His tone indicated that he had no need to, and Storm had to agree. "Who is to say that Tavis has done so? Do ye see any sign that force has been used upon me? I bear no bruises or shackle marks. Do I hold the fear of one much abused?"

"Are you saying that you go to him willingly?"

"Nay, but I have not been hit o'er the head either. Tell me true, sir, an I come with you, do ye mean to make no try to draw me into your bed? Would I not trade one seducer for another?"

Alexander stared into her wide, guileless amber eyes and nearly hated Tavis MacLagan. Here was a woman who used no ploys nor airs but had the straightforward honesty of a man. The passion he could read in the full shape of her mouth and supple lines of her body would come forth as honestly as everything else about her. Tavis was enjoying that, and Alex wanted to taste it. He was, however, beginning to think that he never would, for instinct was telling him that Tavis was getting a lot more than a naturally passionate woman's response to a skilled hand, whether he knew it or not, and Alex doubted that Tavis did. In such matters it was sometimes easier for others to see how matters stood.

Lightly touching her thick braids, he replied, "I would make no effort to place you where you did not want to be."

"But that does not say ye will not try to make me wish to be there."

With a soft laugh, Alex said, "What man would not try to woo a lovely lady?"

"Ye asked that we be open with each other so I will admit that I would no doubt find myself established in your home as I find myself established here. I think ye are well aware of your handsomeness and charm as well as how succcessfully they achieve your aim. Since I feel ye have been no stranger to women, ye would know well how to employ the subtle arts of seduction. I do not feel I add to any conceit ye may have by saying ye feel sure of success nor that ye are right in feeling so. Being blunt, as I am no longer a maid, 'tis merely easier for ye for now I hold no fears to hold me back but knowledge to make my resistance weaker."

"There is openness with a vengence, m'lady. I would, however, be offering ye a choice."

"Nay, sir, merely a change. Subtle ye may be, but it all comes round to the same thing—me, the first born and only daughter of an English border lord, unwed and mayhaps now unweddable, sharing the bed of a Scottish reiver. At least now I am with folk I know and, may my father forgive me," she grinned, "like. I have little wish to change that for the unknown, which will be equally as transitory. At least now, when I return home, I can say, in all truthfulness, that it has been but one man who has put me to shame."

Lifting her hand, he kissed her palm and then kept hold of her hand. "You, Mistress Eldon, are a beautiful woman with a logical mind. 'Tis a combination sure to make any man quake." He caught his breath when she laughed. "Ah, now that is a sound lovely enough to bring any man to his knees."

The warmth in his eyes and the way they lingered on her mouth made Storm feel decidedly breathless. "Ye are flirting with me, sir, and 'tis unsure I am that that is wise." She caught his gaze flicking toward Tavis, noted that Tavis was staring at them and suddenly understood some of Alex's desire for her. "Do ye not think I have far and above enough woes without ye making me a pawn in some male game?"

For the first time in a long while, Alex felt the heat of shame touch his cheeks. "Acuteness of perception in a woman is almost as unsettling as logic. You unman me, madam."

She laughed softly. "That, sir, is an impossibility. Naught but a sword could accomplish that." She gaped and blushed when she realized how outspoken she had just been, but Alex roared with delighted laughter.

He lightly caressed the high color on one cheek with his knuckles. "Tavis and I have oft known the same women. It has long been a game of sorts for us to see which could seduce the lady first or to see if we could seduce her out of the other's bed. It has been this way for nigh on to five years."

Glancing toward Tavis, Storm read far more than competition there. "That is all?"

Again he brought her palm to his lips. "It does not dim my desire for you, Storm Eldon."

"Thank ye, sir, but that is not what I meant. There is something more behind this game ye play."

Alex sighed. "Aye, on Tavis's part, mostly. There was a lady, though I hesitate to call her such, five years past. Tavis believed he loved her." Alex took note of the expressions that flittered over Storm's face with little surprise. "Having been there once myself, I realize how he saw her as near to a saint. He caught us together. He ne'er blamed me, for he kenned I took only what was offered, but such disillusionment is hard to forget." He smiled gently at her. "However, the past need not cloud our future."

"Storm's future isnae your concern, Alex. M'lady, I think ye lose sight of who ye be, a hostage, not a guest. 'Tis time ye returned to your room."

Storm took one look at blue eyes that were pure ice, making his cold words seem almost warm, and swallowed the angry retort hovering on her tongue. With all the dignity she could muster, she rose, bid good evening to Alex and followed Angus to her room.

11

From Tavis's point of view, Alex's seduction of Storm had been well under way and succeeding. To his eyes, their smiles, laughter and hushed conversation looked like a brazen flirtation. The occasional glance in his direction he saw as a guilty one. He was sure Storm was succumbing to Alex as women always had.

As he watched her leave after he had spat his harsh words at her, he was fully aware of having offended as well as angered her. The chill in her eyes and her stiff posture made that clear enough. What he was not sure of and what made him oddly uncomfortable was that he had hurt her. There had been a flicker of what he had read as pain upon her face before it had closed to him, a trick of hers that he detested.

"Ne'er known you to have such a heavy hand with the ladies, Tavis," Alexander drawled.

"She is my hostage, not some filly at court ye can dally with at your pleasure."

"She is also your lover," Alex said softly, finding Tavis's possessiveness fascinating.

"Aye, and this is one ye arenae having, MacDubh. Did ye think I would step aside for the night or mayhaps send her to ye with my compliments? There was little to gain from this seduction."

"Actually, I offered to let her await ransoming at our keep. Thought to mention it to Colin."

Tavis gave a harsh laugh. "And of course ye promised to keep your hands off her."

"Nay, I but offered to treat her as the lady she is. That, and the choice of sharing my bed or nay, which I ken you have not done, my friend. You have simply taken, not requested nor waited for an invitation."

"As any man would do with such a prize taken as hostage. She stays here until 'tis time to return her to Hagaleah."

"And when will that be? There is plainly little rush to gain the ransom."

"It'll come e'en if we maun wait for his lordship to return and send it. Then she goes home."

Alex watched Tavis stride away, delivering curt good nights as he left the hall. The little English lady had the man twisted every which way, but Tavis had yet to see it. Shaking his head, Alex felt a twinge of sympathy for Tavis. The blow he would take from this affair was going to make the one he had suffered over Mary look like the tiniest of bruises. Alex looked up to greet Sholto and Iain with a nod as they joined him.

"That's one he'll nay play the game with, Alex," Sholto said as he sprawled in a chair.

"So I have discovered. What he failed to query was whether or not the lady was playing."

"Was she?" asked Iain.

"Nay, my friend. Not only was I turned down in the most flattering of ways, but the lass caught on to the game and shamed me with it. She sees all too clearly in most respects."

"By the looks of that stiff little back as she left here, there will be a bloody row in the tower tonight," Sholto observed with a laugh. "Shame they took it upstairs, for 'tis a show when they go at it."

"Do neither of them see what is obvious to everyone?" Alex inquired with genuine interest.

Iain sighed. "Nay. 'Tis a shame, but it may not matter when or if they do, for she is Lord Eldon's only daughter, his first-born, and Tavis is heir to this place. Hardly a match with promise."

When the heavy door shut behind Storm as she stepped into the tower room she let loose with a string of curses in her mother's tongue that was vicious enough to make Angus wince and be thankful that he could not understand a word of it. She could not recall ever having felt so furious with the man who was both her captor and her lover. Her chamber seemed a haven for once; it meant that she was not near him.

Undressing provided some outlet for her anger as she flung her clothing across the room. Yanking on her night rail, she hurled herself onto the bed and glared at the ceiling. With intense relish she imagined all manner of gruesome ends and torments for Tavis MacLagan. It always ended with his begging her forgiveness and her grandly allowing him to have it before he gasped his last. She savored the vision.

Storm knew she had as much pride as any man and Tavis had sorely bruised it with his abrupt dismissal of her. His coldness had also hurt her deeply, but she would never reveal that to him. She had little left to her save her pride and dignity, and he had tried to strip those from her in that brief confrontation. There would have to be a great deal explained before she could forgive that. It had been an unnecessary set-down.

Tavis hesitated as he reached her door. "What mood was she in, Angus?"

"It wasnae pretty. She was saying things in that

135

Irish gibberish and 'tis glad I am I couldnae understand it. She isnae going tae be greeting ye with a smile and open arms," Angus added as he walked away.

For a moment Tavis regretted his actions, for he liked the way she always welcomed him to her bed. It would be the first time they had shared the room with bad feeling between them. Then he recalled how she had been seated so close to Alex, letting him touch her and listening to plans to leave him. He entered the room with his temper renewed, slamming the door after him with a force that reverberated through the room.

"Come to have a talk with your prisoner, sir?" Storm asked coolly as she sat up in bed.

"Nay, I have come to have a wee bit of what ye were offering Alexander MacDubh," he hissed as he approached the bed. "Did ye think ye would have enough strength to service us both?"

The increasing thickness of his accent told her the depth of his anger, but his words infuriated her too much to exercise any caution. "You bastard!" She leapt to her feet and stood upon the bed. "Just who do ye think ye are to talk to me so, to make such accusations?"

"I am the fool that stood watching ye cuddle and plot with that cursed Adonis."

"Cuddle and plot? Cuddle and plot?" She stomped across the bed to glare at him. "I was doing no such thing, ye great fool."

"Nay? Did he nay ask ye to come and stay at his keep?"

"Aye, he asked me." Storm hopped off the bed, moved to the table that served as her vanity and began to brush her hair, an action she favored when she was in a temper. "He asked and I said nay, thank ye very much. There is your plot."

Making a mocking noise, Tavis sat on the bed. "And of course ye gave it nay a thought."

"Oh, aye, I fancy a change," she snapped, furious over his distrust. " 'Tis my aim in life to hop from bed to bed. I have decided to follow in my step-mother's footsteps. After all, what is a little whoring to a woman already dishonored? I think I will see if I can outdo Lady Mary in number and variety. There is a fine goal to set for myself."

"God's teeth, dinnae act the offended one with me," he snarled, sent further into rage by the way she was talking. "Everyone there saw how he couldnae keep his hands off ye and how ye didnae stop him."

"He kissed my palm. I have had my hand kissed before. It means naught and well ye know it."

"And touched your hair as weel as caressed your face. There is nay a common practice."

"Nay, 'tis the act of a practiced seducer. Do not tell me ye did not recognize it," she sneered.

"Aye, I recognized it and I recognized how ye were melting for the rogue as weel. I saw the glaze in your eyes as if ye had been knocked half conscious. Sitting so close and listening to all his pretty lies. Staring into each other's eyes like a pair o' mooncalves. 'Tis nay love he offers ye, lass. The man just wants atween your legs," he snapped. "He wants to ride ye as he has half the lasses in Scotland."

"Do ye think I do not know that?" she asked calmly. "I am not stupid. I know exactly what he wanted."

As Tavis had ranted, Storm had felt her anger leave her. Recalling the story Alex had told her of Tavis's first love, she began to understand his distrust. She also began to see something behind all his anger. For a brief instant, when she had caught his eye in the mirror, she had seen a vulnerable boy.

It was almost laughable to her that Tavis MacLagan, a man as important to her as breathing, was unsure of his ability to hold on to a woman. As she thought on it, she realized that his first love's falseness had probably only been the start, that women had pursued him not just as a man but as the heir of Caraidland. There had always been some motive of greed behind their attentions. It was now perhaps a little difficult for him to believe that a woman could want him only for his worth as a man and be satisfied.

Her problem would be to convince him that such was the case with her without revealing all that she felt for him. Storm saw his vulnerability as a result of wounded pride and a crippled sense of self-worth, but nothing concerning her personally, or the fact that she talked with Alex. Her love for him made her want to help him, but her own pride kept her not wanting him to discover why she wanted only him. She decided physical need was the route to follow.

That brought her to the intricate problem of how to accomplish that. Although she had made no attempts to hide her pleasure in their lovemaking, she was always the relatively passive partner. Her contribution to the act was the gift of her passion. He initiated the loving, directed and controlled it. Mayhaps the only way to prove to him that he was all she desired was to take the lead, to be bold for a change and to make love to him.

Still new at the game, she was unsure of how to do that. Suddenly she felt she knew how. She would simply do to him as he did to her. She would caress him, be as thorough in her explorations as he was. For once she would not let modesty and maidenly shyness hold her back. She was either going to thoroughly disgust him or convince him that it was him alone she appreciated and who could stir her passions.

"The same thing ye wanted quick enough," he groused. "I could see weel enough that ye wanted him."

Moving to stand before him, she said quietly, "Alexander MacDubh is a man to stir any woman's blood."

Tavis scowled, so caught up in his anger that he paid no attention to the way she was undoing his tunic. "Did ye fancy spending the night romping with the lad?"

"There is no denying that he is one of the most beautiful men I have ever seen." She unlaced his shirt.

He frowned absently as he watched her. "Would ye have me believe ye felt naught for him?"

"Nay. Ye would not believe me an I said so." She felt him tense beneath her hands. "That man is so perfectly beautiful that he stuns a person. Everything about him is perfectly suited for the seduction of a woman. Soft, beguiling eyes, perfection of face and form, a voice that caresses like the most skillful hands."

"What are ye about?" he snapped as she bent to remove his shoes, piqued at the way she spoke so fulsomely of Alex.

"I am undressing ye, you silly man," she said calmly.

Grabbing her by the arm, he growled, "Are ye verra sure ye are undressing the right man?"

Letting her free hand roam over his bared torso, she murmured, "I was a little tempted to see if he had all he should have as his outward perfection of appearance quickly bred some skepticism."

Releasing her arm, he ran his hand through his hair. "Curse ye, I ken what I saw. Ye wanted him."

Bending closer, she traced his frowning lips with her tongue. Her fingers hesitated before unlacing her gown, for she had never boldly revealed herself to

139

him. He always undressed her. There was also far more light in the room than there usually was. Taking a deep breath to steady herself, she strengthened her resolve. She brushed light kisses over his face as she eased off her night rail.

Tavis's breath caught in his throat. It was the first time he had been freely shown her lovely form. He briefly forgot Alexander MacDubh and the jealousy he refused to recognize as he looked his fill at her supple figure. His hands began to reach for her when he recalled what they had been taking about, and he hesitated.

"Ye would go to bed with him. They all do," he grumbled huskily as her lips explored his throat.

"Only if ye tossed me aside and he was there to pick me up. Only an I still had no kin to seek shelter with and had to go to his keep. Aye, Tavis." Her kisses moved to his chest as her fingers unlaced his braes. "I would most like end up in his bed. I have no doubt that he knows how to pleasure a woman as well as ye do."

A groan escaped him and when her tongue flicked over the hard nubs of his nipples. His hands buried themselves in her hair when she gently suckled. He was so caught up in that new pleasure that he gave no thought to how she removed his braes, merely lifted his hips to aid her. It was the same when she slid off his leggings, for her lips and tongue were playing over his taut stomach.

Out of all the ladies he had bedded in his life, Katerine had been the most skilled in pleasuring a man, knowing where and how to touch. Never had a lady made use of her mouth. That was a skill usually employed only by the high-priced courtesan. Only once had his frugal soul allowed him to pay out the coin for that pleasure, yet it had not set him on fire as the tiny English lady was now doing. Disgust or shock at her boldness was the very last thing on his mind. He simply wondered how bold she would be.

"Do ye think to convince me that ye had no interest in Alex?" he rasped.

"Nay, Tavis. I mean to show ye that until ye turn me away, 'tis only your bed I wish to share no matter whose beauty I might appreciate with my eyes." She took his hand to her mouth, kissing the palms before tracing each finger with her tongue, repeating the gesture on the other hand as she spoke. "These are the only hands I wish to know my secrets, the only ones I want upon my skin." She kissed him. "This is the only mouth I wish upon mine. The only lips I want to taste me." She moved her kisses to his chest. "This is the only pillow I need for my head." She let her tongue play around his navel. "Here is the only belly I want to press against mine, move against it in the most intimate of rhythms." Her teeth nipped gently at his thighs. "These are the only legs I wish entwined with mine, pushing my thighs apart so that this can find its way within me to fill me, satisfy for the moment a hunger that seems to always be with me and drive me to that paradise only ye can take me to."

Tavis gasped, bending over as her tongue teased the length of his manhood. His breath came in ragged gasps as her tongue curled around him, stroked and teased, leaving none of the intimate area unexplored. He doubted she would perform that final intimacy, but cared little at the moment, for his control was already strained near to the breaking point.

Suddenly Storm was grasped beneath her arms and jerked to her feet. To her surprise they did not lie down upon the bed, but he pulled her onto his lap so that she straddled him as she knelt facing him. A gasp that was a mixture of shock and pleasure escaped her as he eased their bodies together.

His hands cupping her buttocks, he directed her

movements until she caught on. He kissed her hungrily, his tongue plunging deeply as his hands moved over her. When he could tear his eyes from the way her lithe form moved upon him or the passion so evident upon her face, his lips feasted upon her breasts. As she cried out, her tremors indicating her release, he grasped her hips to hold her to him, but there was no need. She pressed down upon him, her slim hips rotating gently, increasing the intensity of his own release. Wrapping his arms around her, he buried his face in her breasts and rocked gently as pleasure washed over him and he slowly returned to normalcy.

"God, so good. 'Twas so good." He felt her inner muscles flex and murmured with pleasure. "Nice. Ye are the best I have e'er enjoyed." His gaze settling upon the point where they were still joined, his hands gently rotated her hips, and he felt himself grow taut with a renewed passion. "Ye were made for this, for pleasuring a man."

Storm was surprised by how quickly he was ready to enjoy her again. She was equally surprised at how ready she was to enjoy him as well. With a throaty laugh, she gave herself over to the mutual greed.

The gray light of dawn was filtering into the room when Tavis suddenly found himself awake. A tautness in his loins told him why. Lifting his head from the satiny breast it was pillowed against, he stared thoughtfully at the sleeping Storm as his need grew steadily.

He had no more worries about Alexander MacDubh. She had convinced him that, as long as he still wanted her, she would share no other man's bed. Tavis felt a definite sense of male pride.

It was replaced by an angry regret. Here was a

woman he would feel no qualms about taking to wife. Not only would he have no fears of being cuckolded, but he would not need to seek out another woman, go through all the trouble and expense of seduction and tokens of appreciation. Storm's passion and lack of inhibition in the bedroom would be enough to keep him faithful. There was not the greed, dishonesty or hardness in her that had driven him from one woman to another. It was all for naught, however, for there could never be such a connection between their families.

Shaking off a sudden pain-ridden sense of depression, he eased the covers off of her, letting his gaze linger as he pleased, where he pleased. At last his gaze settled upon the juncture of her slim thighs and, rising, he parted her legs slightly and knelt between them.

There was one thing he had long wanted to, but had held back in respect for her innocence, increasing the intimacies he took gradually. It was an act that he had rarely performed, but had ached to do so since he had first made love to her. He realized with a start that one reason was because he was assured of her cleanliness. Although he had not consciously noted it, a number of the women he had bedded over the years were plainly not all that fond of soap and water. Many truly believed it unhealthy to immerse oneself in water or to bathe with any regularity. Storm washed daily, and he liked that.

Bending, he saluted her breasts, watching as the nipples hardened in response to his tongue's ministrations. She murmured sleepily and stirred, but her eyes did not open as he made his way slowly down her body. His hand went to the heart of her and his eyes went from his fingers, where they tangled in the copper curls, to her face to watch as she and her passion slowly awakened. Suckling gently at her breasts, he let his fingers probe and caress her with a boldness she had not allowed before. When he judged her nearly awake, struggling to sort dream from reality, his gaze returned to the treasures his hands were fully enjoying, watching for a moment as his fingers continued their play. With caressing hands upon her thighs, he spread her legs wider and touched his lips to the center of her passion. When she did not flinch away as once before he knew his unorthodox methods had gained him his prize, and he proceeded to fully savor the sweetness of her.

Storm had sensed his touch early on in the game. Even as she had continued to wake up, her passion gaining strength, she had enjoyed the sense of being in a dream world. It had allowed her to luxuriate in caresses that were bolder than he had made before. When his lips first touched her so intimately the sense of being in a dream kept her from tensing, allowing her to enjoy the pleasure her reticence had denied her. By the time she realized he was lingering as he had never done before, she was already caught in a nearly overwhelming passion, needing the hands that kneaded her backside, holding her steady, as she writhed beneath his intimate caresses.

Again and again he brought her to the very brink of release until she clutched at his shoulders in near desperation. "Please, *acushla*, no more. I need ye, my *fona*." She shuddered with pleasured relief as he slowly possessed her. "*Cushlamochree*."

She clung to him as he sent her spiraling into that land only lovers discover. Her name broke from his lips as he drove deeply to find his own release while she was still in the tight grip of hers. It was awhile before he had the energy to break off their intimate embrace, turn onto his back and pull her into his arms. His fingers traced the newly healed wound on her shoulder, which had kept him in her bed but out of her arms and had added to his current greed for her. Briefly he thought about apologizing for his accusations about Alexander, but he fell into a sated sleep before he could get the words out.

"I love ye, Tavis," Storm whispered, knowing he could not hear her, smiled at her foolishness and, snuggling up to him, joined him in sleep.

12

Tavis heartily wished that he had not agreed to Storm's plan as he looked at her. The lad's outfit she now wore showed her soft curves far too plainly. His men would enjoy themselves, and he was not fond of that knowledge at all. He recognized his possessiveness but told himself that any man would feel so about a woman who gave him so much pleasure in the night and had never done so with any other man. It was a natural feeling that sprang from being the first and the only.

"Ye are looking at me most strangely, Tavis," Storm commented as she tied back her hair.

"I was just thinking that, for a skinny lass, ye are showing a muckle lot of curves."

Storm fought down a blush. " 'Tis a bit snug, but it will serve. I so long for a ride."

"Are ye sure your shoulder is up to it?" He grabbed her by the hair, gently tugging her into his arms.

"Ye did not seem concerned about it last night. Nay, nor this morning."

His lips twitched. "Aye, weel, mayhaps I think ye have done enough riding and need a wee rest."

Pulling free of his hold, Storm started out of the room, remarking haughtily, "Ye are a very vulgar man, Tavis MacLagan. Ye have no concept of how to speak to a lady."

"Show me a lady and my gallantry will ken no bounds," he retorted from a safe distance behind her, and met the glare she shot him over her shoulder with a wide grin.

It was not to his liking to watch the looks the men gave Storm as she strolled out to the stables. Even his dark visage as he strolled beside her did not stop them, only made them look amused or all too knowing. Despite it all, Tavis could not help but feel some pride in the fact that the woman who shared his bed was plainly desirable to a number of men. He also knew that their interest was not all of a carnal nature, but of respectful curiosity about a person who had proven herself, winning people to her side despite the fact that she was an Eldon and English.

Phelan looked her over as they mounted. "Ye do not look much like a boy, cousin."

"Thank ye, Phelan," she said with a grin. " 'Tis a relief to me to know that."

"Do not take them too far, Angus. 'Tis her first ride since her wounding," Tavis advised.

Angus nodded, and Tavis watched them ride out. Storm rode well, and Tavis recognized that she was plainly well accustomed to riding astride. She was rapidly destroying his conceptions about proper English ladies. Lord Eldon had clearly raised his daughter with a light and loving hand. It was a side of the man Tavis was not sure he wanted to know.

A short gallop was all Angus allowed, but Storm did not mind. She realized she had not regained the full strength she needed to control a racing horse for any distance. It was pleasant just to be riding. Angus was a lenient guard, for he had their promise not to try and escape while out on their rides, and he knew their word was bond enough.

When they reached the shores of a loch they dismounted, save for Phelan. With Angus's permission, he disappeared to survey as much of the shore as possible. The boy was still gone when Angus's and Storm's childish game of skipping stones was rudely interrupted by a highly unwelcome source. For the first time in her life, Storm was not pleased to see a rescue party from Hagaleah. Instinct told her she would be far safer staying with the Eldons' old enemy.

There was no time to mount and flee. She and Angus were quickly encircled and Angus, with his sword drawn against the dozen well-armed men, stood protectively before Storm. Storm wondered how Sir Hugh had known to come to the loch, their usual place to pause while on a ride, and the name Katerine MacBroth came to mind. It was the type of thing the woman would do for, with her gone, Storm felt sure Katerine was justified in thinking that she would soon be back in Tavis's bed. He was not a man to go very long without a woman.

"Kill him," Sir Hugh ordered casually, nodding toward Angus.

"Nay!" Storm put herself between the men of Hagaleah and Angus. "Ye don't need to kill him. Just take his horse and leave him bound. 'Twill be a fair long while ere he is found."

"Where's the Irish brat?" asked Sir Hugh, signaling his men to do as Storm said, thinking it could be to his advantage to placate her in this matter.

Storm watched as Angus gave up after a brief struggle and allowed himself to be tied up. It was a relief to know he would not be hurt. Plainly, he, too, had recalled that Phelan was near. With luck, the boy would continue to stay away. Phelan was definitely better off at Caraidland.

"He stayed at the keep today. There were doings there that interested him."

Sir Hugh looked Storm over with obvious contempt. "You dress the whore as well as act it. Get on

149

your horse. An it were not for your fortune, I would leave you here to serve this border scum."

Whatever resistance she felt was useless as one of Sir Hugh's men grabbed her and tossed her into the saddle, handing her reins to Sir Hugh. Before she could say any of the words that burned in her mouth they were off at a gallop. She had to fight to maintain her seat, and it was not long before her shoulder began to protest. This was not the way she wanted to come home to Hagaleah.

Phelan appeared at Angus's side as soon as Sir Hugh had left. He had known to stay away, not only to aid Angus but to be free to help Storm. His stay at Hagaleah had shown him that she was not safe there. It was not only the dismal prospect of her being forced to wed Sir Hugh that troubled him. Phelan had the strongest feeling that Storm would never survive that marriage. Sir Hugh would enjoy the role of a rich widower.

Tavis was just stepping into the bailey when Angus and Phelan returned astride one horse. "Sir Hugh?" he asked when they came up to him. "How in Hades did he know where and when to strike? I refuse to believe that any of our people told him, but I nay doubt that he was told."

"Aye," agreed Angus. "It were too neat." He cleared his throat. "I was thinking jealousy could weel breed a traitor."

A black scowl touched Tavis's handsome face. "Aye. Katerine would do it, burn her eyes." He turned on his heel and strode back into the tower house, Angus and Phelan right behind him, telling him all that had happened. " 'Tis glad I am ye suffered no hurt, Angus. It would all have been for naught." Entering the great hall, he told his brothers and father what had occurred. "There goes the ransom."

"Are ye just going to leave her with Sir Hugh?"

Phelan demanded as Tavis sprawled on a bench and got himself a large tankard of ale. "Ye don't know how it is. He will kill her. I know it."

"Nay, laddie. The man wants to marry the lass. He is hot for her fortune. Aye, and a thing or twa otherwise." Colin noted the way Tavis's face tightened. "He will want his bride alive."

"Aye, but not his wife." Phelan nodded vigorously when that remark caught their attention. "Once he has had a bit o' the other and tired of it, 'tis a widower he will be. That is not all. Ye do not know the man. After he is finished with my cousin she will be fair glad to be killed. Hagaleah abounds in the battered recipients of his sort of loving."

"Lad, I cannae call the men out to bring an English lass back. They'll nay like risking their lives to restore some enemy wench to me son's bed, no matter what she has done." Colin sighed. "I am fair sorry, for I owe her, but I cannae send my men to arms for her."

"Then I will get her out myself! Just give me the use of two mounts. I will return them."

"What will ye do, Phelan? Go tirl at the pin and ask, 'Please may I have my cousin back?' " Tavis drawled sarcastically, already feeling his loss and in no good temper about it.

"Nay. I know how to get in and out without them knowing. Just lend me the horses."

Tavis sat up, glanced at his father, who nodded, and asked, "Ye can get into Hagaleah unseen?"

"Aye, but I am not about to tell you how. 'Tis a bolthole and no use if ye learn of it."

"Phelan," he growled, "if there be a way to get Storm out of Hagaleah, to get into the keep with little risk to the men, then I suspicion I can get a few together to do it." He tried to hold onto his temper when Phelen remained stubbornly silent. "We'll give ye our word of honor that we'll never use the knowledge agin Hagaleah. What is it to be, lad?"

"Your word of honor ne'er to use the knowledge agin Hagaleah and the Eldons?"

'Ye have it, laddie. If we can get the lass away without risking much, we're willing." Colin looked at the ones gathered in the hall and they all nodded. " 'Twas a full battle I couldnae call for."

"Well, I do not doubt I could use a bit of help. 'Tis a tunnel. It goes from the nether rooms of Hagaleah to just beyond the curtain wall. 'Tis for the women and children to flee if the battle is lost."

"Aye. We have one." Colin shook his head. " 'Tis a wonder we ne'er thought to look for it at Hagaleah. Ah, well, come and take a seat, laddie. An all goes well we'll have the lass back here come the dawn."

Tavis thought dawn too late but said nothing. The mere thought of Sir Hugh touching Storm was intolerable, twisting his insides into knots, but he struggled to keep all sign of it from showing in his face. That he would have her back would have to be enough for the time being. Later, he would make Sir Hugh pay for any abuse Storm suffered at his hands. He did not pause to review his feelings. Tavis had neither the time nor the inclination to do any soul searching. He had the fleeting wish that he could see inside the walls of Hagaleah, but decided it was probably for the best that he could not.

Storm sat on the bed in her room and watched Sir Hugh and Lady Mary with a calm she did not feel. They were angry, especially Sir Hugh. She had enough knowledge of them to know that that did not bode well for her. Despite that, she continued to refuse to marry the man. As Phelan had done, she guessed that Sir Hugh did not intend to spend a long life of connubial bliss with her, that her life was in greater danger if she wed him than if she did not. She continued to refuse him and risk his fury. Tavis

MacLagan might be a border reiver, an old foe, a man of quick temper and little love and the man who had taken her innocence as well as a few other things he was unaware of, but at the moment, he seemed a haven.

"You cannot tell us you remain a maid," purred Lady Mary. " 'Tis gallant of Sir Hugh to still offer for you."

A most unladylike snort escaped Storm. "Gallant, my eye. 'Tis my fortune he wants, well I know it."

Hugh glared at Storm, his temper rapidly getting out of control. "You have little call to be so choosy, bitch. We all know you played the whore for the MacLagan heir."

"Do ye now. May I be so bold as to ask how ye know what goes on at Caraidland?"

Lady Mary shrugged. "We were given a full and very colorful report by the woman you replaced."

"I thought as much." Storm wondered if Tavis would ever discover Katerine's treachery.

"I see you do not deny it." Lady Mary wanted a few answers before Hugh's rage burst loose.

"Why should I? E'en an it were not true, e'en an I denied it vehemently, ye would ne'er believe me. What matters what I have to say? Believe as ye will. I care not."

"Do not bother to deny it. Nay, you need not speak at all. 'Tis easy to read upon your face." Lady Mary smiled coldly. "From the heat of the scorned woman's fury, the MacLagan heir must be some stallion, and he has ridden you hard these last weeks."

"Vulgarity suits you, Mother." Storm reeled under the strength of the slap her stepmother dealt her but made no cry, only glared, her hatred of the woman nearly palpable.

"The world will soon know you left your honor in Scotland, dearest daughter. There will be no more swains sniffing at the door. You will marry Sir Hugh and there will be no more nonsense about it."

"Ye cannot wed me off. Only my father has that right. I will not wed Sir Hugh."

"Curse you," Hugh snarled, dealing her a blow that sent her tumbling off her bed. "You may be carrying that bastard's spawn even now. Have you thought of that, slut?" He grabbed her by the arm and pulled her to her feet. "His seed that he regularly filled you with could even now be growing inside this smooth belly." He accentuated his words with a blow to that area.

Above the pain of the blow, Storm felt fear. She had not thought of a baby yet, now that she did, she realized her time was past due. A very natural fear of being beaten was added to by the fear of what it could do to the child she could well be carrying. There was no time to think of the disgrace that would bring her. She had to convince Sir Hugh it was not possible so that whatever beating he gave her, was sure to give her, was to be only one of rage, not one specifically aimed to make her miscarry. Storm was desperate to protect the possible life within her, the child of the man she loved.

"Tavis MacLagan is no fool," she gasped as she fought to catch her breath. "The bitch that talked with ye has been with him for two years, yet has never born him a child. He spills his seed outside," Storm lied and then glared at Sir Hugh, her tongue her only weapon. "E'en an I am carrying the Scotsman's I'd nay wed ye. I'd not give ye a baseborn idiot to father."

Hugh used his fist on her face instead of an open hand. Storm slammed up against the bedpost. Even though she feared for her teeth and her ears rang, her resolve only grew stronger. Now that she knew what she could have, even though that lacked a mutual love, she would never settle for less. Hugh's brutality only enforced her refusals. She was glad that Phelan had not been brought back, for she knew that the boy would have been used to make her say yes.

Storm shook her head to clear it. "Ye do have a way with a proposal, Hugh."

"I will get a yea from you whatever way I can. Give it now, slut, and save yourself some pain."

"Pain? My dear Hugh, marriage to ye would make this seem like heaven." She turned as he swung, thus saving her teeth, but she clung to the bedpost a moment before saying, "Ye forget. I have known a man. The devil will drink holy water e'er I attach myself to an ewe-loving slug like ye." She dodged his swing. "Aye, and ye no doubt have the Crusader's disease."

She was not so lucky the next time, nor the next. When Lady Mary and Sir Hugh stripped her of her clothes she was too groggy to stop them, although she fought them as best she could. They placed her face down upon the bed and tied her wrists to the posts. Storm soon learned not to turn away from the blows Hugh inflicted, for they only landed elsewhere. Her jaws ached from holding back her cries, but each time he asked her if her answer had changed she retorted with words that held all the venom helpless fury can inject.

Soon she reached the stage where Hugh's efforts defeated themselves. Her mind retreated from the pain. A small part of her was aware that she hurt more than she thought was possible, but she paid it no mind, floating in a half-conscious state that brought a false numbness.

"Enough, Hugh," Lady Mary said. "She no longer feels it. We will try again later."

Storm wondered at the odd, husky note in her stepmother's voice. She turned her head to look at the couple only to see them through a blur, her half-shut eyes not focusing correctly. That made her wonder if what she saw was a dream conjured up by her shocked mind.

" 'Tis an odd dream," she mused silently as she watched Mary kneel before a heavily breathing Hugh and, lifting his tunic, unlace his leather riding breeches. "I wonder how I can imagine her doing that to him when I did not know that people did that." She looked at Sir Hugh and saw that he looked as savage in his pleasure as he did in his fury. "At least that is consistent."

"She is watching," Sir Hugh gritted as he caught Lady Mary beneath the arms, threw her onto the bed next to Storm and hoisted up her skirts.

"Let her," Lady Mary purred as she firmly grasped his manhood. "Let her see that our Englishmen are the stallions and the Scots mere colts. Show her how a real man fills a woman."

Their display at her side was not fully accepted by Storm's pain-drugged mind. She remained sure that she was dreaming. Disoriented as she was, she was only partly aware of the fact that dreams do not cause the bed to move nor do they usually come with all the appropriate, if exaggeratedly lewd, noises. She simply watched as they finished, rose, tidied their clothes and left.

For a while she drifted in and out of consciousness. It was not only the pain that put her into such a state but the shock of what had happened to her. The most she had ever suffered, except in a fight as a child, had been a gentle cuff. Her father had used words to direct her, words and love. Even Tavis had never struck her. To be so badly abused in a place where she had known only love, gentleness and affection was hard for her to adjust to.

At some point her spirit recovered. She was first-born to Lord Eldon, a great power in his own right on the border marches and much respected at court.

To lie groveling in her own misery and pain was no way for one who had the blood of both the Eldons and the O'Conners in her veins. "Nor," she thought with a slightly bitter humor, "the woman who could be carrying the child of Tavis MacLagan."

Recalling vaguely that another session had been spoken of and probably another after that until they got the answer they wanted gave Storm the strength she needed. Shaking and sweating from pain and weakness, she edged her body forward and worked at the ropes on one wrist with her teeth. She had to rest often, but she finally freed her wrists. The pain caused by chaffing and too tight bonds was nothing compared to the agony in her body, and she easily ignored it.

Dressing was even harder, for several times she nearly fainted. The muscles needed to don her clothes seemed to all be located in her ravished back. A warmth oozing down from her shoulder told her the knife wound had reopened, but she did not pause in her efforts. That was a problem that could be seen to later. Not knowing how long she had been unconscious made her worry about the others returning. Storm felt like weeping when Agnes entered the room.

"Just what are ye about?" Agnes hissed as she put down the tray of broth, ale, bread and cheese she had brought and shut the door. "Ye should not be up and dressed."

"Nay, I should be bound to the bedposts awaiting another flogging." Storm stood, her hand clutching the bedpost as she fought a wave of nauseating faintness. "I think not, Agnes."

"How can ye get out? Ye'll be seen for sure."

"Not by the route I mean to take. I must be gone. They will soon return, I am certain." Storm wavered as she started toward the door. "Hell and the Devil confound this weakness."

Agnes caught her before Storm fell. "I will give ye a hand. Ye are not used to being afoot yet."

"Just why will ye help me, Agnes? Ye are Lady Mary's maid," Storm said, her suspicions plain.

"For myself. I want Sir Hugh. Ye and your fortune are in my way." Checking the hall and finding it empty, Agnes helped Storm out of the room and in the direction Storm indicated. "An I help ye escape, help ye get away from here, Sir Hugh will be mine again. I will get him to the altar yet."

Storm had serious doubts about the sanity of any woman who wanted Sir Hugh, but exercised a little diplomacy and refrained from saying so. Until she could regain her equilibrium, she needed Agnes even if she did not trust her. She had more important things to worry about at the moment. Things such as where she was going and how she was going to get there.

13

Damp oozed from the walls as they crept through the bowels of Hagaleah. Tavis had never liked the subterranean chambers of a keep. A glance at the grim faces of Iain, Sholto, Angus and Donald told him that they were none too fond of them either. Phelan, however, strode along with apparent calm, plainly at home within the labyrinth although they had barely quit the tunnel so there was still plenty of time to get thoroughly lost. Tavis wondered if he had been a fool to put his trust in a boy.

Donald was wondering much the same thing and he said, "I cannae like this. The lad could be leading us into a trap. He is a Sassanach after all."

Tavis almost laughed at the indignant look on Phelan's small face. "I am Irish. For Uncle Roden I might lead ye into treachery an he dealt in it, which he does not, but not for the Sussex bitch." He paused as he thought he heard a noise. "I seek to free Storm afore their plans for her can reach fruition. Hark!"

The sound of a door opening echoed clearly in the gloom. Dousing their light, the Scots and Phelan melted into the shadows, tucking themselves into a small, doorless chamber. Being so few in number, discovery was the last circumstance they sought. Swords at hand, they waited for the danger to pass. When the footsteps came their way they tensed, only to start in surprise at a familiar voice.

"Ye can leave me now, Agnes. I have no further need of ye." Storm leaned against a wall, uncaring of its cold, damp feel, rather almost welcoming the sensation against the fiery agony that was her back.

"Aye, I'll leave ye," Agnes said softly, and pulled a knife. "This seems as good a place as any."

Storm eyed the knife with scorn, too tired and wracked with pain to be afraid. "Don't be an ass."

Although tensed to intervene and restraining Phelan, Tavis grinned in the dark, amused by Storm's tone and the maid's surprise.

"I ain't having ye take Sir Hugh. 'Tis no bride ye shall be. I aim to stop that wedding."

"I am leaving, am I not? What more do ye require? There is no need to stain your hands with blood."

"You're leaving because ye're angry. Once ye see that Sir Hugh and m'lady were just acting as they ought, ye'll be back, and I will nay let ye have him. If ye be gone, Sir Hugh will wed me."

"I will send ye a bride's gift. Ye are welcome to the man, Agnes. Go. Take him and be wretched."

"Ye don't fool me. Ye will return and take him to wed. What woman could refuse him?"

"This woman. I would rather take myself to London and spread for tuppence than wed Sir Hugh."

Agnes made a scornful sound. "I suppose ye would like me to believe ye return to the Scot's arms."

Tired and in pain though she was, Storm nevertheless saw the way to end the impasse. Convincing Agnes that Tavis was what she wanted was the way to ease the girl's worry that she would return to take Sir Hugh. Giving free rein to her love, Storm proceeded to do just that, blissfully unaware that Tavis stood close by, listening to every word with a mixture of amusement and longing, a longing for it to be the truth and not just a fine cozening act. Phelan bit back a smile as he listened. He knew it all for the truth but would never say so.

" 'Tis just where I plan to go and quickly, before they are filled with another."

"Do not seek to cozen me. The man will not welcome ye back. He'll have plenty to amuse him."

"Unlike Sir Hugh, Tavis MacLagan shares but one bed at a time. An I return quickly, he'll not have replaced me yet. The halls of Caraidland are not filled with his bedmates as Hagaleah's are with Hugh's."

"Ye cannot prefer a heathen Scot o'er Sir Hugh." Agnes's tone was growing less certain.

"Can I not? Ye have not seen Tavis MacLagan. Tall, lean and strong, with hair the color of a raven's wing that begs a woman's fingers to bury themselves within, as mine so often do as he pleasures me. Shoulders so broad and smooth that do not flinch when, in the midst of impassioned lovemaking, my nails dig deep. Those hands that wield a sword so well have another skill that I would blush to tell you."

Worrying that she might be laying it on a bit too thick, Storm watched Agnes as she spoke. The girl was plainly believing every word, her stance growing less and less threatening. Storm wished the process was quicker, for she was using up vital resources simply keeping herself standing and talking. Tavis, too, wished the matter at an end for her imagery was stirring him to the point of discomfort and the palpable, if silent, amusement of his companions told him that they were gathering fodder for many a future jest.

"His eyes are like a summer morning's sky and can seduce at a glance. They can blaze with the heat of a midday or soften like a dewy morn. No woman could resist such eyes. Ah and such a figure of a man. He would leave no woman empty. He makes Sir

Hugh look like a gelding."

"Moon madness. That's what ye suffer," Agnes scoffed, but she put away her weapon. "There be no man with as fine a stature as Sir Hugh. Go to your Scot. I can see that ye will not be wanting Sir Hugh, fool that ye are."

Agnes's satisfaction was short-lived. Just a few hours later Storm's escape was discovered and Sir Hugh quickly discovered who had aided her. It was no lover or future husband that left Agnes broken, bleeding and unfit for any man. That knowledge was what pushed her over the edge into madness, enabled her to drag her crippled body to a window's ledge and sent her plummeting hundreds of feet to the bailey below.

Storm was about to indulge in a much needed collapse when a light flared. At first her heart fell into her boots, but it quickly righted itself when she saw who it was. Her initial delight, something she never would have thought to feel upon seeing a MacLagan, was tempered slightly by the knowledge that he had heard the conversation between herself and Agnes. The broad grin upon his face assured her that he had caught every word, and she glared at her erstwhile rescuers.

"Could ye not have stepped in and lent a hand ere I began to spout off like some whore?" she snapped.

"Now, lass, is that any way tae welcome your gallant rescuers?" Iain chided with a small laugh.

She sent him a disgusted look that suddenly changed as she became aware of the fact that though the MacLagans were within Hagaleah, no alarum had been sounded; there was only one way to accomplish that, and Phelan knew the way. "Oh, Phelan, what have ye done?" she mourned, foreseeing catastrophe for Hagaleah.

"They gave their word of honor they'd not use the tunnel against us, Storm," Phelan said quietly.

Relief flooding through her, she sighed. " 'Tis all right then."

"Ye would accept that, lass?" Sholto asked in slight amazement.

"Would ye not accept an Eldon's word of honor?" she replied, and there was no further discussion on the matter. "Have ye come to take me prisoner again?" she asked with a weak smile.

Sheathing his sword, Tavis took her by the arm, frowning slightly at her weak trembling. "Aye. We havenae gained our ransom for ye yet and I ken ye will be safer by far at Caraidland than here." He felt her shudder, and his grip tightened slightly. "Did Sir Hugh hurt ye, lass?"

"Not as ye mean," she replied, pushing away the unwelcome memories of her brief stay within the walls of a Hagaleah she no longer recognized. "Can we leave now, Tavis? 'Tis not safe to linger here. We are near the stores."

Tavis nodded, and they made their way out of the keep. In the dim light he had seen a hint of the bruises upon her face but, while he suspected she had been knocked about some, she seemed fine otherwise. That she had not been raped was enough for the moment. There would be another time to make Sir Hugh pay for raising a hand to the girl. Frowning, Tavis realized that somewhere along the line she had become more a responsibility than a prisoner. He had become more of a protector than a captor.

Storm grit her teeth against the agony of her body. Instinct told her that only trouble would ensue if she revealed the extent of her injuries. The tone of Tavis's voice when he had inquired about possible rape told her that he could easily be made to seek an immediate confrontation with Sir Hugh. She gave no thought to it being a sign of any feelings Tavis might harbor for her besides lust. The things she had done to aid Colin would be enough to make a MacLagan take up the cudgels on her behalf. Though she would sorely like to see Sir Hugh rent six ways to Sunday, she felt escape was more practical at the moment.

The ride to Caraidland was pure torture from the moment Tavis set her up before him until, with dawn's light, they rode into the inner bailey of the MacLagan keep. There were but eight men, and they rode at a steady pace, none too eager to be caught by a large force from Hagaleah. After a while Storm found herself encased in a numbness; the pain still radiating through her had put her into a state of semi-consciousness. Only now and again did she have to bite down a cry as a jolt caused a shaft of agony to stand out against the sheet of pain she had adjusted to feeling.

When Tavis handed her down to Sholto in a rapidly filling bailey she found her legs unable to support her. For a moment after she had collapsed against him, Storm watched in groggy fascination as Sholto's handsome face shimmered and faded. She had the sinking feeling she was going to faint, but lacked the strength to fight it. All her resources had been used up in surviving the night's ride.

"I do apologize," she said with a formal politeness that was rendered ludicrous by her pain-filled thread of a voice, "but I fear I am about to swoon. Please do excuse me."

Sholto tightened his grasp, his arms encircling her as she gently lapsed into unconsciousness. His hands came in contact with a suspicious wetness as they lay upon her back beneath the heavy curtain of her unbound hair. As Tavis dismounted and stared, Sholto pulled one hand into view. Even in the gray light of a new morning there was no mistaking the blood that coated his hand.

Wasting no time, Tavis pushed aside her hair and ripped open her tunic. While he gave a chilling growl, many another's hand went to his sword hilt, faces tightened with anger at what they saw. Few of them could lay claim to never having raised a hand against a woman, for theirs was a rough life with violence as an integral part, but the visual proof of the brutality visited upon the tiny lady touched them all. It mattered not that she was an Eldon. No man had a right to treat a woman so.

"I will kill him," Tavis hissed as he stared at Storm's bruised and bloody back.

Iain winced as he studied her wounds. "The bluid comes mostly from the reopened wound. Few of these other marks have broken the skin. Whoever did this was nay out to scar her."

Taking her limp body into his arms, Tavis strode into the keep. He neither noticed nor cared who followed him. That the girl had been carried back was enough to draw Colin, who paused long enough to send a maid for a woman who might have some skills in healing. Once in her chambers, Tavis and Iain busily divested Storm of her clothes as Sholto collected whatever he thought might be needed to aid the unconscious girl.

"Sweet mother of God," Colin murmured hoarsely as he moved to the side of the bed and put a comforting arm around the shoulders of a pale, silently weeping Phelan.

There was little of Storm that was not bruised. Colin was able to read the marks like a book. Whoever had done it had plainly used his fists first, resorting to a rod or soft whip afterward. The only good he could find was that few of the marks would leave a bad scar.

"I cannae believe she endured the ride here," murmured Iain as he began to wash her clean of her own blood. "She ne'er said a word, yet it must have been a torture. Who could do this to such a wee lass?"

In a tearful voice that, nonetheless, was filled with hate, Phelan replied, "Sir Hugh and that Sussex bitch." He took a deep, shaky breath as his hand gently touched Storm's bruised face. "I was not fast enough."

"Ye couldnae have been any quicker, laddie," Colin said in an attempt to soothe the stricken boy.

"There's nothing broken," Tavis announced softly, "and there isnae any sign of rape, Phelan."

"She said that had not happened," Phelan remarked, looking improved in spirit.

"Laddie, a man who'd do this to a wee bonnie lass would do near anything, and I cannae believe she didnae swoon somewhen whilst this was being done to her." Colin sighed. "Aye, I only hope that she did."

A small young woman named Jeanne, the maid Colin had sent to find someone, burst into the room. Behind her strode a sturdily built woman of indeterminate age who was the wife of the stable master. While Jeanne's sympathetic dismay was evident, the older woman's plain face registered little emotion. With admirable efficiency, she cleared the room and turned her undivided attention to doing what could be done for Storm which, unfortunately, was not very much. Her injuries were the sort that had to heal on their own, fading with time.

The MacLagans and Phelan retired to the hall. Though they were all grim-faced and angry, none suffered from the seething rage that Tavis did. That for once he cared and cared deeply about what happened to a woman who warmed his bed he put down to the fact that Storm warmed it very nicely, as well as the fact that she simply did not deserve such brutal treatment. A small voice that hinted that he was being obtuse was ruthlessly ignored. No man could look at the destruction wreaked upon that alabaster skin and not be moved.

When the woman left Storm she tersely reported to the MacLagans that she had tended the reopened knife wound but that there was little else to be done. The pain would fade in a few days and a potion or a dram of whiskey could ease that.

"I cannae believe a man could treat the lass so harshly," Colin said after Phelan had been sent to bed. "Oh, aye, she's got a right sharp tongue, but it doesnae deserve such a beating."

"She was witness to the man's humiliation," Tavis said, "and she wasnae too kind to him after he rebuffed the plea she made on his behalf. He also wants to wed the lass, needs her fortune, but she willnae do it. He didnae look an even-tempered sort to me."

"Things have got a wee bit confused," Sholto remarked, frowning into his flagon of ale.

"How so?" Colin asked when his youngest son failed to elaborate upon his observation.

"Weel, when all's said and done the lass is our prisoner, yet it seems to me we've lost sight o' that. 'Tis more like we have taken her father's place as her protectors."

"Aye, but I owe the wee lass my life. She didnae have to save me from Janet's treachery. An I died, I'd been ane less MacLagan to do battle with. I cannae forget that. Eldon she may be, aye, and a Sassanach as weel, but it doesnae mean a thing next to her bringing me back from the brink o' death."

"Father's right," Iain declared. " 'Tis not the time to be thinking o' who she be, only what she has done. Then, too, who she be doesnae mean we can like what has been done to her nor stop me from wanting to rid the world o' scum like that Sassanach what treated her so. This has naught to do with the long-surviving battle atween the Eldons and us. 'Tis a thing apart. Aye, and she's earned our protection."

Sholto nodded. "Do ye think the man will come after her? Finally come out into the open to fight?"

"There's no telling, lad," Colin replied. "We can only wait, but he'll nay get his hands on her again if'n I can stop it." His grim tone ensured that no one questioned the truth of his vow.

Many a plan was put forth to cover all contingencies on the chance that Sir Hugh and his forces came to take Storm back to Hagaleah. As with many of their contemporaries, the idea of battle, especially one with a cause, was invigorating. Their only activity since winter's end had been the raid on Hagaleah, and that had offered little challenge. This offered them grim amusement; Lord Eldon could well return from France to find that his old enemy had rid him of his new one.

Much later, as Tavis readied himself for bed, Storm began to moan and writhe, plainly reliving her ordeal in Hagaleah in her dreams. Slipping into bed beside her, he took her into his arms, ignoring her thrashings as he tried to get her free of the grip of her mind's terrors. Here was the fright she had kept hidden while awake.

"Tavis!" she called frantically as she burst free of the bonds of her nightmare.

Feeling a strange exhilaration at the way she had awakened with his name upon her lips and was clutching him so tightly, Tavis caressed her hair and tried to soothe her. "Aye, lass, 'tis Tavis."

"Oh, God." She shuddered as she sought to bury herself in his protective warmth. "I thought I was . . ."

"Nay. Forget it, sweeting. Ye are back at Caraid-land. He will nay get hold of ye here."

"It hurts so," she murmured, already comforted by the steady beat of his heart beneath her ear.

"Ye'll nay be scarred, lass. Ah, weel, ane or twa, but not badly."

"I care not about that. 'Tis only the pain I wish gone."

"It will pass, Storm. 'Twill just take a wee bit o' time. Go back to sleep. Rest will aid ye most."

She held on to him tightly, disgusted by her fear but unable to quell it. "Stay with me, Tavis."

"I wasnae planning on staying anywhere else. Why did ye anger him so?"

"Hugh was set on punishing me no matter what I did or said. Aye, my words may have added to his rage, something he is prone to, but I could not take the drubbing meekly though I did try." She shivered, and felt Tavis's grip tighten briefly, although not enough to hurt her. "Vicious words kept me from crying out or pleading for mercy. I refused to give him the satisfaction of seeing me quail before him."

Tavis listened in growing fury as she replied to his request for more information about her short sojourn at what had once been her home. Despite that, a laugh of honest amusement, made harsh by the turmoil of his emotions, escaped him as she told of the things she had said. This further proof of her spirit and courage gave him a feeling of pride, especially when he thought of how, despite all that had happened to her, she had found some source of hidden strength to attempt to escape.

Recounting the incidents of the night made Storm recall certain things she had seen but only now began to wonder about. There had been the look upon Lady Mary's face as the woman had watched

Sir Hugh abuse her stepdaughter. As unconsciousness had tightened its grip upon her, Storm had thought she had seen something, but her mind had shied away from the memory. No one could possibly behave so basely. Shyly, but needing and hoping for reassurance that she had been mistaken, Storm decided to speak to Tavis. Since they were lovers, it could not really be wrong to speak to him of such things.

"Lady Mary was witness to it all," she said quietly, her hands enjoying the hard smoothness of his back.

"Put the bitch from your mind," he ordered gently, his lips brushing across her forehead.

"I shall as soon as I clarify something. Lady Mary not only watched, she enjoyed it. There was a look upon her face as if . . . as if"—she felt a blush tinge her cheeks—"she were being made love to."

"Puir wee Storm," he murmured, wondering why he felt such a strong desire to protect her from such ugliness. " 'Tis possible, lass. There be those who do feel so when giving or seeing pain."

"Sweet heaven." Storm buried her face in his chest, feeling slightly ill, for now she doubted he would be able to tell her that the rest did not happen. "Then what I saw as I lay nearly unconscious could have been real," she said in a small voice. "Lady Mary and Sir Hugh might well have made frenzied love. Right there. Right at my side upon the bed where I lay bleeding and wracked with pain."

"Aye, the bastards," Tavis affirmed vehemently. "I wish I could tell ye nay, but 'tis a dark side that exists. Be thankful the animals took each other and left ye alone. Now rest, Storm. Ye'll get better quicker, and I cannae take too many nights o' holding ye without loving ye."

"Nor can I," she said softly and honestly as she closed her eyes.

It was not long before he knew she was asleep, and he wished he could do so as easily. Methodically, he catalogued each emotion that had assailed him in the past eight and forty hours and neatly explained away each one. The reason that kept trying to present itself was ruthlessly ignored for, not only did he not want it but, considering who they were, it was an impossibility.

14

"Lass, it might help to talk about what is making ye so dowie. Have your wounds healed weel? Are they bothering ye still?" asked Maggie, studying Storm's woeful face with honest concern.

"Nay, my wounds cause me nary a twinge, Maggie. They left few lasting marks either."

Another sigh escaped Storm as she watched Maggie knead her bread dough. It was cozy in the small kitchen, and the children had been bedded down or sent off, depending upon their ages, yet Storm was not able to find the lift for her spirits she had hoped for with a visit to the cheerful Maggie. A stranger to melancholy, she was finding it hard, a distasteful emotion to experience.

"Do ye miss your father and kin, lass?"

"Aye. I worry for them as well. 'Twould please me more than I can say to have some word of them, word that they are safe and sound at Hagaleah and Lady Mary's heinous plots have failed."

" 'Tis hard tae worry and nay ken I ken that weel enough, but 'tis nay all that troubles ye, is it?"

Storm shook her head. She had no worry that Maggie would reveal any confidence made to her. Deciding it might help to relate her many worries and pains to another woman, Storm lifted her eyes from the workworn surface of the table and gave Maggie a weak, slightly crooked smile. She simply could not keep it all to herself any longer.

"Nay, 'tis not. I have done a very foolish thing. I have fallen quite hopelessly in love with Tavis."

"I feared as much, lass." Maggie shook her head. "Saw it when the MacDubhs were here."

"Oh, it was well entrenched by then, though I tried to shake free of it." She shrugged.

"But 'tis nay easy when the man is there each night tae hold ye and delight ye."

"Oh, Maggie, I want my father to come home, to be safe and alive, but a part of me hates the very thought of it. When he returns I must leave Tavis." She felt suddenly choked with tears and stared down at the table again, hoping to fight them. "I think 'twill kill me."

"Now, lassie, 'tis nay a certainty that ye willnae stay here," Maggie soothed, but knew she lied.

So did Storm. "Deceiving myself as to how this will end is one thing I have not done. 'Tis bad enough that I am English, but far worse is the fact that I am an Eldon. Mayhaps if my father had other daughters, he'd care little how I ended up, but I am his only girl child. I am his first-born. He brought me into the world with his own two hands, slapped the breath of life into me. 'Tis a bond that few fathers have with their children. I look much as my mother did, and she was the first and mayhaps the greatest love of his life. I do not think he really recovered from her loss until he found Elaine, his mistress. Nay, my father will not leave me here to keep Tavis MacLagan's sheets warm."

"What . . . what if ye were tae wed Tavis?" Maggie asked, her doubt evident in her voice.

"There has ne'er been the option of marriage. For all his pretty words, Tavis has ne'er spoken of love or a future for us. If he mentions the future at all, it is to speak of when I will return to Hagaleah. Then, too, e'en if he did, would it be allowed? My father is an understanding man, but allowing his only daughter to be wed to a MacLagan could well be more than he can tolerate."

"Then, lass, all ye can do is take all ye can while 'tis there for the having."

" 'Tis what I tell myself, what I try so hard to do. Yet oftimes at night I lie awake watching him, and I hurt so knowing that 'tis but for a while. I cannot speak of my feelings for 'tis unsure I am that he feels any such thing for me, and all I have left to me is my pride. I find myself hoping that he will come to love me and work out a way for us to stay together, but there is nary a sign of that. All I can see ahead for me is such emptiness and pain. He has become such a part of me, of such importance to my life and happiness, that I just cannot bear to think of being without him. It frightens me. I am not so foolish as to think I will die without him, but of what quality will my life be?"

Maggie was prepared for Storm's tears when they came. She had heard them in the girl's voice, and had cleaned her hands of flour. Now she stepped over to Storm, put her plump arms around her and let the girl cling to her as she wept. It came easy to Maggie to mother the smaller, younger Storm. There was no thought to Storm's heritage or her far higher station. There was simply a frightened, heartsore young girl who needed some motherly comfort, something Maggie was very adept at.

"I never cry," Storm said, her voice muffled because her face was pressed to Maggie's ample bosom.

"Weel, then, it means 'tis more meaningful when ye do. 'Tis true and frae the heart of ye." Maggie handed Storm a cloth to dry her tears and poured her some ale, lacing it with whiskey. "Drink this now, lass. 'Twill stiffen ye up. Aye, I wish there was something I could say, some hearty words tae gie ye hope, but . . ."

"But there are none." Storm sipped the potent concoction, deciding it was oddly tasteful. "I know that, but of late I seem to be so much less brave. Tears threatened at the slightest turn."

Those words made Maggie's eyes sharpen, and she gave Storm a thorough looking-over as the girl drank from a slightly battered tankard. Considering how long Tavis had shared Storm's bed, the thought that the girl might carry his child seemed a logical one. That the same thought had not yet really settled in Storm's mind was also evident. Maggie decided to keep her suspicions quiet. They would only add to the girl's worries and, if she was pregnant, there was little that could be done.

Storm accepted another tankard of the potent mixture while the two women talked of the similarities and differences in foods either side of the border. Storm decided as she left that visiting Maggie had been a good idea after all, for she did feel less depressed. Her greeting to Tavis as she met him leaving the keep as she was entering was blindingly cheerful.

"But, Tavis," she protested as he took her by the arm and led her back outside, "I was after a small repast."

He held aloft a covered basket. "How convenient, m'lady, it just so happens that I have a bountiful feast hidden in this basket. 'Tis my plan to find a secluded spot where we can feast and"—he looked at her with a very suggestive glint in his eyes—"talk."

"It has been a long time since we have talked," she said demurely as he set her upon his horse.

"Aye," he drawled as he mounted behind her, "but now ye are healed and I intend a verra long discussion."

Leaning against him, looking up at his face and batting her eyelashes, Storm purred, "How enlightening that should be. I much prefer long discussions to short chats."

Laughing, Tavis urged his mount to a fast trot. Standing in the bailey, his family watched them go with a mixture of emotions. It was good to see Tavis shed some of that hard, solemn air he had donned in the last few years, but they wished some other young lovely was the cause. There could only be pain at the end of the road he was now riding.

Storm rested against the hard length of the man behind her and enjoyed the ride. The countryside had a wild beauty all its own, a beauty she realized she had come to love. If things were not bad enough, she realized she was beginning to think of Caraidland as home. It was a depressing thought and, with the lingering assistance of Maggie's tonic, Storm easily shook it away.

The spot Tavis stopped at certainly looked secluded to Storm. It was a small clearing at the edge of a stream. Trees and the gentle slope of the surrounding hills seemed to enclose it. The fact that it was so well suited for what Tavis had in mind made Storm look at him with suspicion.

"Ye can just cease looking at me like that, lass. I found this place when I was a lad, but it only just occurred to me to put it to use for—er—conversing with a lovely lass," Tavis drawled as he saw to his mount. "Do ye nay have a thinking spot at Hagaleah?"

"It used to be where ye found me with Sir Hugh. 'Twill no longer be private, I am sure."

By the time he had finished seeing to the needs of his mount, Storm had shed her shoes and stockings, hiked up her skirts and was dabbling her toes in the clear, somewhat chilly water. Strolling over to her side, Tavis thought she looked very young when in such a pose. He wondered fleetingly if she would always have that carefree air, that touch of innocence that made her so intriguing.

"Can ye swim, Storm?" he asked, looking at her sideways.

"Aye." She also glanced at him sideways, knowing he was about to suggest a swim in nature's own.

He simply quirked a brow, knowing she was fully aware of what he suggested. Storm read it as the dare it was. She looked once at the water, then at Tavis and then began to unlace her gown. It was a bold move that brought the color rushing to her cheeks, but Storm was determined to follow her own and Maggie's advice. With time so swift and so precious, she was going to enjoy what was left, pack as many experiences with Tavis as she could into each day. If nothing else, she would ensure that she was the one he never forgot.

Tavis shed his clothes slowly, his gaze never leaving Storm. He never tired of looking at her, and it was so rare for her to be bold that he relished the change, meant to miss nothing. His breath caught in his throat when she stood naked, slowly undoing her hair. He knew she was playing at being seductive and was not fully aware of how successful she was, thus making it all the more devastating. When she disappeared into the water he flung off the remainder of his clothes and went after her.

Like two children, they romped in the brisk waters of the stream. They splashed and chased each other, laughing and simply enjoying themselves. Just as Storm was beginning to think of going to shore, Tavis caught her tightly in his arms and kissed her, his feet the only ones touching bottom.

"Ye swim like the fishes, nymph," he growled as his lips traveled down her throat.

" 'Tis a skill my father taught all his children.

178

Oh, Tavis," she groaned as his mouth reached her breasts.

"I have ne'er made love in the water," he mused as his mouth toyed with one hardened nipple.

"We should drown," she gasped as he gently suckled. "The stream is too rocky."

"Ye should ken by now, lass, that ye dinnae need to lie on your back. Wrap your arms around my neck and those lovely legs round my waist," he urged hoarsely, his need for her rapidly gaining strength.

They both gasped when he fitted them together. For a moment they stood still, kissing gently, then with an increasing passion. His hands on her hips, Tavis began to move her slowly, then faster and faster until their passion crested and they nearly collapsed into the water.

"We could have drowned," Storm said, trying not to blush as they sat wrapped in toweling on a blanket with the food spread out around them. " 'Tis a bit chill. I should get dressed."

"Nay," Tavis said softly as he handed her a glass. "Drink this. 'Twill warm ye." He touched her drying hair as she sipped the whiskey. "The sun will soon dry ye and the chill will pass."

The whiskey warmed her even as she drank it. They ate heartily, occasionally feeding each other and laughing when they fumbled. A combination of freedom, even if transitory and perhaps illusionary, and whiskey made for very high spirits. Tavis lay back with his arms crossed behind his head when the meal was done, enjoying the sun and watching Storm clear away the food.

Storm sipped her whiskey as she sat by his side and looked at him. She wondered idly why he did not look silly lying there with nothing but a cloth wrapped around his waist. What he did look like was a man she very much wanted to make love to. She wanted to run her hands over every taut inch of his lean body. Thoughtfully, she took another sip of whiskey and wondered if she dared. It was not the sort of thing a lady should do, but then, neither did a lady sit about in so little sipping whiskey with an equally undressed man, she mused.

Blushing slightly, she recalled the only other time she had taken the initiative. He certainly had seemed to appreciate it. Storm then recalled what Lady Mary had done to Sir Hugh. Just because they did something did not make it wrong, for they had made love the same way she and Tavis did. It was simply their attitude that made it sordid. Thinking of how her caresses had so obviously pleased him that time, Storm began to wonder if that further intimacy would also please. If there was one thing Lady Mary knew, it was how to please a man. Storm felt decidedly curious. She also felt that if it was something a man liked, then she ought to do it for Tavis, the man she loved.

Tavis opened his eyes, meeting her warm, considering gaze. He recognized that still look on her face as the one she wore when she was mulling over something. As his gaze drifted over her from the gentle swell of her breasts above the cloth to her slim thighs, he decided he would ask her what she was thinking about later. Reaching up, he loosed her cloth and it fell to her hips, gathering there to give her a rather precarious modesty.

"Ye are one lovely woman, Storm," he said softly, his eyes lifting to see the color tint her cheeks. "Why so modest? Ye are beautiful and 'tis a pleasure to look at ye. I like to look at ye."

"Do ye, Tavis?" she asked softly, her hand moving to caress his chest. "What else do ye like? This?"

"Aye," he murmured as her lips and her tongue played over his mouth before she kissed him slowly.

" 'Tis hard for a woman to know what pleasures a man," Storm said musingly as she trailed kisses down to his chest. "A man learns as he grows from women he pays for or from women who have lovers to teach them. We young ladies are ne'er taught nor told a thing. How are we to know if a man likes this?" she asked huskily as her tongue played over his nipples before her mouth fastened upon one.

His hands ploughed into her thick hair as he rasped, "I cannae speak for other men but 'tis verra fine."

She moved to kneel between his strong thighs, her covering slipping off to lie unheeded on the blanket. Her tongue traced patterns down to the edge of the cloth that still encircled his hips, patterns that her kisses retraced. Every inch of his strong legs were explored by her hands, slowly and lovingly.

"And what is this, Tavis?" she whispered as her lips continued their play over his taut stomach just above the cloth's edge and she felt his hands tighten in her hair.

"A tease, m'eudail," he groaned.

Ever since the MacDubhs had visited, Tavis had thought of the magic Storm could perform with her lovely mouth and intoxicating tongue. It occurred to him that Storm was often on his mind, but he put that down to her natural expertise as a lover. The way she could pleasure a man ensured that she would be well remembered. He would not be able to forget how she could turn his blood to pure fire, make him ache more than he had ever ached for any woman.

"Mayhaps if ye tell me what ye want," Storm purred as she continued her play.

"Ye ken weel what I want, witch," he rasped.

"Is it this, acushla?"

She undid the cloth slowly. Her hand moved over the seat of his passion as her lips drifted to his thighs.

She felt him shudder as she teased and stroked, and knew the power a woman could have over a man. In her case, the power she had came back upon herself. As Tavis's passion grew so did hers, his pleasure increased her own and she surrendered to desire almost as quickly as he did.

" 'Od's blood, woman, ye do ken how to use those beautiful hands. Ah," he gasped as her lips brushed agonizingly close. "Storm, my Storm, maun ye torture me so? Have pity on a man."

"Do ye call this pity, Tavis?" she murmured as her lips took over the pleasant work of her hand.

"I call it heaven," he said hoarsely as pleasure closed his eyes. "Aye. 'Tis heaven."

The sharp edge of his need, a need unsatisfied as she had healed, was gone, so he had the strength of control to simply enjoy. He did not want to rush, wanted to luxuriate in the waves of pleasure flowing over him. That control nearly snapped when her lips engulfed him, performed that intimacy he had never dared ask for. His eyes flew open and he half sat up in surprise.

His violent reaction made her pause, and she peeked at him through the tangled curtain of her hair. "Nay?" she queried in a small voice, terrified she had erred badly.

"Aye," Tavis ground out, urging her back with the hands he had clenched in her hair. Sitting up, Tavis's gaze riveted to the mass of bright hair splayed over his lap. His body trembled as he fought for control. The subservient appearance of her position was a fraud, for he was at that moment her slave. Ecstacy nearly doubled him up until he knew he had reached his limit.

Storm found herself flung onto her back. Tavis's possession of her was savage as he threw himself on top of her and drove into her deeply and swiftly. After the first shock she was caught up in the ferocity of his lovemaking. It was short-lived in its violence as they crested the heights within heartbeats of each other. Her limbs lay heavily around him as he collapsed on top of her, his face buried in the curve of her neck and his breath coming in harsh, shaky rasps.

In silence they parted, each moving to get dressed. There was a tension in the air that made Storm nervous. She could not help but wonder if she had done wrong. Because something gave a man pleasure did not mean he approved of a lady performing it. Storm had recognized the hypocrisy of men early in life.

Tavis's silence was due partly to embarrassment. He knew he had taken her roughly, more roughly than he could remember ever having taken a woman. Never before had he been driven to such a point of white-hot, blind desire. Her ability to do that to him unnerved him slightly. He saw the stiffness in her movments and watched her wince as she bent to pick up the blanket.

"I have hurt ye," he said in obvious remorse as he moved to stand before her.

Holding the folded blanket to her chest, Storm murmured " 'Tis naught, Tavis."

"Ye are a poor liar, lass." He brushed the hair back from her face. "Ye are sore. 'Tis there to see in the way ye move. I am sorry. God, but ye drive a man to madness."

" 'Tis not an unpleasant soreness, Tavis. I felt it not in its making and it will pass."

Taking the blanket from her, he tossed it aside and took her into his arms. The confusion in his mind caused his arms to tighten around her as he buried his face in her silken hair. He had the strongest urge to flee with her, to go somewhere where it mattered not at all who they were. Knowing she would have to return to Hagaleah, he looked into the future and felt chilled by the emptiness he saw there. There was nothing to fill in the space she would leave. Giving himself a mental shake, he tried to convince himself that he was caught up in the afterglow of good loving. Any man would dread the thought of losing such pleasure. It would be a transitory sense of loss.

"Storm?" He pulled away a little to look down at her face, not sure of what he wanted to say.

"Aye, Tavis?" She saw the confusion on his face and wondered at its cause.

"Thank ye," he whispered, and brushed a light kiss over her mouth as his hands gently cupped her face.

"Ye are quite welcome," she said, forcing herself to smile over the twisting pain in her heart, a pain caused by the knowledge that this was all she would ever have of Tavis MacLagan.

15

A crispness to the air foretold the coming autumn and bid farewell to summer. Storm sighed as she prepared to go to the hall. She knew she was pregnant, and the only good thing she could think about it was that she was so far along the sickness had passed and she had been successful in hiding it from Tavis. Now she just had to worry about when she would begin to really show. At the moment she only looked as if she were putting on a little weight. She knew, however, that that was apt to change at any time, for she was too far along to keep it hidden much longer. It had amazed her that Tavis had yet to feel the quickening of his child, for it grew stronger with each passing day.

She had not told Tavis about the baby for she felt it would put a wedge between them. One of her fears was that he would demand that, if she bore him a son, the child stay with him. That was something she could never bear. It was becoming imperative that she get home.

Sighing as she moved to the door, Storm knew that her troubles would not cease once she got home. Eventually she would have to tell her father and in such a way that he did not ride out for Caraidland screaming for blood. There would be the spiteful tongues blaming her for what she had no control over to contend with. With no maidenhead and a bastard child, she would be unweddable. A cold, loveless future stretched before her, and that would be the hardest thing to face, especially now that she had had a taste of love, if unreturned, and the passion it bred. She envisioned endless nights of aching with a shudder.

As she walked into the hall, she thought about the life growing within her. Despite her gloomy thoughts on her future, as well as her current worries, she found a flicker of elation struggling to grow. She would have a piece of Tavis to hold and love. Storm knew that would bring her future pain, but she felt the joy of their child could outshine that. There would be a child of Tavis's body to whom she could give all the love she ached to give to Tavis.

Tavis sat in the hall, drinking ale and talking with his family, but his mind was on Storm, not on what he was saying. Fighting weather was passing even in France, he presumed. Soon Lord Eldon would be coming home. The king could not hold all his high-born knights at his side even if he opted to stay in France for the winter. By now word of the trouble at home must have reached Lord Eldon, and Tavis had no doubt that the man would be hieing it back to Hagaleah to gain his daughter's freedom through ransom or sword. Each day Tavis expected to hear word from the man.

The ransom would be paid, Storm would return to Hagaleah and Tavis's bed would be empty again. The thought brought a chill to his bones. Still, he ignored the small voice that wearily tried to tell him of his feelings. He continued to tell himself that he liked her and relished her passion, a combination he had never enjoyed before. That was why he hated the thought of her leaving. It meant a return to women who satisfied a need at only the most basic of levels.

He had grown greedy of late as thoughts of her leaving crowded into his mind more and more. It did not surprise him that she lingered abed in the mornings. A twinge of guilt assailed him as he recalled how wan she looked at times. That would not stop him from making love to her each and every chance he got, however, but he did think he would try not to disturb her night's sleep as often as he had been. It would not do to send her back to her father looking ill and well used.

Thinking that brought him to wonder what would happen when Lord Eldon discovered that his daughter had slept with her captor. It was ample reason to take up his sword. Tavis knew that his family would be crying long and loud for blood if they had a cherished daughter treated as he had treated Storm. It was a man's responsibility, if nothing else. Dishonor must be paid for in blood.

The only reason he was not positive that they faced a battle with Eldon was because of Storm. It was not vanity that told Tavis she thoroughly enjoyed their lovemaking. Her protests at the start had been very weak and, after that, she had never turned from him; rather she had welcomed him to her bed each night with open arms, a sweet smile and a passion to equal his own.

Would she tell her father how she had been used? If Eldon guessed, would she try to turn aside his natural wrath? Storm did not seem to be the vengeful sort but, because he had offered her no words of love, would she react as a woman scorned and need Mac-Lagan blood to soothe her wounded vanity?

Even as the questions formed, Tavis answered them negatively. Storm would do her best to keep the families from meeting at sword point over her lost innocence. She was a practical, logical person and would not wish any deaths to occur over something that was inevitable and that she had enjoyed. If naught else, she would want to do all she could to keep her own family from battle.

His thoughts were interrupted by her entrance. A slow, enjoyable survey of her as she came toward him told him that no one could say she had been abused. In fact, he thought she looked better than she had when she had first arrived, although there was a sadness in her eyes at times that he was loathe to investigate. Her gentle curves had become more womanly. A lovely smile touched her equally lovely face as she greeted everyone, and he felt his loins stir, causing him to smile crookedly at his own weakness.

Just as he was about to greet her, a messenger from Hagaleah was announced. Everyone tensed, and Tavis noticed that Storm was again looking pale as she sat down next to him. There was no time to puzzle over her reaction, for his father was reading the missive the courier had given him.

Storm had discovered that she was torn two ways. She did need to get away to the sanctuary of Hagaleah, but the idea of leaving Tavis was nearly unbearable. Her personal conflict of emotion was forgotten as she caught the look on the laird's face. The news from Hagaleah was not good.

"They have finally refused a ransom openly?" she asked with a calm she did not feel.

"Aye. They have done that, lass." Colin studied her taut features and knew she suspected the news the missive held, as well as the significance of a refusal of ransom. "Your father and brothers are dead."

"Nay, 'tis not so." She snatched the message when Colin held it out to her.

Lady Mary's scribe had a flowery hand, but Storm managed to decipher her words, and her heart seemed to pound its way out of her chest as she read.

"Lord Eldon and his son and heir met with a fatal mishap as they journeyed here from France. There is neither love nor blood tie twixt his eldest daughter and myself. Hence, I refuse to pay any ransom for the girl who has no doubt lost all honor. Do not think to send thy requests to Lord Foster, for he and his son and heir met the same fate as the Eldons. As they traveled as a group so, too, did the Verner twins. My stepdaughter has none left to champion her. I give thee leave to do with her as thy please. Lady Mary Eldon."

All gone! her mind whispered even as it fought to reject the news. With surprisingly steady hands, she lay the missive on the table before her, her hands palm down on either side of it and her gaze riveted to the words that seemed to run together. Slowly she rose to her feet, although she did not know why. There was no place to flee to escape such tidings. One hand rested on a knife, and with a swiftness that prevented any intervention, she grasped it in both hands. A cry that chilled her audience broke from her as she plunged the knife into the parchment, pinning it to the table.

"I will kill that hell-born bitch," she cried as she started to race for the door, the red haze of a vengeful rage filling her mind, a rage that momentarily held back her grief.

Although everyone in the room moved to catch her, Tavis reached her first. She fought his hold as she spat her hate for Lady Mary in a low, icy voice. Thinking her hysterical, he slapped her. She went still and he released her, staring worriedly into her wide eyes. His look changed to one of amazement as she slapped him back.

"I was not hysterical," she hissed, but then her eyes fixed upon the red mark on his face and she gasped, one small hand covering her mouth briefly before it moved to touch the mark her slap had left upon Tavis's face. "Oh, Tavis," she whispered in a shaky voice as her grief began to flood through her, drowning her rage. " 'Tis not ye I wish to strike."

"I ken that, Storm, but ye wouldnae get near the woman."

She closed her eyes against a wave of pain and slowly sank to her knees. "All gone. They are all gone. What shall I do? There is no one left. I am all alone. All alone. Sweet God, I cannot bear it."

For a moment Tavis stood helpless before the depth of her grief. He had never heard a woman weep so, the sobs tearing through her, threatening to shake her apart. It hurt him to see her in such pain, but he did not stop to examine why as he stooped to lift her to her feet. His arms folded around her in an attempt at comfort when she fell against him, clinging tightly. Out of the corner of his eye he saw Phelan approach, his small face pale and awash with tears.

"She has me," he whispered. "Ye still have me, Storm. Tell her that, Tavis. She's not all alone."

Tavis smiled weakly at the boy. "Aye. She'll ken that when she has spent her tears, laddie." He picked Storm up in his arms, not minding how she clung to his neck, her tears soaking him. "I'll take her to her room. Ye can come to see her when the worst has passed. Go to Colin, laddie," he added softly.

After a last look at Storm, who was still helpless in her sorrow, Phelan raced to Colin. That man's arms were ready to receive him, for Colin was fond of the orphaned Irish boy. Silently, they all watched as Tavis left the hall, Storm's weeping the only sound until it faded completely.

"What will ye do with us now, m'lord?" Phelan asked after a moment, his teary eyes fixed upon Colin.

Leading the boy back to the table and handing him a tankard of ale, Colin sighed. " 'Tis hard to say, lad. Are there no relations left ye can go to, turn to for aid and shelter?"

Phelan shook his head. "The Verner twins' parents died two years past. Their land will now go to the crown, to be allotted as the king sees fit. 'Tis nay a one in Erin, which is why I came to Hagaleah. Matilda Foster may still live, but she is but a child of eleven or twelve years. There is naught that she can do. Storm's half-brothers are e'en younger and in Lady Mary's control now. Uncle Roden's mistress, Elaine Bailey, has fled to the south to elude Lady Mary. We could go to her, for she would shelter us, but 'twould bring her trouble, of that I am sure, and she is unprotected."

Colin sighed as he rubbed his temples. "Curse it. Ne'er had a lass handed o'er to me afore. 'Tis a problem, for I cannae send her to Hagaleah despite the lack of ransom."

"Nay, ye cannae," Iain agreed. "We have seen how they treat her. E'en if we could get Tavis to agree to it, it would sit ill with our own people. 'Twould be as if we cut her throat with our own hands."

"Aye, and I owe the lass my life. That binds me to watch o'er her." Colin shook his head. "I maun think on it. There be no rush." He smiled crookedly. "She's weel cared for at this time."

Tavis lay on the bed holding Storm as she fought desperately to control her sobs, dry now for she had used up all of her tears. Comfort was not something he was accustomed to doling out, but the emotions he still tried to ignore made him an unknowing expert. He truly felt for her in her grief and understood her great loss, because he had but recently come so near to losing his own father. This honest sympathy was conveyed silently to the grief-stricken woman he held and tried to soothe.

He also wondered what would happen now. There was no fear of her being sent back to Hagáleah, ransom or no, for he knew his father would not do that, not when he knew what would happen to her when Sir Hugh got his hands on her. Tavis was ashamed at the small part of him that felt relief, even joy, over the fact that she could now stay with him. That benefit had been gained at too great a cost. He concentrated on stopping her rending sobs.

Slowly Tavis's efforts seeped through Storm's grief. She continued to fight to still the weeping that had totally possessed her. Recalling the struggling life her body harbored helped her. She knew such strong emotion could have an ill effect upon her baby. Clinging to Tavis, she sought to absorb his tender comfort as well as his strength and, slowly, she regained some sense of composure.

Like some broken doll, she lay limp as he cleaned her face and forced some whiskey down her throat. Her slim body still shook with silent tremors even though her tears were spent. Her eyes stayed fixed upon him throughout his gentle ministrations, and the flat desolation he read there unnerved him. He feared her loss had proven too great a burden for her. Such a tragedy had been known to break the spirit or the mind. When he moved from the bed she grasped his wrist with surprising strength and prevented him from rising.

"Stay with me, please," she croaked in a thin voice. "I feel so alone and it frightens me."

Lying on his side, Tavis put an arm around her tiny waist and tucked her securely against himself. "Ye arenae alone, lass. There's Phelan who loves ye and needs ye. Aye, and though ye be an Eldon, 'tis many a friend ye have at Caraidland." He wondered briefly at the look of pain that flickered over her face. "Ye arenae the sort that will e'er be alone."

She closed her eyes so that he could not see how his words hurt even as they helped. Storm had no hopes that he would now declare an undying love, but it hurt to hear him talk of friendships. The one thing that could ease the loss of so many of her kin, as well as her godfather and his son, her friend, was Tavis's love, but that was to be denied her. Straining to draw upon some of her former strength and practicality, she tried to be content with his sincere tenderness and attempts to ease her pain.

"At least I was able to send them off that day with words of love," she whispered.

"Ye speak of love to your family?" he asked softly as his fingers began to idly take down her hair.

"Aye. 'Tis only the truth. I have the comfort of knowing that my family and my dear friends, the Fosters, knew of my love for them ere they died, as I now hold the knowledge that they loved me. 'Tis a feeling to be shared, not held close and secretive. Mayhaps knowing that they were loved and would be remembered eased their minds. The thought that they knew naught of my love for them is not now added to my sorrow. I do not hold a grief for lost chances or unsaid words." She ignored a slight feeling of hypocrisy as she continued to hide the truth of her love for Tavis, for such a declaration would only discomfort him and bring her more pain when her sentiments went unreturned. "We also spoke of our love for each other whene'er we had to part, for each parting could have been the last. I care for ye, Tavis," she said softly, not wanting to leave her heart fully locked and the knowledge forever hidden.

"I ken ye do, lass," he replied as he held her

193

tighter. "Ye tell me that each time we make love. Ye ken that I have a soft spot or twa for ye, that I think ye the best I have e'er kenned. I like ye, Storm, and 'tis something I've nay said to a woman. Aye, I like ye and I trust ye."

"Thank ye, Tavis," she murmured, knowing with an inner delight that eked through her desolation that she had gained more from Tavis than any other woman had. "What will happen to Phelan and me now?"

"Ye willnae be given to Sir Hugh, but other than that I cannae say just now." He caressed the thick, silken cloud of her hair that now hung free. "Dinnae think on it now, lass."

"Tavis? Will ye make love to me now?" she asked softly as she looked into his face.

"Now, lass?" he asked as he fought the sudden rush of desire that flooded him. "Are ye sure?"

"Aye." She began to unlace his tunic. "I feel so lost, so alone. There is an emptiness in me, a black desolation that is frightening me." She met his concerned look. "I fear twill ne'er leave me. I need to know that I can still feel, that I have not been left but an empty husk by my loss. Give me the pleasure and reality of your lovemaking to break its chilling hold. I crave warmth to ease my chill. Is that wrong, Travis?" she asked in a small voice.

"Nay, lass," he replied softly as he shed his clothes and began to unlace her gown. " 'Tis ne'er wrong to want to escape the pain, to seek to prove to yourself that ye are still alive and nay alone. I understand your need. Dinnae feel any shame. No one would fault ye for what ye seek. I only hope I can give it to ye."

When he removed the last of her clothing and held her close to his hard length she sighed and held him tightly. "Ye can, Tavis. I am sure of that if naught else."

He made love to her slowly, taking his time and using all his skill to bring her passion through the heavy layer of her grief. She did not halt him in any intimacy he took, wanting to lose herself in a feast of her senses. Becoming a total voluptuary, she feasted upon him, her lips and hands tasting every inch of him, luxuriating in him, following his hoarse requests and directions without any qualms. She wanted to push away all thought of her loss for just a little while.

Tavis feverishly wondered who was warming whom as time and time again her gifted mouth drove him to the brink only to pause, keeping him at the heights yet never allowing him to descend. He quickly saw that she hoped to lose herself, if only briefly, in a wanton feast of passion, and told her all that he wanted, reveling in the ecstasy that she brought him. His eyes never left her as she pleasured him, the visual heightening the effect of her inborn skill.

When he knew he could take no more he drew her up his body slowly. He kissed her, the taste of himself upon her lips causing him to shudder with need. As his mouth moved to her breasts, his hands traveled over her greedily. He suckled and tongued her breasts until she moaned and ground her hips against him. Then he made his way slowly down-ward, pausing to dart his tongue in and around her navel. He ignored her gasp of protest when he moved even lower to let his mouth pleasure her as hers had done to him.

Storm clutched the bedpost, her eyes closing as waves of pleasure washed over her. His hands caressed her backside as his tongue stroked and probed. She cried out as she neared her peak, but he stopped her attempt to retreat, relishing the gift of her passion, and then skillfully brought her back to the edge of culmination before pulling her shaking body down to fit it neatly to his. His eyes never left her as she rode, his hands moving over her in a restless greed, cupping her breasts and gliding down to touch where their bodies joined. They peaked together, their hoarse cries of repletion blending as she collapsed against him.

"Nay," she begged as he moved to separate them. "Just a moment longer. I need the closeness."

Silently complying with her request, he held her as she fell into a sated sleep. If nothing else, he mused as he settled her beneath the covers and rose from the bed, I have helped her find that oblivion. As he dressed, he studied her, sympathizing with her grief but selfishly pleased to know that she would be staying indefinitely now, would continue to bring him sensual delight.

"How is the lassie?" Colin asked when Tavis was admitted to his chambers.

"The major storm is past, but 'twill be a while ere the pain of loss eases. She will stay?"

"It looks so. There be nay another place for her and the lad to go."

Tavis nodded and turned to leave only to pause in the open doorway as he recalled Storm's words. Colin could be lost as easily and as suddenly as Lord Eldon. He had already come very close to death.

"Father?"

"Aye, Tavis?"

"I love ye," he said quietly and hastened away, feeling lighter of heart but leaving a very startled Colin behind him.

16

Frowning, Tavis watched a force equaling half of their fighting strength ride off to Athdara. It was not that he begrudged the MacBroths assistance, but he was plagued with doubt as to their need. He grimaced, chiding himself for being fanciful only to turn around and meet two sets of worried amber eyes. With a quirk of his eyebrow, he invited them to put voice to their concerns, although he was not at all sure he wanted to hear them. He had enough of his own worries and would prefer them put to rest.

" 'Tis a bad time for ye to be short half your armed force," Storm said, feeling suspicious and worried, but lacking the facts on which to base her feelings.

"Aye, there be no arguing that, little one." Tavis draped his arm over her shoulder. "There has been nary a raid to pay back the one we made upon Hagaleah. The uncertainty of your fate held it off, I think."

"And now my fate has been decided," she said softly, the pain of her loss still fresh, and felt Tavis's arm tighten on her shoulders. "Sir Hugh and Lady Mary need not hold back for the sake of my safety."

"Do ye think Sir Hugh still wishes ye to be his bride?"

Storm shrugged, but Phelan had an answer ready. "Her fortune still remains. 'Tis already in her

197

hands, put aside as her dowry for when she weds or her livelihood if she does not. He could still need that."

"Mayhaps he will wed Lady Mary?" Storm mused, but felt it an empty hope even as she spoke it.

"Mayhaps, but 'twill not gain him much. Ye know your father left most of his wealth and property to his heirs. Her two sons hold that now, though 'twill be in trust 'til they come of age. He said he had made an allowance for me, and he left no small amount to Mistress Bailey and the children they share. Though I doubt he left her penniless, I would wager Lady Mary is far from the wealth she feels a need for."

Tavis's brow creased in a frown at this news. "Then Sir Hugh could well wish to retrieve Storm."

"But surely 'twould be easier to pay the ransom than to try and storm Caraidland?"

"Aye, sweeting, it would, but mayhaps they feel that is just what we would think. They hope to lull us into a false sense of security." He muttered a curse. "I wish I had thought upon all this ere I had sent out my men. Nay. Nay, I cannae think that the MacBroths would deceive us so."

"How far a ride is it to the MacBroth keep?" Storm asked, wishing that Tavis sounded more certain.

"An all goes weel, they will reach there by nightfall. Any mishap and they will need to camp, not reaching there until day's dawning. If there is no trouble at Athdara, the soonest they would return is by tomorrow night. That means at least eight and forty hours at half strength, possibly more. Let us pray that Sir Hugh hears naught of it, for he could, if informed, be at our gates at day's dawning."

In troubled times spies were abundant, and there was one at Caraidland. Although he knew his use as a spy would be ended by the venture, the man made haste to Hagaleah. His excuses for leaving would mean that he could reach Sir Hugh with the news of this opportunity before his absence was questioned. This was the chance Sir Hugh had sent him to watch for.

Sir Hugh was growing very tired of waiting, always waiting and never acting. He lay sprawled upon Lady Mary's bed, frowning up at the ceiling. His devious mind was awhirl with plans to keep most of Lord Eldon's fortune within his grasp by aiding Lady Mary in her quest to hold onto it. He also plotted to regain hold of Storm, whose fortune would be his alone once they were wed. There was no fear of a long stint in the marital noose, for Lady Mary would be more than willing to help him become a grieving widower.

Lady Mary turned from the table where she had been brushing her hair and strolled to the side of the bed. Sir Hugh was her favorite amongst her many lovers, for he was as amoral as she. Her other lovers tended to balk at some of the variations she suggested, but Hugh never did. As she studied his fine physique she tugged her bell rope. A smile touched her face as she thought of the surprise she had for him. This would be a new twist and would momentarily divert his mind from all his scheming. Her bedroom was for entertainment, not plotting.

"Bored, m'dear?" he drawled, his eyes studying her robe, which showed more than it hid.

"You must admit that you have been a little preoccupied of late."

"There's a great deal to think about. Storm possesses a fortune and I want it."

"And her. I think your lust for my dear departed husband's daughter comes mostly from her refusal of you."

"She not only refused me, she insulted me," he growled, his fists clenching, "and she was party to my humiliation. For that she will pay, and pay dearly. No woman does that to me."

"There now, Sir Hugh, your chance will come, but for now, a little surprise." She smiled as a slender, lovely girl of Moorish descent entered the room. "What do you think?"

"Beautiful," Sir Hugh said as his gaze took in the girl's gentle curves, shown to advantage in a nearly transparent gown of the finest white silk. "Where did you find her?"

"My sister sent her to me, for her husband was too fond of the girl." Lady Mary touched the proof of Sir Hugh's own attraction for the girl. "As you could be. Care for a closer look?" When Sir Hugh nodded Lady Mary slowly disrobed the girl. "She has many talents," Lady Mary purred as she watched Sir Hugh greedily eye the slim, brown-skinned girl. "Shall I demonstrate?"

Nodding, Sir Hugh watched as Lady Mary began to caress the girl. He watched avidly as the girl discarded Lady Mary's robe and the two women began to make love in earnest. Moving aside when they fell onto the bed, hungrily pleasuring each other, he briefly envisioned Storm in such a tangle. That proved too much for his already strained control. He moved behind Lady Mary and fiercely possessed her. When the three lay in a damp, sated tangle he grinned at her.

"Your surprises are ever a delight. Who is it?" he bellowed when a knock sounded at the door.

" 'Tis your kinsman, Lawrence, returned from Caraidland. I have news, Sir Hugh," the young spy announced.

The two women slipped beneath the covers as Sir Hugh donned his robe. He curtly ordered Lawrence inside to deliver his message. The young man's eyes stayed fixed upon the bed as he told Sir Hugh about events of Caraidland. He had heard tales of what went on in Lady Mary's chambers, but he had doubted them. As the young man struggled to recall all of his information, he realized the sin-filled, whispered tales were all true.

"So the little bitch still lives?" Lady Mary asked, sitting up and clutching the sheet to her breasts.

Lawrence swallowed hard, for her movement had left the Moorish girl exposed to the waist, and his gaze was fixed with hungry fascination upon full brown breasts. "Yes. She remains Tavis MacLagan's lover."

Seeing how the news angered Sir Hugh, Lady Mary could not resist goading him. "Your prize will be well trained ere you gain it. I wonder what skills a Scotsman could teach a woman?"

That drove Sir Hugh into a tirade filled with bloody vows of vengeance. Lady Mary smiled as he stormed about her room. Then, bored with watching that diversion, she turned her attention to Lawrence. Seeing the direction of his gaze, she let her hands play over the Moor's full breasts until the dusky tips were taut, and Lawrence was plainly having trouble breathing. Slowly, she moved her hand downward, taking the sheet with it. The Moor purred when Lady Mary found her goal, and Lawrence looked near to choking on his own lust as he watched.

Sir Hugh stopped his ranting and watched their games in disgust. "I am off to gather my men. This is too good an opportunity to ignore. I intend to raze Caraidland and send those MacLagans to hell."

Never stopping what she was doing, Lady Mary purred, "And gather your fortune."

"Aye. I will bring that Eldon whore back here on her knees," he snarled. "And on her knees she will stay."

"A position you have a particular fondness for," Lady Mary drawled, meeting his scowl with a smile.

It was hard to think of anything but how those

long, pale fingers were playing over the Moor's dark treasures, but Lawrence managed. "My reward?" he croaked as the Moor arched and revealed more of herself.

"Ah, yes." Sir Hugh exchanged a speaking glance with Lady Mary, who nodded. "A reward you shall have, kinsman, never fear. You have served me well," he said, and he slapped the young man on the back as he left the room.

Finding himself alone with the two women, Lawrence took a tentative step toward the bed. Lady Mary smiled, beckoned him closer and silently invited him to take his enjoyment of the Moor. She watched with a mild interest that grew as he hurriedly shed his clothes, uncaring that he would be observed as he sought his pleasure. Seeing that Lawrence was as endowed as his kinsman, Lady Mary's smile grew, and she slowly removed her thin covering.

"White meat or dark meat, my fine young man?" She arched like the voluptuary she was.

Placing a greedy hand between each woman's shapely thighs, Lawrence drawled, "I have e'er been a man of diversified tastes. What say you to a bit of both?"

A smile crossed Lady Mary's face as she squirmed beneath his touch. "I say prove your worth."

Lying on his back on the bed, Lawrence settled the Moor upon himself. With a grin, he then grasped Lady Mary by her hips and pulled her toward him. She returned his grin as she decided that she would wait a while before she killed him. There were several combinations she wished to try out first.

Sir Hugh knew he would not reach Caraidland by nightfall. The days grew shorter, and his kinsman had used up most of the day bringing the news to him. Nevertheless, he assembled his men, determined to cover what distance he could before dark. If luck was with him, he could begin the attack at dawn's first light. He hoped his move would catch the MacLagans by surprise, but he did not count on it.

When Storm was not returned after the ransom had been refused he had begun to plot ways of attack that would cost him the least while gaining him the most. Lawerence's place within Caraidland, gained when Storm had first been taken, had been one way to help him in that plan. The lad's use was now at an end, and Hugh felt no qualms about being rid of his kinsman. He smiled grimly, knowing how Lady Mary would make use of the unsuspecting young man before she killed him with a heart as cold as his own.

Thoughts of Storm made him grind his teeth in frustrated rage. She was a thorn in his side, in his pride and in his purse. He lusted after her, yet she refused him. Her spirit was the sort that would not allow total dominance, and that drew him, for he ached to crush it, to see the proud beauty grovel before him. Once he had her back in his hands he would show her the true meaning of humility. No woman looked down on Sir Hugh Sedgeway.

Included in his plots for revenge was many a one for the Scottish stallion that had taken what should have been his. The fact that the proud Eldon bitch would take a reiver to her bed before she would take him was an insult that was hard to swallow. He would do his best to see that Tavis MacLagan died, preferably in a slow, agonizing way before the eyes of his English lover. Sir Hugh savored the vision as he rode.

Not all of Sir Hugh's force was pleased to be riding to battle. Lord Eldon's death, as well as the heir's, had put them firmly in Lady Mary's control with little hope of release, a fact they found distasteful. Many of them were trying to convince themselves that their vows of allegience need not extend to the widow, whom many suspected had personally engineered her own widowhood. Unfortunately in this case, they were honorable men, and their oath meant much to them. Disgruntled and unwilling, they nevertheless rode on.

When they camped for the night they were but an hour's ride from Caraidland. Fires were kept small and shielded so that keen eyes at Caraidland would not guess what advanced upon them. Sir Hugh was not surprised when Lady Mary, her new toy, the Moor, and her burly, handsome personal guard arrived. The woman wanted to be in at the start of her stepdaughter's downfall. In her thinking, it was Storm's fault that she had never enthralled her husband. She was also curious to see the man who had dishonored Storm Eldon.

Setting up her elaborate tent, she retired inside with her entourage, later to be joined by Sir Hugh, and indulged herself in an orgy that further alienated their fighting men. Honor demanded that they transfer their allegiance to their liege's widow, but honor was severly strained when that woman was an immoral whore, a woman who belonged in a brothel, not an earl's keep. Many wished for a return of their lord, grieving anew over the unprovable treachery that had brought him down.

•

Lord Eldon was doing his best to reach his keep, but he was still many miles away from Hagaleah. He and his grim-faced troops rode hard for home, eager to face the pair who had engineered the assassination attempt that had been so nearly successful. A false report of the attempt's success had been sent back to his keep and, although he was sorry if the news caused any grief to some of those at Hagaleah, Lord Eldon was eager to see the faces of those who had tried to kill him when he miraculously returned from the dead.

The one assassin they had caught alive had told wild stories of happenings at Hagaleah that chilled the blood. Worst of all his news was the report that Storm was at Caraidland, had been there for all of the summer. Although he ached to head directly for the MacLagan's keep, Lord Eldon knew he had to go home first if only for fresh mounts and fighting men. He cursed the fate that had taken him to France, kept him there while all that mattered to him was brought to ruin.

Another anger burned in him, and that was over the knowledge that his home had become little better than a whorehouse. He had been aware of his wife's voracious appetite, but his presence had always kept it discreet. If only half of what that man had said was true, Lady Mary had thrown discretion to the four winds with a vengeance. He wondered how many of his people had suffered under the yoke of her immoral rule. The whore he had married had turned an honorable, well-respected keep into a place of unwholesome debauchery. For that alone he could easily kill her.

Watching the expressions upon his old friend's face, Lord Foster felt sympathy for Eldon. While his home had not escaped corruption, it did not seem to have fallen so far. That bitch from Sussex had muddied Lord Eldon's name and that of his ancestors. It was an insult the proud Lord Eldon would long grieve over, for it would take some time to erase the stain.

Eldon swore harshly as he sat around a campfire with his son, nephews and friends. " 'Tis bad enough to have married the slut, but now the whole world knows what an ass I was. God's beard, I can almost be glad that MacLagan has Storm. At least she is away from that corruption called my wife."

"That man said that Lady Mary intended to refuse the ransom. What will happen to Storm and Phelan then?" asked Andrew, hoping his father would deny the thoughts that were churning in his head.

He did not, only looked at his son and asked, "If you had a lovely young lady in your grasp for the length of the summer or longer, what would you do?" He sighed over his son's downcast face. "I have little doubt that they were honorable until the ransom was held back. Then, who can say." He smiled grimly. "They have always been the best of enemies."

"They will not kill her when the ransom is refused, will they?" Hadden asked quietly.

"Nay," Eldon answered without hesitation. "They would no more put sword to a lone woman within their walls than we would. The MacLagans have ne'er been murderers of innocents even in the fever of battle. I recall the time a madwoman took up sword against one of them during a raid. He took a wound to the arm, for he fought to disarm her rather than cut her down as he could have done with ease. Nay, 'tis not death I fear for Storm."

"Will we ride against them?"

"I think I must needs wait to see how she fares. 'Tis nay their fault that she was left without protectors. How are they to know what treachery is afoot at Hagaleah? All they see is that none wish to ransom her. If Storm is no longer a maid, does the fault truly lie with the MacLagans? Can I blame a man for seducing a maid who has been tossed into his lap, seemingly deserted by her kin? Nay, 'tis not a simple black or white situation, curse Mary's soul. Aye, if Storm has been dishonored, 'tis more Mary's fault."

He was still of that mind when he arrived at Hagaleah near nightfall of the following day. No challenge was raised as he rode through the gates, and the few who saw him gaped, crossing themselves in superstitious fear until his familiar bellow left them little doubt as to the continued good health of their liege. Hilda was sent for as soon as he entered the hall.

"M'lord," the woman wept, "you live. 'Tis God's sweet miracle."

"Stop your wailing and tell me what is about. Where is that slut that, God forbids, carries my name?"

"She has followed Sir Hugh to Caraidland. He goes to free Mistress Storm so he may wed her." Hilda was so elated to see her lord back and alive that she almost smiled as he ranted in response to that news. "There is a man who can tell ye how it goes at Caraidland. He is a kinsman of Sir Hugh's and was left for dead," Hilda offered when Lord Eldon paused for a breath. "He was a spy at Caraidland."

Lord Eldon was not surprised to find the man in Lady Mary's chambers. He grimaced in distaste as he surveyed the bright silks, lush furs and gilded mirrors. Turning his gaze to the pale young man in the bed, Lord Eldon surmised with amazing accuracy how the man had nearly met his fate.

"Is there a specific reason for Sir Hugh to ride armed against the MacLagans at this time?"

"Aye, m'lord. They are at but half strength." Although Lawrence's voice was weak, it was steady. "Lady Mary sent word that no ransom would be paid for Mistress Storm, that ye were dead, as were all who traveled with you, and that they could do with the lass as they pleased. Sir Hugh hopes to catch them unawares."

"Why does this man wish to rescue my daughter?"

"He wants to wed her, or rather, her fortune. She has refused him in all ways and it sorely angers him. He had her once, and I fear he and Lady Mary treated her harshly, but she escaped back to Caraidland and the MacLagans. 'Tis felt the Scots had a hand in rescuing her. 'Twas indeed the brothers who brought her back to Caraidland, and the lass was in a sore state. When the ransom was flat refused they did not send her back here. Would not."

After venting a boiling rage in some very colorful language, Lord Eldon asked, "How fares my only daughter? Is she ill treated at Caraidland? Have they abused her or the boy in any way?"

Lawrence met Eldon's steady gaze. "They are both in good health and are actually much liked. The laird was being poisoned by his young wife and 'twas Mistress Storm who aided him. The lady knifed Mistress Storm before she was slain, but the lass recovered. So, too, did they nurse her after her treatment at Hugh's hands. She is treated more as a guest, though she is watched at all times. The people treat her with respect."

Although he nodded, pleased with that information, Lord Eldon's gaze remained fixed upon an increasingly agitated Lawrence. "There is more. You will tell me all that concerns her."

"She is no longer a maid," Lawrence said weakly, noting the flare of rage in his lordship's eyes and fearing he would suffer for it.

"Was it rape?" Lawrence shook his head. "Be it more than one? Is she treated as a whore?"

"Nay. After the ransom was refused the first time Tavis MacLagan took her to his bed. There she had stayed the whole time. She is treated well, I swear. Treated as if she is wife to the man. No other man touches her. None would dare."

With a cry of rage, Lord Eldon hurled a vase, shattering one of the numerous mirrors. He strode out of the room, vowing to make his wife and her lover pay, for they were the ones truly responsible.

They had left Storm without protection, given her to the enemy to do with as they pleased.

Lord Foster was waiting for him in the hall, having found things less chaotic at his Keep, and Eldon said flatly, "We ride to Caraidland at the dawning."

"I thought as much, and have brought my men. They are ready to fight MacLagans."

"Then you best have a word with them, for we go after Sir Hugh and my wife, who now besiege Caraidland," said Eldon and smiled grimly at Foster's surprise. "It seems that to save my daughter from Sir Hugh and that Sussex whore, I must needs save Caraidland. I wouldst love to see old Colin's face as we ride to his rescue." For the first time in many a day, Lord Eldon smiled with honest delight.

17

Dawn's meager light was struggling to pierce the darkness when Storm suddenly found herself awake and shivering. Tavis's warmth did not chase away the chill that had invaded her very bones. The very first time she had suffered such a thing was the time her mother had been poisoned. To her the sensation meant danger, was a valid warning not to be ignored. Since her family was gone, that meant that Caraidland was in danger. Without considering the chance that he might treat her feelings with scorn, Storm shook Tavis awake.

"Mmmm?" Tavis nuzzled her breasts as he woke, and then sleepily began to suckle upon one.

"Are ye awake, Tavis?" she asked inanely as she strove to keep her mind on what she wanted to say.

After looking at the hard tip of her breast and admiring the results of his attentions Tavis moved his eager mouth to her other breast to tease the nub of that awake with his tongue before his mouth fastened on it. "Increasing. 'Tis early, m'love. Ye havenae opened your eyes so early for a long time."

"What?" she queried blankly, her mind caught by passion's haze as his mouth continued to play over her breasts and his hands moved intoxicatingly over her body. "Oh. Have ye posted extra guards?"

"Aye." He slid the covers down, following their slow progress with his mouth. "Why do ye ask?"

"Ye may think 'tis foolishness, but I sense danger, trouble. I woke up chilled to the bone." Her words came out in husky gasps as his lips played over her stomach. "I feel we should beware."

"Nay, 'tis not foolish, and we do watch. If trouble comes, we will hear the warning." He knelt between her slim thighs, his own breathing unsteady. "All the men can be armed and ready in no time." Resting his palms on either side of her, he ran his eyes over the slim body he was about to possess. "Dinnae fash yourself, little one. Now, if ye maun talk, ye can say, 'Oh, Tavis,'" he said with a grin.

She did just that several times. Dawn's light was much stronger when Tavis finally rose from her arms, watching her stretch like a contented cat, displaying an unconscious sensuality that never failed to stir him. He was half seriously considering rejoining her in bed when a half-dressed Sholto burst into the room. Sholto took a fleeting but thorough look at Storm, who hurriedly gathered the sheet around herself.

"Enjoy yourself?" Tavis growled as he moved to stand before his younger brother.

Thinking of the full alabaster breasts that were as perfect as any he had ever seen, Sholto grinned. "Aye."

Tavis sent Storm a quick, repressive look when she giggled despite her embarrassment. "What has brought ye racing in here?"

"The watch ye sent to the forest has just arrived at full gallop. There is a large force o' men moving our way. They are from Hagaleah but fly not the Eldon banner. Ah! Father sounds the alarum."

"'Tis that bastard Sir Hugh, no doubt." Tavis placed an arm around Storm's slim shoulders when she paled, and tangled his hand in the thick, glorious hair Sholto was openly admiring. "His men number more than ours?"

212

"Twice, mayhaps thrice as many. He comes equipped to try and storm our walls."

Giving Storm a brief, hard kiss, Tavis began to get dressed. "Ye stay within the keep, Storm. Maggie will be here ere long, and ye can lend a hand to her. Come, Sholto, I must needs stop by my rooms," he said as he left the room, still lacing up his braes.

"That's some verra sweet lass ye have there, Tavis," Sholto said as they raced down the steps.

"Aye, too sweet for some Sassanach dog," growled Tavis as they bolted through the hall.

"Aye," Sholto agreed heartily, excitement already surging through him at the promise of a battle.

Even though she dressed hastily and did not bother to do up her hair, simply ran a brush through it and tied it back, Storm was unable to catch Tavis. She had barely started to aid the women in preparing the hall for the wounded who were sure to come when it was clear that Sir Hugh's forces had arrived. The moment Maggie's attention was diverted, Storm raced for the battlements.

"Send the Eldon girl out, MacLagan. You cannot wish to shed Scottish blood for an Englishwoman. You are outnumbered and my victory is certain," Sir Hugh boasted.

As Colin answered that boast in very colorful language, Storm looked over the force gathered and gasped as her gaze settled on a small knot of people to the right. "God above, Lady Mary herself."

"What the devil are ye doing up here?" Tavis bellowed, grabbing her arm and angrily shaking her.

"Where is she?" Sholto asked, his eyes trying to locate the infamous countess and ignoring Tavis's anger.

Although breathless from Tavis's treatment, Storm answered, "O'er to the right. The bright cart."

Curiosity getting the better of him, Tavis looked as well. Bright was a subtle description of the cart and its occupants, as well as the four horsemen at its sides. It was a ludicrous sight on a battlefield. In their attire of yellow and red, the four horsemen looked like well-built jesters. Tavis thought, with a grimace of distaste, that those horses were not all those men were hired to ride.

Seeing the direction of Tavis's disgusted look, Storm said, "M'lady's handmen." She grinned when Sholto laughed, but then grew serious. "Ye must hand me o'er to Sir Hugh," she said, although the words choked her and the very thought twisted her insides with fear and loathing, "an it will keep this battle from being fought. I am nay worth a battle."

Tavis stared at her, his eyes resting briefly on her full mouth, before meeting her gaze. He could read the fear there, yet he knew she meant what she said. Terrified though she was of Sir Hugh and fully aware of his plans for her, she would go to the man rather than have any blood spilled for her.

"Nay, lass. As my father now bellows, we'll nay hand ye o'er to Sir Hugh. Lady Mary gave ye to me to do as I pleased and," he lowered his voice, "I am nay done being pleased yet. Then, too, he asks for more than ye. He asks for the return of all we stole in the last raid and then a bit more for sparing our poor wee lives. Nay, lass. We fight. A bit for your sake and a bit for our own."

When a volley of arrows was Sir Hugh's reply to Colin's last retort Tavis shoved Storm down none too gently. "Not get your wee backside into the hall and keep it there," he growled. "And put some cursed hose on," he added when he noticed that her slim legs were bare.

"Aye," Sholto agreed, patting one exposed and very pretty thigh. "Ye could catch a chill." He grinned when Tavis shoved his hand away and tugged Storm's skirts back down.

Cupping his face in her hands, Storm gave Tavis a slow, loving kiss. "Take care, *cushlamochree*."

Watching her as she returned to the hall, Tavis murmured, "I wish I kenned what that meant."

"Vein of my heart," Phelan offered as he passed by with a bucket of water, "or darling. Ye can choose."

Tavis fought down an urge to chase after her and ask if she meant it. He turned his full attention to the battle, which soon grew from an exchange of insults and a few arrows to full warfare. For all his other faults, Sir Hugh proved to be a formidable enemy in battle. He knew the Scots were lacking manpower and he worked with slow but definite success to cut the number down even more, making no move to breech the wall. Sir Hugh wanted the odds fully in his favor before he did.

Storm soon had more work than she needed. Men who had only small wounds were patched up and went back to fight. The need for fighting men was too great to allow any pandering. It was not only grief for a lost friend or relative that was felt as the inevitable dead slowly added up but the fear of how each new loss weakened the defenses of Caraidland. Each man lost put the odds more in Sir Hugh's favor.

When Sholto was carried in with an arrow wound in his leg Storm was first at his side. She did not question her very real relief when she discovered it was little more than a graze that had bled freely. As she finished bandaging the wound, she felt his hand touch her hair and looked at him.

" 'Twas a temptation too great to resist," he said with a grin that made her think of her brother Andrew with sad, fond remembrance.

She laughed and impulsively kissed him only to

be caught by Tavis, who was bringing in yet another wounded man. "What the devil are ye about?" he growled as he helped the man onto a pallet.

"Did ye ne'er have your hurts kissed better when ye were a child?"

"Sholto's mouth looks fine to me," Tavis grumbled, his glare doing nothing to dim Sholto's grin.

"Aye, 'twas his thigh that was wounded. If ye wish, I will kiss . . ."

"Do and I'll see to it ye ne'er sit for a week," he snapped, glaring at her and then at the two men who laughed despite their wounds. "Get off with ye, wench." His lips twitched when she winked at him before moving away, but then grew serious. " 'Tis bad, Sholto."

"Aye. The bastard kens his business. He makes no move that'll let us even the numbers a wee bit, kenning that he only needs to wait 'til our numbers be fewer, too few to hold him back."

"If he keeps whittling our numbers down, he can stroll in ere nightfall on the morrow."

"Then give him the Sassanach lass," cried the woman who was tending the man Tavis had brought in.

"Nay," spoke up the stablemaster's wife before Tavis could respond. "I want no part o' giving a wee lass tae a man what beats her near tae death. I saw her wounds and no man did that. 'Twas an animal, a beastie no Christian deals with. The man will taek her and still taek us. Ye cannae trust a beastie like that tae act with honor or mercy."

Everyone stared after the usually taciturn woman as she strode away. The other woman turned her attention fully upon the man she was tending and said no more. Briefly, Tavis pondered upon the many and varied friends Storm had quietly acquired while at Caraidland before he turned back to present Sholto with a plan he knew would not meet with approval, speaking so as not to be overheard.

"The man must needs leave off fighting when night falls. I will try to go for help."

"Nay, we are encircled. They will be watching for such an attempt. Ye'll nay get past his watch."

" 'Tis a chance I must take. Our men could be on their way back. E'en if they arenae, an I ride long and hard this night, I can reach Athdara and fetch aid back here ere night falls on the morrow."

"If they have solved their own troubles."

"Aye, but can ye give me another choice?" Sholto's silence told Tavis he could not, and Tavis nodded. "I will slip away as soon as 'tis dark. I have told none but ye. Keep it that way."

As Tavis had expected, Sir Hugh left only a token force around Caraidland when night fell, the rest withdrawing to the camp to rest, yet near enough to be called up quickly if needed. There was nothing to be gained in fighting blind in the night. More would be gained by allowing his forces to recoup some strength for the fight on the morrow. There could not be any escape from Caraidland, of that he had made sure.

Only the wounded were allowed to rest at Caraidland. There was always the chance, however small, that Sir Hugh would try to storm the walls during the night. It would be out of character, for it would risk a high loss of men, but an unexpected move was the one to keep the closest watch for. Lacking patience, the man could be driven to make such a rash move.

Dressed in black and leading an equally black horse, Tavis crept out a side gate. It was a very chancy venture he embarked upon, but there was no other choice. They needed more men and that meant trying to get to Athdara. He could only hope that, if he reached there, whatever trouble there had been at Athdara was now at an end, allowing him to return with not only his own men but perhaps some sword-wielding MacBroths as well.

It was not the best night for trying to creep through an enemy's line of watch. Caraidland's own watch fires cast out unwanted light. There was also a moon, its light unfettered by clouds. It was a little difficult to keep both himself and his horse in the shadows as he edged toward the wood. Tension and the need to be as quiet and careful as possible made what was but yards seem like miles, and minutes like hours.

When he was just inside the wood he mounted, but kept his steed at a walk. To spur his horse to a gallop when he was still so close to Sir Hugh's ring of watches would be foolhardy. Slowly, he made his way through the wood, working at an angle through its dark tangles that would eventually bring him to the road that led to Athdara and, he prayed, far enough along it to be beyond sight and reach of Hugh's minions.

The sigh of partial relief that escaped him when he reached the road got caught in his throat as two horsemen entered the road in front of him. It was almost as if they had been waiting for him, but he knew it was just sheer bad luck that had brought him through at the spot where Sir Hugh had placed a watch. The fact that the men were far beyond the usual place for a guard only proved how wily Sir Hugh was. He had guessed what would be tried and had undoubtedly placed his strongest guard on this side of Caraidland. Tavis cursed, for it also meant that Sir Hugh knew exactly how short of men they were and why.

Although the chance of success was dim, Tavis whirled his horse around and raced for the besieged keep. If he could get near the walls of Caraidland, there were ways to get back in. There was no chance of getting to Athdara, but perhaps he could return to Caraidland, thus saving them the painful loss of yet another man. When they did not immediately loose an arrow his way, his hopes rose, for he realized that Sir Hugh had ordered that anyone trying to slip away was to be brought back alive.

He could see the watch fires of Caraidland when the men chasing him suddenly called out. Two more men appeared in the road directly in front of Tavis as if by magic, and he realized that Sir Hugh had set a guard at several points along the road. The sudden appearance of two horsemen caused Tavis's horse to rear. His own surprise contributed to Tavis's lack of control and he was thrown. As he hit the ground, his last thought before blackness engulfed him was of Storm.

Storm lay in exhausted sleep crowded upon a pallet with Maggie. When night fell and the fighting had ceased the work had shifted from tending the wounded to feeding the men. Maggie had urged her to seek her own bed, but Storm had refused. She wanted to be near the wounded who might need her, near the battle so that she could know when and if it changed in any way and near Tavis. Maggie had ceased arguing and let her stay.

Suddenly, Storm sat up, Tavis's name upon her lips. She wrapped her arms around herself as she shivered, the cold chill of foreboding she so detested seeping into her bones. Careful not to wake Maggie, Storm rose from the pallet. She had to find Tavis and assure herself that she was only suffering from nerves and exhaustion, that he was all right and not in any real danger. Being caught in the middle of a battle could easily make her see danger and tragedy where none existed.

The battlements were lined with women as well as men. Wives, lovers, daughters and mothers stood watching in their men's place while they lay sprawled at their feet in exhausted slumber, still in full battle array. If it were not for the lack of fighting men, such arrangements would never be allowed, but the men knew that the women's eyes were as keen as theirs and that, if trouble came, the men would be ready, sending the women off the battlements. This way the men could catch some much needed sleep and be more ready to face the battle at the sun's rising.

Pausing by Jeanne, who held the watch for her betrothed, Storm asked, "How goes it, Jeanne?"

" 'Tis a verra great bore. I cannae help but wonder how fit for battle Sir Hugh's troops will be, for 'tis a wild and noisy revel agoing on at their camp. Can ye hear it?"

"Aye," Storm replied with a grimace. "I suspect 'tis my father's wife. She has a fondness for orgies."

"What's an orgy? 'Tis sinful, eh?" asked Jeanne in undisguised interest.

Nodding, Storm elaborated. " 'Tis a whole group of men and women drinking and wenching together. Lady Mary prefers the men to outnumber the women. 'Tis naught but lust and lasciviousness."

"Never," breathed Jeanne, her eyes wide with fascination and horror.

"Aye, lass," came a sleepy voice from behind their feet. " 'Tis a fitting description." Ignoring the gasps of embarrassment from the ladies, Jeanne's betrothed asked, "Does she really hold orgies?"

The dark erased most of Storm's discomfort. "Aye. She held them often at Hagaleah. I would lock myself in my chambers with my old nursemaid, Hilda, and a few maids who were not interested in joining such revels."

"Did ye ne'er keek at such goings on?" asked

Jeanne, nudging her lover with her toe when he chuckled.

"Of course not," Storm replied haughtily. "Why should I wish to see naked people bathing in milk and doing lewd things in nearly every room in the keep?" She turned to walk away, but Jeanne halted her.

"Did they really bathe in milk? Stop that tittering, Robbie."

"Aye, they did. I did see that, and a fair bit more, that I'll ne'er tell ye, afore Hilda caught me and dragged me back to my chambers by my hair." She left the young couple laughing softly.

It took her a while to find Sholto, Iain and Colin. The latter two were asleep, but Sholto stood staring out over the battlements. What immediately struck Storm was that he spent as much time staring toward Athdara as he did at Sir Hugh's encampment. She wondered if he expected the momentary arrival of aid from their old allies or the expedient return of all the men they had sent out.

"Ye shouldnae be up here, Storm," Sholto admonished gently. "Ye should be getting some rest."

"Where is Tavis, Sholto?" she asked, not liking the way he avoided looking directly at her.

"He maun be off sleeping," he mumbled, staring out toward the sounds of revelry.

"Sholto, I have looked everywhere and cannot find him. Please, Sholto, where is he?"

"I dinnae ken," he snapped, but then sighed when he caught her expression, which was a mixture of crestfallen and determination. "Here now, lassie," he said gently as he put an arm around her and drew her to his side, "Tavis is a grown man. Ye need nay fear for him."

"Ye do not understand. I woke up so cold and calling his name. 'Tis not a good sign. Please, Sholto . . ."

"Nay. Now, look out there and tell me what that infamous Lady Mary of Hagaleah is up to."

" 'Tis sinful," she mumbled, still afraid for Tavis, but not wanting to press Sholto.

"Ah, a subject dear to my heart and sure to keep me alert. Tell us all, lassie," he said teasingly.

While Storm proceeded to fulfill Sholto's request by reciting all she had ever seen and heard, despite the occasional awkwardness and embarrassment such a recital caused, Tavis was coming to in time to be tossed to the ground before a tent. What he saw when a man briefly lifted the tent flap and stepped out made Tavis wonder if his brains had been rattled. Before he could decide whether or not he had really seen a tangle of naked bodies, he was yanked to his feet. Held roughly between two men, he found himself face to face with Sir Hugh, the very man he ached to kill.

"Well, well," Sir Hugh gloated, rubbing his hands together in glee, "Tavis MacLagan himself. They will give that little redheaded whore now. In fact, she will probably turn herself over to me."

Hugh called for torches and, leading a wristbound Tavis by a rope leash, he marched with ten men toward the walls of Caraidland. They went under a white flag, for Sir Hugh intended to parley. He was confident that he would walk away with Storm in but the time it took to suggest the trade. Then he could take Caraidland on the morrow as a *coup de grace*.

Tavis hoped no trade would be made. He did not want his error to be paid for by Storm. There was little chance that he would be killed, for Sir Hugh would recognize his worth in ransom if, by what now could well take a miracle, Caraidland did not fall. He shrugged away the intruding thought that Sir Hugh could kill him out of spite or even rage, a state in which he reached near madness. *C'est la guerre*, as the French said, he thought wryly, as he struggled to stay upright and turned his gaze to the walls of Caraidland.

Seeing movement in the camp, Storm halted in her telling of sordid tales about Lady Mary. She strained to see clearly, to determine what was going on. Suddenly she tensed and grabbed Sholto by the arm. "Look, Sholto, there is a group approaching with torches and a white flag. Sir Hugh wishes to parley."

As Sholto woke his brother and father, Storm noticed the man on the leash. It was another moment before she recognized who it was that Sir Hugh led. Her heart seemed to stop and she turned stricken eyes to an ashen-faced Sholto.

" 'Tis Tavis. Sir Hugh has Tavis."

18

"MacLagan," Sir Hugh bellowed as his group stopped within feet of the walls of Caraidland.

"No need to shout. I see ye," Colin replied sardonically, causing Tavis to grin slightly.

Yanking Tavis forward, Hugh called, "As you can see, I have your son and heir, Tavis."

"Aye, I can see that just fine." Colin looked at Sholto and asked softly, "How in God's great name did Tavis fall into his hands? Tell me in as few words as possible what that young fool was doing outside these walls."

"He wanted to reach Athadara," Sholto said quickly. "We are sore in need of fighting men."

"Send out the Eldon girl, MacLagan, and I will give you back your son."

"Where the devil are ye going?" Colin snapped as he grasped the arm of a retreating Storm.

"Out to Sir Hugh," she gasped as he yanked her back to his side, "so that he will release Tavis."

"Dinnae be so daft, lassie. Do ye really think Tavis wants that? Nay, lassie, there willnae be a trade." Storm watched speechlessly as Colin replied, "Nay, Hugh, no trade. See, lassie," he added when Tavis waved his bound hands in agreement.

Hugh swore harshly in fury and disbelief. "Let me see the girl. Mayhaps you have naught to trade with."

Colin signaled two men to step forward as he undid the ribbon that held back Storm's hair. "That will leave him in no doubt o' who ye be, lassie. Go on. Step forward and call out to him."

Storm had no idea how well she stood out with her brilliant hair tossed by the wind and the torchlight illuminating it fully as she leaned on the battlement and called, "Did ye wish to see me, Sir Hugh?"

"Aye, I wished to see you," Hugh said, mocking her polite tone of voice. "I have your lover here, Storm."

"Ye cannae let him ken that ye care, lassie," Colin said quietly. "Play it hard, child. Play the cold bitch."

"So ye do. How goes it, Tavis?" she asked idly as she sat down, straddling the parapet.

"It has been better, little one," Tavis called back and, seeing the white of her slim leg against the wall added, "Ye have nay put on any wretched stockings, ye fool lass."

"Mayhaps I thought to incite Hugh's troops to riot," she replied, slowly swinging her leg, causing the people upon the walls to snicker and Tavis to grin fleetingly before an angry Hugh gave a vicious tug on the rope.

"Come out, Storm, and I will release your lover to his family unharmed."

"Why should I when his own father has said 'tis no trade?" she asked idly. "I care not to come to ye."

"Do you care not what happens to your Scottish stallion?" Hugh refused to believe that he had failed, that holding the heir to Caraidland would gain him little.

"Aye, I care, for 'tis a fine stallion he is but, though it will sore grieve me to lose his, shall we say, affections, he is nay irreplacable." She caught Sholto by the hand and tugged him to her side. "I have a wide choice of stud, Sir Hugh." Sholto obligingly put his arm around her. "I will survive the loss." She

226

fought down the embarrassment of speaking so crudely.

"Am I to believe that the proud Storm Eldon has become naught but a whore to the Scots?" sneered Hugh, unaware of how close Tavis had come to attacking his captor, bound wrists and all. "Are you now to be ridden by all?"

" 'Tis a sort ye know well, Sir Hugh. Nay, I merely see no point in giving myself over to a gelding. 'Tis a love of the horses Sir Hugh has," she murmured to Sholto, who laughed as he began to toy with her hair.

Sir Hugh clenched his hands and snarled softly before he shouted, " 'Tis your last chance, Storm Eldon. Come down to me and I will return Tavis to his family. You are the price for his freedom."

"Here is my final answer to your offer, Sir Hugh," Storm called back as she slipped her arms around Sholto's neck and proceeded to kiss him, finding a little too much cooperation on his part.

Tavis was surprised to find that he was not jealous, that he clearly saw it as only part of the little farce being played out for Sir Hugh and that he had absolutely no fear that Storm would really bed Sholto. Sir Hugh looked near to having a seizure as he watched the pair upon the battlements kiss to the hearty encouragement of their fellows. Storm could not have chosen any better way to convince the man that there was no chance of a trade or that she cared little for her lover's fate.

"Methinks ye play the game too seriously, rogue," Storm murmured to Sholto when the kiss ended.

"Play your whore's games then, bitch," Sir Hugh roared. "I will see you crawl yet."

"Only away from ye, Sir Hugh. Always and ever away."

"Think of what I am doing to your lover whilst

you enjoy your new rider, Eldon slut."

Storm did not see Sholto wince as her grip upon his arm tightened convulsively. "I would keep Tavis away from dear Lady Mary, Sir Hugh, or she will see what a wee man ye are."

"Have ye any words of advice, Tavis?" Sholto called as Sir Hugh stormed off, leaving someone else to bring Tavis and causing several of his men to stumble over each other as they tried to light his way.

"Aye," Tavis called as he was led off, "if ye get a bit weary, ye let her do the riding. She likes that. Aye, and Sholto, ye have inherited a mouth worth a king's ransom."

He was not surprised to hear a burst of angry Irish flow from the battlements, although he did not like the way she was standing upon the parapet to hurl the words at him, despite how glorious she looked up there. It was also not to his liking to talk of her that way, but it was necessary to the game. She was playing the cold-hearted whore for Sir Hugh's benefit, and so he had to act as if she were one. A sigh of relief escaped him when she was yanked down from her precarious position and he turned to watch where he was going.

In the dark of the wood on the south side of Caraidland, a lone watcher shared the laughter of the Scots. Hadden had reached his viewing place with ease, for the guard was weak on that side, as no one expected a threat from that direction. He had a long ride before him, but he started on his way with a light heart. Storm was safe and there was clearly no chance that she would be handed over to Sir Hugh.

"Lord, lassie, ye near stopped me puir old heart, standing up there like that," said Colin as he sat next to a now calm and somewhat despondent Storm. " 'Tis a wonder your father's hair wasnae snow white if ye carried on so at Hagaleah. Just what were ye shouting after that impudent son o' mine?"

A weak smile touched her wan face. "Let us just say that, if my curses take, he will be a changed man." She clasped Phelan's hand when he came to sit near her. "Sir Hugh is not a sane man when he is enraged."

"Aye, I ken that weel, lass. Still, 'tis sure I am that he'll nay kill the lad. The possible ransom will tempt him. I ken he is a greedy man, and Tavis is like coin in his hand. He'll nay toss it aside." He patted her shoulder. "Go and rest, lass. Dawn will bring a fair bit o' work for ye ladies."

As he watched her leave with Phelan, Sholto murmured, "That Tavis is one lucky bastard."

"I kenned ye were enjoying that kiss," Colin said with a chuckle. " 'Tis a sweet mouth, I ken."

"Lord, it turns a man's bones to water. Are we to leave Tavis in Sir Hugh's hands then?"

"We maun do so, lad, though it grieves me. Sir Hugh will not kill the lad. He'll have an eye to the possible ransom," Colin mused, voicing Tavis's assumptions. "They will be awatching for an attempt to free him, and I cannae lose e'en one fighting man. When the battle begins in the morn he may e'en be safer there."

Storm thought that Tavis was in extreme danger, although she, too, felt that Sir Hugh would not kill him. She sat drinking ale with Maggie and Phelan, her mind picturing all that Sir Hugh would do to Tavis. The man might not kill Tavis, but he could have Tavis praying that he would. At long last, an idea came to her. Maggie needed some hearty persuading, but soon not only provided them with what was needed but even told her and Phelan of a way to slip out of Caraidland.

Sholto saw a small figure dart to the stables and frowned. Thinking Iain asleep, he quietly left his post to follow. Iain watched him through half-closed eyes and, after a moment, followed him. He, too, had seen the small figure, and he knew that Sholto's admiration for his eldest brother's lover had been deepened to a dangerous level by the kiss and the tense yet stirring atmosphere of battle. They faced a fight and, quite possibly, death on the morrow. Iain feared it would make Sholto reckless.

At the back of the stables Storm busily cleared off a trap door. It opened up to a tunnel that would lead her out into the wood on the Eldon side of Caraidland. Maggie had explained that it had been used for slipping out during a siege and raiding the Eldon camp. It would serve her purposes excellently.

It was not until she flopped on her back upon a pile of straw that she realized she was not alone. Wide-eyed, she stared up at Sholto. His gaze was busily surveying her attire of a black tunic, snug black breeches and soft dark boots. Her hand nervously clutched a black knit cap and black gloves. Neither saw Iain slip into the stables and find a spot to watch from, yet not be seen.

"Planning to go somewhere, lass?" Sholto drawled, his gaze lingering on her heaving breasts.

Too distraught to fully notice desire's hold on Sholto, she replied, "Aye. To get Tavis."

"Nay. I cannae allow that." His gaze drifted to her glorious hair and he ached.

"Why not? Do ye have any better ideas?" she snapped, her annoyance at being caught winning out over diplomacy.

"Aye, I do, lass," he said softly, "but they havenae a muckle lot to do with rescuing Tavis."

Too late she recognized the look in his indigo eyes. She gasped in surprise when he pinned her down onto the hay with his lean body. He took ready advantage of her parted lips. To her shame, his kiss brought a response from her. He was very experienced and she was very vulnerable.

"Nay, Sholto," she groaned as his mouth worked its way to her throat, but she had no strength to fight.

"Aye, Storm."

His nimble fingers found and quickly undid the laces of her tunic. To his delight, she wore nothing underneath. First his eyes, then his hands moved over what he thought of as perfection. The hardened nipples tantalized his palms and proved her desire. He tore his gaze from her breasts to look into her eyes. A shaky, indrawn breath hissed through his teeth as he met eyes of molten gold, a sight that had always sent Tavis reeling. There was, however, more than desire to be read there; there was desperation.

"Do not do this," she pleaded softly even as she arched against him in reaction to his caress.

"Ye want me," he said huskily as his thumbs teased the taut ends of her breasts until she moaned. "Your body tells me that in a dozen different ways." His fingers unlaced her breeches.

"My body has been well taught. Aye, it screams yes, but my heart and mind scream nay."

" 'Tis not them I seek to possess," he growled as his hungry mouth played over her breasts.

Storm nearly sank beneath a wave of indiscriminate desire. Iain felt for her. He knew her emotions were running high and that she was vulnerable. The man she loved, and he was sure she loved Tavis, was in serious danger. The man she loved had also never spoken of love. She was in the midst of a battle, caught on the inside with her hereditary enemies while a new and more dangerous foe lurked outside. She was also alone, her kin and friends dead. It was not fair of Sholto to take advantage of that extreme vulnerability, yet Iain could understand it. On the morrow they could die. Just once Sholto wanted to taste all he had admired from a distance. Iain had felt the urge himself, but had concealed it. He would see that Sholto controlled his desire as well, but he could not break in yet. It would be better for them to resolve it themselves.

"Please, Sholto, do not," she gasped as his hand slid inside her breeches to caress that which only Tavis had ever known. "I do not want this. I do not," she stressed, but her voice was husky with desire.

He lifted his head from the breasts he had been savoring to stare at her, one hand brushing the hair from her face while his other continued to caress her womanhood. "Your mouth says nay, but this"—he felt her squirm beneath his gentle, seductive probing—"this says aye. 'Tis warm and ready for a man."

She tried to pull his tormenting hand away, but when she clutched his arms her fingers would not pull, only grip. " 'Tis just that I have no control. There is so much troubling me, making me weak. Do not take advantage of that. Heed my words, not my body, for it betrays me. This is so very wrong."

Cupping her face between his hands, he settled himself between her thighs and moved against her with a subtle urgency that made her tremble. "Is it? Feel what ye do to a man. Is it wrong for me to want to satisfy that? I want ye and I want to satisfy that craving ere I meet what could be my last dawn."

"That is unfair," she whispered. "First ye play upon my passions and now my sympathy."

"Lass, an it will get me inside, 'tis little I willnae do. He doesnae love ye," he said, and suddenly knew that he lied.

"I know."

"He willnae wed ye. Comes the time or the choice, and ye will be on a horse back to England."

"I know that too."

"Then why, lass? Why deny the wants of our bodies? The pleasure we could share?"

It was difficult to keep from weeping, but she replied in a small voice, "I love Tavis."

Sholto went very still and studied her. Then, with a groan, he collapsed upon her, burying his face in her breasts, and his hands clenched into fists at each side of her head. She lay still for a moment to see what he would do next, but then she shifted a little beneath the weight of him.

"God's teeth, woman," he rasped. "Dinnae move. Lie as still as the dead. If ye wriggle, I'll be at ye again."

Storm lay so still she nearly forgot to breathe. It was a few moments before he rose to his knees and began to do up her laces. His face was pale and drawn, and Storm felt both sorry and guilty. If she had not responded, he would not be suffering the ache of unfillfilled desire.

"Ye would have hated yourself afterward," she said softly as he moved off of her to sprawl on his back at her side.

"I ken that. I'm nay too fond of meself now." He took a deep breath. "I am sorry, lass."

" 'Tis naught, Sholto," she murmured, and meant it, as she tucked her hair into her cap. "Phelan will be along soon."

"Oh, aye?" Sholto sat up. "Ye arenae going out o' Caraidland, lass."

"I am. Phelan and I are going to bring Tavis back."

"Nay, 'tis foolhardy. He'll be all right. Sir Hugh willnae kill him. He's worth a high ransom."

"Aye. I am sure Sir Hugh will keep Tavis alive for that. At least until he is certain of victory. 'Tis not that which I fear. Ye do not know the man as I do."

"I ken that he's a bastard what beats wee lasses near to death and consorts with an amoral whore."

Sholto grabbed her gloves away before she could don them. "Tavis can hold through a beating, lass."

"I am sure he can, though I have little wish that he must needs prove it. That, too, is not what I fear. The man wants me for my fortune, though I think 'tis also because I say nay to him. That enrages him. It enrages him that another man has had what he saw as his. The way Tavis humiliated him that day also enrages him. Sir Hugh is not a sane man when he gets into a rage. He also enjoys inflicting pain. He, as well as Lady Mary, are stirred by the inflicting of pain. So stirred that they made love by my side ere they ceased beating me."

"Nay," Sholto breathed, and his grip went lax, allowing her to retrieve her gloves.

"Aye. There is something else ye ought to know about Sir Hugh. When he wants a woman but she says nay and turns to another beating the man is not all he does. Aye, Tavis would be returned alive, but he could well be returned no longer a whole man. Sir Hugh's way of punishing a man who possesses what he wants is to remove that which does the possessing. He has done so to two men that I know of. That is what his parting words meant. He knew I would understand his threat."

"Ye say this to get me to let ye go," Sholto said, but he was deeply shaken by her words.

"Nay. She speaks the simple truth," Phelan said, causing everyone to jump with surprise, for even Iain had not seen him enter. " 'Tis a method that works. Men turn their backs when he reaches for their women, and women all say aye."

Nearly choking on the words, Sholto said, "Mayhaps the deed is already done."

"I think there is time, for Lady Mary could ne'er turn aside a man like Tavis. She will want use of him as a man ere Sir Hugh changes that, mayhaps e'en promise it will not be done an he performs well."

Sholto rubbed his hands over his face. "How can a lad and a wee lass save him?"

"We are very good at sneaking about. Ye did not hear Phelan arrive just now, did ye?"

"Nay, but then, I wasnae expecting anyone. They will be looking for a rescue sortie to be made."

"Aye, but mayhaps not from the direction of Hagaleah. By using this tunnel, we shall circle about upon them and approach from the south. Then, too, they will expect men, not two wee ones."

"I cannae like it. Father said nay to the trade. He doesnae want ye in that man's hands."

"He also expects Sir Hugh to follow the rules of hostage-holding, and the man will not. Sholto, I must go. Surely ye must see that?"

"Aye, but that doesnae make me feel right about ye going."

"Ye cannot lose any more sword arms so ye cannot send fighting men. They would be killed if caught. Phelan and I will not be. We are also not important to the defense of Caraidland. E'en if we were caught, I can see to Tavis's release an only I threaten to kill myself ere Hugh weds my fortune."

"Do ye have a weapon?" he asked, which they all saw as the agreement it was.

Phelan held up two stout sticks. "Shillelaghs. Do not frown. We know how to use them."

"Aye. We know just where and how to strike to send a man down with nary a grunt." Storm held out a short, straight, double-edged dagger. "A skain. A good old Irish weapon. 'Twas my mother's. I know well how to use this too. Papa showed me. Just as good, I can make a man believe I will use it. Do not worry for us."

"I begin not to. Go then, lass, and take care. I will ensure that our watch doesnae cut ye down when ye return. What are ye doing now?" he asked as they smeared soot on their faces.

"Ensuring that our wee pale faces do not give us away." Storm opened the hatch to the tunnel.

"Who told ye o' this?" He watched as Phelan lit a covered lantern.

"Ne'er ye mind. We swore not to tell a soul, so it matters not."

He caught her hand as she started to follow Phelan into the tunnel. Already he was suffering doubts about the wisdom of the venture. Pushing them aside, he gave her a hearty kiss, grinning when she blushed.

" 'Twas for luck, lass. I will close the trap and leave it unlocked. Go on with ye."

An instant after he had shut the trap, Sholto heard someone approach. Startled, he looked up at Iain. With a sinking feeling, Sholto had a good idea that Iain knew all that had gone on.

"An anyone can do it, she and that lad can, an only through sheer pigheadedness. Why did ye stop?"

Sholto flushed a little, knowing what Iain referred to. "Three little words."

"Which were?"

" 'I love Tavis.' I kenned then that it wasnae right. She would have been shamed and hurt, and I didnae want that but, God's tears, I did, do want her."

Iain gripped his shoulder in understanding. "Aye. I have felt it too."

"Weel, let us be back to our posts." Sholto stood up. "I will ne'er sleep a wink 'til they are back."

Storm shuddered as they made their way through the dark, cramped tunnel. It was damp and musty, and cloaked in cobwebs. She was glad the light was too weak to show her all that scurried about.

They emerged just inside the wood on the south

side of Caraidland. The entrance to the tunnel was cleverly concealed, yet Storm had no worry about finding it again. She and Phelan began to circle their way toward Tavis.

Within clear hearing distance of the camp, they met their first stumbling block. A one-man watch had been set out, and, although leisurely in his patrol, he was alert. He was also too awkwardly placed to knock out. Nodding to Phelan and hoping he would catch on, Storm shed her cap and stepped boldly forward.

The guard gaped at the apparition before him. Despite the dirty face and male attire, he knew a pretty wench when he saw one. New to work at Hagaleah, he did not know Lord Eldon's daughter when he saw her. Holding his sword at the ready, he edged toward her.

"Who be ye?"

"No one of importance. I seek to avoid the battle."

"Discard all yer weapons."

"I have none. Shall I prove it to you?"

With enticing deliberation, she began to unlace her tunic, then her breeches, calmly watching his lust blind his good judgment. Both items fell open to reveal glowing skin, but she knew she must do more. Swallowing her shame, she slowly bared her breasts. A guttaral cry escaped the guard as he dropped his sword and lunged. Storm hit the ground with a breath-robbing thud, but an instant later she was free of the weight. Phelan had understood, knocked the guard out and pulled him off of her.

Tucking her hair back inside her cap, Storm watched Phelan finish tying and gagging the man. "I hope he is the only one."

"Aye." Phelan collected his club. "Let us be on our way to Tavis."

"I only pray that we are in time."

19

Rescue was something that Tavis found himself fervently praying for. He had not expected any sort of risky sortie, but now he wished for one. Briefly he had wished that the trade had been made, but only briefly, for nothing would induce him to put Storm into the hands of the man who stood before him, not even the bone-chilling terror of the threat Hugh now made.

Still reeling from a flogging, his arms still strapped to the posts, he had glared at Sir Hugh as the man had stepped in front of him. He had thought he would be cut down, if only to be allowed to rest so that he would be strong enough to survive another beating. All his muscles had contracted when the knife Sir Hugh held had nudged his groin. Now a cold sweat came out on his skin, stinging his wounds, but he struggled to give no sign of his very real terror as he continued to glare at a sweetly smiling Sir Hugh.

" 'Tis surely a crime for a lowly border Scot to possess such as Storm Eldon," Hugh mused aloud. "Do you know the quality of the blood in the lady's veins?"

"Nay. It wasnae that I was interested in." Tavis winced inwardly as the knife pressed against him.

"This arrogant fellow has been delving in and out of some of the best stock in all of England."

"And weel he has enjoyed it." This time Sir Hugh drew a little blood, and Tavis swallowed his terror.

"So should have. The young Eldons trace their lineage back to the Conqueror, to Saxon and Irish kings. 'Tis far too rich a mixture for a Scot to be enjoying. What, by sweet heaven, are you doing here, Mary?" he growled when that lady stepped up to his side.

Tavis studied the infamous Lady Mary Eldon and saw nothing that he liked. She was beautiful, with a body any man would want, but her eyes revealed her soul, and that was pure filth. He watched her relieve Sir Hugh of his knife and begin to cut him down. Her nearness only sickened him, but he hid it well. He felt certain she could prove as great, if not greater, a danger to him than Sir Hugh if she was angered.

"Your little games can wait awhile." As two guards quickly bound Tavis's free hands, she purred, "I have need of you now. Let him sweat over his fate for a while."

As Tavis was led to the edge of the camp, he heard Hugh growl, "You do not fool me. I know why you wish his punishment delayed. Have you ne'er had a Scot before?"

Leading him to the tent, Mary replied, "Nay, but I surely intend to ere dawn comes."

From where he was set, Tavis had a clear view inside the tent. The entrance was turned away from the rest of the camp, with one flap turned up to allow for fresh air. He had the feeling they were in dire need of that. There were nearly a dozen people inside, twice as many men as women, and few of them were dressed. The unintentional voyeurism brought him an initial surge of desire as he watched a brown-skinned woman shed her robe, kneel before a young, nearly beautiful man sprawled upon some cushions and begin to leisurely pleasure him with her mouth. That waned as the pair became a trio, then a quartet, until there was a veritable tangle of naked bodies.

"Aye, it soon loses its attraction," the guard at his side grumbled, and Tavis nodded.

It was awhile before Lary Mary, wearing a revealing robe, stolled over to Tavis. She knelt before him, her eyes greedy. Here was a man, and it enraged her that Storm had such a lover. Lady Mary fully intended to sample his skill and virility before Sir Hugh ended it. Her tongue ran over her lips, revealing her hunger to taste such lean, muscular perfection. She was unaware of the eyes that watched her from the enshadowed wood, unaware of how close she came to dying had not Phelan restrained Storm.

Placing her hand upon his manhood, she purred, "The gentleman is at rest for the moment."

"It only salutes a lady," Tavis said coldly, flinching when her caressing hand brought a sharp pain.

"You should be careful, Scotsman. I could be your only chance to save this poor fellow. Come with me now and let me show you how a woman handles a man. You have tasted but a child, who could not begin to appreciate the stallion you are. Come to my tent now and let me show you true pleasure."

"I wouldst rather spill my seed into a man." Tavis could not hide his very real pain when her hand became a fist that left him doubled over and gasping.

"Fool." Mary surged to her feet, enraged by his rejection, verbal and physical, for her expert hand had brought no reaction. "You have 'til the hour before dawn to change your mind. If you still say nay, I will gladly sharpen the knife Sir Hugh will use to make you a gelding, and I will see that the cut is not quick and clean, but slow, tiny piece by tiny piece until naught remains. Think on that, border reiver."

For a while Tavis could only think of sheer agony

in his loins. He rolled about doubled over for a moment, until he came to rest against a tree, his forehead pressed against the rough bark. Something caused him to open his eyes, and he briefly glimpsed amber ones. When the guard bent to offer him a drink of ale Tavis feared he was going mad. The guard's next words eased that fear.

"Lass, ye should not be this near to Sir Hugh. Ye and the lad scamper away now."

Storm peered at Matthew, edging out of the bushes and keeping to the shelter of the tree. "How did ye know, Matthew?"

"Ye and the lad be the only things human with a cat's eyes that I know of."

"What fool let ye out of Caraidland, and what in the name of God have ye got on your faces?" Tavis hissed.

"Such gratitude. 'Tis ash to hide our fair skin. We have come to get you away from here."

"Ye will have to touch me with them clubs o' yours first, lass. I can't be left awake ere he leaves."

"I feared that." She began to cut the ropes binding Tavis's wrists, Matthew's bulk shielding her actions.

"I was sore grieved to hear o' the fates o' your kin and the Fosters."

Despite her efforts, a lone tear streaked a trail down Storm's begrimed cheek. "Thank ye, Matthew. There, Tavis."

Rubbing the numbness from his wrists as subtly as he was able, Tavis said, "This is madness, little one. 'Twill be but one moment ere they see that I have fled. Get yourself out o' here now, love."

"Ye give me no credit for brains do ye, Tavis? I have thought this out well." She caught the wrapped bundle of rushes Phelan edged toward her. " 'Tis shadowy here. This should serve to fool them for a while. I shall place this blackened rope 'round

Matthew to hold him to the tree and he will appear to still be awatch." She suited action to words with Matthew's compliance, and Tavis's eyes showed his growing admiration. "That 'tis Matthew I must deal with makes my plotting work more smoothly," she added modestly. "Forgive me, Matthew," she murmured, and dropped a kiss on his cheek before she hit him, silently sending him into blackness.

The switch of the bundle for Tavis was made quickly and neatly. But an instant later the trio were loping through the woods toward Caraidland. Thoughts of the fate awaiting him at Sir Hugh's hands gave Tavis strength despite the pain in his abused back and the soreness in his loins. He flicked a glance at the trussed-up guard as they passed him, and he shook his head. The little pair was a wonder.

A heavy covering on the floor of the wood allowed them to leave no discernible trail, and they were glad of that when sounds of pursuit reached their ears. If luck was with them, they could reach and be in the tunnel before they were spotted. Tavis did not ask them how they knew of the tunnel as they dove for its haven, shutting and bolting the hatch after them. All he could think of was that he was free, free and whole.

Colin fixed a stern eye upon the group gathered at the table set in one of the few empty spots left in the great hall. He had had no idea of what was afoot until an uproar broke out in Sir Hugh's camp. Iain and Sholto had fled for the stables while all the guards on the south walls had readied themselves as if for an attack. Though he rejoiced with the rest over the clever, successful rescue of his heir and had been made aware of the horror Sir Hugh had planned for Tavis, Colin felt he ought to make some stand against such disobedience.

"I ken I said there wouldnae be any attempt

made," he growled, glaring at them all.

"But, me' lord ye gave Phelan and me no such command."

He stared into two pairs of wide, guileless eyes and two surprisingly innocent, if begrimed, faces and burst out laughing. The rest soon joined in. To Storm's intense embarrassment, she found herself the center of attention. Even worse, Phelan began to blithely recite the full tale of how they had managed to silence the watch. Sholto eased that some by relating an absurd plan to use the same ploy on the whole of Sir Hugh's army when they began the attack anew at dawn. She soon forgot most of her embarrassment in all the laughter at his nonsense.

Tavis awoke to the fact that time was swiftly passing by. All too soon he would be back upon the walls to fight Sir Hugh. Their numbers were so few, it was doubtful they could hold out all that long. He knew just how he wished to spend the remaining time before dawn. His back still burned, but that seemed to have no effect on the desire for Storm that suddenly surged through him. Grabbing her by the hand, he excused them from the table and hurried her off to their chambers.

Sholto sighed as he watched Storm's slim hips sway gently out of the hall, her long, thick hair keeping rhythm as she walked alongside Tavis. He had stopped himself from making love to her, but he had not stopped wanting to. An excess of guilt over what he had done and still wanted to do plagued him. A grinning Iain refilled his tankard. Laughing ruefully, Sholto did his best to empty it.

Lying on his side, wearing only his braes, Tavis watched Storm wash up. She had risked all to come and save him. He suddenly craved knowing why, exactly what she felt for him. Neither cursing himself for a maudlin fool nor reminding himself that he had little to give in return did much to fully kill that craving.

"Storm?" he called softly.

"Aye, Tavis?" She padded over to stand by the bed, looking down at him.

" 'Tis an awful risk ye took coming after me as ye did." He reached out to play with a lock of her hair.

"I could not leave ye in Sir Hugh's hands. I understood his parting threat, ye see."

"I'm nay ashamed to admit I was in a cold sweat for a time there. Got a good keek at how they carry on. 'Tis a wonder ye came away from that unsullied."

"Am I unsullied, Tavis?" she asked softly.

"Aye, little one. It doesnae matter what I have done, that I have had my pleasure of ye."

" 'Twas my pleasure, too, Tavis," she murmured as she reached out and gently touched his chest.

"Shed your clothes, *m'eudail*," he ordered softly in a voice already thickening. "Nay, dinnae blush so. Put aside your modesty for what little is left of this night. It could be my last," he said, mostly to himself.

Storm fell to her knees and placed trembling fingers over his mouth. "Do not speak so, Tavis."

He watched as her eyes overflowed with tears, and reached out a finger to brush one from her cheek. "And would ye grieve for me then, lass?"

"Aye, Tavis. Sorely."

Wondering why that should make it easier to face the dawn, he gently kissed her. "Undress for me, Storm. Stand boldly before me just this once."

Slowly, she got to her feet, jesting nervously, "I may be standing, but 'twill nay be too boldly."

Tavis smiled, knowing how hard she had to fight her innate modesty to fulfill his request and inordinately pleased that she would do so for him. His pleasure changed direction as she shed her clothes.

Fire and candlelight glowed over her skin, and he thought her glorious. When she at last stood naked before him his gaze moved hungrily over her full, high breasts, tiny waist and slim hips, lingering on all his most favorite places. Reaching out, he took the same survey with his hand.

"Sweet heaven, lass, but ye are bonnie. 'Tis nay wonder that man went wild ere ye showed him these." He cupped each breast in turn, his gaze locked with hers. "They fit in a man's hands so perfectly, the tips rising quickly, begging to be tasted, rolled about on my tongue. Skin like silk," he said as his hand continued its journey down her body. "It caresses a man. Hips but gently rounded, and such slim thighs, but they cradle a man so weel, drive him mad. But this is heaven's gate, these silken, copper curls hide a haven a man would kill for. Undress me, little one, and take me into your warmth."

His hands, eyes and husky words were all caresses stirring her past caring about her nakedness. Her hands shook as she unlaced his braes. The continued movement of his hand over her body made her fear she would soon buckle at the knees. When he was as naked as she he pulled her down onto the bed. She had just begun to wonder how they would manage when he cocked her leg around his waist and eased into her, his mouth possessing hers hungrily as they became joined.

They rode to the height slowly and deliciously. It was a ride they took again and again, until sleep stole their need for each other. Tavis lay sprawled across her, his head nestled upon her breasts. One of Storm's slim legs was bent at the knee and resting against his hip. Her arms held him close even in sleep as her cheek rested upon his hair. Tavis's body was her only covering.

Getting no answer to their knock, Iain and Sholto stepped quietly into the room. They both stared at the couple upon the bed, each wishing it was he in such a soft haven. For them the time past had been spent curled up with a plaid. There was no sweet, loving woman to ease the wait for dawn.

"Ye would think his backside would freeze," Sholto whispered as he slowly approached the bed.

Iain chuckled softly. "Mayhaps he overheated it."

Opening one eye, Tavis looked at his brothers. "Humor at this hour is near to sacrilege." He grimaced when Storm murmured his name in her sleep, her small foot briefly caressing his calf and one small hand sliding down to rest at the base of his spine. "If ye twa fools will turn around a moment, I will rise."

"I suspicion ye already have," Sholto murmured as they turned, and Iain laughed.

Tavis grunted at the truth of that as he carefully extracted himself from Storm's embrace. The way she only turned upon her side, still asleep despite the disturbance, showed how exhausted she was. Even if he had the time, he did not think he had the heart to wake her up just to satisfy his lust again.

"Ye can turn round again," he told his brothers as he picked up his breeches.

"Dinnae ken why I bothered, an all I get to see is ye." Sholto's eyes danced at the plain evidence of Tavis's desire for his sleeping lady. "Greedy man, arenae ye." He laughed off Tavis's disgusted look.

"Aye." Tavis reached out and gently caressed Storm's tangled hair before he abruptly headed out the door. "Any sign that the enemy prepares a new attack?" he asked as they went down the stairs.

"The sound of their preparations echo clearly in the still dawn," Iain replied.

"Curse it. We are so few. Weel, luck may be with us and help will arrive in time," Tavis said, expressing the hope of every soul still alive within the walls of Caraidland.

Lord Eldon scowled into the darkness in the direction of the besieged Caraidland. He had not liked sending young Hadden out to recconnoiter, but there had been no better choice for the job. Whether by skill or sheer luck, Hadden had the ability to come within spitting distance of the enemy, watch and leave unseen. Lord Eldon was more worried about what sort of news the young man would bring back. When his nephew finally rode into camp Lord Eldon nearly yanked him from the saddle in his eagerness to hear the news. Whether it was good or bad, he needed to know, and know immediately.

"How goes it at Caraidland?" he asked his nephew as they sat around a campfire sipping mulled cider.

"They are putting up a gallant fight considering they are only at half their strength. I would prefer not to admire the MacLagans, but I can do naught else at this time. Hugh makes no rushes, no attempt to storm the keep. 'Tis a slow picking off of the Scots he is working for."

"Do you think he is succeeding in that strategy?" asked Lord Foster.

"Aye, there were women upon the battlements taking the night watch."

"Which means MacLagan has no men to replace the holes made, none to take the place of the weary so that they might rest. All his force is upon the walls." Eldon shook his head. "Without men they could have to fall back to the keep itself, lose the outer bailey."

Hadden nodded. "Spread too thin and the wall could be scaled. Hugh may try just that on the morrow." He took a long drink before announcing, "I saw Storm."

"Upon the walls?" asked Eldon, not truly surprised. "They have not given her o'er to Hugh?"

"Nay, and I think you need not worry that they will. While I watched, Hugh approached to parlay. Seems an attempt was made to go for aid, but the man was caught. Hugh wished to trade the man for Storm."

Eldon's brows quirked high upon his forehead. "MacLagan refused the trade?"

"Aye. Hugh was rather taken aback for, you see, his prisoner was MacLagan's heir, Tavis MacLagan himself."

Among Hadden's audience only Lord Eldon did not gape, though it was hard for him not to. "That lad said they were fond of her, but this goes beyond all hope. Mayhaps that explains her place upon the walls."

" 'Tis possible for they put her forward to make plain to Hugh that she cared little for the fate of her—" Hadden stopped abruptly as he realized what he was about to say to Eldon.

"Lover," Eldon completed, the word hissed from between tightly clenched teeth. "I am aware of the place my daughter holds at Caraidland. How did this Tavis take to the refusal of the ransom?"

" 'Twas plain he approved fully of his father's refusal. Raised his bound hands in agreement. Hugh had the man on a leash. Storm sent Hugh into a rage with her refusal to come out in exchange."

"Convinced him she was not concerned o'er Tavis MacLagan's fate, did she?"

"Aye, Andrew." Hadden grinned. "She did look glorious, straddling the parapet with her hair down and blowing free. Tavis scolded her for wearing no stockings and she said she hoped to put Hugh's troops to riot." He was relieved to see that even Eldon laughed. "Hugh said he would see her crawl and she said, 'Only away from ye.' "

"How did she convince Hugh that she cared not what fate Tavis McLagan met?" Eldon asked.

Hadden was reluctant to tell just how; however, his uncle's gaze pressed him to. "She convinced him she had a replacement already. Kissed one of the other sons afore all, with the Scots cheering her on. Sent Sir Hugh into a near blind rage, it did. Stormed off to his camp and Lady Mary."

"Did you see aught of my dear wife?" Eldon turned his frustrated rage upon the one he saw as the cause of all his daughter's troubles.

"Aye. She had set up a large tent and, well . . ." Hadden shrugged and blushed.

"Is whoring away the hours," Eldon said succinctly. "There is no need to mince words, lad. What of their men?"

"It was hard to see. Sir Hugh has a sizable force. It seems Lady Mary has bought herself one as well. I recognized some of your old guard. A quarter, mayhaps a third, could come o'er to us. You are their liege lord still, and I cannot believe all of them enjoy what has replaced you for a time."

"Let us hope 'tis a third, for we are few. Get some rest, lad. You did well."

As the younger men rose, Andrew paused to ask, "About Storm? Have ye thought on her and Tavis MacLagan?"

"Little else, son. Hadden's news shows that they protect her from Sir Hugh, who would do far more than dishonor her. What is her virtue compared to her life? Was she not left without protectors? A ransom refused makes all the rules of hostage-holding invalid. I have decided to go by what she says or does."

Andrew frowned in slight confusion. "Meaning?"

"Meaning I will do naught an it is her wish. She has lived with these people many long months and a close watch upon her being all that distinguished her as a prisoner, not a clan member. An I took up sword against the MacLagans, it could hurt her more than anything they have done. If she cries for vengeance, she shall have it; otherwise, I begin to think I will take her back to Hagaleah and let it all be forgotten. By shielding her from Hugh they have granted her a life in exchange for her virtue. To me, her father who loves her, 'tis a fair enough exchange."

"I would also rather have her alive than virginal and dead, seduced and unwed than raped and beaten in marriage. Good night, Father."

After the others had departed Foster studied a pensive Eldon. "Do you speak what is truly in your heart and mind or simply what you wish or think should be there?"

" 'Tis truly how I feel. I treasure her life far more than her virtue, even her honor or mine own. The feeling is bred upon the idea that she has not been abused. If she comes to me hurting, physically or in her heart, I will run a sword through the bastard."

20

Tavis looked up from the sword he sharpened, and his eyes narrowed as he saw guilt and embarrassment reflected upon Sholto's handsome face. A vision of Sholto and Storm kissing upon the battlements filled his mind, and he suddenly grew cold. Part of him flinched from the confession he could see forming upon Sholto's lips, from the pain he knew it would bring, while another part demanded it.

"This isnae easy for me to say, Tavis, but, seeing as a man always faces death ere he picks up a sword, I have to say it. 'Tis a guilt I maun get out o' my heart."

"Go on." Tavis's hand clenched his sword hilt until his knuckles whitened.

"God's beard." Sholto looked around briefly, then returned his gaze to Tavis. "I tried my fiercest to have your woman, Tavis."

"Tried?" The chill began to leave his bones.

"Aye. Tried. Och, she's a warm lassie, and I'm nay being vain when I say I ken how to stir a woman, but she ne'er stopped saying nay. She was right in saying I'd hate myself. I do, and I didnae e'en get what I was after. It wasnae right going after her the moment ye werenae about, but I wanted her that bad, I didnae care whose woman she was."

Standing up, Tavis sheathed his sword as he faced Sholto. "Did her eyes grow warm?"

"Like liquid gold."

Clasping Sholto's shoulder, Tavis said, "If ye looked into eyes like that, I cannae see how ye pulled back."

"It wasnae easy," came Sholto's heartfelt reply.

A grin touched Tavis's face, and he said, "Ye could have taken her but ye didnae. 'Tis naught."

"Would it have mattered an I had?" Sholto asked out of curiosity, knowing he had been forgiven.

"Aye. Ye could have taken Katerine right afore my eyes and I wouldnae have cared but"—he shrugged, for he did not understand his feelings—"Storm is mine. 'Tis how I see it."

"Yours until ye tire o' her or she returns to Hagaleah?"

Curtly, Tavis nodded. It was not a subject he liked to dwell upon. Sholto sensed that and asked no more questions.

They were about to mount up to the battlements when Storm dashed over to them. Tavis watched Sholto's eyes flicker with banked hunger, and his arms encircled her with a more evident possessiveness when she flung herself into them.

"Ye tiptoed away without a word," she murmured, trying to hide the tears that threatened.

"Ah, ye would rather I stomp," he said seriously, his eyes alive with laughter.

"Your concept of humor eludes me," Storm said dryly, but then discarded teasing and held him tightly. "Send me to Sir Hugh, Tavis, and put an end to this. 'Tis my battle, not yours."

Resting his chin upon the top of her head, Tavis replied, "Nay, lass. He has raised a sword against Caraidland no matter what the cause, and that makes it our fight. Just as every soul here kens how 'twas ye who saved the laird's life, so do they ken what that bastard means to do with ye. 'Tis not our way to repay a life by giving up one to certain death. Ye have no kin, and Lady Mary gave ye to me. Weel, what is mine stays mine; an I maun lift sword to keep it, so I will."

Her hands gripped his shirt at the back as she fought against speaking the words that crowded into her mouth. It was not right to send a man off to battle with tears and expressions of fears for his life. A woman must be brave, act as if she is certain that her man will return alive. She felt his hands caress her hair and forced her very real fear to recede for the moment. Out of his sight she could weep and wring her hands as much as she wanted to. She looked up at him.

"Oh, well, there is none that can say I did not give it a try. Ye are a stubborn man, MacLagan."

"That I am, Sassanach. So are ye. Stubborn as a summer's day is long, so I will have a promise from ye here and now. Ye'll nay go tripping out to the man. Swear to it, lass." He quirked a brow when she clamped her lips together. "I will tie ye and that tiptoeing cousin o' yours to a keg an I must. Swear that ye will stay within these walls and nay do anything foolish."

"I swear," she muttered. "Ye play unfair. 'Tis no fun to be read so well. I had this plan . . ."

"Aye, I kenned that. Tend to the wounded, lass. 'Tis where ye are truly needed, not hurling yourself into the fray like some ancient sacrifice. Now, off with ye. There is a battle that willnae wait on me."

When he touched his mouth to hers her hands delved into his hair, holding his mouth to hers for a kiss that held all her love for him. Finally releasing him, she pressed her cheek to his. Suddenly, it was important that he know how she felt. Pride was an insignificant thing at such a time.

"Ye are the sun of my world, Tavis MacLagan. Without ye all would be cold and dark. I love ye."

She slipped free of his arms, arms grown lax from sheer astonishment. Sholto, who was looking at his brother in obvious puzzlement, had his turn to be surprised when she pressed a brief kiss upon his mouth. She then swiftly disappeared into the keep, not wanting to wait around for any possible discussion over her impulsive admission. That, with luck, would come later.

"What did the lass say to leave ye looking as if ye have been pole-axed?"

"Naught, Sholto," Tavis replied, shaking free of his shock, yet discovering that he did not want to believe his own words. "Only sweet words to make a man fight all the harder so that the battle will end and he can be back with her. They didnae mean more than that."

"Are ye certain?" Sholto had an idea of exactly what Storm had said.

"Aye. She says such things because of what I maun face." He started toward the battlements. "That which we best get to ere it begins without us."

All was tense and quiet upon the walls of Caraidland. The men watched Sir Hugh's forces gather with an eye to guessing his strategy. Each one knew that they were weak, were up against great odds and could well lose the day. Although each knew it, they faced the knowledge bravely, prepared to fight to the last man. The bringing down of Caraidland would cost Sir Hugh dearly indeed.

Tavis's eyes were fixed upon Sir Hugh's men, but his thoughts were with Storm. He wanted her words to be true, wanted her to be bound to him in that way. It was more than the way she could heat his blood with just a look, then cool the fire in the most satisfying way he had ever known. Never had he liked so much about one woman, from the color of her eyes to the extent of her independent nature. Not since Mary had he thought of settling to one woman, of marriage and family. If Storm truly meant what she had said, was not just mouthing sweet words to give him added strength of spirit to face the battle, all that could be possible. He could feel secure in binding himself to her, for he knew that, if Storm truly loved him, he need never worry about another man.

He forced his mind to concentrate upon the battle he faced. Distraction at such a time could prove fatal. More than ever before he was reluctant to die. He had too much to live for, too much left unsaid. There had to be time left to him to speak to Storm, to speak of more than how much his body continually craved hers.

Sir Hugh mounted his destrier as Lady Mary looked on. As the time of battle drew near, her blood ran hot. At times she wished she were a man so that she could join in the fighting. However, she gained more than enough satisfaction from watching the fight and could be content with that. She could stand at a safe distance and savor the sight of men fighting a life and death struggle, revel in the violence and death played out before her eyes. It left her with a voracious carnal appetite and, with her husband now gone, she could be completely free to sate it as she saw fit. The need for some discretion in the past had severely curbed her creativity.

"Slaughter them to a man, Hugh," she said coldly.

Although he had been savoring that very plan, he resented her ordering him to do so. "I was just about to offer them a last chance to surrender. 'Tis customary to do so."

"Then do so. They will say nay. I know it. E'en if they say yea, should that stop you? An I have learned anything in this wretched land, 'tis that the English here feel it their Godly duty to slay the Scots. No one would fault you if that is what you fear."

"I do not care for what others think." He scowled down at her. "There are rules to follow in war, Mary.

Whate'er else I may be or have become, I am a knight." He could not bring himself to offer terms of surrender and then, if they were accepted, cut down the unsuspecting.

"They are Scots. 'Tis not necessary to deal honorably with them. It seems to me that you take up or toss aside these rules as suits you. These are MacLagans, border reivers. You do not deal honorably with such scum. If you rid the world of the curse of their presence, you will only be thought a hero. None will question how it was done.

"I want them dead, Hugh. I want that ugly pile of rock razed to the ground. They are naught but a burr in my side. I grow tired of trying to shake free. They have stolen from me, and I mean to take everything from them. 'Tis a fair payment to my mind.

"Do you forget how they have injured you? Do you forget that shameful ride back into Hagaleah, all the laughter at your cost? Do you forget that they stole the fine, costly stallion you had only just gained? They also stole the mare you meant to breed, and I speak not of the four-legged ones but of Storm. Tavis MacLagan rides your mare, mayhaps e'en sets a MacLagan foal in her belly. By holding her, he also holds your fortune, holds the land you crave but have never owned. They, too, laugh at you. How much scorn must you bear before you act as you should and avenge yourself?"

"No more," he snarled. "Cease your speeches, woman. You have won your way. E'en an I must draw them from Carailand through treachery, I will see them all dead. This day will mark the end of the arrogant, troublesome MacLagans. This land will turn red with their blood."

She smiled as he rode off. Soon the MacLagans would bother her no more. She had no doubts about who would gain the victory today. Hugh was a skilled fighter and the MacLagans were greatly outnumbered. She had spied the women upon the battlements taking the night watch and knew what that meant. What men did remain to fight for Caraidland were a weary lot with no hope of much rest unless they could defeat Sir Hugh. Her forces were well rested and alert. She wondered, as she moved to sit in her shaded cart, if the coming battle would last long enough to stir her passions. It would be disappointing, if convenient, if Caraidland fell too quickly. She hoped she could count upon the MacLagans' fighting skill and obstinacy to provide her with a satisfactory show before she claimed the victory she so craved.

Storm studied the women and small children gathered together in the hall. The tension as they waited for the battle to begin was almost a tangible thing. They all struggled to hide their fears and worries for their loved ones facing the army Sir Hugh drew up before Caraidland. Even the children were quiet. Storm found it a painfully familiar scene. So it was at Hagaleah before a battle. On either side of the border it seemed a woman's place was to wait and hope that her man, be he lover or kin, would return alive.

In this instance she knew the fears ran deeper than usual. This battle was at the very threshold of their home. It threatened the children, the innocent and the weak. They must now view at first hand the horror of battle, hear every sound as men tried to kill each other.

"I cannot bear it. I must stop this," she whispered, starting to rise.

Maggie grasped her by the arm and kept her seated upon the bench they shared. "Ye cannae stop this. The swords hae already been drawn and blood spilled."

"I cannot sit here and allow blood to be spilled because of me. I am not worth dying for."

"Weel, I suspicion there be a few what would argue that but, wheesht, lass, 'tis nay longer for ye alone. I am thinking it ne'er was. Oh, aye, ye are a part of it. I cannae say ye arenae. 'Tis also a battle for Caraidland, a fight agin a man who deserves tae be destroyed."

"But Caraidland could fall," she whispered. "All this could be destroyed."

"Aye. We all ken it. We hae but half our men and they are weary. We hae faced that foe afore and God has left us live. Mayhaps he'll look kindly upon us agin. We can but pray 'tis so."

"I have been praying, but it does little to still my fears."

"Lass, that man tirling at the pin doesnae mean tae stop if we let ye go. Ye ken it as weel as any o' us. We hae all heard our men talk. With sae much agin us, they would trade ye if they thought it would save us, save our bairns and women. They ken it willnae. We will still be slain if 'tis possible and so will ye, just not so quickly."

Storm shivered and closed her eyes. She knew all that Maggie had said was true. Giving her to Sir Hugh would not end the fight. She had tried to find an easy solution, a quick end to what she knew was going to happen and a way to stop any pain or loss of life. Although she was still a bone of contention, she was no longer the whole of the reason for the battle, maybe never had been.

"He will offer a chance for surrender," she said desperately, clutching at one last hope.

"Aye, he will. 'Tis the way of it."

"But it will be refused." She sighed, for she knew that was how it would be.

"It will be. There be no honor in surrender."

"There is life."

"Do ye really think so?"

After only a moment of meeting Maggie's gaze

Storm looked away. She could not bear to read the truth in the woman's eyes, could not bear to see what she already knew. It was a truth she wanted to vigorously deny but could not.

"Nay,' she finally whispered. "Nay, I do not really believe that."

"Guid. Tis nay guid tae try and deceive yourself, lass. Not now. Facing the truth will gie ye the strength tae go on."

"I suppose 'tis truth that has my innards so twisted up that I fear to be ill."

"I ken the feeling weel, lassie. I e'er feel it when my Angus gies tae fight and 'tis worse now, for me bairns face the sword." She shook her head when Storm paled. "Nay, lass, 'tis not your doing. Ken this, I'll nay blame ye, ne'er blame ye, for whate'er happens. 'Tis Sir Hugh Sedgeway I will be cursing an a sword cuts down any o' mine. Him and him alane.

"Lass, we both ken that he wants all we Mac-Lagans deid. Whate'er he offers, unless 'tis death, he'll nay mean tae keep his bargain. He but tries tae make us set down our weapons sae that he can slaughter us like sheep. We'll nay let that happen. If God means tae see us deid, we'll gie down fighting to the last unweaned bairn. Sir Hugh will find victory o'er us one hard fought for. I pray tae God that that beast is the first to die."

"There would be a blessing. I am so torn, Maggie. I have friends on either side of these walls. Some of my father's old guard follow Hugh, though they like it little. They are fighting men and must go when ordered whether they like it or not."

"I ken it. Our laird is a guid man, but he could hae been ane like Sir Hugh. My Angus would hae had tae follow e'en so. He is bound tae Caraidland. He kens naught else. I dinnae either. Ah, lassie, how I wish 'twas your father out there, and I ne'er thought tae e'er be saying that."

A weak smile curved Storm's lips. "I think more than one MacLagan has said the same."

"Aye. Lord Eldon be a man ye can trust, his word be his bond and he would ne'er kill the innocent, the unarmed. This man cares only for his ain skin and doesnae honor his word. Och, weel, what will be, will be. Ye cannae fret o'er God's will."

"Easier said than done."

"Keep trying, lassie. That is where ye will find a bit of peace."

Storm studied the women and children around her. She sensed that Maggie spoke for all of them. Not one had an accusatory word or look for her. They quietly went about the business of preparing for war. They silently but firmly included her in their number, as just another woman doing what she could to help the men who were soon to be fighting. She wondered how many knew that she, too, held the fear of losing a loved one, that her prayers were not really for any of the English outside the walls of Caraidland, but for one tall, dark Scot standing upon its battlements, bravely facing the overwhelming odds.

Inwardly, she grimaced and tried to concentrate upon the salve she mixed. She would not be surprised to discover that every woman there knew how she felt about Tavis. Love was an emotion most women could easily recognize in another. It would not really surprise her to discover that they had seen how she felt before she had.

Briefly, she wondered what Tavis thought about the words she had spoken to him. Did he believe her? Did her confession make him happy or appall him? Was he wondering how he really felt about her or if there was a future for them?

A soft curse echoed through her mind, and she told herself not to be such an idiot. He was standing upon the walls of Caraidland looking at a gathering force that was more than twice the size of his own. He had no time to think on a few whispered words. Lives hung in the balance; perhaps the end of the MacLagans and Caraidland was drawing near. What one small woman felt or said was not something he would ponder as he faced that. Even she could understand how, at this moment in their lives, what she felt for him and he for her was insignificant.

She tried very hard not to think of him, at least not constantly. It only made her fear for him grow. Nothing could make her stop being afraid for him, stop worrying about what he faced, but she knew it was time to concentrate upon other things. Very soon there would be work that needed doing, people who needed help. She had to stop being so distracted or she could fail them, fail to carry her share of the burden.

After the battle we will talk, she told herself. The MacLagans have to win and, Papa, if ye are watching, I know ye will understand why I wish our enemies to be the victors. I swallowed my pride and told him how I feel, Papa. I could not let it stay a secret when death stares us in the face. I hope ye understand something else, Papa. I have begged God to let Tavis live, e'en if he cares not a drop for me. I need him to live e'en more than I need him to love me. But, Papa? An all goes awry and Hugh does as we all fear, if he wipes the earth clean of the clan MacLagan, please help me. Hugh will take me alive and within me is growing a new MacLagan, hope for the future of the clan and a part of the man I love. Help me keep the child alive, Papa, I beg it of you.

Her silent conversation with her father came to an abrupt halt. The sound reaching her ears told her that the men of Caraidland no longer stood silent and waiting. She grasped Maggie's hand.

"It begins."

21

"MacLagan, do you hear me?"

Colin stared down at Sir Hugh, who had ridden forward, flying a flag that indicated he wished to talk, and flanked by two men-at-arms. "Aye. Do ye come to ask me terms o' surrender?"

Hugh spluttered with outrage. " 'Tis no time for jests, fool. Do ye yield?"

"Nay, Sassanach dog. Caraidland will never yield."

"Then it will fall. Look about. Can you deny what your eyes see? I have many men, many more than you do. Near to twice as many."

"That makes us about equal then."

"You fool," Hugh screamed. "Do you mean to condemn your whole clan for but one girl? Is your son's whore worth the loss of Caraidland, the end of your clan? Give her over to me and I will spare your people. Do not force me to spill the blood of your people for an English slut."

"The only blood that will run today is Sassanach blood."

"I will bring this keep down around your ears, you fool."

"Then cease yapping, cur, and get on with the business."

"You die today, MacLagan. You and your whole clan, the rest of that thieving scum." He hurled the truce flag down, trampling it in the dust as he rode back to his army.

"The man has nay control o'er his temper, eh?" Colin grinned at his sons, who flanked him, as Hugh rode back to his men and began to scream orders. "He doesnae have old Eldon's skill with a taunt. There was a man who kenned how to wield a word."

Sholto laughed and shook his head. "Ye talk as if ye miss the man."

"Aye, I do and will. 'Tis rare in a man's life to face a man like Roden Eldon. Ye kenned ye could trust his word. Unlike this whoreson, Eldon wouldnae slay the innocent. Eldon would give up a victory ere he would take sword to the unarmed, women and children. Ye knew where ye stood with Eldon. If he took hostages, ye could trust him to treat them weel. All ye needed to fash yourself about was the ransom and how to raise it. Aye, I will miss him. I could trust and respect that Sassanach more than I can trust some of me own kin."

"Aye, he was a fine enemy," agreed Iain. "Ah, the whoreson begins to move."

"But will it be a full attack?"

"This time I think it will be, Tavis," Colin replied as the English force bellowed their battle cry and surged forward en masse, picking up speed as they went.

Beneath a murderous hail of arrows, the English force pressed on. Time blurred for the Scots as they fought to cull the English force and keep the walls of Caraidland from being breeched. They had barely enough men to hold the walls and all knew that if those walls were scaled, they would lose in the resulting confrontation. Falling back to the keep was an option, but it was also an admission of defeat and none of them wanted that. Such a retreat would also bring the enemy closer to the women and children.

Tavis moved along the parapets, viewing the battle from every possible angle. He did not need to urge any man on. They all knew they were fighting not only for their own lives but for the very future of the clan. No one doubted Sir Hugh's threat nor that any offer he made to deal for clemency or surrender was a lie, that he only sought to trick them into letting down their defenses. They had all taken a true account of the man he was, that he was not a man one could trust, not even if he swore on all that was holy to every man.

He reached one point where there was one man dead and another badly wounded. There was no one left to push the scaling ladder away, although the wounded man struggled valiantly to get to his feet and shove the ladder down. Tavis grasped the ladder even as the first man scaling it reached the top and desperately tried to stop him from pushing the ladder away.

As he started to push, Tavis looked into the man's eyes and wished he had not. There he read the fear nearly every man held, the one of falling. The man stared death in the face and could do nothing, only wait for his body to finish plummeting to the ground. Tavis felt something inside of him twist with horror at the thought of what he was about to do to the man.

"Ye have twa blinks of an eye to get closer to God's earth, man," Tavis growled even as he wondered what madness had seized him, a madness that was giving his enemy a chance to live.

The man blinked, then gaped in amazement, and then began to scramble down the ladder. He screamed at the others to hurry and back down. They hastily obeyed as Tavis began to push the ladder further away from the wall. When he judged them a relatively safe distance from the ground he shoved the ladder away, watching it and the few men it still held topple to the ground. He noticed that they made no attempt to put it or another up against the wall.

"Why did ye do that?"

Glancing at the wounded young man, Tavis frowned. "I dinnae ken. I looked into the man's face and . . ." He shook his head. "I dinnae ken. I saw his fear . . . I . . ."

The young man nodded before Tavis finished stumbling through his disjointed explanation. "Ye cannae look at them. It isnae like wielding a sword, with the blood lust in your veins. Ye maun ne'er look. Just push." The young man's eyes closed and he groaned softly.

Yelling to a few men, Tavis soon had the weak spot covered. He put an arm under the wounded man's arms and nearly carried him into the hall. Upon entering the hall, he nearly screamed with frustration. There were too many wounded. He knew there would soon be more weak spots along the wall than men able to fill them.

Storm was told that another wounded man had been brought in and hurried to lay out a pallet for him, a blanket all they had left to use. She did not realize Tavis was the one aiding the hurt man until she had spread out the blanket and looked up to see if she could help to lay the wounded youth down. For a long moment her gaze devoured the sight of his begrimed face as her mind reveled in this proof that he was still hale. It was another moment before she realized that the wounded young man was Jeanne's betrothed.

"How goes it?" she asked Tavis after calling for Jeanne and starting to cut away the blood-stained tunic young Robbie wore.

" 'Tis hard to say," he answered with a weary honesty. "So many wounded, yet the scaling ladders still clatter against our walls."

"But Hugh is upon none of them."

"Nay. The bastard rides about at a safe distance and drives his men on. I cannae help but think that if we could cut the whoreson down, it would end this attack."

"Aye, I think it would, and mayhaps he does too. 'Tis mayhaps why he stays away." She grimaced, hating to say anything that might be seen as even remotely favorable to Sir Hugh. "He is a low piece of scum, but I have ne'er noted that he suffered from cowardice."

"Nay, I dinnae feel he is a coward either. He cares little for his men's lives, though, simply keeps hurling them at our walls. Och, weel, I should be grateful that he has not the weaponry to hurl anything else at us." He shook his head as Jeanne arrived, and Storm let her take over the care of Robbie. "We hold, but 'tis all we do."

" 'Tis enough, is it not?" Storm moved to stand before him, as worried about possible defeat as he.

"Aye, if we can keep holding, but"—he looked again at the many wounded, few of them able to be patched up and quickly returned to battle—"I fear there will soon be more weak spots upon the wall than we have men to fill them."

"An I go to him . . ." she began, still hoping that there would be some way to stop what was happening.

"Nay." He gently gripped her shoulders. "Nay, little one. 'Tis more than ye being bickered over now and all ken it, e'en ye. He means to end the clan. When he cried that he would bring Caraidland down about Father's ears, that he would see us all dead, he didnae boast, nay, nor make an idle threat. He but spoke the truth, a truth we all kenned ere he put it into words. For mayhaps the first time in his life, Sir Hugh spoke honestly. E'en had we been fool enough to agree to his terms of surrender, he would have slain us all. Ye are the only one he means to keep alive. We fight for our very existence, for the survival of the clan.

269

"Do ye ken? For a while I faulted meself for all o' this. An I had let ye be, mayhaps none o' this would have occurred. But, nay, I ken it would have. We would have raided Hagaleah again and brought him to our gates. 'Tis better to have brought it on because o' a fair wee lass than for a herd of cattle or a few mares."

"He is mad, I think."

"Near to, mayhaps. Mayhaps 'tis the pair o' them, he and Lady Mary. She, too, is the sort to demand such a vengeance. I maun get back to the walls." He pulled her into his arms, caring nothing about their audience, although almost everyone in the hall was too busy to be interested. "Say it again, Storm." He kissed her and whispered, "Say it again. I find I have a craving to hear the words."

"I love ye," she said softly, coloring deeply but unable to refuse him his request. " 'Til the sun ceases to rise of a morn and beyond."

He said nothing, simply kissed her fiercely and left. She stared after him, wondering if it meant that much that he liked to hear her speak of her love. Shaking her head, she returned to the grisly, sad work of tending the wounded that continued to flow into the hall. For now it would be enough that her admission had not pushed him away from her as she had feared it might. Later, and she refused to think that there could be no later, she would find out what his liking of the words meant to her.

The sun was nearly at its apex in the sky before Sir Hugh allowed his troops to draw back long enough to allow Caraidland any rest. Tavis sank down to sit where he had stood. The air carried the smell of blood and death. He felt that he did too. When Phelan paused by him with the water Tavis poured a dipperful over his head before taking a long drink.

"There will be a lot of widows and orphans at

Hageleah," Phelan said softly as he peered over the walls and viewed the dead and dying strewn over the land.

"Aye. This is a costly way to do battle, a bloody waste of good fighting men. The attackers must toss away many a life to end that o' but one o' those upon the walls. That is why Eldon e'er preferred an acre fight. He didnae see his men as naught but fodder for Scots' arrows and swords. He would ne'er have wasted lives so."

"Nay. He cared about the welfare of e'en the lowest peasant." Phelan smiled sadly. "For all he bellowed and cursed. It grieves me sorely that I could not know him longer and better."

"Aye. He was the best of enemies."

"And Sir Hugh is the worst."

"Aye, laddie. The worst. His word isnae e'en worth spitting on. He will slaughter the bairns at their mother's breast and think naught of it. I wonder what fool knighted him."

"He saved the life of an important man. I think there was little choice. There had to be a reward."

"True. Such a thing cannae be ignored. 'Twould be a black deed, blacker than the knighting of a man like Sir Hugh."

"Can Sir Hugh win?" Phelan asked softly.

"I fear he can, laddie. We ready ourselves e'en now to fall back to the keep, to give up the outer wall and the bailey. Some of the bairns were slinked away out o' the tunnel, but we daren't move too many or 'twould be seen and all lost. We cannae hold against many more attacks. Too many wounded, though, by God's sweet grace, few dead yet." He grimaced. "Mayhaps 'twould be best if they were dying upon the walls. If Caraidland falls, I think Sir Hugh willnae kill us all with any mercy."

"Nay," Phelan whispered. "The man has a liking for torture. Lord Eldon's men are sickened by it, but they can do little, for Sir Hugh and Lady Mary rule. Also, each of them has their own guard who help them hold their rule, enforce their ways. No word of the rest of your men?"

"Nary a whisper. Go on, laddie. Give the men their water. 'Tis all in God's hands now."

Sir Hugh drank deeply of the wine Lady Mary served him. He was hot and weary, wishing only to remove his clothes, his heavy armor and soak in a bath. It was too hot for a battle, especially one that was lasting far too long. The MacLagans had already held for far longer than he had thought they would. He had also lost more men than he had anticipated. It grew harder and harder to drive his army against the walls of Caraidland. As the dead piled up, the living grew hesitant. They were unwilling to face what was apparently a sure death, especially when, as far as they could see, they were gaining nothing. Even the fear of the retribution he would deal out to any who disobeyed was barely enough to keep them doing as he ordered. He had drawn his personal guard nearer as he had sensed the growing rebellion of his troops. Hugh wished he could look inside the walls to see how matters stood within Caraidland. For now he could only make guesses about where the weaker points of defense were and hope that the breakthrough would come before his men turned upon him.

"You are taking a considerable amount of time to bring down the MacLagans."

He glared at Lady Mary. "Would you like to have a try, m'lady?"

"I daresay I could not do any worse."

"You cannot seduce the Scots from the walls."

"Hugh, you grow tedious."

"Heed me, woman, stay to what you know—murder and the arts of the bedchamber," he hissed. "You

272

know naught of battle, never have, save that it makes your nether eye weep with want. That hulking lump of stone is not just a place to eat and sleep. 'Twas built to resist just such an attack as this, and built with skill and art."

"Then try another form of attack."

"There is this or there is a siege. Do you wish to rest here for months?"

"It would not take months to break them." She looked around with clear distaste.

"Aye, m'lady, it could. We would suffer more than they, for we would be out here with winter closing in upon us. I assure you, they will have ample food and water within those cursed walls. There is no way I can judge how much, how long they could hold out against us. The longer we sat here, the greater the chance that we would meet the other half of their forces. I mean to avoid that."

It galled Lady Mary to do so, but she had to admit that Sir Hugh was right. She had forgotten that the MacLagans were at but half their strength, that the other half of their fighting force was at Athdara and could return at any moment. It was true that she knew little of war and the ways of fighting, but she decided she would learn as soon as possible. Never again would a man talk down to her as Sir Hugh was doing. She would not allow it. It robbed her of some of her power.

"Try not to kill all of our forces in the taking of that place," she said nastily before she moved away, returning to her shaded cart.

Cursing viciously, Sir Hugh watched her go. He realized he had shown her that she had a weakness, and he knew well how she would feel about that. Until he could soothe her ruffled feathers, he would have to watch her closely and eye all he ate with great care. She could easily decide to be rid of him, if only out of spite.

He turned his angry glare toward Caraidland. It and its defenders were proving far stronger that he had thought they would. They had cost him a lot of men, yet he was no closer to victory. If he kept losing men at such a rate, he would soon lose the numerical advantage he had arrived with. He would wait awhile and try again. Let them realize their own exhaustion. Without the stirring effects of battle to keep them going, they would soon feel how weary they were, how weary he knew they had to be. Then he would hit them again. If luck was with him and he timed it right, they would fall to him quickly, for they would not have the strength to repulse him.

Taking a moment from pondering his strategy, he ordered men to go and watch the way to Athdara. It had been unwise to pull the guard from that duty. He could not afford to be caught between two forces. The last thing he needed was some foe coming to strike at his flank.

"What is that whoreson doing now?" asked Colin as he joined Tavis upon the walls.

"Waiting."

"For what?"

"For our weariness to weigh us down, I think."

"Aye, that seems right. We are feeling it right enough."

" 'Tis unfortunate, but I feel the man has some skill. He seems to ken what to do and when to do it." Tavis glanced around at the men slumped along the wall. "They will soon find it hard to lift a sword."

"And that Sassanach bastard will swoop in to see that they ne'er lift another one. It has been a long time since I have faced such as this, and I could have gone to my grave happy without doing so."

Soon Hugh tried again. The MacLagans valiantly fought back the first wave of Englishmen that tried to surge over the walls of Caraidland. It cost them dearly, however. No matter how many Englishmen he took with him, each Scottish life lost brought Caraidland closer to destruction. They no longer had anything to hurl over the walls, could only continue to push the scaling ladders down, but the hands needed to do that grew fewer and fewer.

When Sir Hugh struck after another brief pause Tavis tasted the bitter gall of defeat. The English brought forth a battering ram, the machine well covered. He could almost wish they had chosen one of the many other siege weapons despite how deadly they could be. Scottish arrows were unable to penetrate the thick hide. Over the screams of men and the clang of steel against steel came the constant ominous sound of the battering ram. Unless it was stopped, it would soon break through the gates.

Tavis knew with a cold sense of certainty that they could not stop it. He began to order the men to fall back even as he heard the chilling sound of the thick wood of the gates splintering, accompanied by a cheer of triumph from the attacking forces. The English knew they would soon be victorious.

Storm cried out in surprise when Tavis and two other men suddenly burst into the tower room. She felt her heart enter her throat, for she realized what it meant. Sir Hugh had broken through, his men were taking or had taken the inner bailey. The Mac-Lagans were now down to to their final line of defense. The people she had come to like and—she looked at Tavis—love were one step closer to slaughter. She desperately fought a strong urge to weep. The last thing the exhausted men needed was a hysterical woman on their hands.

"Get down with the other women, little one," Tavis ordered, and felt a shaft of pain go through him as he wondered if this was to be the last time that he would ever see her.

"Sweet Jesu," moaned one of the men at the

window, "the English dog has fresh troops coming."

"Nay, it cannae be," cried Tavis as he raced to the window, refusing to believe that fate could be so cruel. "Could it be our men returning rom Athdara?"

"Frae the south? Nay, 'tis mair Sassanachs. Aye, fresh and hot for battle. Listen tae them."

Having hesitated in obeying Tavis's order to leave, Storm made her way to the window. "Let me have a look. I might know who they are."

Even though he let her through to look out of the window, carefully shielding her body with his own, Tavis said, "I cannae see that ye would ken one I didnae."

"Nay, I suspect ye know most all of the families in the Marches, but there is e'er that chance. Whoe'er it is, he has caused great confusion in Hugh's troops. I can think of none who wear strips of blue, like some lady's favor, upon their arm either." She suddenly paled and clutched Tavis's arm. "The man to the fore. Oh dear sweet God, Lady Mary lied. Look to him, Tavis. 'Tis Papa."

"Sweet Jesu, 'tis Eldon. But does that mean we are to be saved?"

22

"Do we have to wear these things?" Andrew grumbled as he tied the strip of blue cloth onto his arm. "I feel like some fool of a lovestruck knight parading m'lady's silly favor."

" 'Twould be more foolish for us to ride in there with naught to mark us as not of Hugh's forces." Eldon glared at the light blue cloth upon his arm and then glared at Lord Foster. "Why carry this cloth to battle? Do you mean to have such a pretty shroud?"

"I had no time to unpack the supply cart and it was in there. 'Twas for little Matilda, for a gown."

Looking at all the men wearing the strips of blue, Eldon drawled, "One gown? 'Tis enough for a score of them."

"Well, Matilda is very hard on gowns and she loves blue. Here comes Hadden." He frowned. "He does not come alone, yet does not appear to be a prisoner."

"Hallo, Uncle. I brought some added troops." Hadden grinned as he indicated the dozen men with him.

"Matthew, you old dog." Eldon clapped his old man-at-arms on the back. "A battle wound?"

"Nay." Matthew touched the bandage round his head and explained how he came by the wound. " 'Tis naught. I bandaged it to make it look worse."

"She rescued the heir?"

"Aye, m'lord. I felt 'twas right to aid her. The man didn't deserve the fate Sir Hugh planned for him. He has taken good care of Mistress Storm," he added softly. "Hugh meant to geld the lad. As a fellow man, I could nay stomach it. I also knew the wee lass was safer with them Scots."

Eldon nodded. "It pains me to agree but, aye, she is. I will owe them for this no matter what else has happened. They have kept her alive. How goes the battle?"

"Well," replied Hadden, "if ye wait much longer, Sir Hugh will have rid you of the troublesome MacLagans. They were within one blow of breaking through the gates into the bailey. I think the Mac-Lagans were falling back to the keep."

"That would make it easier for us. With the Mac-Lagans in the keep, we need not fear that one of them could strike one of us down, either by error or out of habit."

"If ye wait, there is no chance that any MacLagan will do aught."

"What do you mean, Matthew?"

"Sir Hugh has cried havoc, m'lord. No mercy. Not e'en for the wee babes. He means to slay every man, woman and child in Caraidland, strip it of all worth and raze it to the ground. If his men break into that keep there will be a bloodfest. He means for only Mistress Storm to walk out of there alive. I have the feeling the MacLagans know it."

"Did he not offer them a chance to yield?"

"Aye, but he only thought to make it easier to kill them all and they know it, I be thinking."

"Tie a piece of blue about your arm," Eldon ordered. "We want no confusion as to what English force we are. Take an extra strip or two for those who may wish to come to our side. Haig, you take some men and be sure that none of Sir Hugh's or Mary's people get away. Drive them toward the

MacLagan keep. There is too much to be answered for to allow any of them to escape."

"So we really are to save the MacLagans," Andrew mused as Haig rode with ten men toward Sir Hugh's and Lady Mary's encampment.

"Aye. I will not have murder done in the name of Eldon or Hagaleah. I have ne'er held with the murder or abuse of the innocent. The bastard plots a merciless slaughter and I will stop it, be it MacLagans or nay." He looked around and saw that all the men were ready. "To Caraidland, men. And remember that we fight Sir Hugh and my cursed wife this day, not the Scots. You are not to cut down a MacLagan unless he tries to kill you. For this one time, they are our allies. Now, ride!"

By the time they reached Caraidland, Hugh and his men were inside the bailey. The arrival of Eldon and his men caused a brief hesitation in the battle. An instant later it became clear to Hugh's men that this force of Englishmen was not there to assist them. To add to their dismay, nearly a third of their force changed sides, donning blue ties and turning against their former master, Sir Hugh. The few Scots left in the bailey quickly saw that, in this one instance, Englishmen were going to aid them, and a weak cheer went up amongst their decimated numbers, for they could also see that the tide of battle now turned against Sir Hugh.

Tavis watched the scene below and, slowly, the bitter taste of defeat left his stomach. Sir Hugh was good, but Lord Eldon was better, his skill gained from years of fighting. When so many of Sir Hugh's force rushed to join their liege lord it was more or less a *coup de grace*. Defeat now faced Sir Hugh and had from the moment Eldon had swooped into the bailey. The desertion of so many men simply ensured that the defeat would come more quickly.

He and the other two men raced from the tower

room, eager to rejoin the battle. It did not surprise Tavis to find the men who had managed to reach the security of the keep milling about in some confusion. Not only was Eldon supposed to be dead, but it was hard for many to comprehend that he would do anything to help them.

"I cannae see clearly," Colin said as he reached Tavis's side. " 'Tis truly Eldon?"

"Aye. 'Tis Eldon. The man has not only risen from the dead, he has come to our rescue." Tavis laughed with enjoyment and relief. "Tell all the men to strike no man wearing a blue tie upon his arm."

When Tavis reached the bailey he smiled with grim pleasure. Already a number of Sir Hugh's men were yielding. He caught sight of Sir Hugh and raced toward the man. Although he could see that Eldon struggled to get to the man as well, Tavis did not hesitate. It would be courteous to allow Lord Eldon the pleasure of slaying Sir Hugh, but Tavis held too strong an urge for vengeance to be courteous.

Sir Hugh read his death in Tavis MacLagan's eyes. The knowledge that he had lost, especially when he had been so close to victory, enraged Sir Hugh. With a scream of fury, he lunged for Tavis.

The fight was fierce but brief. Tavis's fury was cold, allowing for clear thought and smooth action. Hugh's rage was mindless, lessening his usual skill with a sword. All too soon, as far as their grim-faced audience was concerned, Hugh gave Tavis an opening. In the blinking of an eye, Tavis pondered toying with the sweating, ranting man for a while longer and discarded the idea. He struck, cleanly piercing the man's heart and killing him instantly.

For a moment Tavis simply studied the corpse of the man who had nearly brought about the total destruction of his clan. He felt almost disappointed that it had been so easy to kill him. Then he sensed someone at his side and turned to face Lord Eldon.

One look into the man's eyes told Tavis that Lord Eldon knew everything. He saw the man raise his sword and tensed for yet another battle, one he had no wish to fight, but it never came.

"Papa! Papa!" Storm raced through the quieting battle and flung herself into her father's arms. "Oh, Papa, she said you had all died. All of you. I thought my poor heart would shatter."

Holding his daughter close to his heart, Eldon said, "I caught the murderers before they could do what she had hired them to do. One lived, and we learned of all that has gone on."

Haig, pushing a furious Lady Mary toward her husband, was briefly diverted as he watched the reunion between Storm and Lord Eldon. Lady Mary glanced at Sir Hugh's body, then glared at her husband and his daughter. She knew she would be lucky if all Eldon did to her was banish her to some remote nunnery. The realization of how completely wrong all her plans had gone made her hiss with rage. She pulled her dagger out and raised it, a cold smile curving her full mouth as she thought of how she was going to bury it deep into Eldon's broad back. There would be a loss she was certain would dim the glee they all felt.

Sholto saw the glint of steel in the woman's hand and guessed what she was about to do. There was no time to cry out a warning. Even as he moved to ensure a more accurate aim, he pulled out his dagger and hurled it. It troubled him as he watched his dagger bury itself deep into her chest, for she was, after all, a woman. He forced himself to remember all she had done and all she had intended to do.

Lady Mary felt a searing pain, and her dagger fell from her suddenly lifeless fingers. She stared dumbly at the hilt of the dagger protruding from her chest. Even as she sank to the dirt, she could not believe she was dying. A curse against Eldon formed on her tongue, but her life slipped from her grasp before she could utter it.

Eldon, his arm still draped around Storm's shoulders, looked down at Mary, then at Sholto, who had arrived to collect his knife. "God's toenails, I grow weary of owing you MacLagans a life."

"Take comfort, Eldon," drawled Colin as he joined the group. "We owe ye ours."

"Aye, you do. Where have all your men gone? Has Sir Hugh killed so many? Or is it true that he struck when you were at but half your strength?"

"At least half our men rode to Athdara. Now, about that ransom," he drawled.

Staring at the man, Eldon wondered a little wildly how a battle-scarred, dark-visaged Scot could look impish. A low chuckle started deep within him and quickly built to roaring laughter, which Colin shared. It soon spread to all around, save for the prisoners, who felt this hilarity in the face of their devastating defeat was somewhat callous. Another group that did not laugh was the newly returned force of men from Athdara, who had seen the clear signs of a fierce battle that was evidently over and had raced into Caraidland afraid of what awaited them there. The call to Athdara had been a false alarm, and they knew now that it had been part of a trap sprung upon Caraidland. They wondered at the sanity of their laird, who stood with an ancient enemy laughing and slapping backs as if they were the oldest and dearest of friends.

Tavis did not laugh either. The battle was over. Because of Eldon's part in the saving of Caraidland there would be no ransoming. Storm would simply leave with her father. He fought the urge to grab her and race for the hills, to kidnap her once again.

As the bodies began to be cleared away, women served ale to the men. Eldon had to smile as he saw how the Scots and the English stayed more or less separate and eyed each other warily. He then turned his full attention to the matter of Storm. She still stood with him and the rest of her family while Tavis stood at a distance, neither moving nor speaking. He wondered if they were going to resolve a great many problems by simply turning their backs on each other.

Storm looked toward Tavis, wondering why he stayed so far away. She felt a chill enter her blood as it seemed that he was staring right through her. Even as she told herself not to imagine the worst, to wait and give him more of a chance to speak up, she found herself bracing for the blow.

"We will take some of our dead home, MacLagan," Eldon said, "and what we leave behind is yours to toss away as you will. I recognize a few of the men. Hugh and my wife gathered some true scum round them. A troop of traitors, thieves and murderers. Hagaleah is choked with such refuse."

"Weel, I thank ye for saving us from that refuse. We had our backs to the wall. I admit it."

"While we are being so disgustingly honest, I will admit that I thought on waiting."

"I can understand why. Best way to weaken your enemy—sitting back and letting others do it. Why did ye change your thinking? Your lassie?"

"Nay. My nephews had reported that you would not trade her, and I knew that Sir Hugh would not kill her until the wedding vows were secured. I changed my mind because I was told that he had cried havoc. Not only is that forbidden, but I wanted no murder of women and babes to stain the name of Hageleah or Eldon." He looked at Colin curiously. "Why would you not trade her for your son?"

"Did ye hear that that whoreson had grabbed her once?" Eldon nodded. "Then ye ken why. I couldnae give her o'er to that. Nay, especially not when I owe her my life. My wife was poisoning me and the lass kenned it, catching me back from the brink o' death and naught less. It seems we share a deadly puir taste in the women, Eldon."

"Speak for yourself, MacLagan. I have found me a fine one and now I can wed her. Aye, and I should hie to it. If she hears that I have returned and naught else . . ." He grimaced.

"She is not at the cottage, Papa. Ye have time. She also knows of the troubles, for they reached out to her, but she and the babes are well," Storm hastened to add. "They stay at her sister's."

"I think you have a tale or two to tell me, but it can wait. There are other things to speak on ere we go." He studied her carefully, yet kept a watch on Colin, who looked only mildly curious, but was in fact tensed for confrontation. "Do you have anything to talk to me about?"

It was hard, but Storm resisted the urge to look at Tavis and struggled to look mildly bewildered. "Such as?"

"Very well done, m'girl, but do not think to play that game with me. More than one has told me how things stand here, all that has gone on. What is done is done. The question I ask is what is to happen now?"

Storm looked at Tavis. It was up to him to speak. She felt her heart contract, break apart piece by piece as he stood silent. There was no need to speak of what her confession of love had meant to him. His silence was answer enough. As she had always feared, he had simply used her. She forced her pain aside so that she could face her father with some calm.

"We go home, Papa," she said quietly, suddenly needing to get away from Caraidland.

"Are you sure, sweeting?" He frowned, for she had gone somewhat pale.

"Very sure, Papa. When do we leave?"

"As soon as the horses are done being watered."

"I will be ready. Just let me go and see that I leave nothing behind."

She hurried off to the tower room, stopping briefly to bid a fleeting, tearful farewell to good friends she had made. It occurred to her as she hugged Maggie that she would probably never see any of them again, and she came very close to wailing like some starving baby. So, too, did she realize that she had hoped, even before she had heard that her father was dead, that her new friends would always be at hand. Even though they were but a few miles away it might as well be thousands.

When she reached the tower room she decided it had been a mistake to return to it. She hastily gathered up the few things she felt could be considered hers, anxious to leave a place that was choked with memories. The urge to hurl herself upon the bed and weep was almost too much to resist, but she knew she had to. If her father saw that she had been crying he would ask her why and, if she answered truthfully, there could be a great deal of trouble.

As she bent to pick up a hairpin, she felt her amulet shift beneath her gown. Slowly straightening up, she pulled it free and stared at it. It was supposed to be given to the man she loved. She would never love another man as she loved Tavis. Carefully, she removed the amulet and set it upon the pillow. When he saw it he might finally understand, but she would not allow herself to hope. All that mattered was that she loved him, would probably always love him, and so the amulet was his to wear if he chose to.

"He might as well have it, he has all else that is important to me save for my kin," she murmured bitterly, then shook her head. "Oh, Mama, why him?" She smiled faintly. "I imagine ye, and most like your kin as well, asked much the same. I tried to make him love me, Mama. No one can e'er say I did not try. It was not enough. I just hope that I can be healed of this wound."

She practically ran from the room, modifying her pace only when she felt there was a chance of someone seeing her. If nothing else, she would leave with dignity. No one would know how deeply she was hurting, nor guess that she had been fool enough to fall in love with her captor.

Andrew helped her secure her meager belongings to her mount. She was glad of his chatter and teasing, for it helped her in her desperate effort to maintain control. Usually he was very perceptive, but he was young and full of tales about his adventures in France. She tensed when Iain and Sholto arrived, for she feared they would speak on the very matter she sought to ignore.

"I dinnae ken what goes on," Sholto began, only to have Iain cuff him to shut him up.

"Take care, lassie." Iain hugged her and gave her a brief kiss, laughing softly when Sholto hurried to do the same. "Ye werenae too hard to bear, considering ye are a Sassanach."

Somehow she managed a weak smile in response to his teasing. So too was she able to smile for Colin when he bid her a gruff farewell, even though his eyes told her he saw more than she wished him to. He made no move to alter the way things were headed, however, and moments later she rode away from Caraidland with her family. She did not look back, fighting the urge and trying to believe that it was all for the best, that such a pairing could never have worked out.

Eldon frowned as he studied his daughter. She was pale and far too quiet. There was pain flickering in her eyes when her calm poise occasionally slipped. She said nothing; made no demands concerning Tavis MacLagan. Eldon began to wonder if the pair had really been lovers, but then he shook his head. Too many people had said they were. Mayhaps they were taking the most sensible route, the one of the least difficulty for either of their families. It was best for all of them, but Eldon withheld judgment for the moment. She might yet have something to tell him or ask of him.

Colin watched the Eldon group ride away. For whatever reasons, he owed Roden Eldon the life of his whole clan. He felt it might be for the best if the ancient antagonisms were finally laid to rest. It was something to think about. He turned to look at Tavis, who still stood in the same spot.

"Tavis," he began as he moved toward his son, who looked very pale and much as if he were in shock.

"Nay," Tavis rasped as he suddenly moved. "Nay, not a word. I willnae speak on it, Father."

He hurried away before his father could press him on the matter, ask for explanations. With each step he took he gained speed until he was racing through the halls of Caraidland. When he found himself in the tower room he was not really surprised, but cursed viciously, for it was the last place he wished to be. Moving quickly to the window, he stared toward the south, but not even the dust raised by their passage lingered behind the Eldons. They were really gone, on their way back to England and Hagaleah, riding even further out of his reach, even deeper into hostile territory.

Groaning in despair, he pressed his forehead against the cool stone. Eldon's arrival had been both a blessing and a curse. The man had ensured the survival of the MacLagan clan, but he had taken Storm.

"But what could I do?" he asked of the empty room. "She is a Sassanach. She is an Eldon. Twa enemies bound togother in one wee lass. She doesnae belong here. The man woundnae have let her stay. Nay, not to warm a Scot's bed. There was naught I could say," he moaned as he fought to banish the memory of her stricken face when she had turned to him, waiting for him to speak, and he had remained silent.

It hurt, and he had the chilling feeling that now, when it was too late, he understood. He felt as if a large and important part of him had been torn away. It was a deep wound, and he began to fear that it was one that would never heal quite right, that what scar remained would always be easily scratched open to bleed freely again. The worst of it all was that he felt sure the wound was mostly self-inflicted.

His gaze fell to the bed and his breath caught in his throat. Slowly he moved to the bed and, with a trembling hand, he picked up the amulet. A convulsive sob wracked his frame as he clutched it. She had meant every word she had said. Unable to stop himself, he began to weep, for he saw with agonizing clarity all he had just let ride away.

23

Storm glared at her reflection in the mirror. It told her exactly what she did not care to know. Her hand rested over the swell of her abdomen and then clenched into a fist. She could no longer hide the truth. The pregnancy she had fought to conceal now defeated her, her belly rounding more every day at a nearly alarming rate, or so it seemed to her.

Suddenly, she was swept by a wave of desolation. She sat on the edge of her bed and covered her face with her hands as she fought the urge to weep. The man who had planted the seed, the man she loved, ought to be with her. She should not have to hide the fact that she carried his child, should not have to fear making the announcement to her father. It should be a time of joy and anticipation. She found it easy to curse Tavis for stealing that from her as well.

It was with great effort that she put aside what she felt was harmful self-pity. There was too much to do and she needed strength to face it all. If nothing else, her father would at least gain a good reason for why she had refused two attractive betrothal offers, begged him not to make the arrangements, and continued to dampen the interest of any and all young men who looked her way. She was lucky she had a father who allowed her such scandalous freedom in the matter of choosing a husband.

She grimaced as she thought of those young men.

There had been a few who had thought her free for the grabbing, but mostly it seemed her stay with the MacLagans and her undoubted loss of chastity was accepted as a battle casualty. She suspected her family's wealth and power had a great deal to do with that unusual tolerance. So, too, the fact that her father let most any man court her if she had no objections, asking only that the man she chose be a good man. Many a landless knight saw what a rare opportunity that was. The tolerance was nice all the same, no matter what lay behind it.

She had, however, not even tried to soften toward one of the suitors. Although any could accept that she had lost her chastity, she was certain none of them would accept a MacLagan bastard. Neither could she take a husband when her heart and passion were still held captive at Caraidland.

Straightening her shoulders, she told herself firmly to cease dawdling and tell her father. She did not get very far before she decided to speak to Elaine first. It would not hurt to have an ally.

A faint smile touched her mouth when she found Elaine with her young half-brothers. The woman spent as much time with them as possible. Lady Mary's two sons were already accepting her as their mother, soaking up the love they had never gotten from their own mother.

Within a week after their return from Caraidland, her father had wed Elaine, ignoring the sweet woman's plea to wait for a decent mourning period to pass. Despite her time as Eldon's mistress, Elaine was a very modest, proper lady. What she had done had been out of love, aided by the certainty that Eldon's marriage was no real marriage at all, that she was not stealing a man from a woman who loved or even wanted him. Her acceptance at Hagaleah had been immediate, and she did not bemoan the hastiness of her marriage any longer.

After a brief tussle with her brothers Storm gently sent them from the room. She stared at a curious Elaine for a moment as she searched for the right words. Announcing that she was carrying a MacLagan bastard was no easy thing to do. Storm doubted that there was any way to break such news gently.

"I am with child."

Elaine stared at her husband's eldest child. As the meaning of Storm's words slowly penetrated, Elaine's soft gray eyes began to widen. She paled slightly, for she could already hear the crash of swords as Eldon and MacLagan hurled themselves at each other.

"Are you certain, child?"

"Very certain, Elaine." She took the woman's hand and placed it upon her belly, smiling faintly when her increasingly active child moved beneath Elaine's touch and the woman gasped.

"Oh dear God, this cannot be."

"So I have said, over and over and over again, but my belly continues to round. I must tell Papa."

"Aye, but how? He has not e'en spoken of what must have happened to you. Methinks he tries to ignore it. This will ensure that he cannot. That no one can."

"He will be in a rage. There is no doubting that. I was hoping you would aid me in the cooling of it."

"Can it be cooled? This is no small thing, child. He will wish for blood to avenge the shame."

"Please, do not say shame." Storm's hands covered her belly as if to protect her child from hearing the words. "My child . . ."

Putting her hands over Storm's, Elaine said quietly, "I speak not of the child. The child is innocent, though many think not. I speak of the abuse of you, an innocent hostage."

"I was not abused, Elaine."

For a moment Elaine stared at Storm, then she asked softly, "Did you go to the man willingly?"

"Nay, not truly. I asked that he leave me be. Only asked, though, Elaine, for I knew that I had no will to push him away. I asked that he show the strength I did not have, is all."

"You love him?"

"Aye, though he feels not the same, is naught but a wencher. I looked to him when Father came to get me, but he said not a word, just let me go. Will ye speak to Papa with me?"

" 'Tis not really my place," Elaine murmured, aching to help the girl, but not wishing to step beyond what was her right as Roden's third wife.

"That is foolishness. Ye are family. I do not ask that ye speak for me or take sides, only that ye come with me to ensure that our tempers do not make this more of a woe than it is."

With an inner grimace, Elaine thought of the confrontation to come. It would be loud and the language blunt, perhaps vitriolic. She had always known that Roden was a man of strong emotion, but in her short time at Hagaleah she had come to realize just how strong. His children were as he was. Even the worst of outbursts was tempered by love, however, and slowly she was adjusting to the abundance of life at Hagaleah, to all that unfettered emotion. She did not know if she was ready for as great a confrontation as this one promised to be, but she nodded, willing to face it for Storm's sake.

Storm smiled in relief and gently teased, "One would think ye are afraid, Elaine."

"I am some. Not of ye or Roden, but I am unused to your ways as yet."

"You mean our bellowing and ranting."

Elaine laughed softly. "Mayhaps I do. I am not yet accustomed to such honesty of emotion."

"It can be difficult. Shall we go and put this confrontation behind us?"

They reluctantly went to speak to Lord Eldon. Neither doubted how he would react to such news. The only question they had was whether or not they could stop him from racing to Caraidland, a sword in his hands and blood in his eyes, eager to spit any MacLagan that came to hand.

A thousand words tumbled through Storm's mind as she faced her father, but they refused to form into coherent and clever sentences. Her father had never spoken to her of her stay at Caraidland, except to have her assure him that she felt no need for vengeance, had not been treated cruelly in any way. He did seem to wish to ignore the fact that she had been Tavis MacLagan's lover, even though he must have been told. Now she would have to tear away those blinders, tell him that there was proof of her dishonoring that a blind man could not ignore. It hurt her to think of how it was going to hurt him.

For a brief moment she thought of Tavis, then inwardly cursed. He had made it very clear that he was done with her. It was past time that she was done with him. The man had brought her only trouble and woe and now that woe was going to reach out and pull in the rest of her family. A bastard was a hard thing to hide.

But it did not have to be a bastard, she suddenly thought. She was fairly certain that she could count on Colin MacLagan to support her if she demanded the MacLagan name for her child. Things might not be as dismal as she had thought. It would be hard to be Tavis's wife in name only, but for the welfare of her child she would do so. Even though he would be a Scottish man's child living amongst the English, it would be better than being a Scottish man's bastard in the same place. The fact that his grandfather would be Lord Roden Eldon would help a great deal.

"Did you come here to speak to me or just to stare at me?" Lord Eldon drawled, smiling a little at his wife and only daughter, who had entered the small room he often used to confer with his steward, a servant he lacked at the moment. "There is a reason for this visit, I presume?"

"Aye, Papa," Storm said quietly. "I fear there is a reason, and ye will not be liking it much."

Eldon tensed. Looking closely at the women made him tense even more. There was only one thing left that could happen to Storm. He had not forgotten how her time at Caraidland had been spent, and now he felt sure that she was about to tell him that they had not been able to leave that woe behind when they had ridden away.

Storm could see the realization harden her father's face. "Papa, I am with child."

"I will kill the bastard. Slowly."

Elaine and Storm put themselves between him and the door when he made to leave. Storm thought he looked very much like a raging bull as he stood before them. She felt sure he would never hurt her or Elaine, but it was unnerving to stand firm before so much fury. The extent of his anger made her fear that nothing she or Elaine could say or do would quell it.

"And what will that accomplish, Papa?" she asked softly.

"It will avenge this loss of honor."

"How? I doubt not that it might make ye feel better, but I will gain naught from it."

"This insult to us cannot go unpunished," he growled as he began to angrily pace the room.

"Spilling blood will not gain me back my lost maidenhead nor take this babe from my belly. All it will do is kill men, mayhaps ye or Drew or someone else I love."

" 'Tis the way of things to avenge insult with bloodshed," he bellowed.

"I do not give one pile of cow droppings for the way of world," she yelled back.

"Curse you, girl, the man abused you . . ."

"Seduced me."

"What matter? He . . ."

"And he did not have to seduce me too hard," she finished softly. "Hardly at all."

Whirling about, he stared at her. "What say you? You willingly bedded him?"

"He bedded me. My unwillingness was that I asked him not to. That is all. I but tried to stop what could not be stopped. If he had but waited and wooed me, he still would have had me. He only rushed matters."

"Was he the only one?" he asked tautly.

"Aye, Papa. The child I carry is Tavis MacLagan's. It can be no other man's. He was the only one to touch me in all the time I was at Caraidland." She fleetingly thought of Sholto's attempt to seduce her and decided she was not really lying.

"By God, I should have cut the man down whilst I was there."

"Why?" She blushed slightly, but knew it was a time for complete honesty. "For taking what was his more or less for the asking? I could not refuse him, Papa. I knew that ere he touched me. 'Twas why I asked him not to, not because I did not want him but because I did. Can ye really justify cutting a man down because of that? He awaited the ransom first."

"I know," Eldon spat out, his fury at his late wife briefly renewed. "Are you speaking the full truth, Storm, or do you tell me what you hope will stop a battle?"

"I tell you the full truth, Papa. Then, too, I do not wish a battle, for I have friends at Caraidland, good friends who helped me, and though I might ne'er see them again, I can fear for them."

"And I owe them your life." His voice revealed how much he wished he did not owe that debt, for it did work to tie his hands, made it easier for her to talk him out of a rightful vengeance.

"Well, they owe me Colin's life and his sword arm. I think such debts are well paid on either side. In truth, 'tis they who owe us, for Hugh came very close to slaughtering the lot of them."

"Then I can cut the bastard down and not feel guilty," he said, and watched her very closely, easily reading her paleness and stricken look. "You love him."

"Aye," she answered quietly. "I fear I do. 'Twas foolish of me, for the feeling was ne'er returned. He has but one use for women. He chose badly the first time he gave his heart, and I think he decided to lock it away. He was kind to me, Papa. I simply wanted more than he had to give. Ye cannot cut a man down for that either."

"So he lives and you are left with a bastard soon to be born."

"We can care for the child, Roden," Elaine said, relieved that there had not been as great an uproar as she had feared. "Mayhaps if we plan carefully, it could be hidden in some way, disguised."

"Nay. That rarely works. If the secret does not slip out, then the secrecy turns about to hurt the child."

"Papa, I have one idea," Storm ventured warily.

"Why do I feel I will not like this?"

"I could wed Tavis MacLagan."

Eldon gave vent to a string of colorful curses as he renewed his pacing of the room. Elaine blushed furiously while Storm smiled faintly with amusement. Her father had a way with words.

She frowned then, her amusement fading as she continued to watch her father pace the room, venting his frustrated rage. It did not look at all promising. Her father looked less amiable with each step he took. He did not look at all accommodating. She feared she would be proven right, that her father's tolerance would stop at the thought of his only daughter being wed to a MacLagan. Storm doubted that it would help at all that she intended a marriage in name only. That she and his first grand-child would carry that name would probably seem to him like one long slap in the face, inflicting its sting every time he looked upon her or her child.

"Papa, if ye would just heed me for a moment . . ." she began with false courage.

"Heed you?" He glared at her, not truly angry with her, but needing some tangible target for his frustrated rage. "With each word you say I but ache all the more to run the bastard through with my sword, but you cry nay ere I speak on it."

"Because it will help naught. There would be no gain, only loss. Dear friends and kin would die, but I would still be here, still unwed and with child. Now, an I wed Tavis . . ."

"No daughter of mine will e'er wed a MacLagan."

"But, Papa, it would give my child a name, take away the taint of bastardy."

"Better to be a bastard than a MacLagan."

"But, Papa, 'tis the child who will suffer more for being a bastard than I will for bearing him. Aye, he may suffer for carrying the name MacLagan, but at least he would have a name, would be fighting for the name he did carry and not for not carrying one at all. All I ask is to give him a name."

"Fine. Give him one, but not the cursed name of MacLagan."

Before she could argue further he firmly, if gently, pushed her and Elaine out of the way of the door and then started to leave. Storm found it hard to believe that he would deny her the chance to try for legitimacy for her child. Shaking free of that shock, she hurried after him, a worried Elaine at her heels. She had to keep trying to change his mind.

The whole of Hagaleah soon knew what the trouble was as the argument between Storm and her father raged through the halls. Elaine tried a few times to stop it, seeing that the chance of any secrecy was swiftly being lost, but had to give up. She saw that nothing could put a stop to this argument, that both Storm and her father were set on banging heads, as set as each was not to back down. It was hard to see how such a deadlocked confrontation could end. Defeat or compromise was required, and neither was willing to accept either.

Sheer exhaustion and a raging headache made Storm halt the argument. She accused her father of heartlessness, of caring nothing for her child, his first grandchild, and then sought sanctuary in her chambers. As soon as the pounding in her head was eased she would start again, plot yet another way to approach her father on the matter and win. It was clear that argument and anger were not the way.

"Roden," Elaine ventured softly when she caught up with her husband in the west tower.

"Do not begin where she left off, Elaine. I am fed up to the teeth with the matter. Leave it be."

"I do not mean to stand with either your or Storm; I can see and understand how both of you feel. There is the trouble, though. I think the two of you do not try to see or understand each other's position."

"You do not think I understand what she battles for, Elaine?" he asked softly, but kept his gaze fixed upon the bailey below the window. "She fights for her child as would any mother. Had I been unfettered by the chains of marriage to that Sussex whore, I believe you would have pressed me long and hard to put my name upon the children we share."

"And you would have given me that name. Do you not think the MacLagans would do so?"

"Why should they care what shame an English lass must bear? Or a child who is half English? Half Eldon?"

"Could you not even inquire?" she asked softly.

"And have them refuse?"

"They may not."

"And well they may. Then what do I do? Ask again? Go to the gates of that cursed pile of Scottish stone and ask again? Nay, Elaine. No Eldon will crawl so before a MacLagan, not even for the sake of an only daughter and first grandchild. Let that be an end to it. The child will be born an Eldon and, though he be a bastard, 'tis a name he can feel pride in."

Elaine accepted that as his last word on the matter and soon wished that everyone else would. Instead, Hagaleah was quickly divided into two camps, retainers and family alike. Some stood firm with Lord Eldon in the belief that no name was better than the name MacLagan and just as many stood firm with Storm, feeling that if there was any chance of gaining a name for her child, even if that name was MacLagan, she should be allowed to try for it. For the most part, the line was drawn between male and female, the men with Eldon and the women with Storm. Elaine began to feel like she was caught in the midst of a massive marital argument.

The larger Storm grew, the harder she and her allies worked to convince Eldon to try for a marriage. With the visual proof of her pregnancy and the encroaching birth, the long-running argument took a more subtle turn, however. Even Eldon was more cautious, for no one wanted to do any harm to the child they all so vehemently argued about or cause

Storm too much distress. It seemed as if they would argue the matter until the baby was christened.

Storm was very close to the time of birth, as nearly as they could figure the time, when a short reprieve came for a beleaguered Elaine. Roden was to leave for a little while, to help one of his vassals to still some trouble at one of his demesnes. Elaine prayed that the break in the quarrel would be enough to end it.

24

With what she considered agonizing slowness, Storm made her way to the top of Hagaleah's sturdy walls. She felt like she was carrying far too much baggage. So, too, did she question her wisdom. The weight of her pregnancy made her feel unbalanced, which made her feel afraid of falling, but she struggled onward. She was determined to see her father and his entourage leave Hagaleah. For once it was not simply an urge to wave a final farewell, although she intended to do that, too, if she reached the walls in time. She wanted to be sure that her father was going.

A weak smile split her face when she finally reached her goal. The two men stationed there were startled into open-mouthed speechlessness when she appeared at their side. They eyed her warily, as if they expected the exertion of her climb would have her giving birth to her child right there. One of them finally broke free of his shock and, mumbling a respectful excuse, hastened away. Storm was sure that he was racing to fetch one of her kin either to get her off the walls or to be there in case she had the impudence to give birth. Her smile widening slightly, she moved to the wall to look down.

Her father and his entourage began to ride out a moment later. She felt the usual twinge of pride as she watched him, the slighter Foster at his side as ever. Whenever she saw him so she knew why her mother had risked life and limb to get to him. Although many thought forty an advanced age, especially since few seemed to reach it, Eldon was still tall, straight, lean and muscular, still youthful.

Suddenly she found herself thinking of Tavis. He was never far from her thoughts, but she fought a constant battle to at least keep him from the forefront of her mind. However, as she watched her father, she found herself thinking that Tavis was another such man. He would probably keep his strength until the last, still be attractive to women far into his life.

When her father glanced up she waved. Although he waved back, she could tell he was cursing, complaining about her foolishness, and she grinned. Lord Foster smiled sweetly and waved, apparently oblivious to his friend's anger. Impulsively, she threw him a kiss and saw him laugh.

She continued to watch her father until he was out of sight. As always, she would worry about him until he was safely back at Hagaleah. The trouble he went to sort out was only a small annoyance, but danger lurked at nearly every turn, from accident to murder. Nevertheless, she was relieved that he would be gone for a while. Turning, she met her brother Andrew's scowl with a sweet smile and demurely asked him to help her down. There was planning that needed to be done and, she expected, a great deal of convincing needed before she could put her plans into action.

"That child will be the death of me yet," Lord Eldon grumbled as he rode.

"I sometimes think she is the life of you, Roden."

"Do not go cryptic on me, Hastings." He scowled at Lord Foster. "Do I not have enough woe on my plate?"

"You know well what I mean. Children such as we have, though mine are of a milder nature, keep a man alert, keep his mind sharp and his blood flowing. Few do that as well as little Storm Pipere."

"These last weeks she has become nearly tedious, battering away at me night and day."

"So why do you not give in?"

"Hastings, she asks to wed a MacLagan."

"She asks to wed the father of her child."

"I should have cut him down. Curse tolerance. Curse debts owed. He dishonored her."

"He seduced her, and your own daughter told you that he met no challenge in doing so. Do not look so choleric, old friend. At least she speaks the truth to you. I think, deep in your heart, you are glad that she does, that she did not have you bloody your sword with an innocent man's blood. Aye, innocent. Do not act as if he did aught that not one of us would do or has done. You seduced her mother and left her, though I know you would have gone back for her. She simply acted first."

"Is there a purpose to this rattling of old bones?"

"Since the MacLagan boy is mostly innocent and because of all else that went on, the lives owed and the goodness done by both sides, why do you so adamantly refuse her request to wed Tavis Mac-Lagan?"

"Because I believe that 'tis a thing he will need to be forced to and that will cut her deeply," he admitted reluctantly. "I gave them a chance to speak with me, for him to approach me, but there was naught done. I kept my mind open, was even ready to ignore the fact that he was a Scot, a MacLagan, but he stood there like a cursed post and said naught, let me take Storm away from him, from his bed, without a word. Unlike me, mayhaps he was not willing to set aside that she was English and Eldon, mayhaps his family or clan could not. Or," he said curtly, "mayhaps he but enjoyed himself with a comely lass, caring naught for her. I will not bind her to that. Better she faces the trouble of bearing a bastard child than the pain of an uncaring husband."

"But Storm feels she would rather bind herself to such a man, feels it is more important to give her child a name. Is that not her choice to make? She is no longer a child but a woman grown, soon to be a mother."

The logic of that stung Roden and he growled, "Leave it be, Hastings. I want a rest from it."

"As you wish, Roden, but do not slip too deeply into a rest from it. Storm will not leave it be."

Andrew scowled at his sister, then began to angrily pace her chambers, although the freedom to pace was severely hampered by the presence of the Verner twins, Phelan and the Fosters. He should have guessed the reasons for her calling a meeting, especially when she insisted that they keep it secret from Elaine. It had been foolish to think the matter of the quarrel would leave Hagaleah with his father. He wished now that he had gone with his father, but then admonished himself for being cowardly. It was going to be hard to talk her out of her plans, especially when he was sympathetic to her plight as well as her desire to gain a name for her child, even though he had staunchly backed her father in his stand against the marriage.

Inwardly, he grimaced. Clever words would be needed to forestall her long enough for their father to return. He knew he was not lacking in wit and glibness, but all that seemed to fail him now. No clever arguments or persuasive words came to mind. It was suddenly very easy to understand what drove his father to rant and rave. A good bout of cursing and swearing, of seemingly aimless fury, might clear his head, allow him to think with sharp accuracy.

"Our father has made his displeasure on this matter very clear," he finally ventured to say.

"Oh, aye, very clear." Storm mused that Andrew was looking very much like their father at the moment. "Do not think I feel he is wrong or do not understand him. I do understand, and in many ways feel he is right. Howbeit, so am I. There is no compromise to be made here, Andrew. There can never be. Equal amounts of right and wrong exist on both sides. I fear my only choice is to disobey him."

"If ye feel there is so much right behind ye, why do ye hide all this from Elaine?"

"Ye know why. She is our father's wife. Better she be kept in ignorance, mayhaps feel that she did not watch close enough, than be caught between Father and me, forced to stand with one against the other. In a way, I do her a kindness, for I will end this too old quarrel that has kept her torn."

"She would ne'er go against our father."

"There is a chance she would, though 'twould sorely grieve her. She is his wife, but she is also a woman and a mother. Her children are bastards, still face the trouble that mark can bring though Father has claimed them, made them legally his in the eyes of the church and the law. She understands too well what I fear."

Her hand rested over the nesting place of her child. "I crave a name for my child. Each time he stirs within me I hear the scornful whispers aimed at a bastard. It tears at me to think I will bring that woe to my child. I ask naught else. Just the name. Do I truly ask for such a great thing?"

"Nay," said Hadden, moving to sit by her upon the bed and placing his arm around her. "Haig and I are with you, Storm. 'Tis wrong to fault a child for what he had naught to do with, but faulted he is. We have seen it. I cannot bear to think on the pain that will bring you, for I know you will feel the sting of each cruel word, mayhaps more than your child."

"He truly speaks for you, Haig?" Andrew asked.

"Aye, and I mean no disrespect to your father, nor do I savor the idea of disobeying him. In truth, doing so pains me deeply, for he has been more than good to us. Howbeit, I go with Storm. What matter the name of the man so long as it rests, by church blessing, upon the child he bred?"

"But 'twill be an empty marriage. Is that not so, Storm?"

"Aye, I fear 'tis so, Andrew."

"Do you speak from your pain, cousin?" Phelan asked quietly.

"Mayhaps in part. I will not deny that he near tore the heart from my body when he stayed silent that day. Nevertheless, he ne'er spoke of future or love. I foolishly held hopes, though I tried not to. Still, when I can look past the hurt, past the foolish hopes so cruelly dashed to the ground, I can see that he is not a man who craves marriage and all it entails. There are many such men."

"If that is so, do you not fear he will refuse to give ye the name ye seek so avidly?"

"Not really, Andrew. He is an honorable man, and I do not believe he would wish the product of his seed to suffer from the taint of a bastard. In truth, I may offer an arrangement that pleases him mightily. He will have a wife and an heir, yet not need to play the husband, will still hold all a bachelor's freedoms."

"And what if ye do not give him a son but a daughter?"

" 'Tis a boy child I carry. I am certain of it." She smiled faintly. "I have chosen a girl's name, though, despite what my feelings tell me. It troubled me some to place such complete confidence in but a feeling. Nay, Tavis MacLagan will have his heir. I but hope that he will not try to hold the boy at Caraid-land."

"We would tear the keep down stone by stone to gain back the child."

"I know ye would, Haig, which is one reason I hope he will not try such a thing. I should not care to see it come to that. In truth, I hope ne'er to see Eldon fight MacLagan again. Too much that I value lies on both sides of the border now. Aye, e'en Tavis, though I oft curse him most viciously." She sighed, shook her head and looked at Andrew. "If ye decide ye cannot go, I will understand, but recall that ye swore that all we talked of here would be kept secret."

"Aye," he growled, feeling she had tricked him in a way. "How go ye, Matilda?"

"With Storm."

"And ye, Phelan?"

"With Storm."

"I guessed it so. 'Twas a waste of breath to ask." He sighed and prayed that his father would understand as he said, "I am with ye, Storm, curse ye and myself for a fool. When and how do we go?"

"I feel ridiculous," Andrew hissed as they crept into the stables the next night at an hour close to dawn.

Glancing at Andrew, Storm had to stifle a giggle. The monks' robes had been difficult to gain, and there was one very nervous young man praying fervently that they would be returned before the monks discovered they were gone. They all looked a bit silly, but it would not be wise to let a bad-tempered Andrew know that.

"Hush, Drew. I do not wish to chance discovery when we are so close to victory."

It was relatively easy for them to creep away

from Hagaleah, horses and all. The watch was for an enemy trying to creep in, not for anyone leaving. They also knew their home as few others did and could find the best way out unseen and unheard. If the need arose, they could find their way back inside with as little notice being taken.

Progress was slow until dawn's light was strong enough for them to ride safely. Looking at the small group as they mounted, Storm had to smile. It would not only be Tavis who was surprised.

The thought of Tavis made her heart contract. She did not know what she would face when she confronted him. She was almost afraid to do so. He could be wed. He most certainly had not remained celibate. Would she have to face his new lover or wife? Would it be, God forbid, Katerine MacBroth? Would he deny their child? Would he refuse to wed her and mayhaps need to be prodded to the altar at swordpoint, if his kin and clan would ever allow such a thing? Just how much pain was she riding to collect?

Seeing the confusion upon his sister's face, Andrew asked, "Do ye change your mind, Storm?"

"Nay," she answered softly. "I suddenly feared at what cost I would gain what I seek."

"Cousin," Phelan ventured, "what if he not only agrees to wed ye but asks that it be a real marriage?"

"I have tried not to think on that. I have had enough of shattered hopes."

"Would ye not e'en consider it?"

"Aye. I do not want to think upon it now when 'tis naught but a chance, a small chance."

Phelan said no more. He did not understand why the pair was separated at all. Those at Caraidland had accepted Storm. There would have been no trouble within the clan if the future laird had taken her as his wife. Phelan had felt sure that there had been a lot of them who wished that Tavis would marry Storm. He also felt certain that Tavis had deeper feelings for Storm than the lust of a man for a pretty girl. He shrugged to himself. It was a mystery to him, but adults held a lot of mystery about them. They did seem to make the simplest things complicated.

The ride to Caraidland went slowly. Several times they had to stop so that Storm could walk off her discomfort or relieve herself, her body seeming to have lost all ability to hold water. She held no joy in riding at the moment, the heavy weight of pregnancy making it difficult and uncomfortable. Her companions began to eye her swollen belly, not completely hidden by the flowing monk's robe, with easily read wariness. She did little to try and ease that, for she was not all that free of worry herself. Babies had been known to arrive early, and her calculations could be wrong. What arguments and soothing words she had were needed to still her own fears. Nevertheless, she began to feel an urge to reach Caraidland for more than a name for her child. At least there she would have a soft bed and a midwife if the need arose.

"There squats our destination," said Andrew quietly.

Feeling almost homesick, and quelling a sudden urge to bolt back to Hagaleah as she viewed Caraidland, Storm nodded. Despite all that had happened to her while she had been there, the tower house held a lot of sweet memories. For a brief moment those memories overwhelmed her, and she desperately fought the need to weep. Caraidland and Tavis had dealt her the bitter as well as the sweet. She should not allow herself to forget that.

Fighting an increasing tension and trying to look casual, they rode to the gates of Caraidland. She knew they would be safe, but also knew that nothing she said would stop her brother, cousins and Robin from growing more tense, their hands hovering near their swords, concealed by their robes. They had been well trained to fight Scots, not to ride into their hold as if they were trusted friends.

She was dismayed when Sholto and Angus arrived just as they were dismounting within the bailey. As she tried to keep her voice low and disguised, she watched recognition flicker uncertainly in their eyes. It did not really surprise her when Sholto finally bent slightly to stare full into her hood-shaded face, and she smiled slightly as she saw full recognition widen his eyes.

"God's tears, 'tis really ye, Storm."

"Aye, 'tis really me."

"Lass, what brings ye here?"

"I plan a surprise for Tavis," she answered with a crooked smile.

"Are ye armed?" Sholto asked as he eyed the others warily.

"Of course we are. Only a fool would ride from Hagaleah to Caraidland unarmed. Thieves and rogues abound. I mean no harm to any person here."

"Do ye swear that, lassie?"

"Aye, Sholto, I swear it, and they would, too, if ye but ask."

"Nay, I will take your word for it, little one. 'Tis enough for me."

"Thank ye. Is Tavis here?"

"Aye, lassie," answered Angus, wondering if he should tell her who else was here, only to decide that he really did not want to be the one to be the bearer of such news. "Do ye wish me tae take ye tae him?"

"Aye, my surprise will be short and direct. I mean to take as little time as possible here. I must needs return to Hagaleah ere my father does. Or before Elaine discovers what I have done," Storm added silently, then squared her shoulders, braced as if for battle, and started into the keep.

Elaine stared at the nervous young maid before

her. She knew her mouth was hanging open but could not·seem to get it to close. The news the girl had given her was a complete surprise. As if to compound her difficulties, Eldon's page had arrived but moments before to say that her husband would arrive in a few hours. Her initial joy had been turned into total dismay by but a few words.

"Are you very certain?"

"Very, m'lady. The pack of seven's gone."

"The pack of seven?"

"Aye. 'Tis what they be called for they always, well, most always, act together. They used to be called the pack of six, but then that Irish lad came."

"Of course. Gone?"

"Aye, m'lady. 'Tis felt they left near or just afore dawn. Old Matthew did not track them down, but he did say that their trail wended to the north, m'lady."

"To Caraidland," she groaned.

Her mind whirled as she tried to decide what to do. The only clear thought she had for a long while was that Eldon would be furious. She then decided to take the coward's way out. Hastily, she penned a note to her husband, then sent his page off to deliver it. Eldon would head straight for the MacLagans. She would be left out of what she had begun to term the great battle. Part of her hoped that matters would work out to her husband's satisfaction, but another part of her hoped Storm was successful. She also hoped that, whatever happened, the great battle would finally come to an end.

When the page from Hagaleah arrived at the Eldon camp and handed Lord Eldon a message from Lady Elaine, the first reaction of the men was one of worry. A moment later Foster's eyes widened as he listened to Eldon rage. The man possessed a hair-raising turn of phrase. Instinct told him that the note from Elaine concerned Storm. He was very curious

311

but waited patiently to be informed. Mayhaps, he mused, the girl was already wed. He shook away his musings, feeling that they might muddle the facts he would soon be given. It was clear from Eldon's manner that the news was not of a tragic nature, and that was enough for the moment.

Clenching the missive in his hand, Eldon turned blazing eyes upon Lord Foster. "We do not ride for home just yet."

"Ah. Where do we ride to?"

"Caraidland."

"God's teeth, ne'er say the lad has come and stolen Storm away again?"

"Nay. She rides to him to get his cursed name for her child."

"Mayhaps I had best withdraw. 'Tis a private matter."

"Not so private. The pack of seven went. Your two eldest. I suppose I should be grateful she did not tow the wee ones along."

Sighing, Lord Foster prepared himself for the long, hard and undoubtedly fast ride ahead.

25

The great hall of Caraidland was not wholly winning its battle against the encroaching winter's damp. The man seated at the table, a constantly full tankard making numerous trips to his mouth, took little notice. In fact, the gray dismal weather blended nicely with the mood Tavis had been in for far too long. That he was more than halfway drunk had become far too common an occurrence as well.

Katerine hid her annoyance as she sat at his side. For two long weeks she had forced herself to be the most amiable of companions. Although when she had arrived she had felt enough time had passed both for him to forget their differences and work up a sizable appetite for a woman, she had not yet found her way into his bed. She decided it was time to grow a little bolder.

Ever since Storm had left, Tavis had wavered from loving her and wanting her back to hating her and thinking himself well rid of her. Neither attitude helped to ease the hollow ache that seemed to be a permanent part of him. Even when he was hating her he was missing her.

Unthinkingly, his hand went to the amulet he wore constantly beneath his tunic. The moment he felt it, he could recall all too clearly how Storm had looked when he had let her leave with her father with no word. In that one moment of silence he had belittled everything that had gone between them. The hurt he had inflicted had been plain to read on her face even though she had quickly subdued it.

That thought started him growing angry again. If she had been hurt, if she had loved him as the leaving of her amulet suggested and she had claimed, then where was she? She should realize that a man had his pride to consider, that he could not go chasing after her. It was not too much to ask that she understand that it had been an inopportune time for him to consider her and him together. They had just fought a battle, her father had saved Caraidland even if it was mostly because Storm was inside its walls, and they were not allies. He could hardly have told the man then that he had been bedding his daughter and was rather loathe to see her leave. She should have explained matters to the man and then returned.

A saner part of him told him that he was being ridiculous, but Tavis was in no mood to listen to reason. To listen to reason meant that he had to admit that he had made a mistake, had been fool enough to let go of something he could never replace. No man could comfortably admit such uncomfortable things. It was easier to blame Storm for his pain, for his unending ache, his sense of being adrift and his long, far too empty nights.

It was time he started to do something about the nights. Celibacy was not healthy for a man, he assured himself as Katerine pressed against him, her fingers caressing his neck. Katerine was plainly willing, and she would ease some of his torment.

"Ye look troubled, Tavis," purred Katerine, recognizing the considering light in his eyes.

"Aye, and I ken ye have a cure," he murmured, sliding an arm around her shoulders.

Katerine smiled, seeing success coming closer. "Aye, one that's worked oft in the past."

Tavis waited for his senses to stir when Katerine's capable hand slid over his thigh. He decided the ale had dulled his passions. Katerine would have her work cut out for her. Sprawling back in his seat, he pulled her toward him and kissed her. With determination, he forced away the image that came to mind, forced his mouth to accept the taste of Katerine instead of the one he craved. When they finally parted for air he was beginning to foresee success. Anticipation was cut short when a knife skewered the chair between their faces. Katerine screamed, fainted and slid ungracefully to the floor.

"I think 'tis time ye got a new mistress, Tavis MacLagan. That one is a bit cowhearted."

The voice was painfully familiar and, in confusion Tavis looked at the small knot of monks near the door of the hall, thinking that his liquor-soddened mind was playing tricks on him. "Storm?" he whispered.

"Shocking behavior before men of the cloth," drawled one of the tall monks as the group moved to the table, nearly double their number in Tavis's men hovering behind them.

"Is no one going to pick up the lady?" asked a high, girlish voice.

"What lady?" drawled the monk that Tavis was sure was Storm. "I see none."

Just when Tavis felt inclined to succinctly demand who his visitors were they pushed their hoods back. There was no mistaking Storm and Phelan. Tavis knew the ale had fogged his mind when he realized that he had not noticed the distinct lack of height of several of the monks.

"What? No greeting? All wenched out, are ye?" Storm gave into impulse and kicked at the unconscious Katerine.

Storm was in an icy fury. She had not really expected him to have remained celibate. Nevertheless, it was not a theory she had wanted to see verified before her eyes. She reached forward and yanked her knife out of the chair. The look in her eyes as well as the way she held that knife told Tavis how tempted she was to use it on him.

"I believe ye know my companions, though the years may have changed them a bit and ye took little note of some of them the day they helped rout Hugh."

Keeping an eye on the knife she held on him with a false air of casualness, Tavis looked at the others. It was a moment before he could see past the seven years of growing to the children once held for ransom by the MacLagans. The boys were all growing into very fine young men, strong, tall and handsome. Little Matilda could be only about eleven, yet she showed promise of being a very attractive woman. Storm evidently still led the group of friends and kin.

Colin entered, but was halted in his advance by his youngest son. "What the devil is going on here?"

" 'Tis a private matter atween Storm and Tavis. Dinnae fash yourself, she willnae kill him."

"How can ye be so sure, Iain? She doesnae look to be feeling too friendly," Colin drawled. "The heirs again?"

"Aye," Sholto answered. "I cannae think why she has risked returning. All she told me and Angus when we kenned who it was, was that she intended no harm to anyone, only a surprise for Tavis."

"Weel, keep a close eye on her. The lass isnae a killer, but there's nay telling with a lass hurt and set aside." He nodded toward a slowly recovering Katerine. "I suspicion he was wenching as well."

Sholto laughed softly. "Aye, and she got that dirk right atween them. A good, clean throw it was."

"A reunion, is it?" Tavis asked quietly, trying to distract Storm, for she was holding the knife with too serious an intent and he saw with angry disgust that his family was not going to aid him.

"Ye could say that." Storm was taking a perverse pleasure in his evident discomfort.

Katerine dragged herself back into her seat. She saw at a glance who wielded the knife and feared for her life. Her eyes widened when she saw that Tavis's family plus a number of other important men of Caraidland stood apart, clearly not intending to do anything to aid their kinsman. For a moment she contemplated making a run for it, but then decided she was safer if she just sat quietly.

Storm knew the woman was awake but kept her eyes on Tavis. The reminder of Katerine's presence produced the clear image of the two kissing and touching each other. At that moment she hated Tavis, hated him for showing her heaven only to hurl her into hell. She had given him her most precious gifts, her love and her virtue, only to have him toss them away. At times she feared that the memory of that wound would never pass. She often feared it was mortal, so much did it hurt.

"It has been months, Storm," Tavis said quietly as he tried to think of a way to obliterate past hurts and a present misconception, but her cold, angry eyes did not encourage him.

"Aye, and I can see how ye have pined for me," she snarled, and buried her knife in the chair between his strong legs and very close to the seat of his virility, that which she both hated and ached for.

Tavis moved faster than he had ever done. He nearly flew from the chair and moved to put it between him and his angry lover. Her action had caused him to break out into a cold sweat. He watched her yank her knife free and slowly move after him. Unlike his family, he did not feel all that confident that she would not do him any real harm.

"Ye should be more careful with that knife, Storm," he said inanely.

"Aye. I should adjust my aim," she purred as she stalked him. "Sure 'n I am sore tempted to remove that part of ye that ye distribute so freely. That would surely curtail your drinking and wenching."

"Isnae anyone going to do anything?" asked Katerine, unable to keep quiet any longer.

"If that bitch says another word, ye pin her to the chair, Cousin Hadden."

"My pleasure," drawled that young man as he drew his sword and stood next to Katerine.

"Now, Storm, ye got no call to do that. Kate is innocent in this."

"Kate was ne'er innocent. She was born in a bed and decided to spend all her days there in active service. I would be doing the women here a kindness an I skewered the slut here and now."

Tavis cursed as he stumbled slightly on his backstepping away from the stalking Storm. He was still too muddled with drink to be able to take her dagger away quickly and cleanly. He could see, almost feel, the hurt in her, mixed in equal parts with her rage. Even so, his mind could not leave the problem of avoiding her knife long enough to think on a way to placate her. In all the dreams he had had about her return, he had never imagined it this way. He ached to take her into his arms, but in the mood that she was in he had little doubt that she would slip that knife between his ribs.

"Do ye think we ought to put a stop to this?" Sholto asked softly.

"Nay," said Colin. His eyes had studied Storm thoroughly and he had noticed something the others had not seen yet, so he added, "She isnae here to kill him. Let her vent her rage. She is due that much."

"Why have ye come here, Storm? 'Tis plain ye wish naught from me," Tavis said quietly.

"Nay, I do not want anything from ye," she lied, "but 'tis not what I want that brings me here, ye rutting bastard. If there had been a choice, I would have stayed at Hagaleah and seen to it that every sword there had your name upon it. 'Tis necessity that brings me."

Backed against the wall, Tavis wished fervently that his head would clear more quickly. "A necessity?"

"Aye, there is something that ye have that I require, Tavis MacLagan."

"What is that?" It was hard for him to see her so cold toward him.

"Your name." Storm refused to see the sadness in his bewitching eyes.

The fumes of too much drink faded a bit from his mind, but he remained confused. "What?"

"We will be married today. If ye have nay a priest, ye best send for one. I will not settle for handfast. 'Tis a union sanctified by the church that I seek."

"But why? Ye hate me. 'Tis there to see in your eyes."

The touch of desolation in his voice plucked at her, but she hardened herself against it. "Am I not a woman of rank? Was I not a virgin when ye bedded me? Aye, I did not fight ye, but neither did I invite ye. By all the rules of chivalry ye must wed me, replace the honor ye stole."

"We discussed this before, Storm. Ye are pretty, young and rich. There will be many a man who will care for ye, care not that ye are no longer a maid. Aye, and those who will understand."

"I know that, MacLagan, for proof I have had these last few months." She wondered by what right he had to look jealous. "Aye, and a fair number willing to show me that a Scotsman is only good for rutting like a boar, that 'tis an Englishman who knows the fine art of loving." She met his glare with an icy calm, purposely leaving him to wonder if she had tested the veracity of those claims.

"So ye dinnae need me. Get yourself a braw Sassanach husband," he snarled.

"She kens just how to goad him," mused Colin with laughter in his voice, a laughter that was echoed in the eyes of a number of men around him.

"He is right, though, so why does she want to wed him?"

"Ye'll soon see why, Malcolm," Colin replied softly, sorry that the pair continued to be kept at odds by Mistress Fate, but enjoying the confrontation, for they were evenly matched.

"Well, it seems there is a limit to their tolerance," she drawled as she signaled to Robin and Andrew who, along with Haig, moved to keep Tavis at swordpoint. "That ye took my innocence they could understand, and too, the fact that I may not have put up much of a fight, but"—she began to remove her monk's robe—"there is something ye left that they cannot overlook. Nay, nor do they want anything to do with it." She let the robe slide to the floor.

There was a indrawing of breath from the Scots. Katerine cursed violently but softly. All the color drained from Tavis's face as his gaze fixed upon her altered figure. There was no mistaking the swell beneath her gown. Only Colin remained unsurprised, for he had seen through the camouflage of her monk's robe to the child-swollen figure beneath. It was plain that Tavis's seed had taken root early in their affair and the fruit was nearly ready to drop.

Tavis could not understand how he had not noticed. She had to have been several months gone with child when she had left. For all the time they had been together he had never been denied her favors due to the arrival of her monthly time. Despite his experience, he had never noticed the lack of it. If she had suffered any of the sickness of a pregnant woman, she had hidden it well. When he realized his seed had been growing within her when Sir Hugh had nearly beaten her to death and perhaps even when Janet had tried to end her life he shuddered even as he felt a surge of wondrous pride over the strength of both his seed and the vessel that carried it.

"A bairn?" he croaked stupidly as he touched her swollen belly with a shaky hand.

"Obviously," she drawled. "Ye should not be so surprised. Ye worked hard enough for it."

Katerine forgot the sword still held on her. All she saw was that Storm had accomplished what she herself had failed to, that her plans to be Tavis's wife were still doomed to failure. Her jealousy and rage boiled up inside her. She leapt to her feet, startling Hadden, and rushed to where Tavis stood, his hand still resting upon Storm and the swords still aimed at him. She stood on the outside of that circle.

"She's out to trick ye, Tavis, to make ye give your name to some other man's bastard. Can ye nay see what she is up to?" she wailed, knowing her accusations were false even as she made them. "She's naught but a Sassanuch slut."

A strong backhand sent Katerine sprawling to the floor. Andrew was only fourteen, but he was a tall, strong lad, and his blow had been as good as any full-grown man's. So, too, did his beardless face hold the cold, hard fury of an adult as he looked at the woman weeping on the floor.

"I suggest ye leave, madam, ere ye say anything else and I forget ye are a woman," he said icily, and watched as Katerine hastily withdrew in honest fear for her life.

"Do ye doubt 'tis yours?" Storm quietly asked Tavis, wishing she could remove his hand but afraid of what that might tell him.

Tavis felt his child move within her and found it hard to speak around the emotion choking him. "Nay, lass. I ken not what ye have done since leaving here, but no man's seed could have grown so in so short a time. I was the only man to touch ye here and none had touched ye ere I did. Nay, 'tis mine and I will give the bairn my name an it is what ye want."

"Aye. I'll not have my child labeled bastard and hear his mother labeled whore."

"Ye were ne'er that, little one," he said softly, and sighed when she jerked away. "An it is a son, he will have all his heritage gives him right to. I will ne'er deny him."

"And if 'tis a girl child?"

"I will see that she ne'er wants for anything and is given a fine dowry."

Storm nodded. She had all she had come for, yet she felt like weeping. "Do ye have a priest?"

Colin strode over. "Sholto will fetch one, lass. Malcolm will show ye all to rooms so ye can wash up and rest if ye have a mind to. Ye shouldnae have set on a horse," he admonished softly.

"My child will be no bastard," she reiterated quietly.

"I understand, child." He gently touched her braided hair before urging her toward Malcolm.

"But," Tavis protested, only to stand watching Storm and the others leave, his father's grip firm upon his arm. "I have to talk to her."

"The time for talking was long past," Colin said, not unkindly. "Ye maun go soft and slow right now. I will go and have a word with the lass. She wants naught but your name for the bairn now." He shook his head sadly when he read the pain in his son's eyes. "Go clean up and clear the ale from your head. Ye may yet mend things."

Awakening from a nap several hours later, Storm found Colin sitting by her bed. "The priest, m'lord?"

"He has just arrived, lassie. How do ye feel?"

"Fine, but could ye give me a hand? I have found it very hard to rise of late."

Laughing softly, Colin helped her to sit up. "What do ye plan to do after ye have wed my son?"

"Go back to Hagaleah. 'Tis only his name I have come to collect. There is naught else here for me."

"How can ye be sure?" he asked. "Ye gave him nay a chance to talk to ye."

"He had a chance to speak when I first left. He has naught to say now that I want to hear." She checked her hair in the mirror. "In truth, I do not e'en want to talk about him."

Colin sighed. "Then ye willnae have much o' a marriage, lass." He watched as her hand clenched upon the brush until her knuckles whitened. "Ye will be neither wife nor widow nor maid."

" 'Tis better than staying here and watching him wench," she snapped as she opened the door. "Shall we go? I must not lose any more time or my father may well come home and guess where I have gone."

Shaking his head and commenting on the trials of fatherhood, Colin followed her, catching her up to take her by the arm. "Should ye be so hasty? Can ye nay give it a chance?"

"Nay," she said softly. "I only just survived his last rejection. Do not ask me to chance another."

Squeezing her arm gently in understanding, Colin said no more. She had told him what he wanted to know. A woman did not fear hurt if she was without feeling. If Tavis wanted her, he had a chance, but it would take a fight. As they entered the hall, one look at Tavis told Colin that his son would fight. The problem was going to be the vast amount of pride each of them had.

Tavis tried to speak to Storm, but it was the wrong time to try to break through the icy shield she had erected. There were too many people hovering around and speaking to them. Even the priest thwarted Tavis, for the man was anxious to have the service over with. Sholto had dragged the man away from other important business, allowing for no refusals.

Things looked no better after the vows had been spoken, for there was a sudden commotion at the door. A large group of armed men surged into the hall. The people of Caraidland had been so intent on the hasty wedding that the keep had been breached with only a few heads knocked together. Over the sound of swords being drawn by the Scotsmen gathered in the hall, Storm's surprised cry was barely heard. It was enough to cause a hesitation, however.

26

"Papa! Ye are back early!"

"Aye, but not early enough," Lord Eldon growled as he strode over to his daughter.

"Quite right," she said calmly, although, inwardly, she was trembling. "We are now wed by a priest."

"I should still cut the bastard's heart out. Aye, and a thing or two more." Lord Eldon's brown eyes glittered with icy rage as he and Tavis faced each other over the length of their swords.

Storm rolled her eyes, revealing a woman's disgust for this male posturing. Grabbing the nearest object to hand, which happened to be a many branched candelabra, she brought it down hard on their swords. She watched calmly as the swords were knocked from their hands, as much by surprise as from her blow, and they both swore softly but colorfully. Their glares were turned upon her at this sign of disrespect for a man's business, but she ignored them.

"Ye cannot kill him, though I must say there is a part or two of him I'd not mind seeing cut off."

Tavis wondered a little wildly if everyone at Hagaleah had the desire to go about threatening a man's private parts.

Lord Eldon's lips twitched, but he kept his tone cold. "I told you not to do this." He looked at her cohorts in the escapade. "And you lot. Trooping along after her as always. You look ridiculous."

At this, Lord Foster stepped up to speak in the group's defense. " 'Tis a good guise, Roden. Worked well."

"So it did," Lord Eldon said dampeningly. "It got Storm here so that she could wed this rogue." Taking his sword, which Lord Foster had picked up for him, Eldon pointed it at Tavis again. "I will still kill the bastard."

"Ye cannot, Papa. Tavis is kin now. He is your son-in-law." She almost laughed at his expression.

"B'God!" he bellowed, waving his sword around dangerously. "Eldons have fought MacLagans since first we set eyes upon each other. We have been spilling each other's blood for generations."

"Then 'tis time ye ceased," Storm said loudly, trying to be heard over the sudden swell of voices. "I am certain ye can each find someone else to clash swords with," she said into the equally sudden hush.

"You are an impertinent wench and I did not beat you enough," drawled Eldon, but Storm ignored him.

Glancing around, Storm became aware of a definite mixture of feelings. Men were plainly creatures of habit and the idea of ceasing what they had done for generations was not an easy one to contemplate. Some men looked confused, some looked mildly belligerent and some looked as if they did not care one way or the other, but were vastly interested in the confrontation. There was no real dispute between the families other than one of nationalities. Storm decided it was not too much of a deprivation for the two families to cease hacking at each other.

"Just think on this," she said, looking at her father but speaking to everyone. "An I have a son, your grandson will be heir to Caraidland, a future

326

MacLagan." Again she almost laughed, for the shock on a number of faces showed that not many had thought of that. "Why, if none of your sons has sons, the son I may bear could well inherit both Caraidland and Hagaleah. Think of that." She looked around briefly at the sound of laughter, and saw that its source was Colin and Iain.

"That's enough out of you," growled Eldon.

"I was merely elucidating," she murmured. "These things should be thought about."

"Aye, and speaking of things to consider, you should ne'er have been on a horse."

" 'Twas fine, Papa. We went at a nice, easy pace."

"You should have waited 'til the babe came instead of risking your wretched, impudent neck."

"I wanted a name for my child. It will not be named bastard," she snapped.

"You are as bad as your mother was. She came traipsing o'er from Ireland in the dead o' winter for the same reason. Naturally her daughter must needs gallop o'er the countryside but weeks from her lying in."

She had little defense save the one she had already given, so Storm tried another tactic in hopes of dimming her father's rage. "Ye should not bellow so at a woman in my delicate condition," she said weakly, placing one hand upon her abdomen and the other on her forehead.

"You will get nowhere with that ploy," Eldon scoffed, halting Tavis's concerned move toward Storm. "You are as healthy as a horse. I have had three women bear me seven babes, so do not try to fool me."

Storm recovered immediately. "Leave it to a man to insert boasts of his prowess into every discussion." She jabbed a finger at Tavis. "Ye and your new son-in-law should compare. He may top ye."

"Now, Storm," Tavis protested, "I havenae had

any bairns. 'Tis my first that ye carry."

"Hah! The way ye dabble about, ye probably have dozens."

"Nay. Nary a one. I was muckle careful about that." He immediately wished the words unsaid as both Storm and her father leveled murderous glares upon him.

"Phew!" breathed Sholto. "I think the ale still addles Tavis's brains. He's nay thinking too clearly."

"Nay," Colin agreed in a voice choked with laughter. "The lad's digging a muckle great hole for himself."

"I suppose I should feel blessed," Storm hissed, thinking immediately of all the women he had probably been careful with. "If ye can save the rest of your anger for a bit, Papa, I wish to go home."

"Storm." Tavis caught her arm as she started to move away. "Stay awhile. We should talk."

"Should have done a bit more talking and a little less of the other," muttered Eldon, but his eyes were studying Tavis and he was swiftly noticing a few things that altered his outlook on the situation.

Wrenching her arm free of his hold and furious over how much even his most casual touch could affect her, Storm snapped, "We have naught to talk about, MacLagan."

With as much haste as she could muster without looking ungainly, Storm headed for the door, her cousins and friends falling into step around her. She wanted to get away as quickly as possible. Just seeing Tavis had brought back all the feelings she had thought she had begun to bury beneath the pain. Every time her baby stirred, she recalled how it had been created. When it happened with him but a step away it only heightened the aching emptiness. She had had enough.

Tavis strode after her and grabbed her by the arm again. "Just a few minutes is all I ask."

Whirling around to face him, Storm's hot words were stopped by the sight of what hung around his neck. "My amulet."

"Do ye want it back?" His hand drifted toward it as if he would prevent its retrieval.

"Nay," she whispered, and met his gaze. "Nay. I want it no longer. Toss it away, Tavis MacLagan. Throw it aside as ye did all it stands for." She yanked free of his hold and strode away.

Lord Eldon paused before Tavis and with one look at the young man's pale, desolate face had his suspicions confirmed. It was not a case of a man using a maid as he pleased, then tossing her callously aside. He had no idea why Tavis had let Storm go, beyond the very obvious, such as who they were, but it was plain that the man loved her. This day's work would not put an end to the affair. Lord Eldon briefly touched the amulet, knowing well what it said about his daughter's feelings for Tavis MacLagan and for an instant recalling where and when he had first seen it. Shaking away a brief sadness for precious things lost, he looked straight at Tavis, seeing clearly the haunted look in the younger man's eyes.

"I should still kill you. Last thing I need 'tis another fool in my family." His gaze fell upon his son, Andrew, still attired in monk's robes and hovering in the doorway. "Take that cursed robe off. You look ridiculous and 'tis no doubt near to sacrilege for a depraved soul such as yourself to wear it." He strode out of the hall.

Andrew hastened after his father even as he struggled to get the robe off. " 'Tis unfair of you to call me such."

"Hah!" came Lord Eldon's voice. "Ever since that wench in France, you have had your backside bared to the sky more than you have put your mind or hand to any work. You'll wear it out, lad."

Lord Foster stepped up to Tavis, the only one not

laughing, although the ghost of a smile touched his lips. Foster knew he was neither as hot-tempered nor as clever as his longtime friend Eldon, but he, too, could read Tavis's look. Understanding how a woman could hold a man's soul, Lord Foster sought to give the young man hope.

"The Eldons are ones of strong emotion. 'Tis the hair, mayhaps. They are not above forgiving, though."

At his side, little Matilda stared at her father, her eyes wide. "Papa, Storm would not like you telling him that. She says he is a rutting bastard whose braes unlace at the mere sight of a wench."

Over the laughter, Lord Foster took his daughter by the hand and started out of the hall, saying, "I foresee a great deal of trouble with you." He paused by Colin. "I cannot say I will miss fighting with you."

"Ye go as the Eldons go?" asked Colin as he strode out into the bailey with the Fosters.

"Aye. It has ever been so." Lord Foster led his daughter to her horse as Eldon stepped over to Colin.

Glancing at Tavis, who stood a short distance away, his eyes fixed upon Storm, Eldon said, "I think 'tis not the end of this, that there is a great deal more to come ere 'tis finally settled."

Colin nodded. "Aye. Shock, ale and the knowledge that he carries the blame for any pain has dulled his wits, but 'tis a man of action Tavis is. Though pride may bring a hurdle or twa, he will soon be fighting for her. I will be urging him on. There's nay another I'd be so proud to have carry my grandchild."

Lord Eldon bowed his head in acknowledgement of the compliment. "Hold off until the babe comes. It could do her harm to suffer an upset now. Little fool should ne'er have tried this escapade."

Tavis had stepped closer in hopes of speaking to

Lord Eldon without a sword in his face, and he quailed at the man's words, for they played upon his concerns for the woman he loved. "Is there aught amiss?"

"Nay, though she is small and she carries large. 'Tis ne'er good to cause a woman with child distress of any sort. She will be fine. Storm's strong, healthy and an Eldon," he added.

"And an O'Conner," piped up Phelan, who had come to say farewell to Colin and the others.

Rolling his eyes, Lord Eldon drawled, "A fact you will ne'er let me forget." After Phelan had said his farewells and left Lord Eldon said musingly, "I will have to try and foster the boy out again after Storm has the babe."

"Ye have trouble finding ones to take the laddie?" asked Colin, genuinely interested.

"Aye, he is Irish and few want him for that." Lord Eldon shook his head over that thought.

" 'Tis a clever, healthy lad he is. Aye, and he has spirit. A little training and he'd be a fine fighting man. 'Tis said the Irish and the Scots share a common stock," Colin drawled, one brow quirking slightly.

"Is it now," murmured Eldon, his eyes showing that he understood Colin very well.

"Aye. Mayhaps we can discuss it further after the bairn is born. Suspicion it will have red hair."

Lord Eldon grinned. "You could do with a bit of color in the clan. The sky holds a warning. We had best be on our way." He looked at Tavis. "I will send word when the babe is born." He went to the horses and mounted behind Storm, ordering one of the men to take the reins of his mount.

"I can ride perfectly well by myself," Storm protested indignantly. "Ye need not guide me as a babe."

"You have no more sense than one at times," Lord Eldon said dampingly as they started off, and he

331

observed how she strove not to look back at the man who was now her husband. "You should never have wed the rogue, but you have, and now you ride away from a husband. You will not give the marriage a chance?"

"Nay. There is naught there to work with," she said quietly, forcing herself to believe her own words. "He will be glad to be left free. I would only hamper his wenching and I will not stay about to watch it."

"Wenching, is it? 'Tis not like you to accuse a man without proof."

"I have proof of his wenching. 'Tis no idle charge I make. Katerine was there. She was his mistress for two years and she turned me o'er to Hugh to get me out of Tavis's bed. She has ne'er stopped trying to regain her place."

"Lass, you were not about for a long while and did not look to be returning. Celibacy ill suits a man."

"I know that. There was naught said betwixt us when I left so I did not expect faithfulness. A man needs more than a memory. When I rode back into Caraidland I think I hoped that now we would speak of things, that the child I carry would bridge the chasm betwixt us, the chasm of birth and history. Still, 'tis different to actually see him at it." She did not see her father wince. "But, curse it, fool that I am, I think I could have ignored it an it was not that bitch, Katerine. What does that groan mean, Papa?"

"It means I understand. Recall the time Elaine was called to her father's side?"

"Aye. Oh," Storm breathed, "and my brother Tristram was born nine months later to Lady Mary."

"I nearly lost Elaine for that and could not understand. With a man's logic, I had not seen it as being unfaithful to use my wife. Elaine eventually listened and explained how she saw it. A whore in the village is naught but a convenience, an unknown vessel for relief much as a chamberpot, but my wife was one she knew and one who would do her utmost to see that Elaine ne'er forgot I had lain with her." He laughed softly. "Not that Elaine was very fond of me using some tuppence whore. An I think I cannot last another day, I ride to where Elaine is no matter how far. Saves a lot of trouble in the end."

Storm laughed softly. "I can hear by your voice that ye do not really understand. Aye, ye see how it can matter about what woman, but not truly about the other. Ye see it as naught, for ye do not give of the heart, soul or mind, only your body. 'Tis a simple easing of an ache. Would ye want Elaine to do the same, to seek an easing of an ache?"

"God's teeth, it ain't the same for a woman," he growled. "Elaine is my woman. No one else shall have her."

"Then 'tis strange that ye cannot understand how she can feel the same, that 'tis painful for her to think of ye in the arms of another e'en if only briefly and in callous use. She cannot see it fully as a meaningless thing, for 'tis not that way for her. Elaine sees only the pleasure ye give her and cannot bear to think of ye giving that to another while she lies alone. When ye return to her arms she must wonder whose breasts your lips have touched and whose curves your hands traced and did you find more satisfaction there than with her. Just as ye would wonder if she had lain with another. Ye would wonder when that man would try to take her, for surely she gave him the pleasure ye thought solely yours, and that mayhaps she would go, for he had found a way to pleasure her better. Mayhaps she was e'en comparing the two of you as you loved her."

Lord Eldon scowled at the back of his daughter's head. "A woman does not need as a man does."

"That is foolishness, Papa. If she enjoys the

bedding, then why should she not miss it? Do ye think a woman's passions fade upon request? God alone knows I wish they could. Do ye think a woman has no memory, does not lie alone in her bed and remember, feeling her blood stir yet again only to know that ache that comes when there is no one there to cool it? Do ye not think that after so many nights of knowing that unfed hunger that a woman does not turn her eyes to another man and wish that her heart and mind would not question right and wrong and that she could just use him to fill some of that void? Ye want us to be on fire when ye are about, but ice when ye are not. Ye also expect us to suffer as ye do, but not complain when ye seek the relief ye deny us."

"Is that how you feel, princess?" he asked softly.

For a long time Storm did not reply, then said softly, "Aye, and I could kill him for that." She drew a deep, shaky breath. "Tell me, Papa, does the pain e'er fade?"

"Aye, it will fade, though you might still get a pang if you think on what might have been."

Storm thought that a mere pang would seem heaven next to the agony she now felt. Leaning against the strength of her father, she closed her eyes. She was so tired and she felt all torn up inside. The edge of her memories, which had begun to dull, would now be razor sharp again. She did not savor the bleeding that would cause.

Later, as Eldon lay in his bed, Elaine snuggled up in his arms, Storm's words echoed in his mind, stirring his curiosity as to the depth of their truth. "Elaine?"

"Mmmm?" She lifted her head from his chest to look at him. "I thought you were asleep."

"Nay." He brushed the hair from her face. "Answer me true, Elaine. Do not fear that I seek to judge. Storm said something on our return from

Caraidland, and her words prey upon me. I need to know if 'tis really true."

"Then ask what you will, Roden. You will have naught but the truth from me."

"When I am not with you do you want me in the night? Do you feel a need for my loving and ache because 'tis not there? Do you hunger, and does it grow until you could bed another man, any man, just to ease the hunger if only your heart and mind would let you? Do you think on the loving and ache for it?"

"Aye," she replied quietly. "Did you think I would cease to want simply because you were gone from me? Aye, Roden, I ache, I burn and I hunger until I fear to go mad." She smiled a little when he enfolded her in his arms, holding her tightly. "I can judge how bad I have grown by where my eyes rest whene'er I see a man." She laughed with him, relieved that he saw the humor of her remark.

Eldon grew serious again. "When I return do you wonder whom my lips have tasted or my hands have touched? Do you think that I have found greater pleasure mayhaps with some other woman? E'en if you know 'tis but a whore and my use of her callous, does it hurt to think another has held me if only briefly? Do you think upon me easing a base need but see it as me giving another pleasure, the pleasure you crave but cannot have because you lie alone?"

"Aye, and I could kill you for it at times," she said softly. "Then when you return I fear to show you the full strength of my hunger, thinking 'twould repulse you just as I fear you will not be able to meet it, for you have eased your own while you were away." Her hand idly caressed his broad chest as she spoke.

"Since the time I almost lost you there has been no other woman, none, not even when we have been long apart. I have feared that I would frighten you with the strength of my hunger so have held back," he said in quiet wonder, and then tossed her onto her back. "Just how hungry are you now? 'Tis my first night home for days and ere that you had your woman's time."

"Ah, well, if you think of it as a meal, I have barely finished the first course." She laughed as, with a growl, he kissed her, and her last clear thought was " 'God bless you, Storm. I hope Tavis MacLagan is wise enough to know what a treasure he could have in you.' "

Tavis MacLagan sat drinking and cursing Storm Eldon in as many colorful ways as his ale-soddened mind could come up with. He was prone to cursing a vast number of other people as well, including his kinsmen who sat at the table, wondering if they would have to carry him to his bed. Under all his anger lay a gnawing hurt and a deep concern for the tiny woman who would soon bear his child. In truth, he was afraid of her.

"God's beard," he muttered, glaring into his ale. "The first time I didnae speak and the second time no one would let me. It seems I am fated to e'er see her ride away with that cursed Eldon."

Colin smothered a laugh. "The man does seem to e'er be about. Aye, an I had a daughter like Storm, I would be quick to horse too. The lass does seem to have a way o' getting into the thick o' it."

"Matters might have gone more smoothly had ye not had your hands all o'er that bitch, Katerine."

Slamming his tankard down on the table, Tavis snarled, "Was I to become a monk, Sholto? There was no reason to think Storm would return or e'en send word. Should I sit and pine like some untried boy?" He slouched in his chair, looking very much like a sulky little boy. "She isnae pining for me."

" 'Tis certain that I have no great opinion of the Sassanach gentlemen, but I cannae see them hovering o'er a woman whose belly is swollen with child, another man's child," Iain said dryly, and laughed at the expressions crossing his brother's face. "Aye, and a Scotman's bairn as well."

Confusion had changed to realization and then rage inside of Tavis. "Blood and thunder, she did it to me again."

"Nay, ye do it to yourself, lad," Colin said. " 'Tis easy to see the lass isnae wanton, that she wouldnae hop from man to man, but ye always think the worst. She but plays on that. If ye mean to get her back, ye are going to have to curb your temper, not let her goad ye so."

Finishing his drink, Tavis stood up. "Ye're right. An I stay calm, she will have to listen to me in the end and then she will see that here is where she belongs." He strode out of the hall with a gait that was amazingly steady considering the amount of drink he had consumed, adding as he went out the door, "If that doesnae work I will simply drag the wench back here by the hair."

27

Three weeks passed, winter settling in with an intermittent vengeance. Storm awakened on a stormy morning, instinct telling her that she was going to continue to follow in her mother's footsteps. She had not felt comfortable for many a morning, but somehow this discomfort was different. Nevertheless, with her maid's assistance, Storm rose, dressed and made her way down to the hall. She had seen, even aided in the birth of enough babies to know that there were many hours yet before her work really began.

By the time the evening meal was laid out, she knew she could no longer hide the fact that she was in labor. Elaine and a number of the women serving in the keep had been watching her so closely that Storm felt sure they would not be surprised. She found it slightly amusing that, due to the celebration of Andrew's birthday, the Fosters were now caught at Hagaleah by the storm. The Fosters and the Eldons always seemed to be together when something momentous happened in either family.

It was not simply maternal pride that made Storm think of her child's birth as momentous. In but hours, the blood of two warring factions would burst forth united in one living entity. The future heir to the MacLagan stronghold would call the lord of Hagaleah grandfather or, in the far future, uncle.

She realized she had continued to be certain that she would have a boy, and smiled crookedly. It would hardly surprise her, what with Colin having three sons and her father having six. Daughters were the rarity in both families.

"Papa," she said, and then had to clench her teeth as a strong contraction gripped her, revealing that her child's patience had finally run out.

Silence fell, and every eye was turned toward Storm. Roden Eldon needed no more than one all-encompassing glance to tell him the baby was on its way. He soon had his servants working with the precision of his troops. As Storm tried to stand with Elaine's help, he strode over and picked her up.

"I have grown a bit large of late, Papa," Storm protested as he carried her along.

"Left it a bit late to tell us 'twas time," he growled as he mounted the stairs to her rooms.

Gasping slightly from the pain of another contraction, she said, "I thought I had hours yet."

"So did your mother and, an I had not taken the stairs two at a time with her in my arms, you could well have been born upon the very table we were seated at tonight."

As soon as he had lain Storm down upon her bed, Elaine tried to get him to leave, saying, "There is naught for you to do, Roden. 'Tis woman's work from here on."

Lord Eldon looked scornfully at the young girls bustling around. "Bah! I have brought more babes into the world with these two hands than they have. Begone, the lot of you. I want none here but Lady Elaine, Hilda and myself." He smiled with grim amusement as the maids fled the room.

Though it was hard to speak with Hilda vigorously removing her clothes and her contractions gaining in strength, Storm said, "Someday they will realize that you are all snarl and no bite, Papa."

"If they discover it, I will send them packing," he said as he sat on the bed beside her.

When her next contraction came she was glad of her father's large hand holding hers, and clung to its strength. For a moment she wished he was Tavis, but she forced that thought away. It was no time for sadness or weakening longings. Bringing her child safely into the world would require all her strength and concentration. She could not waste it upon a man who was not there nor wanted to be.

Seeking to help her keep alert and, with luck, distracted from the pain, Eldon began to tell her tales of his time in France. A number of the tales were not the sort to tell a gently bred lady, but even Hilda refrained from protesting when she saw how well they kept Storm from being caught up in her own pain. Eldon knew that it was more than her pain he had to keep his daughter's thoughts from, that one Tavis MacLagan could not be allowed to haunt her. It was not easy, for he was on the minds of them all.

"Bearing a child lacks a certain dignity," Storm drawled as Hilda and Elaine peered between her legs yet again.

Roden laughed. "Most definitely. It will not be long now, Storm. Follow the pain, sweeting. Do not fight against it, for that only makes it harder to bear." He gently bathed her face with a cool, damp cloth.

" 'Tis torture upon my back," she ground out. "Must I lie so? Can it not be done another way?"

"Well, a horse stands, but you could kill the babe when he slid out." Lord Roden grinned when Storm gave a weak laugh. "Mayhaps if you got up upon your knees. 'Twould ease your back."

Hilda and Elaine protested but were ignored. It was awkward, but Storm was soon upon her knees, her father sitting before her to give her both support and something to cling to. Elaine complained that it

341

was not easy to see what was happening, but she admitted that they could manage well enough. Storm was far too pleased to have the pressure off her back to really care if she inconvenienced anyone.

"Papa, an anything should go wrong . . ." she said weakly as the pains began to blend together.

"Do not speak so, child," Roden scolded softly, hiding his own very real concern, for she was so tiny and the labor was taking so long. " 'Tis bad luck, I am certain."

"Nay, I must say it. 'Twill ease my mind. Ye must take the child to Tavis. He may be a rogue inclined to toss up near every skirt he spies, but he will be a very good father. E'en for a girl. Swear it?"

"Aye, sweeting, though there is no need. 'Tis merely that you grow weary." The sound of the wind pounding against the walls came to his ears, and he smiled faintly. " 'Twill be as it was with your mother. It was storming thus when you came into the world. Hilda and I were there to hear your first cry. 'Tis fitting we will do the same for your babe. A grandchild. I begin to feel my years."

"Never that, Papa. Ye will e'er be young. Ye will no doubt be spry and sour for your grandchildren's children."

"God forbid. Push now, Storm," he urged even as he felt her whole body begin to work.

Faintly, Storm realized that she no longer had control. Nature and her body's instincts held the reins. The pain was there, yet she was not fully aware of it. All she did know was the need to push, to strain with every ounce of strength she had and more. Every inch of her was concentrated on birthing her child. She knew when the baby was free of her body and held her breath with the others until a lusty wail filled the room.

"A sturdy boy, Storm," Eldon announced in a slightly unsteady voice.

Too tired to speak, Storm nodded and smiled, but even as she did, she knew something was wrong. The contractions should have ceased, yet they were still as strong as ever. Her belly worked as if it still meant to expel a child. She looked at her father's weary face, confusion easy to read upon her own.

"Something is wrong," she gasped, and watched all the color fade from her father's face. "I do not feel finished."

Eldon's hands went to her stomach, finding it still hard and large, contractions rippling through it. For a moment he was stunned into speechlessness. Elaine and Hilda sprang to life, and he laughed shakily.

"You are not finished. There is yet another to be born. I should have realized, you carried so heavy. Be strong, little one, this must surely be the last. Then you can rest and enjoy your accomplishment."

After her daughter was born Storm thought collapse was what she did, not rest. She stayed limp, her gaze fixed upon her babies as she was washed, the linen changed upon her bed and a clean nightdress put on her. When they were put to her breast one at a time tears filled her eyes. Her heart was filled with a loving wonder even as it was tattered by the pain loving their father had brought her.

The boy had a thick crop of reddish hair, and she knew she would be impatient to see what color eyes he would have. Her daughter had a mass of black hair and, again, she was anxious to know what color the eyes would be. Although smaller than her brother, the girl looked no less healthy.

" 'Tis like Tavis and I reversed," she said softly as the twins were laid in the cradle, and then she met her father's worried eyes. "Do not worry. I will survive." She closed her eyes with a sigh, feeling sleep come up on her like some unstoppable tidal wave. "God, I could have loved him so."

Lord Eldon brushed the hair from her sleeping

face. "You will yet, sweeting. You will yet."

"Do you really think that, Roden?" Elaine asked softly as she moved to his side.

"Aye, and if Storm had not been so blinded by past hurts she would think it too." He shook his head. "He had no chance in hell of softening her the day they wed, for she caught him in an embrace with the woman who had shared his bed before her." He put an arm around Elaine's shoulders.

Elaine's eyes filled with tears of sympathy. "Oh, the poor child, to know that blow so soon in life."

"I could have killed him. Taking her innocence was cause enough, but I knew she spoke the truth when she said he could have had that at any time, with patience could have gained it without even the faintest of refusals, and who am I to condemn a man for taking a woman he desires who does not repulse him? Nay, it was the pain he dealt her that I wanted to kill him for, the pain that she carried night and day. God, e'en then I had no idea of how tortured she was until the ride home the day of her wedding."

"All children must grow, must suffer. 'Tis life. A parent cannot shelter them from all of life's wounds," she said quietly, trying to ease his sorrow. "What chanced to change your desire to kill him, Roden?"

"He was in agony, his soul no less tortured than hers, so much so that he could no longer hide it. It was there for all to read. He could see all that he had thrown away and might ne'er regain. I could not run the man through for not knowing his own heart. He had wounded himself enough."

As they turned to leave the room, Elaine asked, "So what is to happen now?"

"The weather will hold him in Caraidland until Storm's full strength returns, but then I have no doubt that the man will be battering at the doors. There is a son to think on now."

"You seem to think it important that Storm is up to her full strength."

"Aye. 'Twill be no good for either of them if he gains the prize too easily. They must air their feelings and clear up all misunderstandings." He grinned. "Storm shall not be placated easily."

"Why, Roden, I think you look forward to the confrontation."

Roden laughed softly. "That I do. Ah, but Storm is glorious in full battle. Now," he said as they entered the hall, "where is that wretched Scot that has been lurking for near to a forthnight?"

Angus had rather enjoyed his stay at Hagaleah. After a few sore heads and bruised bodies were left behind the men of Lord Eldon's guard treated him like an equal. Though they would probably never fight side by side, he was now rather glad that they would no longer meet sword to sword.

When Roden was able to break free of relatives, friends and men-at-arms Angus was still in a bemused state over the news. A son for Tavis was all they could have hoped for, but two bairns at one go was near to miraculous. Twice he asked for the news to be repeated, only to shake his head.

"Has the lass decided on names for the bairns?" Angus asked at last.

"I imagine so, but she has not told me as yet." Eldon glanced out at the raging storm. "You will know e'er you can set out for Caraidland. I will write a letter for MacLagan that I ask you to give him."

"He will be here as soon as travel is possible."

"Aye, he will want to, but he will wait until her lying in is over."

"Want the lass in fine battle trim, do ye?"

Roden grinned. "Aye. I do not want those two starting out their marriage with all that is between them."

"Nay. The board needs clearing, 'tis sure. Weel,

soon as the weather clears I will be away. The lad maun be sairly bedeviled ere now, what with nay kenning what is aboot with the wee lass."

Bedeviled was a mild word to describe Tavis by the time Angus made the difficult trip back to Caraidland over a week later. He had spent the month anxious to hear news of Storm, any news, but when he saw Angus he did not want to hear anything.

Clutching the arms of the chair on which he sat, Tavis waited in an agony of apprehension for Angus to enter the hall. Although men were not involved in the birth of children, they were not ignorant of the process or the dangers. Often the screams of the women could be heard far from their origin. Too often for anyone's liking the mother died, either from an inability of anyone to stop the bleeding or a fever that came all too commonly afterward. At times her sacrifice was for nothing, as the babe was stillborn or sickly, lasting not long after its mother.

All these catastrophes haunted Tavis. He did not recollect her obvious strength or good health, only how small she was. The thought of her lithe frame wracked with pain tortured his dreams. At times he was glad that he would not be there to see, but more often he wanted to be at her side, as if his presence and added strength could ease things for her, hold off the shadows that hung ominously over a child bed.

When Angus finally entered with a large group at his heels Tavis's tension eased a little. It was not possible that they would smile so if anything were seriously wrong. Angus had grown too fond of Storm to look so gleeful if she had come to harm. Because of that and because of the fact that Angus would not have returned to Caraidland unless the baby had been born, Tavis felt excitement stir within himself.

346

"Storm?" he choked out when Angus stopped by his chair.

"The wee lass is fine, though her temper is a wee bit short frae being coddled and forced to play the invalid. An I was leaving, she sent her brother Andrew to his heels, a chamberpot aimed at his head."

"Angus," Tavis groaned, "has she had the bairn?"

"Aye. Why else would I be here?" Angus judged by Tavis's darkening face that he had teased the young man enough. "Aye, ye hae a son." He waited for the cheers to die down. "A fine, braw laddie he looks tae be. Has red hair and promises tae hae your eyes. She named him Taran, which means thunder in Welsh." He grinned. "Lord Eldon's mother was Welsh. 'Tis her grandfather's name, or is that the grandfather's father? Nay matter. I ken it suits. Lusty cry Taran's got. Truth is he has a string o' names. Taran Roden Colin MacLagan. Lass said it would save some arguments."

Blindly, Tavis accepted a tankard of ale and was jostled by many a slap on the back. "God, a son."

"I wasnae finished," Angus bellowed, and the noise faded abruptly.

"But ye said Storm was all right," said Sholto, voicing the confusion that Tavis felt.

"Aye, that she is. Looks a wee bit o' a thing, but sturdy as an ox."

"Then what else is there to say, ye old gowk!" bellowed Colin, losing patience with the man's games.

"Tavis has hisself a daughter."

"Curse it, Angus, ye just told me I had a son."

"Aye, ye do that, but ye hae a daughter as weel. Here now, laddie, taek a wee dram. Ye look peakish."

Tavis felt peakish. "I have a son and I have a daughter." He took a long drink. "Twins?"

Angus nodded. "Aye. Twins. The lass has black hair and her eyes look tae be like her mother's. A bit small, but the bairn is hale. Called the bairn Aingeal after her own mother. Aingeal Vanora O'Conner MacLagan. Got your ain mother in there as weel. Bit quieter than the lad she is, but nay meek."

"She wouldnae dare to be meek with such a set of parents," murmured Colin. "And Storm such a wee lass. 'Tis hard to believe she would bear twins, live, healthy twins. Ye sure, Angus?"

"I hae looked at the bairns meself. Aye, and Storm is looking fine and healthy as weel," he reiterated, anticipating Tavis's question. "Now, Lord Eldon sent ye a word or twa."

Staring at the packet before him, Tavis almost laughed. "A word or twa, eh? Looks to be a book."

With a sigh, Tavis began to read the long missive from his new father-in-law. The others in the hall celebrated the new heir and his sister quite merrily without the new father's participation. If there were any among them who had harbored qualms about the match, they did no longer. Storm's heritage faded into insignificance compared to the fact that she had born Tavis's heir, had, in fact, born two healthy bairns her very first time. This astonishing feast they naturally attributed to her Irish heritage and Scottish lover.

Tavis felt both amusement and annoyance as he read Lord Eldon's letter. The man was swiftly shaping up into someone Tavis was almost sorry to have drawn a sword upon. There was still a touch of reproach to Eldon's words, but Tavis could understand that. Eldon was being forced to accept a man as kin that he should have, by all rights, run through with his sword.

Every detail of the birth was related, for which Tavis was truly grateful. It was the next best thing to being there. He felt both resentful and grateful toward Eldon. Tavis recognized that he was jealous of Eldon's part in the birth, yet could not help but be thankful that the man had been there to give Storm his strength. He was also jealous of the very obvious closeness between father and daughter.

Those feelings paled into insignificance when Tavis read further. Eldon wanted him to wait even longer before seeing Storm and his children, almost another month. As if to rub salt into open wounds, Eldon proceeded to give him advice on how to handle Storm when he finally saw her.

"The cursed man is telling me how to handle Storm," he growled, tossing the missive to Colin.

"Weel," drawled Sholto, "ye maun admit ye havenae done a verra good job of it so far." He dodged Tavis's lunge.

"Here now, Tavis." Colin spoke over the laughter. "The man makes some verra good points."

"Does he now. He also tells me I cannae see her for near to another month. I maun still wait."

"He gives a verra good reason for that, a reason that shows he is thinking on your benefit. 'Tis verra true that a woman behaves verra emotionally after bearing a bairn. Ye neednae face her when she is nay apt to be using her head. Ye want her to listen to ye. There's less chance o' that right now. So ye wait."

"Storm's always been emotional," growled Tavis, recalling laughter, sorrow, rage and passion all openly displayed.

"Aye, but 'tis different when a woman be carryin' a child and for at time after she bears it," said Malcolm, the father of six, and a number of men who were married and had children nodded in agreement. "A woman that ne'er weeps will turn into a waterfall and a woman that ne'er gets angry will snap and snarl. There isnae any reasoning with it either. Ye can only soothe, try tae keep your temper and wait 'til it passes. 'Tis nay a time tae sort out problems. Eldon's right aboot that. Ye could only make things worse. Wait as he asks."

Colin looked at Tavis. "From what he writes here, lad, ye have a muckle lot to gain by the waiting."

Tavis sighed and massaged his temples. Eldon had related the conversation between himself and Storm on the ride home after the wedding. The knowledge of how Storm felt stirred him to the point of extreme discomfort. It was difficult to think that a woman felt such things, yet he had no disgust, did not think her shameless or wanton, only wanted to get her into his arms. That, of course, was a very good reason to wait for a while longer. Storm could not be bedded yet, and he doubted he could near her without wanting to for at least several days running.

"God," he groaned, "it seems I have done naught but wait for a chance to make amends."

"Ye are waiting to gain what some o' us ne'er find," Iain said quietly. " 'Tis worth it."

A nod of heartfelt agreement was all that Tavis could manage.

28

Storm walked toward the hall, her son in her arms and Phelan at her side. Elaine followed with her daughter, Aingeal, gurgling merrily. At three months, the twins were growing plump and lively. Unlike others, Eldon had no firm rules as to the use of the hall. He felt there ought to be one place where all mixed freely, so women sat with men and there were often children running about. If there was a need of serious discussion between himself and his men-at-arms or anyone else, he simply cleared the hall. There were a few eyebrows raised at this arrangement, but only by those not of Hagaleah.

The winter had been hard, but it was surprisingly mild for mid-March. Spring was just around the corner. Storm refused to recall a mild late March night a year past. Memories only gave her pain, and she felt she had had more than her share already. Even so they engulfed her as she neared the hall, causing her to pause in her advance. She could hear the low sound of men talking and found herself straining to discern one voice. Elaine's face revealed nothing to her.

"What is it, Storm?" Phelan asked when he saw that she was not going to continue on her way.

"I am not quite sure. 'Tis just a feeling that tells me that I will not like what I find in the hall today."

Struggling to put aside her qualms, she continued, only to stop in the doorway and glare at those gathered there. "My feeling was right."

For a moment she simply stared at Tavis, trying to sort anger out of the maelstrom of emotions she felt and cling to it. It was not easy, for she knew she still loved him, still ached for him. Knowing who had let her husband come to Hagaleah, Storm turned her glare upon her father, meeting only a guileless smile that she did not let fool her for a minute and that only added to her anger. Elaine's soothing noises did no good at all.

Tavis paid little attention to her obvious anger. His eyes drank in the sight of her lithe form like a starving man. In an attempt to control the desire that shook through him, he turned his gaze to his children. Emotion choked him as he looked from his son's bright head to his daughter's dark one and back again many times. Acceptance of his fatherhood had been hard to gain, but now it flooded through him.

"Why are ye here?" Storm snarled at Tavis as she strode to the table. "Have ye run out of whores at Caraidland and come marketing here? Ye are too late. Elaine cleaned house months past."

"A simple well met will do, Storm," drawled Roden, but there was laughter in his voice.

Tossing a glare at his family, who snickered with the others, Tavis looked at Storm and fought to keep his temper in check. "I have come to see my bairns and to speak to ye."

Sitting down next to her brother Andrew, Storm looked at Tavis icily. "Here they are. Look your fill." She pushed away all feeling as he approached. "When ye are done looking ye may leave."

Taking the seat Andrew gave him, Tavis held his hands out for his son. "May I hold him?"

Storm handed him the child without a word. She could see the glitter of anger in his eyes, yet his voice remained calm. This sign of control unnerved her more than anything else could have, for it showed that Tavis was determined to have his way in this matter. A Tavis set on having his way was a formidable foe, so formidable that Storm began to feel afraid, something she strove to hide from him.

Just sitting near him was causing her insides to curl and melt. It was hard to keep up her icy attitude. What she longed to do was hurl herself into his arms and stay there until he doused the fire that had burned in her for months. Simply breathing in the clean male scent of him was driving her to distraction.

For a while at least Tavis knew relief from that torment. The first time of holding his son and then his daughter had cleared his mind of all else. With a sense of wonder, he touched them all over, from their silky curls to their tiny toes. In a time when a healthy baby was a blessing he found himself with two.

In an age where men had little to do with babies, Storm noticed there was yet another similarity between her family and Tavis's. The MacLagans felt no shame in holding a baby and taking delight in him. Her children were soon making the rounds amongst their Scottish kin. As she had with her father, Storm watched large calloused hands that could wield a sword with deadly precision handle the babies with gentle, loving firmness. The MacLagans, as Eldon did, saw that the future lay in these babies, that there was no loss of manliness in the enjoyment of children who were God's promise of the continuity of man.

With his arms now empty of child, Tavis rapidly regained the need to wrap them around Storm.

Sitting at his side and sipping a tankard of ale, she gave him no encouragement to do so. It was hard to believe that she had ever lain awake aching for him.

"I have held my bairns. Now I wish to speak with ye."

"Are ye sure there's time? The day hastens on. Ye must not get behind in your wenching."

"God's teeth, Storm, I havenae been wenching," he ground out, his hands clenching into fists.

"Really?" she drawled, glaring at him. "I suppose ye were just counting Katerine's teeth with your tongue to save getting your fingers wet." She was mostly unaware of the badly smothered laughter her remark brought.

"Now it starts," murmured Colin as he sat down next to Eldon, and there was laughter in his voice.

"I enjoy Storm in full rage," mused Eldon. "She does have a way with words."

"Takes after her father," Colin said quietly, and grinned when Eldon sent him a mock scowl.

"Nay," Tavis snapped, "but I willnae explain that afore all these people. I want some privacy."

Storm finished her ale, slammed her tankard down upon the table and leapt to her feet. "Ye can have all the privacy ye wish, but I will not join ye. Well do I know your tricks, Tavis MacLagan."

"So ye should," he sneered as he rose to stand before her, "ye askit for them oft enough."

"E'en the mundane is craved when one is bored," she purred, forcing herself not to blush.

Elaine gasped softly. "Roden, is this not getting very personal? Should you not send them out of here?"

"Nay, personal is the best sort of argument," Eldon replied gleefully, grinning when Colin nodded in vigorous agreement. "Worry not, Elaine."

Realizing that his temper was rising, Tavis

fought to rein it in. "I do not want to argue with you."

That was not good news to Storm. "And I do not wish to talk to ye. Not at all."

"Weel ye will, bitch, and ye will heed what I say." Tavis gave up trying to keep a hold on his temper.

"Oh, aye, and well do you know bitches since ye have no doubt come from the arms of the greatest one in all of Scotland. Well, if ye have any pretty lies ye wish to spout, I am sure Kate will listen well."

" 'Od's wounds, woman, I havenae seen Kate since ye and your brother threatened to skewer her."

"She called Storm a whore," murmured Colin when Roden sent his eldest son a reproachful look.

"Oh, that makes a difference." Roden smiled at Andrew. "Has he been bedding this Katerine?"

"Nay," Colin replied as Storm dramatically expressed her regrets concerning Katerine MacBroth's continued good health. "I think Storm caught him making his first effort. She was only about for a fortnight. The lad's had no other woman since he set eyes on Storm that day. I would swear to it."

"If ye had listened instead o' hurling dirks," Tavis began as he followed her retreat to a window.

"I did not want to listen to ye. I do not want to listen to ye. I listened one too many times. 'Tis all empty words and useless promises." She stared out the window, saying softly, "When I craved your voice it was silent. The second time I was prepared to listen, hoping for even empty words, ye had your mouth otherwise occupied."

Tavis paled slightly. That was a piece of news that Roden had not put into his letter, believing it too cruel to let Tavis know that he had missed yet another chance. Nor had he told Tavis that it was more his choice of wench than his wenching, but Tavis had begun to see that for himself. To know that one kiss that he had had to work at to enjoy had brought him yet another four months of hell, had kept him from Storm's side when she had borne their children and had caused him to miss their birth, tore at his insides. He wondered if any man had paid so dearly for such a minor thing. The knowledge did very little for his tenuous grasp on control.

Whatever he might have answered was lost as their son set up a wail. It mattered little to the baby what important subjects were being discussed. He was hungry. His cry started his sister's face to crumbling as she recalled how long it had been since she had eaten.

Sighing, Storm went to collect Taran from his uncle, Sholto, who looked startled at the boy's volume. Elaine collected Aingeal and followed Storm out of the hall, wondering what would happen next. Storm was simply glad for the diversion and the chance to elude Tavis.

"Are you going to just stand there like a pile of cow droppings?"

Glaring at his father-in-law, Tavis snapped, "She has to feed the bairns."

"I am sure she will reveal naught that you are unfamiliar with," Roden said dryly. "Unless you are a complete fool, as I begin to suspect, you will realize that it will occur to her that her chambers, securely locked, are a good place to be if she does not want to hear you any longer."

For a moment Tavis stood torn between defending himself against Roden's softly spoken insult and following the man's advice. "I can see where she gets it from," he growled, and strode out of the hall.

"What do ye think his chances are?" asked Sholto

after Tavis had gone.

"Storm cannot avoid him with a babe at her breast, and she will try to stay calm since she will be holding a babe. That gives him a good bit of an edge." Eldon grinned. "Then, too, soon as her arms are empty of child, he can jump her. When it comes to wives if all else fails, seduce them." He raised his tankard along with the other laughing men. " 'Twill be a while ere we see those two again."

Seduce was a mild word for what Tavis wanted to do when he saw Storm with Taran at her breast. He shut the door after Elaine's retreating figure and tried not to lunge at his wife. For an instant he was fiercely jealous of his son, whose small hands touched that ivory fullness, whose mouth worked greedily at the nipple and whose plump little body was held so lovingly in slim arms, all of which Tavis ached for. Telling himself not to be absurd, he forced his eyes to meet hers and his mind to think of other things.

The fire was still in his eyes, however, and Storm, recognizing it, felt her body flare in response, which did not please her at all. "Do ye not recognize when a battle is lost, MacLagan?"

"Is it lost? I prefer to think not. Listen to me first, little one. It cannae hurt."

Her gaze fell to her son's head and stayed there. She did not want to listen, but she knew she was caught. Tavis faltered briefly, unsure of how to begin. Taking a deep breathe, he simply plunged in.

"I kenned as soon as ye set off after the battle that I had made a verra great mistake. But think, Storm, your father had just aided us in saving our keep no matter what his reasons. Was I to say all that had gone atween us when the blood lust o' battle still flowed hot through all o' us? The blood o' both our families would soon have stained the ground."

"Ye would have me believe ye acted out of noble reasons?" she queried in soft sarcasm.

"Nay, though 'twas part of what held me silent. I will be honest, Storm. I wanted ye in my bed, didnae want ye to leave it, but I didnae ken that I wanted any more than that. Thinking that, I couldnae speak to Eldon. Ye cannae ask a man to let ye use his daughter, his only daughter and first-born child, as your mistress. I didnae ken what I wanted until ye were gone and then, e'en then, 'twas awhile ere it was verra clear."

"Yet ye sent me nary a word." She put a drowsy Tarran in the cradle and began to feed Aingeal.

"What I wanted didnae change anything as I saw it. Ye were still Eldon and still English. E'en had he kenned we had been lovers, your father would nay welcome my suit. An English Marcher lord doesnae wed his only daughter to a Scot, a border reiver, be he of equal rank or nay. Ye cannae fault me for thinking that."

She stared down at Aingeal as she thought over his words. It all seemed very logical. Tavis said nothing, letting her think for a time, for he knew the strength of that particular reasoning. It was all the rest of his actions that would be harder to explain.

"Ye did not grieve long, though, did he, Tavis."

"I did, lass. From the time ye rode off with your kin until ye appeared to tell me I would soon be a father, I was ill tempered and soddened with drink near all the time. I cursed ye for leaving, then cursed myself for letting ye go. At times I thought ye should come to me while other times I wanted to besiege Hagaleah to get ye back. I hated ye one instant and unmanned myself with the wanting of ye the next, yet kenning that it was all over for us."

Storm stood up, placed Aingeal in the cradle and, with her back toward Tavis, gently washed her breasts. "And so ye decided to bury this grief in the woman who nearly saw to my death at Sir Hugh's hands. Aye, and your babe's too."

"Nay, Storm." He moved to stand before her when she sat upon the bed to relace her bodice. "Kate had come to Caraidland but a fortnight ere ye did. She was all that was sweet and understanding."

"I am sure she was," Storm snapped. "Quite prepared to soothe your ˙much-battered soul, I wager."

"Aye, but I took little notice of it until that day, curse my luck." Storm had abruptly halted her relacing to stare at him, and he fought to ignore the exposed swell of her exquisite breasts. "I spent far too many nights sleeping with the memory of something sweet I thought lost to me forever. Then, too, I was in one of my moods o' hating ye, cursing ye for putting me through such a hell. God's wounds, Storm, I ached for ye, lay awake nights twisting with it. I lived with that ache for three months. Dreams couldnae ease that."

The tone of his voice as well as the fact that he was describing a hell she knew intimately held Storm enthralled. Even so, a cold tongue of fear curled around her insides, fear that he would soon reveal that he had made use of the very available Kate. Understand she might, but that understanding would not lessen the blow.

Tavis read the fear in her wide eyes and reached out to touch her face. He felt a flare of hope when she did not jerk away, but remained still, amber eyes locked with his own. It was proving easier than he had thought it would be to reveal so much of his inner self. Easier still when such a coveted reward drew nearer.

"I'll nay deny I planned to use her." He felt her flinch beneath his fingers. "Aye, I was telling myself

359

the lie that I could ease the intolerable nights, wear myself out in Kate so that I could sleep at last without ye torturing my dreams. It was going to be a struggle, little one. I kenned that ere I finished kissing the woman. I had to fight to ignite a tiny spark, but I was determined to end my days as a monkish fool tied to a dream. Ah, Storm, I swear I have touched no woman since ye. On my honor, I swear it."

She believed him then. Slowly, her fingers as unsteady as the ones that traced her upturned face, she began to unlace her gown. He said nothing as she stood and shed her clothing piece by piece.

"Ye look a hungry man, Tavis MacLagan," she said softly as she began to unlace his tunic.

"Near dead o' starvation," he rasped as his hands moved lightly over her lithe frame, and he pried his shoes from his feet using the toe-to-heel method. "This vision is all that has kept me sane."

Her lips moved over his chest, bringing feral sounds of pleasure to his throat. Unlacing his braes, she let them fall, hearing him kick them away. Sitting down on the bed, her kisses moved to his taut abdomen as her hands unlaced his chausses. When they fell and he kicked them away she made no attempt to hide her admiration for him. Reality was so much better than a dream.

"A vision of this, Tavis?" she murmured as her tongue played with his navel, her hands moving gently over his taut backside. "Or this?" she whispered as her kisses moved lower.

A strangled cry escaped him as her gifted tongue paid homage to his passion. When he felt her draw him into the moist heat of her mouth he nearly fell to his knees. It proved too much for his starved senses. Burying his hands in her hair, he pulled her away, bending to kiss her gently. He then crouched before her, aching with the need for possession, but needing even more than that.

Storm shuddered as his mouth moved hungrily over her breasts, latching onto each hardened nub with ill-concealed greed. Her hands touched all of him that she could reach. When his kisses moved over her stomach and lower she tensed, still unused to that depth of intimacy, but he forestalled her attempts to push him away.

"Nay," he rasped as he nuzzled the silken, copper vee. "I need to ken the taste o' ye again."

The hands that caressed her slim thighs pushed them apart as he knelt by the bed. Storm blushed beneath his gaze. As his hand caressed and probed, she sat engulfed with embarrassment even as she felt exhilaratingly bold and beautiful. When his lips touched her she cried out and fell back onto the bed, her eyes closing with the pleasure that flowed over her in waves, bringing his name to her tongue in a moan of need.

Tavis held her steady as she bucked and writhed. He was insatiable. Storm felt the culmination of their passion upon her and tried to move away, but he held her still.

"Tavis," she groaned as she fought to control a passion run mad. "I am . . . God, 'tis time. Ye must cease."

"Nay, give it all to me. I have such a thirst. Let go and quench it. Ah, aye, 'tis the sweetest of nectars."

He drank deeply of her love as she cried out his name and gave herself over to her ecstasy. Then he leapt to his feet. Lifting her hips, he drove into her languid body, bringing it to life once again. Bracing himself with his palms flat on the bed on either side of her, he bent his head to her breasts. His suckling was in rhythm with his thrusts. The dual assault brought Storm to the heights yet again. When he felt her passionate inner tremors he drove deeply, finding his own release, one that had been so long denied him.

When they finally lay wrapped in each other's arms beneath the covers he said, "I have kenned many women. Nay, dinnae stiffen, lass. Hear me out. Ne'er has it been so good. I didnae crave them, just the act. Once done, I would leave their arms ne'er caring to linger. I had had all I wanted o' them."

"Even Katerine?" she asked softly, her hand moving with loving awe over his hard chest, touching her amulet that he wore with pride.

"Aye, e'en Katerine. I kenned in my heart e'en as I tried to ignore it that ye were far more. The first time I saw ye, fighting off Sir Hugh, I wanted ye. Not just a lovely woman but ye, Storm Eldon MacLagan. It was a while afore I saw the difference. I wasnae lusting for a woman only, but for ye alone."

"It was a near mortal wound when ye held silent that day," she whispered.

"I ken it. I near killed myself as weel. 'Twas an awakening that came too late." His voice grew hoarse as her fingers idly traced the arrow of hair that trailed from his chest down to the seat of his passion. "My lust was still there, but it responded only to the memory of ye."

"And mine to ye alone. I let no other man touch me, Tavis, though they offered." She felt his sigh of relief. "I lied to hurt ye as I was hurting when I thought ye back in Katerine MacBroth's arms."

"I hoped 'twas so, but I kenned that I deserved no faithfulness. I had neither asked it nor offered it."

" 'Tis yours despite that. I cannot stop my love for ye, though I did try to." She felt his hold tighten.

"*Am pos thu mi?*" he asked thickly, feeling nearly unmanned in his love for her.

"What does that mean, Tavis?"

"Will ye be my wife?"

"I am now."

"Nay, ye but hold my name. Will ye hold my heart as weel?"

"Oh, Tavis, 'tis a most precious gift, and I will cherish it as it deserves," she whispered huskily, and proceeded to show him so to the best of her ability throughout the night, an endeavor that Tavis did his best to reward in kind.

None of those in the hall were surprised to see nary a sign of the pair as day proceeded into night and edged toward day again.

ConnieMason

The Laird of Stonehaven

He appears nightly in her dreams—magnificently, blatantly naked. A man whose body is sheer perfection, whose face is hardened by desire, whose voice makes it plain he will have her and no other.

Blair MacArthur is a Faery Woman, and healing is her life. But legend foretells she will lose her powers if she gives her heart to the wrong man. So the last thing she wants is an arranged marriage. Especially to the Highland laird who already haunts her midnight hours with images too tempting for any woman to resist.

Taken by You

CONNIE MASON

English nobleman Morgan Scott pillages the high seas. When he and his crew attack the *Santa Cruz*, he sees the perfect opportunity for revenge: an innocent Spanish nun whose body he can ravage to spite her people. But Morgan quickly finds himself torn between this act of vengeance and the passion incited by her fiery spirit.

Even as Luca Santiego fears her fate at the hands of the powerful privateer, she fights the feelings of desire he inspires with his sparkling eyes and muscular contours. She may be posing as a nun, but the emotions she feels in his strong arms are anything but pious, and she soon longs to be taken by him.

Lionheart
Connie Mason

Lionheart has been ordered to take Cragdon Castle, but the slim young warrior on the pure white steed leads the defending forces with a skill and daring that challenges his own prowess. No man can defeat the renowned Lionheart; he will soon have the White Knight beneath his sword and at his mercy.

But storming through the portcullis, Lionheart finds no trace of his mysterious foe. Instead a beautiful maiden awaits him, and a different battle is joined. She will bathe him, she will bed him; he will take his fill of her. But his heart is taken hostage by an opponent with more power than any mere man can possess—the power of love.

THE SELKIE
MELANIE JACKSON

While the war to end all wars has changed the face of Europe, some things stay the same; the tempestuous Scottish coast remains a place of unquenchable magic and mystery. Sequestered at Fintry Castle by the whim of her mistress, Hexy Garrow spares seven tears for her past—all of which are swallowed by the waves.

By joining the water, those tears complete a ritual, and that ritual summons a prince. He is a man of myth whose eyes hold the dark secrets of the sea, and whose silken touch is the caress of the tide. His very nature goes against all Hexy has ever believed, but his love is everything she's ever desired.
